ALTAR EGO

Kathy Lette

BLACK SWAN

TRANSWORLD PUBLISHERS
61–63 Uxbridge Road, London W5 5SA
A Random House Group Company
www.transworldbooks.co.uk

ALTAR EGO
A BLACK SWAN BOOK: 9780552775922

First published in Great Britain
in 1998 by QPD, by arrangement with Picador,
an imprint of Pan Macmillan Ltd
Black Swan edition published 2012

Addresses for Random House Group Ltd companies outside
the UK can be found at: www.randomhouse.co.uk
The Random House Group Ltd Reg. No. 954009

The Random House Group Limited supports the Forest Stewardship
Council (FSC®), the leading international forest-certification organisation.
Our books carrying the FSC label are printed on FSC® paper. FSC is the
only forest-certification scheme endorsed by the leading environmental
organisations, including Greenpeace. Our paper-procurement policy can
be found at www.randomhouse.co.uk/environment

Typeset in 11/14pt Palatino by Falcon Oast Graphic Art Ltd.
Printed and bound by CPI Group (UK) Ltd, Croydon, CR0 4YY.

2 4 6 8 10 9 7 5 3 1

For my sisters, with love

Contents

Part One
The Wedding

1

I Do

Query: Would it be a serious breach of etiquette to run out on my own wedding? That was the question I asked myself as I put a leg over the window ledge of my parents' bathroom, grimly regarding the ten-foot drop into the putrid metallic depths of the dustbins below.

The mirrored cabinet was perfectly positioned to eye-witness my own pathetic escape. I stared in disbelief at the meringue dress which I had drunk only skimmed water for four weeks to fit into. (The tradition for wearing white at weddings doesn't seem to have been dented by the fact that the bride holds the Girls' Night Out record for the shortest amount of time between meeting someone and shagging them – nine minutes.)

Across the Crescent directly opposite my parents'

crummy Islington flat I could see the idyllic stone church, the coiffured, confetti-clutching guests, the gleaming chauffeur-driven Rolls ... This was a fairy-tale wedding, all right. *Scripted by the Brothers Grimm.* How the hell did I, Rebecca Steele, man-izing, feisty, thirty-*ish* New feminist (with a small f – a member of what Julian, my intended, called 'London's Muffia') get into this God-awful mess?

Actually, it all began with fellatio. The getting out of it, that is.

The previous evening we'd been having the traditional Girls' Night Out – you know, where you lie to each other that you look great in stretch lycra, swap mascara-de-blobbing techniques, compare breasts (whose are biggest) and bottoms (whose have dropped) and stretch marks ('you think *yours* are bad ...'), acupuncture your nostril with a minuscule umbrella every time you take a sip of cocktail whose name is spiked with an innuendo you're drunk enough to find funny, discuss male partners' anatomical details at length (or not) – including width (imperative for any mothers in our midst), only to regain consciousness twenty-four hours later in the jockstrap of a spent Gladiator.

About midnight, the mandatory 'where's the weirdest place you've ever had sex?' conversation had lurched on to techniques for getting out of swallowing.

'Listen, doll, I just say to the guy that he's *so* big, it's making me gag. And when I gag, I always get the urge to *bite down*,' money-bags Anouska admitted, emboldened by the wine she was slopping down the front of her size-8 Prada suit.

'That's *pathetic*.' Kate had to raise her slurred Aussie drawl above the throb of the male strippers' backing tape. 'He actually swallowed that?' This was followed by the witch-like cackling which characterizes these all-girl gatherings.

'My sister,' Anouska went on, 'you know, Vivian . . .'

There was a collective moan. Vivian is Anouska's older, plainer half-sister; an arugula-d, aerobic-ed kind of person universally detested for her competence.

'. . . *She* tells her hubby that she can't swallow because she's trying to lose weight, you know after the baby . . .' Anouska paused, dramatically. 'He's seven.'

Cue witch-like cackling. Kate laughed so hard that pina colada jetted out of her nostrils.

The giant ashtray that went by the name of the 'Tooltique' was pulsating with females baying for full-frontal nudity. The disconcerted strippers looked for help from the female bouncers only to discover them making the crudest catcalls for more crotch. They needn't have worried. Women go on Girls' Nights Out for the psychological striptease.

'But if you're not in the mood –' I paused, lazily decapitating a maraschino cherry with my teeth '– why do it?'

'Mood?' queried Anouska. 'Nobody's ever in the

mood. Fellatio is just something you put up with, doll. Like the weather . . .'

'Absolutely.' Kate tore open a packet of salt and vinegar crisps with her teeth. 'Men only like blow jobs because they know we can't talk with our mouths full . . . Proof of how insane men are. I mean, if you were a bloke, would you put it in a *mouth*, where there are *teeth*? The teeth of a female who's been discriminated against for *centuries*?'

It was then I made my mistake. 'I like fellatio.'

There was an awed silence while this shocking information was fully absorbed.

'Oh, yea, penis-breath,' my two 'besties' (best friends) Kate and Anouska chorused.

'No, I do.'

'You're just saying that 'cause you're not married. Once you're hitched you can stop pretending to bloody well like it,' Kate asserted.

'Yeah,' Anouska groaned, 'the rest of us have *gallons* of ejaculatory fluid still to be endured.'

'Marriage is just something to do when you're too bloody tired for sex,' Kate gloated. 'It's copulating, under quarantine.'

But I was the only one listening. Every other eyeball in the club had catapulted out of its socket and on to the stage. Even Anouska had roused herself from her face down position in the guacamole.

The trouble with nude male dancing is that not everything stops when the music does.

I chucked Kate's chin towards the undulating dancers. 'Just because you have no libido . . .' I teased.

'It's not a lack of sex drive, you big boofhead.' Kate brushed away my hand defensively. 'It's just an over-abundance of celibate feelings. I have nothing against half-naked men . . . Hell. I wish I did . . . It's just marriage I hate.' She tossed a fistful of crisps into her maw with alarming savagery.

As well as being my best friend, and my boss at the Institute of Contemporary Arts, 35-year-old Kate is a Zeitgeist surfer. She hadn't always been a professional sceptic. A failed love affair – she'd followed her English lover to London, only to find out he was MWC (Married With Children) – had given her the ability to disbelieve anything. She'd mastered the power of Negative Thinking. According to Kate, the end of absolutely everything is nigh. She only eats in restaurants that have resuscitation diagrams on the walls and worries about aeroplane passengers flushing their toilets directly above her head. Kate McCready likes nothing more than optimum brooding conditions.

'The medical term for a woman paralysed from the waist down and the neck up is "marriage", you know,' Kate killjoyed. 'Matrimony should be avoided with precisely the same zeal that one accords . . . I dunno – British beef.'

I was used to Kate's Feminazism, but still, it was a bit rich the night before my wedding.

'Oh, fuck off,' I said, proving yet again that a career in Avon-Ladying was definitely beyond me.

Anouska, picking avocado out of her tawny corkscrew curls, backed me up. 'Marriage is the new rock and roll . . . Look at Spice Girl thingo . . . and . . .'

'Huh!' Kate turned the blowtorch of her exasperation upon Anouska. 'You only say that because *you're* bloody *desperate* to get a hubby.'

'How do *you* know that I want to get married?' a singed Anouska whinged.

'Gee, I dunno,' replied Kate sarcastically. 'Highlighting chapters seven to sixty-two of the *Complete Wedding Handbook* could have been a *clue* . . . Over half of marriages end in divorce. If marriage was a horse, no self-respecting gambler would take a punt on it. Why the hell do you want to get married?' she demanded through a mulch of chewed crisps. 'Hmm?'

Kate and Anouska have nothing in common – except me. Kate is chairperson of at least ten pressure groups. The only political gesture Anouska ever made was to join the Harvey Nichols 24-Hour-Opening Lobby. While Kate has ambitions to be the youngest female prime minister ever, with maybe a couple of Nobel prizes for services to humanity thrown in, Anouska's entire aim in life is to make the 'Bystander' section of *Tatler*.

'Well?' Kate barked, her short blonde hair lacquered so severely into a helmet that even I nearly saluted.

Anouska, shrinking, replied feebly. 'I'm . . . I'm just programmed that way, okay?'

'Programmed to become obsessed with china patterns?'

'You're just jealous,' Anouska rallied, 'because nobody's ever asked you to get married!'

'Wearing taffeta after the age of twelve is embarrassing.'

'E . . . E . . . Everybody should marry,' Anouska spluttered. 'It's natural. Unless you've got a very good excuse, you know, that you're a lesbian or a eunuch or are so visually challenged that you need to get your mirrors insured!' she said pointedly.

I blanched on Kate's behalf. Don't get me wrong, Kate had started pretty, but since university had been taking Ugly Pills – shit-kicker shoes, no make-up and nipple hair you could weave into macramé hanging baskets. Kate McCready's idea of protection in bed is to take a small, perfectly formed handgun.

But if she was hurt, she didn't show it.

'I do *not* want to perform my personal hygiene routine in front of anybody, thank you very much, I want to know that the pubes on the bloody soap are my own. Savvy?'

I laughed at her then. 'You can't reject love on the basis of autonomous toiletries!' I fumbled an olive pip out of my mouth. 'People marry for security and . . .'

'Security! Huh.' Kate contemptuously shoved her red-framed specs up the bridge of her slightly hooked nose. 'England has the highest divorce rate in Europe, you big galah!'

'It's the greatest commitment you can make, isn't it? It's a –' I tried to remember the way Julian phrased it '– a public display of a private passion.' I gloated inwardly. Eat that, Feminist-breath.

'Oh,' Kate purred flippantly, fluttering her eye-lashes, 'It's a Hallmark card moment . . .' The sweetness in her voice evaporated. 'But why bloody marry? Couldn't you just *lease*?'

'You're so lucky getting married, Becky,' said Anouska covetously. 'You can get fat and hairy now.'

Anouska was an It Girl, fast becoming a Past-It Girl. At twenty-nine, party invitations were starting to dry up. She'd worked in the Press Office at the Savoy, been the muse of a Haute Couture Designer, even once Done Something With The Queen's Pictures. Recently she'd passed herself off as a Fashion Therapist, advising rich women that gold was the 'new silver', and brown was the 'new black'. But marriage was the next career move. Nicknamed the Mountie, 'cause she always got her man, Anouska's motto had always been 'guys I can't get, are guys I've not met'. But her downfall was that she was tiara-hungry. This was a woman who wanted to buy tiaras in six-packs. Having always been the most beautiful girl at school, she'd held out for a Royal and had actually dated Prince Edward for a while. But when thirty loomed its ugly numerical head, and with her dad, the South African arms dealer, under investigation for sanction-busting, and constantly pilloried by *Private Eye* magazine, she'd been forced to downgrade her marriage expectations to Marquis, Earl, Viscount – even *Honourable* of late. A marital limbo dancer, she just kept getting lower and lower.

'These days if your skin's cleared up, you're too old to marry, doll. Men are walking down the aisle with a foetus in a veil.' A great sob rose in Anouska's pale, pearl-entwined throat. 'I'm approaching the age of being dumped for a younger wife and, and I'm . . . I'm not even married yet!'

Her blubbering increased in intensity, just as the dancers reached a delicate moment of soulful groin gyration. As Kate propped her up and I mopped her up, rubber-necking revellers were shooting our table death rays.

'Hey!' I said, cheerily – it was time to get this Girls' Night Out back on hedonistic track. 'What's the difference between men and pigs? . . . Pigs don't get drunk and act like men!'

Kate rolled her eyes. 'It's pointless telling chauvinist jokes,' she counterblasted, 'when you still marry them.'

As the strippers pelvic-thrust themselves into a lather, one bronzed hunk slipped and fell. The atmosphere, so frenzied and incendiary, became suddenly maternal. As women rushed forward to cradle and coddle, my thoughts turned to my wedding day . . . I was a woman who'd been on the go, but going nowhere. A 'new direction' for me had always ended up horizontal. I'd left a tub ring of men high and dry and been thrown out with the bath water by just as many. But I wanted to be a fish *in* water for a change. Julian, with his buttery blond hair, caramel-toffee eyebrows, burning-blue gas-flame eyes, and that succulent mouth from which rolled a judicious voice – Jules Verne deep, vowels as plump and round as plums – was my chance for a centred, sane life . . . and by hell was I going to take it. I'd never been so sure of anything in my life.

2

I Don't

Getting *married*? Was I *insane*?

The next morning I'd woken, in the bed I'd slept in as a child, to a different feeling altogether. There were so many reasons *not* to. Was marriage really romance's prophylactic? I never, ever wanted to become a Fellatio Refusnik; to make love to a man out of duty. Okay, sex was good now, but what if our orgasm warranty expired? What then, hmmm?

I'd made it through breakfast okay, even with my dysfunctional parents, but by the time I was in the shower, I was suppurating with anxiety. All my life I'd found it hard to avoid temptation. Soon it would be impossible to *find* any.

Negotiating my knee topography with a disposable razor, I thought how 'cruising' used to mean a late-night trawl through the Café de Paris for a Stud Puppy

. . . Soon it would mean hunting for a parking spot outside Peter Jones. All my married friends, that's where I saw them now, cruising round Sloane Square in their orthopaedic People-Movers, an urgent look in their eyes – a lust for linen and light fittings. Ugh. No, I did *not* want to become one of them. Never. Ever.

The blood loss, as I hacked mechanically at my leg hair, was now rivalling the shower scene from *Psycho*. Would I never again get the urge to lambada naked in front of my pets? Never again perform a strip karaoke? Never again seduce the tumble-dryer man with the washboard tum and torn jeans bum? Never again be a painter of towns? Never steal a friend's fiancé? . . . Never again give him back again?

No. Now my life would be consumed by much more Important Issues. Locating lost dry-cleaning tickets. Taking dogs I loathed for dental descaling. Perusing Sainsbury's Homebase stores on Sunday mornings in search of paint-stripper and Polyfilla, before brunching with people I hated merely because our children had a mutual fixation on *Bananas in Pyjamas* memorabilia.

By the time the eyelash-curler was clamped in place, I could clearly see my future (thought admittedly not much else): *obsessing about whether my washing machine has a double-duty agitator, as I run my fingers through what would be left of Julian's hair and wonder how I ended up living with a man who could wear a tartan flannel dressing-gown, without irony.*

Sweet Jesus. By now I was towelling sweat. After my lip de-fuzzing, hair-gassing with Maximum Hold and Sepia Remembrance eyeshadow application, I perched on the closed lid of the toilet in my tatty silk robe and tried not to have a cardiac arrest. I took deep, even breaths. In . . . Out . . . In . . . Out . . .

Yes. I felt much calmer now . . . I then flossed my face and powdered my teeth and ran a bath through my hair.

On the tenth attempt I threaded my legs into white silk stockings. But as the blue satin garter snapped on to my thigh, a horrible realization besieged me. I'd never told my single years how much I loved them.

Tutoring my breasts into uplift with merciless underwire, it hit me that I really was too young to get married. I had a pimple. I still got crushes on pop stars. Hell. I still wanted to be a catwalk model . . . The fact that I was five foot three, thirty-two-years old and would rather drink battery acid than be seen in a bikini had done nothing to dampen the dream.

But Jesus Christ – I slammed my palm against a sodden forehead. *Was* I really young? When my parents were my age, they were old. My parents. Ugh. Now *there* was a happy marriage: husband and wife, grinding together like teeth; my father wearing that slightly baffled, I-want-my-money-back expression he'd worn all his married life. Perhaps like him, I'd develop marital Alzheimer's and just forget how miserable I was? Holy Hell. It was *then* I'd clambered on to the bile-green tiles of my parents' bathroom ledge, left leg flapping out the window as though trying to pick up a short-wave radio signal.

But the frequency being transmitted was all too familiar.

'Rebecca?' it was my mother. 'Reb-ECC-A?' her knuckles rapped resolutely on the bathroom door – an irritated maternal Morse code you didn't need an Enigma machine to decipher.

My armpits spurted into each embroidered socket – proof that I'd completely bypassed the apprehension stage and gone directly to panic. The streak of hair-sprayed misery I dimly recognized in the mirror as myself (Mum had insisted on putting up my chilli-pepper red hair, so I looked as if I had a brioche baked on to my head) pitched backwards off the sill, caromed off the towel rack and whimpered pathetically. 'Ye-es?'

She jiggled the handle. 'What in God's name are ya doin' in there?' The key plopped on to the mat and I knew her eye was at the hole. 'Re-grouting?'

Since my mother had storm-trooped her way back into my life, dragooning me into all the baroque grotesqueries of a white wedding, I'd reverted to little girl-dom. On progeny autopilot, I immediately re-instated the key and unlocked the door.

Parents can be a disappointment to their children. It's such a shame when they don't fulfil the promise of their early years. My mother was wearing a micro-mini two sizes too small and dressed for cleavage. She'd always done this, upstaged me. She liked nothing better than to spend the evening as the centre ornament of an arrangement of my boyfriends, most of whom were a head shorter than her and happy to be so. My father, on the other hand, drew underwear on the natives in the National Geographic magazines. He has no neck, as though constantly cold and has never kissed me in his life.

'Well, kiss the b . . .' she nearly said 'beautiful', but giving me the once-over modified it simply to 'bride'. She unceremoniously shoved my father over the pastel threshold. He tried to kiss me but got the muscle groups confused and merely collided, teeth bared, with my ear lobe.

By way of a little joke, my mother had dressed him in a long-sleeved T-shirt stencilled with a dinner jacket. That was her technique – endless little digs until both were buried alive in a marital grave. He'd retreated into plane spotting, eyes constantly skyward – 'Oh, it's the BA 52. Right on time,' and reporting neighbours to the 'Beat a Cheat hotline.' When my father first met Julian, he treated him to a home movie of the damp-proofing of the tool shed. Grounds for divorce before we even got married, really.

'Now get a move on, girl.' She tapped a snakeskin stiletto, which her pet Chihuahua named Brutus, licked morishly. 'All ya relations are waitin' to take a look at ya.'

Oh great. *There* was an incentive. Uncle Fester meets the Clampetts.

As my mother finger-licked my hair back into place, reshaped my torn nail and verbally catalogued who'd spent *what* on *which* presents, yet more nightmares engulfed me. My parents were hideous enough. But what about *his*? The Blake-Bovington-Smythes? What the hell did I know about *them*? *Really* know – besides the fact that the upper class have the same number of chins as surnames. What if Julian was a carrier for genetic diseases like Huntington's? My God. That was something I'd never asked him. And who were all those mysterious business contacts he was always going to meet? . . . Maybe he had debts? Maybe he had ex-wives? Ex-names, even? Hell, maybe he had an ex-*husband*? Which might mean Aids. Maybe he was an Aids-carrying bankrupt of bad character? With one hour till the wedding ceremony, was it too late for surveillance? Was there still time for him to be followed, photographed and ultimately befriended by a private investigator? How on earth could I have contemplated marriage without a pre-wed? By now I was hyperventilating. My foundation had started to slide off my face. I readjusted my breasts in their cups, as though wearing red-hot underwear.

'All right, love?' (I didn't take it affectionately. That's what my mother calls everyone.) 'That under-wire's far too tight . . . There.' She re-hooked my Wonderbra on to a less asthma-inducing notch, re-zipped my frock and tucked her little canine accessory under her arm. 'Feel better?'

Yes. Like an astronaut on a space walk who can't get back into the shuttle.

'Yeh. Great. Fine. Fab.' A fake grin rictused to my face.

'Now get ya skates on, Rebecca. I'm gunna go do an infantry of the guests.' My mother was always getting words wrong. The premature baby was in the 'incinerator'. My cousin had a low sperm count meaning his wife had to have an 'FBI' baby. And her own sex life was ruined because my father was 'imminent'.

As she went sighing into the kitchen, on some further stage of mother-of-the-bride martyrdom and I unsutured my smile, a fresh attack of the 'Will It Work?', 'Is He *The* One?', 'Will He Now Expect Me To Iron His Shirts?' ambushed me. But come on, I castigated my reflection as I wiped the brush back and forth across the blusher compact. We'd lived together, bought a microwave and shared a genital infection. Marriage was surely the next logical step?

But Jesus. I rouged more ferociously. Should love be logical? My mother said that marriage was a natural progression – yes – but *forty to fifty years' progression*? From honeymoon to tomb? Forty to fifty years of looking at the cheezels and chips stuck in his fillings every time he laughed . . . Shit. By now I either had too much rouge or not enough cheek. With palsied palms I rubbed off the blusher I'd just applied.

Why tinker with a relationship that's working? Why didn't we just stay in unwedded bliss? . . . Stop this marriage! I want to get off! . . . and I was back on another Window Ledge Odyssey.

Riding the weathered sill side-saddle, asphyxiated by the cappuccino froth of my frock's lace and tulle, I cased the Crescent for witnesses to my escape. The part of North London where I grew up is architecturally book-ended by the Hospital for Infectious Tropical Diseases and Pentonville Prison. Tall, elegant Georgian houses fraternize (well, slum it really) with the sort of squat, grey-brick bungalows in which my mum and dad live. Meek and defeated, their council flat at 2, Coventry Crescent is the home I'd fled at sixteen, and to which I'd returned in this ludicrous act of wedding-day rapprochement with my parents. It was Julian who kept telling me that blood was thicker than water. But hey, so was egg-nog.

Pulling myself up by the sash cords, I was just jockeying into position to test Newton's Law, when a kerthump of car chassis on kerb heralded Anouska's arrival. Her Mercedes sports car had lurched into the Crescent at breakneck velocity. Anouska believed that the speed limit should be quadrupled in visually challenged places. Kosovo, Slovakia, Croydon and everywhere north of Bond Street were tackled at the speed of light.

'I nearly *died*, doll. I thought I'd missed it,' she trilled, alighting in a swirl of silken Voyage – the upmarket Bag Lady look currently championed by London's Celebritocracy. The only skill Anouska had learnt at her Swiss Finishing School was sports-car-alighting with minimum knicker-flashing whilst balancing a copy of *Who's Who* on her highlighted head.

'No. But *I* might.'

I'd met Anouska through her half-sister Vivian, one of Julian's law firm partners, and had liked her immediately. She was considerate (the woman faked orgasms 'cause she didn't want to be impolite), deliciously quixotic and endearingly erratic ... but not about to be headhunted by a Space Research Centre. Which is possibly why she hadn't noticed that I was half out of a window, my wedding dress tucked up around my waist, stockings laddered, tears Niagara-ing.

'I CAN'T GO THROUGH WITH IT.'

She blinked her false eyelashes. Anouska's Mac lashes are so long that when driving, she gets mascara streaks on her windscreen. 'WHAT?' She re-knotted her Hermés scarf with such agitation that she nearly garrotted herself. 'But, doll, marriage is so fashionable now. Think of Uma Thurman, Sharon Stone, Brad Pitt and Jennifer what's-her-name.' She retrieved her brocaded bridesmaid's dress from the passenger seat. 'Don't move, doll. I'll be right up.'

But the voice at the door moments later was Antipodean, rough, tough, good in a crisis. Kate looked up at me with horror as she barged into the bathroom. 'Why are you wearing those rid*i*culous shoes . . . ?' She nudged the door shut with her bum and plonked a magnum of Moët on the fluffy pastel bath mat. 'You'll get nosebleeds up there. You'll need to chew sugar to keep your energy levels up.'

Yes! Maybe *that* was it? Maybe I wasn't suffering from existential angst at all, but altitude sickness! From vertiginous heels. That was why I felt so light-headed?

'High heels,' I retorted, 'were invented by a woman who got sick and tired of being kissed on the fore-head.'

Striding towards the window, Kate planted a wet one mid-brow, then frisbeed a paperback of *How to Do Your Own Divorce* at me with such force that I nearly made my appointment with the pavement. 'Why not save time and money and just marry a divorce lawyer?'

'It's just as well I don't have sensible shoes. If I *did*, it would be time to take my shoelaces away.'

Kate's eyes flickered on to high beam. 'Really? Why?'

'What else can a woman do, who's running out on her own wedding?'

'You little beauty! . . . I did wonder why you're half out the window. Atta girl.' She dropped her crumpled bridesmaid's gown on to the toilet-pedestal splash mat as though it were toxic. 'Peach is *not* my colour.'

'But God, Kate. *Julian*.' I buried my face in my damp palms. 'I love him so much, but isn't there some other way I can prove it? If only he'd get sick, so I could give him a kidney . . . I mean, what a betrayal.'

'Not being true to *yourself*. That's the ultimate betrayal; the ultimate infidelity. If you're apprehensive about getting married then…'

'I'm not apprehensive about getting married. I just don't want to be married.'

'You have a great job, a great boss,' she winked, '. . . a fully charged vibrator, a car that rear-demists and a washing machine that only floods the kitchen two or three times a month. What the hell do you need a bloody husband for?'

'Right now I need a drink,' I said. 'Just one.' One magnum, that is. Clambering off the ledge in my clonky white shoes, I broke a varnished nail popping the gigantic cork and swigged as though rescued from the Sahara. 'What the hell are *you* wearing anyway?'

Kate's only interest in clothes was that they were flame retardant. Today, her Cumberland sausage thighs were squeezed into ill-fitting trousers made from natural fibres. But before she had time to lecture me on the misogynistic superficiality of the fashion industry, the door wheezed on its hinges once more.

Anouska scurried into the bathroom, kicked the door shut behind her, searched in vain for an ashtray before upending the soap from the dish, closed the toilet seat, sat down on it, rummaged in her cavernous bag for a fag, swilled down some champers, crossed one perfectly waxed leg over the other and lasered me with her coloured contacts. 'Bottom line, you can always get divorced.'

'Don't be silly.' Kate removed her red-flamed specs. 'Have you got any Band-Aids? . . . You make it all sound so quick, so easy. A drive-through McMarriage,' she admonished, rifling through the haemorrhoid and foot-fungal creams in the cabinet. 'Husbands are disgusting. They shed more nose hair than a moulting Labrador. *Drain-clogging* amounts of nose hair.' She retrieved a packet of plasters. 'They dribble piss on the porcelain . . . Post Urinal Drip Syndrome. Matchsticks covered in earwax; clipping toenails during foreplay . . .'

'Oh, right. Like *you'd* know,' I interjected. 'You think Mutual Orgasm is an insurance company. Give me a fag, Annie.'

'But you don't smoke, doll.'

'I do now.'

Kate perched on the edge of the bath and waved away Anouska's cigarette smoke with a windscreen-wiper motion. 'I've just had a dry spell . . . That's all . . .'

'Um . . .' I corrected her, 'it's called a decade.'

'Success puts men off,' Kate said, truculently. She confiscated Anouska's cigarette, stubbed it out on the bath enamel and flicked it window-ward.

'Ugly women who can't get laid always say that,' snapped Anouska.

'Some men find me very attractive, I'll have you know.' Kate peeled open a Band-Aid and wrapped it around the bridge of her glasses before pushing them back on to her nose. 'Not that it bloody well matters of course . . .' she said defensively, commandeering the champagne.

'Yesterday's spinster is today's feminist.' Anouska ostentatiously lit up another Cartier. 'I do *not* want to have to hastily organize another Girls' Night Out on Valentine's Day so that I won't be tempted to kill myself, okay?'

From across the Crescent came the warble of an organ gasping into life. 'Oh God,' my voice see-sawed with emotion. 'What the hell am I going to do?'

'Flee!' Kate demanded. 'Do a runner.' She started peeling me out of my wedding dress.

'Stop that!' Anouska clawed at Kate's dirty, dish-water-blonde hair. Kate swatted her away. Anouska sprang back. A Feminist and an It Girl wrenching either arm, I accordioned between them. It was like Strindberg meets Mr Bean. Which is how my mother found us. She took in my chipped varnish, the clumps of my red hair caught on a nail by the window, the skew-whiff lipstick, the low tide in the champagne bottle, one false eyelash dangling like a suicidal caterpillar from a smudged and tear-swollen eye.

'What the flippin' hell's goin' on?' Her eyes glinted

like metal. Her painted talons strained around a tumbler of lager and lime. Brutus snarled menacingly.

'. . . Mum.' I gulped in air, a palpitating fish on the deck of a boat. 'I'm . . . I'm having second thoughts . . .' I blurted. 'Not second, really. 142nd.'

'*What?*' She growled, sounding suspiciously like her pampered little canine. 'Of course ya goin' frew wiv it, Rebecca.' Her voice set me on edge, like a knife scraped on a plate. 'You've lived with Julian for five bleedin' years. Ya love him, don'cha? Love should end in marriage.'

'Oh believe me,' muttered Kate, 'it does.'

'Marriage, well, it's a natural progression, ain't it? And then kids . . .'

'God! Just because I'm in my thirties everyone keeps asking me when I'm going to have my first baby. Why? Just because you're sixty, do I keep asking when you're going to get your first incontinence pad?'

I bit my lip. Another Doris Day Mother and Daughter moment. It brings tears to the eyes, it really does.

'I am *not* sixty!' my mother huffed, vacuuming in her cheeks all the better to pout her collagened lips. 'This . . .' she sniffled into her lace handkerchief, an escapee from a Jane Austen novel, 'is ya chance for Once In A Lifetime Joy.'

'Oh for God's sake, Mum. I'm thirty-two. I've found Once In a Lifetime Joy *zillions* of times . . . But before, I could always leave him if the sex went off.'

'Ya silly cow! Sex is *not* the most important fing in a marriage!'

'Maybe not for your generation. I mean, if the sex was bad, *you* wouldn't know. We're the first generation of wives who've had a lot of sex before marriage. Been there, licked that. We *know* what we'll miss . . .'

'You've 'ad a lot of sex before marriage?' my mother interrogated, tartly.

'Mum I know that the kind of cloud nine, euphoric feeling of love will pass . . .'

'Yeah,' Kate slipped in acerbically. 'Maybe even by the first morning of the honeymoon.'

'How *much* sex before marriage? Who . . . ?' My mother's kohl-rimmed eyes narrowed. 'The fact that yer damaged goods is even more of a bleedin' reason to marry quickly.' Brutus, mimicking his mistress, bared his furry fangs in contempt. 'Exactly how shop-soiled are ya?'

I felt a cold wave of malevolence rise in the pit of my stomach. 'Remember, when I was fifteen, that thing I told you was an elbow moisturizer? Well, it was my cervical cap.'

'Elbow moisturiser?' Kate guffawed. 'A diaphragm looks more like a Frisbee for your Mum's Chihuahua.'

'Or a rubber yarmulka for a tiny Jewish doll,' Anouska giggled.

Anouska, Kate and I spluttered into helium-filled laughter. We bent double with illicit chuckles and chortles.

'You people are sick . . .' My mother's eyes were hard as boiled sweets. 'You lot need psychiatric help. I want you and yer 2,000 quid dress out that door and up that aisle, pronto.'

'Yoo-hoo.' The smile on the well-groomed head that bobbed around the bathroom door epoxy-resined in place at the sight of the mayhem within. 'What's going on?' asked Anouska's half-sibling, Vivian.

'Cold feet,' explained Kate wearily, lowering her bulk into the empty tub and lolling, spreadeagled. 'Nuptial frostbite. Lost all feeling from the knee down – maritally speaking.'

Vivian shook her hennaed head in sad disbelief. Although looking like one of those women who come to your house to demonstrate something, she is actually a highly respected solicitor, Earth Mother of two, charity fund-raiser, skilled dinner-party hostess and housewife superstar (she has damask linen napkins and *launders them herself* after every meal). What can I tell you? The woman sun-dries her own tomatoes. She obviously employs a team of people to sleep, eat and have sex on her behalf. Vivian had her last baby induced so that she could make a meeting. Networked the labour ward, then went back to court twenty-four hours after her episiotomy – making every other Working Mother bite right through her briefcase. Vivian is a good woman – in the worst sense of the word.

'Talk to her!' my mother yapped, her bouffant listing perilously.

The whole room strained to hear Vivian's words of wisdom. 'Um . . . did you like the Magimix?'

'Abou' the flippin' marriage!' said my mother in a voice brittle enough to qualify for osteoporosis pills. 'You are the Matron of flippin' Honour, ain't cha?'

Julian's idea. Vivian is not my friend. Like his collection of Bartok and Boz Scaggs albums, I'd simply acquired her by cohabitation.

'You young people are so impatient,' Vivian condescended. 'You move on because you can't keep up the romance,' said the Woman Who Does Everything More Successfully and Fabulously Than Every Other Woman in the Known Universe. 'But that first flurry of passion evolves into something so much richer.'

'This from one half of a couple whose idea of foreplay is to give each other enemas,' I retaliated.

If we'd been sitting at a table, Anouska would have kicked me under it. 'Becky!' Anouska scolded, 'I told you that in confidence.'

Vivian gasped. 'You *told* her?' Suddenly arctic, she flounced to the door. I was tempted to put Vivian into the blender she'd given me as a wedding present and press 'puree'. 'I'll get Simon. He's trained in dealing with . . .' she looked at each of us in turn, '. . . emotional retards.'

The only person who didn't live in constant fear of Vivian's enthusiasms was her husband Simon – a high-octane Harley Street marital psychotherapist.

They have two 'gifted' children. (Vivian, who ingested gallons of fish oil during pregnancy to optimize brain development, seems unaware that an Infant Prodigy is nothing more than a rug-rat with unbelievably ambitious parents.) Simon is a Dad Evangelist; they have genitalia consciousness evenings with their toddler, for God's sake. Another thing Anouska shouldn't have told me.

My mother seized me by the shoulders and looked into my eyes as though trying to diagnose glaucoma. 'Now listen here, Rebecca. Ya farver and me,' she enunciated in a spittle-saturated avalanche, 'have been 'itched for near on firty-five years . . .'

'God,' *sotto-vocce*'d Kate from the bathtub. 'You don't even get that for first-degree murder.'

'Oh shut up, Kate.' Anouska balled Kate's gown and over-armed it at her head. 'That's admirable, Mrs Steele. You should get some kind of medal.'

'Or maybe remission,' Kate's muffled voice added.

'Ya can't back out now . . .' My mother's plea trailed off so plaintively that I faltered and turned to her, actually expecting heartfelt emotion. 'Ya'll have to give back all them presents!'

'Oh, mum . . .'

'I've done everyfink right for ya Special Day . . .'

'*My* special day. This is not my day, Mum. It's yours . . . You chose the guests, the cake, the vicar with halitosis . . .'

My mother appropriated the champagne bottle and

chug-a-lugged indignantly. 'What about the caterers? I've given them a £2,000 deposit already. The dress, the invites. The sugared almonds! The booze, *magnums* no less, of bloody Frog stuff! The bleedin' photographers . . .' She scoffed another gulp. 'The cake. It's a bloody great cake with four tiers' – she stopped pacing for a moment to address the toilet-roll holder, wistfully – 'linked by stair-bloody-ways with little figures of blokes in dinner jackets and brides-maids in white and a fountain! Spoutin' champers! . . . Have ya any bleedin' idea what I've spent on you?' Her voice pitched to incredulity.

'*I* didn't want this wedding, *you* did,' I retaliated. 'All that talk about shelf-life. All those veiled, cosy little chats about which of my old friends were getting hitched and who'd had a baby . . . I wanted a registry office, with joss sticks and Mozart where we wrote our own vows about not hindering each other on our personal journeys . . . But oh no. You had to have the Big White Wedding . . .'

'Oh-oh, Vivian Alert,' Kate warned. 'Ten o'clock high.'

We turned to see my Matron of Honour practically ripping the bathroom door off its hinges in her desper-ation to bring her orthodontically enhanced, ruthlessly amiable husband to the rescue. Best man Simon launched into one of his upbeat lectures. If there's one thing I hate, it's pissants who can see the bright side of other people's troubles.

'Are you in touch with your inner self on this, Rebecca?'

Simon was big on 'getting in touch with' your inner anything. The only inner self I ever got in touch with was during tampon insertion.

'It's common to get all tied up in knots about tying the knot,' he clichéd. It struck me for the first time how much Simon, bald, pale and tubby, resembled a giant mozzarella. 'Whatever your emotional misgivings, you and Julian can work them out.'

Kate groaned. 'Why is it that people are always using the word "work" next to the word "marriage"?'

Simon loomed over Kate in the bath tub. His tie, patterned in what appeared to be leashed Dobermans, whipped her face. 'Kate McCready, you're a commitment phobe. A pathetic individual who's never got over being rejected by some married man and is jealous of anyone else enjoying a normal relationship.'

'Normal? Like you, you mean?' Kate yanked on his tie, strangulating him. 'Mr *"Toddler Genital Awareness Workshops"*!'

Simon, stunned into uncharacteristic silence, wheeled around to glower at his wife.

'Anouska!' Vivian, shoving her anger-gorged visage into her half-sister's face, lost no time in getting in touch with her Inner Bitch. 'You little cow!'

'You're right. If only I'd married a Marquis. But oh, no. I just had to hold out for the Duke.' Anouska mopped up the mascara rivulets on her cheeks. 'The

Marquis Who Got Away . . . story of my life. And now look at me. My only friends are my looks . . .'

'Yes,' retaliated Vivian. 'And they're leaving.'

Anouska dissolved into a torrential downpour of tears.

Word of my volte-face seemed to have reached the congregation. I could see them across the road, craning in our direction. Delegates were being gingerly dispatched to the flat to dip an investigative toe in the familial waters. The organist, having worn holes in the keys playing hymns, lurched wittily into 'Why Are We Waiting?' . . . Oh, that was just what we needed – an organist with a sense of humour.

'The expense!' my mother kept incanting, positioning her formidable cleavage in Simon's face. Honestly, my mother would flirt five minutes before the Apocalypse.

A knock heralded the arrival of my father. 'It's time, um, to um, give you away,' he yelped, strengthening his resemblance to a startled Pekinese.

Kate snorted in derision. '*Give you away*. You see? Marriage is nothing but an institution invented to protect the property rights of patriarchs over land and cattle and . . .'

My mother, leaning over Kate, turned on both taps. As Kate clambered, swearing like a trooper, on to dry land, the Humorous Organist switched to what sounded suspiciously like a Liberace medley. The crowd were oozing out of the church. The doorbell buzzed maniacally.

'Becky, what are you going to do?' Anouska pleaded.

My eyes jumped around the room. Another Happy Couple were due to be married in half an hour. Brides were probably backing up around the block. 'I don't know!' Sweat was squeegee-ing out of me, my beaded tiara was askew.

'Well, ya better hurry up and bloody decide.' My mother's lips secateured the sentence with brutal efficiency, sending shredded words flying. 'The salmon starters will have swum upstream by now.'

Kate ferociously towelled her hair. 'What the hell do you intend saying when the vicar asks if you'll take this man to be your lawful wedded husband? ... "*Um ... Gee ... Can I sleep on that*?" Just say "*No!*" And say it now!'

Anouska embraced me. 'Think of it, doll. The hush of the guests as you enter. The beating of your heart. The caress of the veil. The swish of silk around your legs ...'

All eyes were focused expectantly on me now.

'Look ...' I began. How could one person produce so much sweat in April? I splashed cold water on the back of my neck. 'In some ways I agree with Kate ...'

'Hallelujah!' Kate gloated.

'What? You can't be serious.' Anouska shrieked. 'Don't trust her. The woman's not natural. I've been to her house. *She doesn't have bathroom scales!*'

'. . . and in some ways I agree with Annie. Sex with the Right Man,' I continued, 'is a beautiful and moving and lovely thing . . .'

'Absolutely.' Vivian beamed at Simon and squeezed his hand, appeasingly.

'. . . and sex with a stranger on a train in the dead of night is even better.'

'Exactly,' whooped Kate. Her victory jump brought her down hard on Brutus's tail who rocketed, yelping, from the room.

'For God's sake, stop crying on your veil,' hissed my mother. 'Use toilet roll!'

'You've done that?' an astonished Anouska asked me.

'What . . .?' The alcohol was kicking in. 'Had sex with the right man?'

'. . . No, with a stranger on a train? Why didn't you ever tell me? . . . I tell *you* everything . . .'

'Obviously,' snapped Vivian, sulkily.

'Rebecca!' shrilled the Cleavage with whom I reluctantly share a genetic inheritance. 'Ya just throwin' away the Happiest Day Of Ya Bleedin' Life!'

Hmmm. I thought about what she'd said. Watching all my friends get drunk on cheap champagne then making contrived, innuendo-laden speeches about wedding tackle while my relatives danced badly to cover versions of The Clash, simultaneously wolfing down food which could either be prawn cocktails or tent tarpaulin as ex-boyfriends threw up on their shoes – was this really love's greatest possible manifestation?

'If ya won't fink of me,' my mother added tragically, 'fink of Julian! . . . What's he supposed to do? Marry one of the bridesmaids?'

My heart flopped like a pole vaulter into a mattress. Although wearing the thick butterscotch emulsion of foundation, my face in the mirror was wedding-dress white. I couldn't run out on him. That would take, not exactly balls, but iron ovaries. I looked around the room, at the chaos I'd caused. I couldn't back out. What had I been thinking of? Imagine it – my darling Julian's heartbreak and humiliation; the 'How could you possibly do this to my son?' recriminations from the Blake-Bovington-Smythes; the cost, already running into thousands of pounds, the disinheritance dramas. . .

Besides, hadn't I sewn enough wild oats to feed a large continent? It was time to make a clean sweep of a dirty mind. And marriage does have its good points, I rationalized, confronting my reflection once more. What a relief not to have to get naked in front of a stranger ever, ever again. Not to have to bikini wax every five seconds. Or lie on my side to make my breasts look bigger. A husband is the person who knows all about you and still likes you anyway. Of course I should marry. I'd done everything else. Except bondage. And I didn't particularly want to do that. Marriage is an immunization against loneliness . . . Isn't it? Okay, living alone meant I could sleep diagonally, but who would I beat at Monopoly? Did I really want to become one of those females who pretends to be fulfilled by the new medieval-history lecture series they've signed up for? I'd turn into one of those women who got bath salts every birthday and Christmas. A Gobi Desert of bath salts. Forever doomed to tick the box marked 'Single'. Spending my child-bearing years in a board meeting then trying to conceive with a turkey baster at the age of forty-five? Forever doomed to wear full make-up and high-rise heels to the supermarket *just in case I met somebody*. No. No. It was enough to make your nipples go numb.

The very thought of having a husband was starting to relax me – like looking at tropical fish. Besides, Engagement, Marriage, The First Baby – weren't these the traditional greetings-card milestones of life? Well, weren't they? Especially with Julian. My darling had a very high MIQ – Marriage Intelligence Quota – unique in pre-millennium man. I had found my Duke of Right, a man who shopped and mopped. A man who'd located my G and *his* E spot. Yep. Julian had a well-read penis and he was emotionally articulate. How rare was that in a red-blooded bloke? Then *what the hell was stopping me*? I looked at the sapphire cluster ring glistening on my engagement finger. Of *course* I was going to get married.

'Shit,' I said, looking down. 'My face is on my frock.'

I daubed at the foundation stains on my wedding dress.

'We can fix that, love.' My mother brightened. In a paroxysm of good cheer, she started fussing and clucking.

'God,' I acquiesced. 'My hair!'

Anouska descended with mousse and root lift. Vivian pared down my torn nails and reapplied Estée Lauder lacquer while Mozzarella Man jettisoned Kate out of the bathroom. My mother attached the stain-edged veil and blotted at her blue-eyeshadowed orbs.

Restored to my former pristine condition, with something old (bra), something new (a polo mint to disguise alcoholic consumption), something borrowed (Anouska's Janet Reger G-string), something blue (a joke about wedding tackle I'd saved up for the reception), I waited until friends and family had vacated the bathroom, took a deep breath, then launched myself out of the window, like an acrobat through a flaming hoop; tumbling through space like Alice, only missing giving my mother's hideous Chihuahua a cardiac arrest by a measly half centimetre.

3

The Undress Rehearsal

Julian rounded the corner of Coventry Crescent in his black morning suit, looking like a band leader who'd lost his orchestra.

'Becky?'

I stared up at him in mortified silence from my prone position amidst the dustbins.

'Rebecca?'

I gawped at him some more, my mouth opening and closing soundlessly, like a fish.

'Something's wrong,' he joked. 'I can tell by the tone of your voice . . .' Wearing an expression of mild, donnish surprise, he leant down and detached me from the pavement, scraping old tea bags and vegetable shavings from my posh white frock.

'Well, that's it. We can't get married now,' I said, two octaves higher than usual. 'It's bad luck to see the bride before the wedding. Besides . . .' a throb of a sob was lurking behind my tonsils, 'half of all marriages today end in divorce, did you know that?'

'Yes. And more ought to.' He held his six-foot-two frame erect, as though posing for an invisible camera.

'God, if only I could divorce my parents . . . Parents really should be seen and not heard, don't you think?'

'Is that what all this is about?' He brushed the gravel and grit from my palms. 'Is that it?' His verbal approach was not unlike a bomb defuser's advance on an anti-personnel landmine.

'We can't get married, Julian. Your parents hate me.'

'Who cares?' His fingers pressed into my shoulders – pale, tapered, pen-wielding fingers. 'We love each other.'

'So did Romeo and Juliet . . . And look what happened to *them* . . .' The low brutish clouds bulged with rain. I was freezing cold. But cold in a way that had nothing to do with the weather. Julian took in a big swig of damp, chill air. I leapt in before he could speak. 'Everything's turned out to be so *ordinary*, Jules. Why couldn't we have had an underwater wedding, wearing aqualungs. Or parachuting nude. Or . . . Marriage is a state of mind, anyway. And in my mind, we're already married. So why bother with a stupid ceremony?'

'It's not a state of mind,' Julian said patiently. 'The wedding kiss signifies the union of souls, exchanging the breath of life . . .'

'No, no Julian.' I backed away from him and straight into a tepid pile of dog shit. I'd forgotten how much there is in Islington. Most of it Brutus's – a case of old familiar faeces. 'You're a *man*! You're supposed to be vile and cowardly and refuse to commit.'

I plunged into the alley, a long, undressed wound behind the Crescent, overlooked by beady-eyed windows. Julian followed, his new leather shoes exhaling sadly with each step.

Catching up, he turned my face to his and gave me one of those looks that men have polished over the centuries. That 'Oh God. Is This Really The Only Other Sex Available To Me In The Universe?' look. He sighed deeply. 'On the whole, if you're going to get cold feet about marriage, it's best to put the wedding on ice a day or two *before* the guests Concorde in from the four corners of the globe. Or, at the very worst, the morning of, before relatives have had their hair done and heart operations postponed.'

The wind mourned through the solitary tree marooned in the cracked asphalt. 'I . . . I . . . just can't go through with it.'

Julian's fists clenched into two tight balls. 'Don't you love me any more?' His breath steamed.

'Of course I do.' And I did. And had done from the moment we'd first met five years ago when Kate, who was then Events Director at the ICA, had booked him to give a lecture on torture in Turkey. Julian is a human rights lawyer. He airs the world's dirty linen for a living. His job is to ferret out illegal arms dealers and major fraudsters and, more often than not, remove them from the House of Commons. Julian is my Rebel *With* A Cause My Knight in Shining Armani. He's front-page news making. He saves lives, rights wrongs, frees the world's underdogs from their kennels. How could you *not* fall in love with a man like that? And he loved me because I was an antidote to the grimy sombre side to his life. He loved me because I made him laugh. Because I had 157 synonyms for sex. And a penchant for dancing naked in his father's full-bottom judge's wig. I was his Eliza Doolittle in a leopard-skin miniskirt.

'Then *why*?' Julian looked at me, eyes wide with dismay.

'I'm sorry,' I pleaded with a thin, tin-opener voice I didn't recognize. What the hell was wrong with me? Nothing an exorcism couldn't fix. It was as though my brain disc had been wiped, and the cerebral software of, I don't know, Sarah Ferguson installed in its place.

'Look, I'm used to your contradictory, impulsive nature, Becky. In fact, I love you for it. But you suddenly appear to be sporting a personality borrowed straight from Scarlet-bloody-O'Hara. Why in God's name are you doing this?'

How could I tell him that I loved him too much to marry him? Because I'd make a totally lousy wife. Which meant that it was best for me to marry someone

I didn't like much so I didn't feel too shitty about ruining his life.

Clocking Julian's devastated face, I tried to dredge up feelings of remorse, truly I did. If only I could get in touch with my Inner Adult. But the further I got away from that bloody church, what was blubbing to the surface was euphoria, liberation, relief. I couldn't get over the notion that a wedding is just like a funeral – except you can smell your own flowers. I had PMT – Pre-Monogamy Tension. And I had it bad. But how to broach the truth, in all its wounding complexity?

'Well, it's all to do with being a Fellatio Refusnik . . .' Julian's eyebrows collided on his forehead. I'd just have to let actions speak louder than words. Clinging to his arm like melted marshmallow, I steered him through the corroded gate into the little weed-choked wood that runs by the canal.

I kissed him deeply. 'Look on it as an undress rehearsal,' I said, hand on his fly.

The fact that he didn't freak out, of course, is the very reason I should have hightailed it back to the church and married him then and there, that split second. But hell – I must have been taking Bimbo pills, or something.

4

Send In The Crones

Guides to correct protocol are so out of date. What we millennium girls need is an updated manual on modern manners. There are so many social dilemmas just not catered for in traditional etiquette texts. For example, what sort of small talk to make to the gynie while he has his hand up your twat? What, I wonder, is the correct conduct when you crap on your obstetrician, then meet him socially at a cocktail party? Or bump into a man whom you can't quite remember whether you slept with or not? Or attend a Swinging Singles evening only to run into your husband? What do you say then, hmmm? And, most tricky of all, how do you greet the man you've just jilted at the altar over breakfast next morning?

'I hope you notice that I'm still not discussing that thing we're not discussing,' Julian volunteered when I shuffled groggily into our recently renovated, urban-minimalist Conran kitchen with concealed white goods and handle-less drawer units for which we now had no implements, having sent back all our wedding presents. 'Our parents don't want to discuss it either.' He worried a teaspoon around a cup of cold, teak-coloured coffee. 'Actually neither side of the family are speaking to you.'

'Oh well, that solves Christmas.' I hazarded a tentative smile.

Julian raised one weary brow, then sipped despondently at his Nicaraguan Workers Co-op blend. 'Are you ever going to grow up?'

'What? And become the bewildered recipient of all those weird envelopes with cellophane windows? God, I hope not.' I touched his arm timorously. He shrank away. I ground more beans, drowning out the clangorous silence.

Julian crammed some files into his briefcase and prepared to depart for the twenty-minute minicab ride from Belsize Park to the Inns of Court. Some case had come up overnight involving the usual battered Algerian unipeds or banned Lebanese lesbian political mime troupe. So instead of basking on a beach in Sri Lanka in wedded bliss, he could now embark on yet another unpaid stint as saviour of lost souls. Julian had even chosen our honeymoon destination to coincide with a cause: he only ever took me to countries where I ran the risk of being taken hostage by some guerrilla band or other. Our hotel bedrooms were invariably bugged, which didn't matter as we were more often than not sharing it with bodyguards anyway. Most of our honeymoon I suspected, would have been spent in the cells of detained Tamil dissidents on the nearest death row to the beach.

I grabbed hold of his sleeve. 'Yell at me, Jules! Tell me what a bitch I am! Hate me. I'd hate *you* if you'd jilted me. I'd hate you more than I hate Woody Allen for marrying his daughter. I'd hate you more than I hate the bastard Eurocrat who put VAT on tampons.'

'I don't hate you. And I could never leave you.'

He stood, crumpled, over his soggy cornflakes. That was the trouble with 1990s Prince Charmings. They were too fucking charming. There was no swash-buckling left in the poor bastards.

'Jesus, Julian. Why can't you be cruel and vindictive like a Real Man? Throw something at me ... Throw me out even! You haven't even asked for your engage-ment ring back ...' I tugged at the sapphire cluster ring on my left hand.

Julian picked up a dishcloth. For a moment, I thought he was going to chuck it at me, but he simply mopped up a coffee ring I'd made on the counter.

'By the way, can you please stop using the floor wet-tex on the counter tops?' he said. 'It's unhygienic.'

'Can you please stop holding wash-cloth seminars? You're supposed to be on your goddamn honeymoon!'

'When you *do* work out why we're a romance

fatality' – Julian rocked back on his heels, as though addressing an especially dim-witted jury – 'a chalked outline in the marital stakes ... you will tell me, I trust?' He turned quietly and slouched out of the house.

It was typical that, despite his PLT (Personal Life Trauma), Julian would go to work. It underlined my misgivings about the marriage. When I'd first met him, it was his passion and politics that had magnetized me. He was a psychological Spiderman, weaving webs of words to catch evildoers. He was like the Caped Crusader minus the bionic underpants – Action Man in the IQ equivalent of combat khakis. A Superman, who fought for truth, justice and the legal way. When it came to tracing the bank accounts of corrupt African governments or crooked Scotland Yard detectives, mild-mannered Julian transmogrified into The Terminator.

At first I'd Lois Laned to his Clark Kent; I'd Nicole Kidmaned to his Batman. I nobly sacrificed holidays, candlelit dinners, and gave up nights we might have spent cocooning in front of the TV, consummating our love in a variety of spine-realigning positions. I pretended I didn't mind flying solo socially. I made excuses for his absence at posh parties and bought frozen dinners for two in M&S so as not to look too desperate.

But as he burnt gallons of midnight oil, whole Iraqi oilfields of the goddamn stuff, weekend after weekend, Christmas break after Christmas break, my foot gradually drifted further and further towards the stirrup of my high horse. What was the point of living together if I never bloody well saw him? Gradually my exquisitely sautéed gourmet spectaculars involving peeled grapes and marinated bats' balls gave way to grilled chops. Peekaboo teddies to white bloomers. What was the point of buying Janet Reger if there was no one to linger longer over such lingerie? Crotchless knickers lay undiscovered between disappointed thighs. Chocolate body paint coagulated in its jar. Pretty soon I stopped making excuses for him at my work functions and his family reunions. 'Julian *who*?'

When he cancelled the anniversary of our first meeting, I did actually swing up into the saddle of the old high horse, but one word from Captain Marvel – 'But darling, I have to prepare a case that could save 250 people on death row in Jamaica' – and I was forced to dismount again.

After he missed our second anniversary, I got a friend at Amnesty International to take a black and white photo of me in the window, looking dejected. I inked barbed wire around the frame captioned 'FREE THIS VICTIM OF TYRANNY FROM DINING ALONE. LIVES WITH HUMAN RIGHTS LAWYER.'

By the third missed anniversary I'd developed quite a different response to his 'I've got 250 people on death row' spiel. 'Oh, let them die. See if I care.'

The year after that I offered to fly on out there and hang them personally.

And then he asked me to marry him.

And I did still love him. The little place behind his ear that made him melt when kissed. The sweet way he cut the crusts off his sandwiches. The constellation of freckles on his broad chest, upholstered in pale down. The way he sang Broadway musical numbers, off key, in the shower. His wit – I'd never met a man who could thrust away for so long with his rapier. The way he filled his soliloquies with huge, majestic words. They steamed full bore into every sentence, a fleet of lexico-graphic ocean liners.

I, meanwhile, remained linguistically landlocked. My entire education was osmotically linked to Julian. He'd taught me about chamber music, Wagner, five-star hotels, cuisine minceur, poetry, literature and love. Okay, he lived in an ivory tower. But, hey, for a girl from an inner-city comprehensive – what a Des Res.

I knew I should have been crippled with remorse for leaving him at the altar like that. Hell. I should have been taking my place in the International House of Self-Serving Bitches. So why did I feel like a kid who'd just been given a day off school? Why was I as light-headed as a maximum security prisoner who's just tunnelled to daylight?

The truth was, I didn't want to grow up. I was too young to grow up. I still had posters on my wall, for God's sake! Not walking down the aisle had given me a renewed zest for life. Christ. I felt more alive than Kate's cystitis-curing Greek yoghurt. But little did I know that Life was about to crowbar some fissures into my new-found confidence . . .

It began over coffee with Anouska. I *had* contemplated donning the sackcloth of lycra and punishing myself for the wedding debacle with a severe workout. But, hell, the hardest thing about push-ups is trying to keep your cigarette alight. And this was a morning I needed to smoke. A lot. The wedding-dress shop had just refused to take back the frock. 'I'm sorry,' the manager had said snidely, 'but company policy stipulates that a refund can only be made if the customer has died.'

'But I have, socially,' I'd pleaded. It was true. The only people who hadn't white-exed me off their Christmas-card lists were Kate and Anouska. So, instead of exercising at the YMCA, I met Anouska for breakfast in South Molton Street. When I say 'breakfast', I mean the glass of designer water and fag she calls a meal. Personally, I prefer the Seafood Diet – you see food and you eat it. But Anouska was busy chewing over other things.

'Oh God, doll,' she sobbed into her espresso. 'I've had the most hideous morning.

I wasn't too alarmed. The woman thought she'd had a tough childhood because she'd had to walk three feet to her Dad's Volvo for the drive to primary school. 'Why?'

'Tressida's just found out she's got ME and Tabitha's got ovarian cancer.'

'What? Two It Girls at one blow?'

'If *they* can be given charity balls to organize, why can't *I*? Because I'm not married, that's why. Not even engaged . . .!' Her haywire hair corkscrewed from her cranium, as though she'd had a million brainwaves simultaneously.

'It won't take long. Literature's full of Willoughbys and Wickhams prowling for heiresses . . .' I daubed cappuccino froth from the tip of my nose and abstemiously pushed away the doughnut remnants. 'You'll meet your perfect man one day, Annie.' She should too. Anouska had been on more laps than a portable PC.

'Perfect!' she shrieked. 'Who said anything about perfect? Interestingly flawed would do. Vaguely bearable.'

'Two corpses short of a serial killer, even, in the case of Darius.' What shocked me about Anouska was not how much she expected from a man, but how little. Her latest representative of the Ring-Buying Sex, Darius Gore, possessed everything that makes the English upper class so interesting: an attic-dwelling, Hitler-sympathizing sibling, a recent political scandal and looming bankruptcy. If there's one thing the Nouveau Poor need, it's a niche with the Nouveau Riche. After leaving Vivian's mother, Mr Johannes de Kock made a fortune in armaments, meaning that Anouska fitted the bill, literally.

63

Somewhere in the dim recesses of Anouska's strange brain, it suddenly registered that raising the marriage topic with me was akin to asking a paraplegic if he was running late. 'Um . . .' she curled one leather-trousered leg up beneath her butt. 'You know I don't agree with what you did, doll, but it must have taken a lot of bottle.'

'It did. Moët Chandon.' I polished off the doughnut in one bite. 'I know everybody thinks that what I did is totally immature, but hey,' I grinned, 'at least I've never deluded myself into thinking I'm an adult.'

She pushed her plate towards me. 'Do you want mine as well?'

I shook my head virtuously. 'Look, I'm not a bad person, Annie.' (I noticed that she didn't rush to agree with me.) 'Okay, I'm not Mother Teresa . . . But, hey, I'm probably somewhere between her and Hitler . . . right?' No response. 'Well, aren't I?'

She stared at the floor directly in front of her Charles Jourdan sandal.

I inhaled her untouched doughnut with the speed of an industrial Hoover.

The second blow to my confidence came in Selfridges, at the make-up counter, awash with deeply sensual scents, shapely bottles and exotically coloured vials.

'Doll, you've just bought a one-way ticket to

disaster and you're worried about skin elasticity?' Anouska had whined as I dragged her into the colonnaded edifice in Oxford Street,

'Yeah, but at least I'll look good on the way . . . Night cream, please. Light.'

The Estée Lauder make-up assistant appraised me, sucking her teeth as though about to make an urgent, whispered phone call to a surgical dermatologist, '*Light*, madam?'

Madam?

'I think it might be time we moved on to a more . . . nourishing cream. The Super Strong Ultima Extreme for Mature Skin is very good . . .'

Mature?

She swivelled the magnified mirror towards me and I was confronted by an elephantine version of my own face. 'Wrinkles. Etched either side of your mouth. This cream contains marine algae to boost circulation and . . .'

'They're not wrinkles. They're fellatio lines,' Anouska explained helpfully. 'App*a*rently.'

'Freckles, dry patches, blotches, loss of pig-mentation, broken capillaries . . . A neck cream would also be advisable . . .' The wind-up, white-coated doll prattled on with a lot of euphemisms for the war against decrepitude – refining, enriching, recovery, rejuvenate, protection . . .

I glowered at her.

'I'm just trying to give you a clearer view of your

flaws and provide helpful hints on how they can be overcome.'

'Oh truly, your selflessness knows no bounds.'

'There's also an Electrolysis special on offer,' the android added in that professionally insulting manner they have.

Wielding a cotton bud like a miniature police truncheon, she pointed to one small black hair I'd never noticed sprouting from my chin. It looked, in the magnified looking glass, like a sequoia tree.

'Where the hell did *that* come from?'

'It's normal as we age that . . .'

'Would you stop with all this ageing crap, already. I have one facial hair. It's not as though I'm about to start baying at the moon . . .'

'Well then, why not try this.' Lunging forward, the saleswoman attempted to sandpaper my face off with a brusque rotary action that would have been better employed in the resurfacing of airport tarmac.

'Hey! What the . . .'

'Retin A peels away at the skin . . .' Her voice rasped insistently, a wasp caught against a window pane.

'Eats away at the skin? Jesus. What is it? Eboli in a jar?'

She handed me a refining gel tester for the thigh zone. With that bizarre combination of humiliation and desire that is central to every make-up purchase, I looked at the price tag on the tube . . . Christ Almighty. How could a cream cost more than a dream retirement home?

'There's always liposuction,' Anouska suggested helpfully.

' "Fridge-o-suction" would be more useful,' I said half-heartedly. 'Just suck the food right out of the refrigerator, you know. Go right to the source, Can you believe this woman?'

Anouska eyed me critically. 'Well, doll, your lycra-panel days are kind of over, ya know?'

'I am *not* descending into tan medical hose crone-dom quite yet, thank you very much. Come on, I'm outta here.'

The make-up assistant smiled at me; a complicit, grinning jackal. 'Have a nice day.'

'Sod off,' I told her. 'I've got other plans.'

Having come in for one lousy tube of moisturizer, I left Selfridges ten minutes later so laden down with pungent unguents, enzyme creams and crater-fillers, that I had to sign the credit-card slip with a pen clenched between my teeth. Now all I needed was some shaving foam for the handlebar moustache I seemed to have sprouted, like Jack's beanstalk, over bloody night. It was just as well I didn't want children because I'd obviously be giving birth to a litter of she-wolves. A compulsory broomstick was no doubt waiting for me at Customer Services.

And there was worse to come. Anouska left me with an air kiss on the corner of Regent Street. She was off to prepare for her date with the dreaded Darius. Preparation would involve her usual DIY lobotomy.

Anouska's technique for getting a man was to act happy, busy and swallow at all times. Not a technique that had ever worked for me. Hell, Julian says my neuroses are the only interesting thing about me. (Besides my ability to hook my legs behind my head.)

'If I don't ring by nine tonight, sub-let my apartment, okay, doll?'

I continued my walk to work unaware of the body blow awaiting me. As I approached a building site, I prepared for the sexist onslaught. I mentally rehearsed my barbed ripostes ... And then it happened – or rather, it didn't. Not one whistle. Not even an 'Oy!' I told myself the builders must have been engrossed in some high-tech, hydraulic manoeuvre demanding maximum eyeball riveting – and retraced my steps. I sashayed past again, this time with a little more swing in my hips. Nothing. Zilch. Having raged against building-site harassment my whole life, when it didn't happen I felt inexplicably devastated. I was also devastated about *why* I should feel devastated. But there was no time to dwell on the hypocrisy of the situation. The lack of male response had tapped into a vein; a varicose vein. A few hours ago I'd been vibrant and invigorated. But how could I be feeling my oats and my varicose veins at the same time? Maybe that wretched assistant was right? Yes, the evidence was mounting up. Hadn't I actually gone to bed last New Year's Eve? Why else would I hate jungle music? And hey. You *know* you're old when you no longer laugh at the concept of electrolysis.

Suddenly, here I was in Margaret Rutherford mode. A tweed cape and bicycle beckoned. Any minute now, I'd find myself tremendously exercised about my bowels.

If I were a building, I'd have subsidence. Hell, I'd be listed. If I were a tree in Yellowstone National Park, whole girl-guide packs would be hiking through me. But there was even worse to come.

Reaching the Mall, I stood outside the white, wedding cake of a building housing the Institute of Contemporary Arts and sighed resignedly. The truth of it is, I'm a bit of a shirkaholic. I'm convinced that historians will look upon this era as the Dark Ages Mark 2. All the women I knew were ricocheting from one nervous breakdown to another, leaving a trail of feral, nanny-reared children in their wake, juggling dinner parties and Prozac overdoses and extramarital affairs (because their workaholic husbands are too tired for sex), gushing all the time from their psychiatric-unit beds that they'd be bored if they didn't work. I, on the other hand, have vocational cancer. My ambition's in remission. The only thing I wanted to be when I grew up was young.

Having run away from school at fifteen, I have, in my time, scraped the bottom of the job barrel – from bedpan emptier to buxom serving wench. While putting myself through art school, I'd worked nights inserting colour supplements into newspapers just so that I could tell people I was a 'hand inserter'. I've been a kissogram, a cabaret singer and dressed as a human street sign for a gym in Woolloomooloo, Sydney, which is where I'd met Kate. How could you not bond with someone when you're both parading around in promotional sandwich boards that read 'Fat and Ugly? . . . *Want to be just ugly?*'

Ever since the United Nations had declared her love life a disaster area six years ago, Kate had worked at the ICA. When she was promoted to Artistic Director, junior only to God and the Great Barrier Reef, she'd help me fail upwards into a job in the PR department. Although I tried to persuade the nude poets and Mutant Nymphet Sculptresses of the benefits of working without the pressure of success – I still had to turn up at the office occasionally.

The staff were mostly of the 'all sex is rape', 'snot fair Millie Tants variety. What the sign outside the gallery should have read was 'Danger. Extremely Hormonal Females For Next Mile'. I didn't so much receive a wage here. It was more like combat pay. Especially when an exhibition was being mounted.

I pushed through the glass doors and negotiated my way over the layers of artists' legs, woven backpacks, ethnic papooses and the seven vehicle pile-up of prams. My arrival silenced the buzz.

'So?' greeted Kate, readjusting her red-framed glasses. 'How did Julian take it? Did he go ape-shit?

Did you tell him you didn't love him enough? I suppose you couldn't tell him the truth; the male suicide rate is high enough already, right?'

'I *do* love him enough . . . It's just . . .' I glanced at the expectant, eager faces around me. Was I really going to strip off to my emotional knickers here? Like hell I was. 'It's just that there are three billion other men in the world whom I'd like to see naked, you know?' I said glibly.

I trailed Kate to the main gallery where she was supervising the unpacking of the latest exhibition – a feminist collection entitled 'What Women Want'.

I picked up the glossy brochure I'd help design. On the front was a penis photographer dedicated to fighting patriarchy through her series of nude male 'skinscapes'. 'In close-up, from certain angles, the male armpit bears an uncanny resemblance to the female pubic area', read the artist's blurb.

'For the curator of a feminist exhibition, Kate, you really know nothing about women. Women, all women, worry about three things only. Bad Hair Days. Shoe Shopping. And Thinner Thighs. If you renamed the feminist struggle as The Struggle For Thinner Thighs, Firmer Hair Mousse and Perfect Arch Support While Wearing Stilettos, membership would soar, you know.'

Kate laughed. Insulting an Aussie is no fun. It's like water off a duck-billed platypus's back. 'We want for women what women want for themselves,' she said sickly, pointing impatiently at the photographs she'd instructed me to enthuse about for a television arts programme later that day.

What we want for ourselves? Jesus. What *did* we want? A man *and* to be single. A job *and* to be free. Children *and* to be childless. A sensual encounter on a train with a witty, poetry-quoting stranger that leads to a romantic dash by private Lear jet to a Tahitian island so remote it's not in the atlas . . . And then other times, just a quiet night on my own watching *Seinfeld* and eating Mars Bars in flannelette pyjamas. And not to age, ever. One thing today had taught me: I may be young at heart, but apparently I was middle aged in all the other places.

This was confirmed when the Channel Four team arrived and Kate pushed me in front of the camera. The producer, one of those pubescent trendoids who make films that are about as interesting as watching paint dry (he once actually *made* a film about paint drying), looked at me through the lens then asked Kate if she had a presenter who was not so 'chronologically gifted'.

Kate and I looked at him blankly.

'Experientially enhanced?' We still had no idea what he was talking about. 'Look,' he said frankly, 'the exhibition is about young artists, right? And I don't think Ms Steele's giving the right impression.'

My geriatric blood froze in my clogged veins. 'Yeah? Well you're not giving the right impression of a producer either. The only thing *you* could produce is a urine sample.'

Kate dragged me into the foyer before I could do any more damage. 'What the hell's eating you? We need the publicity!'

'It's a sore point, okay? The Beauty Führer at Selfridges this morning suggested that I'm old, ugly and too fat.'

'So?' said Kate. 'Get a wider mirror.'

It didn't make me feel any better. Nor did the Super Babe with skyscraper heels and the shoulder-padded silhouette of an American quarterback that the producer conjured up to replace me. How could any woman look that young? She'd obviously been drinking embalming fluid.

By the time I left the ICA later that afternoon, I was ready to buy some Vaseline Intensive Care, massage it in for about fifty years, then repeat. I was straight off for a boob and lube job.

Okay, so I was older than I thought. But it didn't mean I could no longer bite off more than I could chew – it just meant that I had to chew more slowly.

But I wasn't counting on what Life was about to dish up . . .

5

Bridesmaid Revisited

It is a truth universally acknowledged that a single woman in possession of a good fortune must be in want of a husband. Which is why, a month later, all the usual suspects were gathered at St Andrew's Church, Cliveden, for the society wedding of the season. Finally the Mountie had got her man.

The fact that Anouska and Darius would love and cherish *till divorce do us part* was not in question; Anouska had spent more time choosing her gown than her groom. Her only criterion now, hubbywise, was that he be aristocratic. Darius's obligatory epiglottal lisp, combined with his invincible repugnance for everything and everybody, indicated that he possessed the perfect upper-class credentials.

But the trouble with upper-class wealth is that it doesn't always vouchsafe money. The British landed gentry do have this tendency to leave their fortunes to retirement kennels for hunting canines and cat hostels. Darius came from a long line of dog orphanage donors. Anouska was a woman with money to burn. In Darius she had met her match.

I didn't stop trying to talk her out of the marriage, even in the bridal car. 'He just sees you as a meal ticket,' I staccatoed, as we jounced over the cobbled country lanes. '. . . And believe m-me, A-Annie, D-Darius h-has m-made a lifetime r-reservation a-at t-the R-Ritz.'

'How can you talk that way on my wedding day!'

'. . . I so want you to be happy, Annie, but DARIUS DOESN'T LOVE YOU. Of all people, why *him*?'

'I chose him chiefly on the grounds that *he's a male*.'

'Yeah, with a title. Well I can think of a few other titles he richly deserves. Like Free-Loading Bum.'

But Anouska had convinced herself it was love. After they'd vowed everlasting devotion in the eyes of the Lord, I watched as she folded back the lace veil to reveal a spectacular barnet of brunette profiteroles before turning her hopeful face up to his. Darius, with facial expressions by Taxidermy, went in for the kiss. Making the face of a child rejecting spinach, he dodged her lips and made minimal contact with her left ear lobe.

After we'd all been dandruffed in confetti and posed for photographs on the stone steps, Darius, silk top hat rakishly askew, approached we bridesmaids with what he thought was a swagger but merely looked as though his underpants were too tight.

Having air-kissed Tara, Tania, Tressida, Tabitha and Tessa (it's illegal to be an It Girl unless your name starts with T) he paused before me – marooned, as I was, in a sea of maroon chiffon. 'Ah, the Wedding Reneger. I can't believe the church didn't burst into flames as you approached.'

'Congratulations,' I said to him. 'A wealthy wife . . . quite a labour-saving device. If *I'd* been marrying you, I'd have made you sign a pre-nuptial agreement you could make into a mini-series.'

'Anouska, poppet,' Darius drawled, beckoning his bride, 'has it ever crossed your lovely little mind that your friends resent not being as rich as you? Perhaps it's time you acquired some new chums in a higher-earning bracket?'

He flicked the swallow tails of his grey morning coat and departed with that mincing waddle. Annie, or rather Lady Anouska Gore, tethered to his arm, smiled helplessly over her shoulder.

The reception at Cliveden, a moss-flecked seventeenth-century stately home, set amid a glen and glade-studded Thames-side acreage big enough to support the entire population of Belgium, was doomed from the start. Darius's *old* monied friends and Annie's *new*, went together like, I dunno, caviar and Sara Lee cake.

The tribal dialect of the upper-class trough-monkeys – yawing voices honed by thousands of pounds of private education, clashed atonally with the strident raucousness of Mr de Kock's Euro-trash coterie. I recognized a newly pardoned drug baron, a disgraced former President with humorous cufflinks, an asbestos magnate and Henry Kissinger.

After Julian's matrimonial aspirations had gone into free fall a month ago, I'd been getting the old Trappist Monk treatment. If *he* did deign to speak to me over breakfast, he was excessively polite. 'Please, after *you*.' 'No, no, I *insist*.' 'Would it be too much trouble removing your knife from my back?'

The rest of the time he was in Martyr Mode. Every single sentence he'd uttered since then began with 'Don't worry, *I'll* do it. The man had been inundated with letters of condolence, as though somebody had died. He'd been offering nothing but tea and sympathy to relatives on both sides of the family. But now he was attending the wedding that should have been his, and the guy was ready to burn his boxer shorts.

The façade started to crack soon after we'd been seated in the tapestry-lined dining room, and the wine waiter leant towards me, a white and a red in either hand.

'Um . . . white thanks.'

'Subject, of course, to her indecision,' said Julian sarkily. 'Rebecca can't commit to a wine. As far as she's concerned, the word "commit" should only be used

77

next to the word "murder" ... which is an apt description for living with *her*, actually.'

All fourteen eyeballs at our table focussed on me. 'Julian, do you really think it's best to spin-dry our dirty laundry in public?' I darted a desperate look towards Kate.

'Do you reckon they'll have veggo?' Kate interjected helpfully. 'I can't eat any animal life that can be seen without a microscope.'

'No other dietary requirements?' Julian pondered derisively. 'Like *smoked foreskins*. It's thanks to *you* Rebecca eschewed the band of gold – in my opinion,' he made a mock bow, 'the most stupid bloody thing you've ever done – which is saying something to a woman who once slept with Roman Polanski.'

'Julian, I don't want your opinion ... and neither does anybody else at this table.'

'Don't be ludicrous. I'm a lawyer. Everybody wants my opinion. I'm paid £250 an hour for it.'

'You slept with Roman Polanski?' Kate lip-synched, aghast. 'Why didn't you ever tell me that?'

The It Girl seated to my left craned around me to inspect this £250 an hour jiltee. Her eyes glinted. 'Really? She turned down your marriage proposal?' she purred, leaning right across me to stroke Julian's sleeve. 'A handsome, successful, attractive man like you ...'

'I know,' Julian bantered. 'If only I had a little humility I'd be perfect. And what do you do?' Julian asked the It Girl, leaning across me to cover her delicate hand with his own.

'I'm a Trustafarian, actually,' she trilled. 'In search of some meaning in my life.'

Meaning that she was in search of a husband. I accidentally slopped my wine into her lap. 'Oh, you're an *heiress*. Sorry. I thought you said airhead.'

The atmosphere at table thirteen on this cold May evening became as starched as the tablecloth before us.

'So,' gushed Vivian, desperately trying to inject some merriment. 'What did *you* give them? I had complete gift angst . . .'

'Couldn't you just recycle the gift you bought for us,' Julian queried scornfully.

'I hope you only gave presents in plastic,' I said, ''cause they'll be chucking them at each other in no time.' I slathered a roll in butter – hey, cholesterol was about all I had left in life.

'Simon says that lasting relationships are based on nothing more than common interests,' Vivian persevered.

'In their case,' Kate whispered for my benefit, 'Simon.'

'. . . and joint projects. Like children, isn't that right, Daddy?'

Simon blew her a kiss. 'Yes, Mummy.'

'I'm sorry but I have no intention of dilating my cervix the customary three miles, for the pleasure of spending the rest of my life in bathrooms applauding bowel movements. Ugh.' I devoured the entrée in three bites. 'No. Thank. You.'

'Personally I want lots and lots of children.' The Trustafarian said, looking doe-eyed at Julian.

'Really? Me too.' Julian laced his arms behind his head and rocked back in his chair. 'I can just see just myself sitting cross legged at a cubs' campfire.'

I bristled. 'Really? I hate children. How can you not hate anyone who can eat sweets without putting on weight?'

'Working mothers have a much greater risk of heart attack and going bonkers than childless career-women, you know . . .' Kate contributed.

'Well, *you* don't need to worry,' Julian retaliated. 'Not with *that* haircut. That's a haircut that needs a number under it.'

'As long as Duracell continue to manufacture, I'll be okay,' Kate said. 'Much more reliable than a man.'

'You must have the sort of vibrator that requires a lorry drivers' licence,' Simon scoffed. 'Warning. Wide load.'

'Yes. Just like mine.' I rallied on behalf of my friend. 'I'm surprised we haven't chipped our teeth! Now leave her alone.'

A knife tapped on a glass as the Best Man rose to his feet for the ritual Humiliatingly Indiscreet Speech By Groom's Soon-to-Be-Ex-Friend.

'*You own a vibrator?*' Julian interrupted the silence in horrified amazement. Surrounding tables gawped at us, simultaneously. *'When did you get a vibrator?'*

Now, even the Best Man was looking in our direction.

'Julian . . .' I shushed him.

'I just can't believe that you'd wait till now, five years into a relationship, to tell me you don't want children and you own a vibrator.'

'Maybe you're insufficiently in touch with your feminine side?' Simon, the Red Adair of Relationships, suggested.

'Oh fuck off,' I said, femininely.

'Would you *mind*?' hissed someone's great aunt, two tables over.

Oh, nothing like a wedding to bring out the best in people. Much more of this and I'd develop a facial tic. After the lame speeches I was just contemplating finding a bathroom window I could escape out of again, when I first laid eyes on Zachary Phoenix Burne. It wasn't hard to spot him. The collective female 'phwaah' that filled the room as he took to the dance floor could have been the give-away. I had never, ever seen anything quite like his cardiac-arresting combination of tangled black hair, pernod-coloured, stray-cat eyes, straining Levi fly buttons, silver-stud earring and musculature last seen on George Clooney in his rubber Bat suit. Each bicep was the size of a guest bedroom. On the left hibernated a death adder, which reared to strike whenever he flexed. This guy wasn't just sexy, he was a crotch-moistener. A mammary-achingly, take-me-now-you-brute, drop-dead dreamy hunk of spunk. But . . . in an understated kind of way. The tear in his black jeans, situated just below his butt, was in the shape of a sly smile. No. More like an eye that winked as he moved. And moving was what he did best. 'Dancing' is too tame a word. It was more like floor-carving. The guy could give dancing lessons to Michael Jackson. It was as dirty as you could get without latex. A girl could get up the duff just by jiving with a man like that. If he was trying to come over as a hot-to-trot stud puppy with buns of steel, then he'd definitely scored.

'Okay, Kate. Have I got a *guy* for *you*.'

'I don't want a guy, you big galah . . . Bloody Hell!' Even Kate was dumbstruck when I swivelled her towards the dance floor.

'We have a ten.' I mimed the actions of an Olympic Judge holding aloft the score card of a parallel-bar performer.

'And a half,' adjudicated Kate.

When Zachary Burne left the floor, the sound of a hundred women tearing their eyes away from his body was like Velcro.

'Do you want to dance?' I asked Julian, curling my fingers around his arm.

'You know I can only do two types of dances. One of them is the funky chicken and the other one isn't.' Julian brushed aside my hand as though it were a hive of hornets. '*You own a vibrator?*'

All around us, on chandeliers and banisters and chair backs, there were reclining carved cupids, lyre-plucking Hymens, naked Apollos and Adonises lounging lasciviously. 'Come on, Jules. Dance with me . . .'

'What I really want to do is hail the winged chariot.' He yawned, peering at his watch. 'Jesus, what are you people? Vampires?'

What makes Julian an unusual human rights activist is that he hates humans. Leaving early was part of his People Avoidance Programme. This was a guy who liked humankind in theory, but not in practice.

'You always want to go early,' I sulked. 'You're a social premature ejaculator, do you know that?'

'Spoken by the woman who climbed out of the loo window on her own wedding day.'

'We never have any fun any more . . . You're such a Grown-Up.'

'Yeah, well. It's time you grew up too.'

'And it's time *you* grew *down* . . . Jesus Christ, we're just like an old . . .'

I nearly said 'married couple' but stopped just in time. The thump thump of the music, the oppressive warmth of the room, the psychological claustrophobia of being at a wedding with the man I'd jilted – made me feel as though I'd been swallowed whole by a boa-constrictor. 'I need a cigarette.' I stood up.

'You don't smoke,' Julian chastised, taking me by the wrist and tugging me back into my chair.

'Oh, Julian,' I said sadly. 'You sound just like a husband.'

If I didn't get outside and fast, I thought I might regurgitate my £85-a-head meal on to the antique woven rugs. Watched by the portraits of censorious ancestors and the dark eye-slits of suit after suit of sinister armour, I wrenched off my shoes, hitched up my frock and ran through the hall, down the stone steps and across the dewy lawn that rioted with tulips, dodging an earie topiary menagerie and assorted architectural follies, deep into a cool, dark glen.

I leant, wheezing, against an oak. I looked up at the tangled canopy, necklaced with dew. Glinting through the trees I glimpsed the dark ribbon of river. I took in the faraway sounds of people laughing, masts clinking, boat engines receding into silence.

I also ever so slowly realized that I was listening to someone else's breathing.

At the sound of a match striking, I wheeled around. A flickering orange ember illuminated a male hand. I peered through the hungry shadows, trying to discern the interloper.

'Wouldn't it be sad if there are no little green men?' said the cigarette end. '. . . Suppose Human Beings are as intelligent as Intergalactic life gets?'

I fired up my own cigarette. The match briefly spotlit the midnight philosopher. Lying supine on a low-slung branch was the Man Who Took Women's Breath Away. He peeled open one eye, barely bothering to blink as he looked me up and down with casual disdain before giving a low, honeyed smirk.

Hormonal Houston. We have lift off. We're going warp factor ten to Planet Passion. I was just wondering if it would be an even more serious breach of wedding etiquette to snog, marry and have children with one of the guests – when my match died.

The symbolism wasn't lost on me as I burnt my fingers.

6

Posh Frock, No Knickers

A micro-second later I re-entered earth's atmosphere. What the hell was I doing? I was practically married. I was now a user of Crone Cream. What's more, up close, this guy was just out of nappies. He looked about twenty-two. Besides, in navigating my way through life, I was no longer keeping my compass in my camiknickers.

'I'm sorry about disturbing you,' I said primly. Who *was* I all of a sudden? Miss Jean Brodie? I unlaced the frilly maroon bodice of my skintight bridesmaid frock. 'I just couldn't *stand* another *minute* of holding my stomach in. This truly is the most God-awful, snobby, excessively pompous wedding I've ever had the misfortune to attend.'

'Yeah?' The voice was American, languid, lazy. 'I

find a good way to relieve "excessive pomp" is to fuck yer brains out behind the altar.'

Did Stud Muffin just say what I thought he just said? It had, after all, been a rather long and fraught day. Now I was having audial hallucinations. Just to be safe, I moved out of the throbbing darkness. 'Nice meeting you,' I farewelled over my shoulder. 'Part of my allergy to weddings is my complete hopelessness at inane small talk.'

'Really?' I heard the soft thud of his feet as he sprang to the ground. 'I'd say yer doin' jes' fine.'

Cheeky bastard. 'Better than you.' I eyeballed him, Brodie-style. '*Your* main conversation no doubt revolves around how long you've got to go in your parole.'

'Con-ver-sa-tion? Um ... That's "words" ain't it? Those things we use to kill time until we fuck.'

Obviously the guy accounted for half the known world supply of Smartass. But little did he know that *I* had the other half. 'I didn't realize that Anouska's guest list ran to pets and other animals.'

Well that was the end of him. I slogged through the wet grass towards the pool. This was the pool where high-class hooker Christine Keeler had cavorted naked with Tory ministers in the sixties. Legs dangling off the diving board, I was just casually pondering whether that made it more of a bidet than a pool, when the Man Who Took Women's Breath Away breezed out of the shadows and perched his peachy posterior on the head of what looked like an ancient Greek sculpture. Obviously not the antiquities type.

'There's one cool thing about weddin's. The ... what do you Brits call it? Oh yeah. The PFNK look.' I raised a quizzical eyebrow. 'Posh Frock No Knickers.' Smiling salaciously, he stretched out one of those legs that started at his ear lobes, and lifted up the hem of my dress with the toe of his cowboy boot. 'Love that look.'

I slapped his leg. 'Um ... dare I use the words "tiny", "cock" and "obviously you've got a" in the same sentence?'

In response, the Eye-Candy leant forward, nonchalantly took my hand and placed it on his groin. This was not a penis. This was a vaulting pole. I'd heard that Americans have a lot of effrontery, but ten inches before we even knew each other's first name? Who did he think he was? ... Bill Clinton? I snatched my hand away.

'Hey, never point a loaded penis at anyone. I could report you to Kenneth Starr!'

'Yeah? Where I come from, it's considered impolite not to have sex with the bridesmaids.' A mutinous grin split his face. 'Besides, it's loaded, sure. But there's a safety catch. I ain't in'erested in any woman who ain't in'erested in me. Although, it sure is difficult to tell the way you females say yes when you mean no and say no when you mean yes. Cigarette?'

'Yes/No,' I replied.

He laughed. God. Even his teeth were perfect. He was what Anouska called a 'good drop of skin'; what Kate referred to as a 'root rat'. Basically, the guy could star in a Diet Pepsi break.

'So, ya mean we've gotta do like, ten dull dinners and talk about Human Relationships in microscopic detail before we can finally rip each other's clothin' off with our teeth?'

'For your information,' I smugged, 'I've never been to bed with a Lowlife and I have no intention of . . .'

'Bet you've woken up with a shitload of 'em, though.' He crackled open a fresh packet of Marlboros.

I studied him with narrow eyes. 'What's *with* you? You're too young to be such a chauvinist.'

'Thank Christ there's a few of us left!' He lit two cigarettes before passing one to me.

'Well, that tells me all I need to know about your brain-cell capacity.' I ostentatiously wiped the filter on my hem before inserting the cigarette between my lips. 'And it's only going to get worse, buddy. It's scientifically proven that as men get older, their brains atrophy.'

'At-ra-what? . . . Trouble with you British babes, you spend so many words saying nuthin' at all. Can't yer just use a normal word now an' again. Just as well us guys are so much brainier to start with.'

'Men? More intelligent? . . . Yeah. Right.' I dragged deeply on my cancer stick. 'Which is why your idea of fun is to snap towels at each others' bottoms. What the hell *is* that . . . ?'

'And why youse chicks' idea of cool is to act like men.'

'*Chicks?*' I picked the expression up with a pair of invisible sterilized tongs.

'Can't fuck ya for fear I'm turnin' gay.'

'I'm sorry. I beg your pardon? Me? Having a carnal encounter with someone like *you*, is about as likely as you being able to find the hypotenuse of a triangle.'

'Hell, I didn't know it was lost.'

Despite being an unevolved Neanderthal, he had charm, you had to admit. Goddamnit. The guy was more disarming than a team of UN weapons inspectors. 'Um . . . it's the end of the twentieth century. Men don't treat women like objects, any more.'

'Hey, I don't treat women like objects. Hell no.' He gave a kind of James Cagney shrug. 'I treat my objects *way* better.'

Like I said – smartass. 'I'll have you know that women can do everything that men can do. The only thing men do better is die earlier.'

'Crap. Men are loads better than women at loads of stuff.'

'Oh, yes? Like what?'

He smirked. The sort of smirk that hints at un-mentionable sexual acts, things you couldn't possibly care for – at first. 'Guilt-free sex and whistlin'.'

I put two fingers in my mouth and forced out a decibel-piercing shriek of air that even managed momentarily to drown out the Dire Straits hit being mangled by the band inside. On the Cliveden balcony, guests pivoted in our direction, eyes straining through the blackness. The Man Who Took Women's Breath Away pulled me out of sight. He rattled the handles on the pavilion doors. Locked. The last door yielded, revealing the pool utility room. I could just make out the folded deckchairs, not yet unpacked for the summer, and a ping-pong table, pyjama-ed in canvas. It smelt mildewed but warm, there in the liquid, sensuous dark. We squeezed inside, close enough to feel each other's breath. He smelt spicy, yeasty, and – it has to be said – divinely masculine.

'Men don't have to go to the john in pairs.'

'Women don't regard sitting on the toilet as a leisure activity.'

'Men don't get PMS.'

'You'd *love* to have Premenstrual Syndrome. Men have PMS envy. Besides being a woman is better because, when we have kids, we never have to worry who the mother is.'

'Yeah, but we get to have kids without havin' to wear floral maternity dresses . . .'

'Men can't wrap things.'

'Women can't tell jokes.' He came closer. Despite his Schwarzenegger pectorals, he moved with an easy grace. He leant a hand on the wall behind me, his bare forearm grazing my shoulder. 'At least men know how to have fun. A chick's idea of fun is to buy those tiny glass animals made from blown glass. Knick-knacks, yeah, that's them. Explain that to me . . . Chicks get all juiced up over upholstery, man . . .'

'Just like men do over gadgets. Actually men are just like those gadgets you buy which read "A little assembly required". Then they sit in the corner all in pieces for centuries.'

'So' – he placed his other hand on the wall, touching the side of my face – 'why are you hot for us, then?'

'Hot for you! Huh! I don't think so.' Hot for him? I was bleeding from the ears. 'How could anyone be hot for the sort of breed who like to drop bombs on urban areas?'

'Yer know, yer right. Men are only good at the little things . . . like runnin' the world and goin' to war.'

'At least we're not always timing ourselves. Oh, that nuclear detonation took 12.6 seconds . . .' I hooked one stockinged leg around his calf and drew him closer to me. Nothing like a touch of IBS (Irritable Boyfriend Syndrome) to make you horny and reckless with a complete and utter stranger. 'Oh look! We did that trip in 1 hour, 13 minutes and exactly 3.6 seconds. And you won't give way to traffic either. Especially to another man.' My fragile dress fretted against his hard denim. 'You'll accelerate past the speed of light, before either of you idiots will give way . . . We can drive a small car and not worry what people are saying about our sexual prowess.'

'Yeah, but garage mechanics don't see *us* comin'.' He slipped his hand down inside my bodice and rolled my nipple between two warm fingers. I drank in the details of his face. This guy was the practice run Mother Nature had for Brad Pitt but the slight flaws – the indecently juicy lips, the sleepy eyes, the scar calligraphied across one cheek – made him even more dangerously irresistible.

'Men don't write thank-you notes. Or remember anniversaries . . .'

'Men never get cellulite. Doan' have ta wax nuthin' neither. Plus nobody will ever ask us to wear suspenders . . . Do yer? By the way?' He ran his other hand up under my dress.

'Not to forget the way you're always scratching yourselves, idly, in the crotch area. You never see a *woman* scratching her genitals, now do you?'

'Maybe not in public.' He nibbled on my neck as he massaged my inner thighs. ''Cause yer not as honest about yer urges.'

'Honest! Huh!' I winkled my finger inside the hole in his jeans leg. The velvet flesh was hot and hard. 'How can you expect me to find a species attractive who lust indiscriminately? Women are capable of not thinking about sex occasionally.' I held my breath, as his fingers strayed higher. 'Men can never find things either.' I groaned again as he sent me into orbit.

'Except G spots,' he grinned.

By now I was liquefying. It was all I could do to keep standing. In the time it took the band to segue from 'Ina Gadda De Vita' to 'Honky Tonk Women', I'd been in orbit so often I started to feel like the Mir Space Station.

It was then the stranger leant down and kissed me. It was a kiss like liquid caramel. 'Kissin' . . . the second best thing you can do with your lips.'

'Second?'

He lay me back across the ping-pong table and disappeared under my PFNK in one fluid, graceful movement. Now that's what I call paying lip-service to love.

It was the first time I'd ever made love with a black man.

7

A Lick And A Promise

'Where've you been?' Julian interrogated upon my dishevelled return. Judging by the stained tuxedos of the wrung-out wedding band on their seventh rendition of 'Jumping Jack Flash', I'd been gone for longer than I realized. I waited for the wave of guilt, but no psychological surf rolled in. After all, what exactly was I guilty of? It was nothing more than a crime of passion. Not even a crime, more a folly of passion; a sexual *faux pas*.

'Walking,' I lied effortlessly, omitting the destination, *on the wild side*: It wasn't a big lie. More like a half truth. I just told him the wrong half. I noticed the squadron of plaster cupids buzzing overhead and, for a disquieting moment, thought they might dive-bomb.

Lord and Lady Darius Gore appeared on the stairs

together for the traditional Bouquet-Tossing-Let's All-Pretend-She-Has-A-Hymen Moment.

Kate and I were just placing twenty-pound bets on how long the marriage would last when I saw, out of the corner of my eye, alcohol-lubricated females hurtling bouquet-wards. But the orchid homing missile was rocketing with ironic accuracy straight towards Yours Truly. It was not so much a catch as a floral facial. There was a muted gasp of breath and muffled whisperings. I peered out from between the fronds to see friends rolling their eyes in embarrassment. I tried to speak, but could only spit out greenery.

'Déjà vu,' said Julian, with droll disdain.

As the queue of well-wishers pressed in on all sides, I kissed Anouska goodbye. She whispered urgently in my ear. 'I think I may have made a mistake.'

'What? With your going-away outfit?' She was wearing a transparent lacy dress with Big Underpants.

'No. With my husband.'

'Anouska, it's the *reception*. Things aren't supposed to sour until oh, at least until you get back to the honeymoon suite.'

Before she could detail her misgivings, she was whisked away to married life. As I sought out Kate to pay up my twenty-quid bet money, I glimpsed Zachary once more before he evaporated into the night. He looked into my eyes just a split second longer than necessary ... enough to make my knees buckle.

'Well, that's a record,' proclaimed Kate. 'It only took you half a second to undress that teenager with your eyes.'

I attempted to drag her on to the dance floor for a bit of pelvis jumping to 'Oh-Oh-Oh-Oh-Stayin' Alive'. Even second-rate cover versions were better than the long drive home with Julian. But there was no holding back the premature social ejaculator.

'So who was the teenager I overheard Kate say you were flirting with?' were his opening words as we gravel-crunched out of the drive.

'Um . . . what time was it . . . ?' I kicked off my shoes and propped my feet on the dashboard. 'You know I'm a serial flirt. But relax, I'm only window shopping.'

I amazed myself at how easy this lying gig was. No wonder men did it so often. My heart executed a kind of clumsy foxtrot in my chest but my face stayed composed; my voice remained level.

I rummaged in the glove compartment and slotted a CD into the player. Pink Floyd wafted out of the speakers. I groaned, stabbed at the stop button and rummaged some more.

'Mike and the Mechanics, the Rolling Stones, The Eurythmics, *Steeleye Span* . . . God, Jules, don't we have anything from this century? We're getting so middle-aged.'

'Becky, we *are* middle-aged.' Rain drizzled on the windows.

'It's not how old you are, it's how old you behave. And you are behaving like a geriatric.'

'I am not.' The wipers cleared the windscreen with a sluggish, petulant swipe.

'You sort your socks on a Saturday night.'

'So what? You're making me out to be the human version of a Dr Scholl sandal.'

'You go home early from parties.'

'I have grave misgivings about the pleasures of rap dancing, okay?'

'Speak for yourself. Personally, I am not ready to have the variety of life of a bloody battery chicken.'

'What? You really want to go back to being young? . . . Hanging bits of lace sarongs on the wall? Wearing shirts that proclaim your philosophical beliefs? Ugh. Petting in the back seat has lost its appeal, Beck.'

'Petting? I can't believe you used that word. Petting? You see what I mean? You're geriatric!'

'If "geriatric" means no longer considering hitch-hiking a means of transport, then yes I am. I like to drink coke – not do it. I no longer wake at 6 a.m. on Christmas morning, either. I can actually be seen with my parents in public. I also find it reassuring to see policemen around the place. You too, Becky, are old enough to eliminate "catwalk modelling" from your career ambitions list.'

'How did you know about . . .'

'And anyway,' he upped the volume on Elvis Costello. 'We still have lots of fun.'

'Fun! Okay, let's think. Exactly what *did* we do last weekend? A whipped-cream orgy perhaps? No. You reorganized the condiments cupboard. I haven't been invited to a party I wouldn't go to in a million years! . . . We have the debauchery of, I dunno, an Osmond!' I ejected Costello with a churlish jab of my manicured nail.

'Hey, I ran a red light in 1996,' Julian joshed. 'And I didn't declare that £500 purchase to Heathrow Customs. Do you remember?'

'I used to be wild! I used to be interesting! I've lost my identity. You've stolen it from me!'

'Well let's go along to a police line-up and see if you can make an ID' he said, tartly.

'It's just that you've become so, well, anal.'

'I am not anal!'

'You arrange my shoes in height-of-heel order. You discuss dietary fibre when it's not even breakfast. You lecture me about which dishcloth I can use on the floor . . . Your main obsession is whether or not your toothpaste has tartar control. You worry about getting ringworm fungi from shared combs, and that staph thing . . .'

'Staphylococcus aureus.'

'. . . from public telephones. You wipe the cashpoint machine with an anti-bacterial cleanser for God's sake. Actually, you're a hypochondriac. You are! You just can't leave being well enough alone.'

'I am not a hypochondriac!'

'Well then hypochondria is the only disease you *haven't* got!'

'You really think I'm a hypochondriac?'

'Oh God. Now you're going to get hypochondriacal about being a hypochondriac. Julian, your ailments are killing me! One measly headache and it's swelling brainstems, one pee too often and it's prostate cancer . . .'

'At least I'm not a *psychological* hypochondriac. You take your emotional temperature all day. Am I happy? Could I be happier? Is he really the right man for me?'

'Yeah? Well, It's time we took the temperature of this relationship. With a *rectal* thermometer.'

The only sign that I'd stung him was the way the car bumped over the road-Braille of cat's eyes. I went down a mental gear. 'All you need to do, Jules, is take more exercise. Look at you.' I patted the pot belly straining against the seat belt with tenderness. 'You're getting podgy, darling. You haven't seen your testicles for over six months.'

'Testicles! Huh! I don't have any testicles! You took them on my wedding day. Need I jog your memory?'

'It's the only thing you *do* jog. When we met, you had buns of steel. Lately your buttocks have the consistency of, I dunno . . . lasagne. Vegetable lasagne. With too much milk.'

'I don't know whether you've noticed, Rebecca, but I'm a lawyer. I conquer the Great Indoors. The only thing I exercise is caution. Which is why I waited until

I was forty to choose the woman I wanted to marry. But since you eschewed the band of gold . . .'

'There you go. Eschewed. Did you have to say "eschewed" at the reception? Why can't you just say "rejected"? Why can't you just use a normal word now and again?' The overhead fog lights had turned us both a toxic orange. 'Why do you always have to show that you're suffering from First-Degree Knowledge?'

'So that's why you resent me? Because my brains have gone to my head?' he asked incredulously.

I groped under the seat for my cigarettes. 'What I resent is the fact that you were at bloody Oxford for so long that you've got ivy growing up the back of your legs. All work and no play makes Julian a dull boy.'

'But all play and no work will get Julian defending serious cases of unlawful parking in Bognor Regis. I work hard so that we can enjoy the finer things in life.'

'Oh yes, like all night unpaid work-a-thons – you haven't charged a client for months. Sex with socks still on 'cause you're too tired to take them off . . .'

Flicking on the dome light and rummaging in my handbag, I thought about Julian's mistress – his work. In a way I'd have preferred it to be another woman. Then I could simply carwash his Saab in hydrochloric acid, bathe in his fine wine collection, and pen the odd piece about 'A Woman Scorned'. But what could I say about a man who lavished love on his law books? It was giving me subpoena-envy, it really was.

'What about all the wonderful holidays I've taken

you on?' he retorted, once we were safely ejaculated into the motorway traffic. 'Would you turn that light off?'

'Yes. In the coup-ridden capitals of the Universe . . . I'm sick of you carrying the weight of the world on your shoulders, Julian.' I turned off the light and punched in the cigarette lighter. 'Get a porter!'

'You're thirty-two, Becky.' Julian snatched the cigarette from between my fingers and extinguished it. 'You've had enough fun. It's time you settled down and started a family.'

'Huh,' I sulked, 'you actually have to have sex now and again to get children . . .' I gnawed on a nail. 'The last time we had any physical contact was when I got that fish bone stuck in my throat at the River Café and you gave me the Heimlich manoeuvre. You haven't given me head for months!'

'Honestly, Rebecca!'; The Saab tyres slurped angrily at roadside puddles. 'Must you speak so crudely? It's not as though you ever asked . . .'

'What do you need? A written invitation? Jesus!'

'Oh, well, while we're at it, what else is bothering you sexually? Why not make a list!'

'Well, okay.'

'I was joking!'

'Your approach to sex could be a little more, um, spontaneous. It's the same approach you have to deleafing the gutters, a task you dutifully undertake, say, once every other week.'

'The spontaneity has *not* gone out of . . . What about when we had sex in Vivian and Simon's house? When we went over to feed the cat?'

'Julian. You hung up your clothes first. You don't talk enough in bed either.'

'I'm a lawyer. If I talk I have to charge.'

'There you go. Why do you have to relate everything back to work? You'll soon have me plea bargaining for foreplay . . .'

'Good idea. Just outline your sexual requirements on a yellow legal pad, will you, and I'll take them under advisement.'

There was a beat while we watched the wipers cha-cha across the windshield, before we both spluttered into laughter. Julian was laughing so hard he had to pull over. When he calmed down, he laid his warm, dry hand on top of mine.

'I love you so much, Becky. I love your chutzpah, your cheek. Your wit . . . Not to mention the best legs in London.'

The tidal wave of guilt I'd been damning engulfed me in one giant roar. I seized his hand. 'I'm so sorry, Jules. I'm a vile, loathsome excrescence. I belong on the bottom of somebody's shoe . . . I've been behaving like Betty Davis on crack. I can't believe you can still love me after all the . . .'

'I'd do anything for you, Beck, you know that . . . Well, anything which doesn't involve sex-change operations in Thailand.'

I squeezed his hand. 'Let's go away. This weekend. And just fuck our brains out. Like we used to. And in between, we can talk everything through.'

Julian winced. 'I can't. Client dinner. Saturday night. Actually, I was hoping you'd come with me . . .'

I groaned loudly. 'Oh no, not the Wife Thing.'

'Please, Becky.' He leant over. The kiss he gave me was sultry and succulent. 'There,' he said, eventually, resurfacing for air. 'Can a vibrator do *that*?' How about some "heavy petting"?' he suggested wryly.

'I think I've finally solved one of life's great mysteries, namely, why men prefer to have sex in cars,' I said, shedding clothes. 'Because objects in the rear-view mirror always appear larger than they actually are, right?'

Julian laughed, unbuckling. The Man Who Took Women's Breath Away, I sighed inwardly, would not *ever* need to make love in a car.

When the car phone rang seconds later, we both jumped. My mother's t-glottalling assaulted our eardrums over the loudspeaker. I wouldn't have picked up except that it was the first time we'd spoken since my non-wedding day.

'So, Anouska got 'erself a bloke then, did she? Why can't I 'ave a daugh'er like 'er . . . Instead of a thirty-two-year-old spinster.'

'Oh Mum. Why do I have to be thirty-two years *old*? Why can't I be thirty-two years *young*?'

'Ya 'aven't gorn and met someone else, 'ave ya?'

I dashed thoughts of my one-night stand from my mind. Well, one-lick stand, really. I also made a vow never ever to breathe a word about Zack to anybody. I didn't understand what I'd done myself, so how could I expect anyone else to? Having so recently jilted Julian at the altar – an act that put me on a par with, I dunno, a puppy vivisectionist – a full carnal confession was not exactly going to win me any points, not even with my girlfriends. Besides if there's one thing I've learnt it's the definition of a secret: something your girl-friends tell everyone not to tell anyone.

'Can't 'old me 'ead up in public.' This from a woman whose only claim to fame is winning every wet T-shirt competition for Seniors the length and breadth of the Costa del Sol. 'I'm tha(t) bi(tt)er abou(t) i(t).' I cringed at the way she strangled her t's. 'I mean, what exac(t)ly do ya fink you're up to?'

I looked at Julian's rapidly detumescing appendage. 'Later,' he promised, re-zipping.

I sighed. 'Not much, Mum.'

Just a lick and a promise.

8

Yodelling In The Canyon Of Love

'I had a fling,' I gushed, flumphing into Anouska's designer sofa. So much for my little secret.

'You what?' Kate's molars cracked on a Japanese rice cracker.

We were at Anouska's posh Chelsea Harbour apartment for the official present opening where, traditionally, girlfriends gather to hyperventilate over colanders and comedy oven gloves. We'd watched aghast, as an eleven-inch-high Francis of Assisi scratching a Royal Doulton dog's nose emerged from its gift wrapping. Why is there such a complete collapse of good taste when it comes to wedding presents? Why is it that normal, sophisticated couples, collectors of Art Deco, subscribers to Interior Design magazines, suddenly feel an overwhelming urge to purchase crockery bullocks carting glow-in-the-dark sleighs or tartan egg-cups from Argos? (Argos is the place I took my friends to show them what I *didn't* want for my wedding.)

'When?' said Anouska.

'With whom?' demanded Kate.

'Where?' they said in unison.

'At your wedding. I don't know his name. By the pool.' I answered them in order.

'What did he look like?' Anouska pored over the wedding list.

'He didn't seem to know many people. Maybe he was a last-minute space-filler? He was tall, sexy, black . . .'

'Black?' Anouska exclaimed, offering pretzels from a ceramic donkey with a hollowed-out back. 'So, is it true what they say? You know . . . about black men?'

'What? That they have black skin?'

'You know. *It.* Down *There. That.*'

Anouska was the sort of girl who, in the heat of passion, referred to her vagina as 'There'. And the man's penis as 'It', 'That' or 'That thing'. 'Touch me there with that thing' was really the extent of her erotic verbal repertoire.

'I can't believe you asked such a stereotypically racist question. 'I nibbled haughtily at a pretzel before gushing. 'Yes. It's abso*lut*ely true! His penis is so big it's in a separate time zone to his body!'

Anouska squealed. 'Balaclava or turtle neck?' she added, boldly.

'Stop. Stop this phallophilic conversation right now.' Kate fumed. 'Honestly, Rebecca! How could you have sex on a first encounter?'

'It wasn't a *first* date, Kate, it was a *last* one. It's not like I'll ever see him again, okay?' I said, crossing one knee-high chunky-soled boot over the other.

'I worry about you, I really do,' Kate lectured me. 'I mean, look at those ridiculous shoes. I don't know how many times I have to tell you high heels dehumanize women. Only deer and cats walk on their toes. And that's what you look like wearing them.'

'Have you no redeeming vice, Kate?' I asked wearily.

Anouska passed me salt and pepper shakers in the shape of cows with big, pink udders from which the desired condiments were dispensed. 'How could you be unfaithful to Julian, Becky?' She primly scissored her legs. 'At least you've got a man who loves you.'

Unlike Anouska, I thought sadly. In a good marriage it takes about a month before you're vertical for long enough to write the thank-you letters. Well, Anouska was writing hers *the day after the wedding*.

'I wasn't unfaithful!' I waved the udder over my tomatoes and basil. 'He only went down on me.'

Kate and Anouska swivelled simultaneously to face me. 'What?' they said in prurient tandem.

'We didn't have sex. He merely yodelled in my canyon of love.'

'Rebecca, since when doesn't that count as infidelity?' Kate demanded.

'Well, that's what *men* always say. "It didn't mean anything. It was only a blow job." Ask Bill Clinton. For some men even 'sticking it in a little way' doesn't count as being unfaithful.'

'So,' Anouska pried, curiosity overcoming her sense of propriety. 'How was it?'

'Now that's a stupid question. What's the worst cunnilingual experience *you've* ever had?'

'Um . . . fabulous.'

'Exactly. Which is just how I felt. It was a genital highball . . . clitoral Tabasco. I had orgasms like a string of firecrackers. I had . . .'

'Okay. Okay.' Kate waved me into silence. 'Jeez, we get the picture . . .'

'No you don't.' I retorted. 'The only thing that ever goes down on you is your computer.'

'Ha bloody ha . . . You really weren't allowed to reciprocate?' Kate sticky-beaked, dumbfounded. 'You really just had to lie there and receive pleasure?'

I nodded. Both women looked at me, gobsmacked.

'Why is it that people already in relationships are the only ones who fuck around?' Kate complained. 'We singles don't have the energy. Too bloody exhausted doing the shopping, picking up the car, completing the DIY . . . God!' Kate scraped her pitta bread across the bowl of tzatziki. 'Now I remember him! The teenager. On the dance floor. I mean how old is he? Twenty-one? Twenty-two? That's about two steps up from sperm. You need a shrink, Rebecca, you really do.'

Why did people keep telling me I needed psychiatric help? I'd dumped the love of my life at the altar, seduced a complete stranger, then confessed all to my girlfriends – having vowed not to. Hell, I didn't need a shrink. I already *knew* I was nuts.

'How could you dump Julian for a piece of jail-bait?' Anouska insisted sanctimoniously.

'Look, I didn't dump Julian for this guy, okay? It was hips that pass in the night . . . A postscript for a memoir . . . except that it's too clichéd to tell anyone – the black toy boy with the gi-normous cream-stick. I mean puh-lease. So let's just forget about it. It's not like I'll ever see him again. Gee, I've forgotten him already.'

My two 'besties' looked at me with a mixture of distrust and disapproval. But, hey, I reassured myself, tucking into the hummus. At least I was deep enough to know that I'm shallow . . .

9

Raw Emotion

... And shallow enough to know when I'm in too deep.

Life is like a restaurant menu; it never has what you order and even if it *has*, you always end up wanting what everybody else ordered anyway. *And*, no matter what's dished up, there are bound to be hidden allergy-inducing, life-threatening ingredients that'll have you hospitalized faster than you can say 'organ donation'.

Which is why I shouldn't have been surprised to look up from my Major Sulk – my normal demeanour when Julian insisted I join him in a tedious client dinner – to see my One-Lick-Stand gliding sinuously through Chez Nico restaurant towards our table.

My heart drilled against my Wonderbra. Ignoring my frantic sideway eye flickers in Julian's direction, Zachary Phoenix Burne swaggered right up to us. He gave me that melt-in-the-mouth look, which, despite my terror, had every single drop of blood in my body saluting instantaneously. As false alibis crashed about in my cranium Julian jumped to his feet and extended a hand.

'Zachary? How good to meet you. This is my partner, Rebecca Steele. Becky, this is my new client, Zachary Burne.'

For one cardiac-arresting moment, I thought he was going to say 'yeah, we've met . . .' But his mouth, no, it wasn't just a mouth – we're talking child-bearing lips – curled into a wide and wicked grin.

'A pleasure,' he said moistly, 'Rebecca.' He rolled my name around on his tongue. In contrast to Julian's hand-stitched Savile Row suit, Zachary was sporting faded Levis, Nike trainers and a T-shirt that ended halfway up his midriff, exposing a muscular, crème-brûlée-coloured abdomen. A medusa of dreadlocks coiled from his crown. A silver ring through his belly button completed the Himbo look just nicely.

Before I could fake a cerebral seizure, Himbo sat down uninvited and smiled engagingly in my direction. I glowered back at him.

'So, Zachary, how are you finding England?' Julian asked, conversationally.

Zachary stretched a leisurely hand in my direction to retrieve the wine bottle. I flinched automatically. He looked at me questioningly. 'Yeah, it's okay an' all,' he shrugged. 'The babes are a bit weird, know what I'm sayin'? Come on real strong then the next time yer see 'em, it's like they've got an iceberg up their ass.'

'Maybe it's just that it takes them a little while to realize how truly arrogant Americans are?' I retorted prissily.

Julian shot me an admonishing look – the same look he gave me the time I used his Beatles compilation CD as a drinks coaster.

Waving away the disgruntled wine waiter, Zachary filled his own glass with Chardonnay. He moved, I noted, with an underwater languor, slow and measured. 'At least meetin' British women I've learnt that ya don't have to be, like, dead, to be stiff.'

Before I could avenge myself with a little penile acupuncture beneath the table with my stiletto, my eye was caught by a hideous, head-turning apparition galumphing across the floor, scattering waiters in its wake. Mid-fifties, five foot three, weighing in at about 190 pounds, it had the sort of face you wouldn't wish on a bull terrier; the sort of face, in fact, you usually associate with Crime and Accident Reconstruction programmes. Stuffed into a Versace suit and completely bald, it had that 'I was a chartered accountant for a Colombian drug cartel' look. What was worse, this porcine Scud missile was about to make a direct hit with our table.

As Julian rose to greet this monstrosity, I turned to Zachary, my whispered rebuke shrill with indignation. 'I am *not* stiff. Just allergic to bumping into *one-night stands* while I'm out with my *husband.'*

'One *night*?' Zachary smiled cockily and rocked back in his chair to scratch his ribcage lazily. 'You'll be back for more.'

'Becky?'

I realized with a jolt that my mouth was hanging open. 'Um . . . Yes?'

'Julian rotated towards me. 'This is Eddy Rotterman, Zachary's manager.'

'What's got four legs an' an arm?' Eddy said, by way of introduction. 'A goddamn Rottweiler . . . So call me Rotty.' He extended his hand. I was reluctant to shake it, not having had a rabies shot.

Julian sat back down. Eddy Rotterman took longer to lower his pachyderm proportions into an ill-fitting leather chair.

'In a fit of political correctness,' Julian explained for my benefit, 'Zachary's latest CD has been seized by Scotland Yard's Obscenity Squad. Mr Rotterman has asked me to act on his behalf to secure its release at a court hearing next week. We will have a difficult task educating the Bow Street Magistrates. Scotland Yard has spent many hours with specially enhanced sound equipment transcribing the otherwise incomprehensible voice of the black ghettos of the Bronx into passable English – no offence.'

'You're a rock star?' I asked Zachary, astounded.

'Kinda.' He looked down at his hands, his lashes languishing on velvet cheeks.

'He's the bomb,' enthused Rotty, cracking his knuckles. 'Matter-a-fact the top labels are creamin' their jeans to sign up America's hottest hero. My main man, Zack, here, is soon to be a household name.'

'Like Toilet Duck,' I said dryly, from behind the menu.

'Don't cha like rock stars?' Zachary enquired, his bottom lip now playing host to a roll-your-own cigarette.

'Rock stars? You mean the sort of person who thinks it's funny to slip his penis between two slices of a sandwich before offering it to an aged relative? Ah . . . no.'

Julian's eyebrows started executing a curious kind of hirsute SOS semaphore.

Rotty scowled before deciding I was joking. 'Nice one, babe.' His guffaw sounded not unlike a backed-up Jacuzzi.

'Actually, it ain't rock. What do yer think of the rap?' Zachary leant back, arms folded insouciantly across his powerful chest and smirked insolently in my direction.

'I find deep sleep an excellent way of listening to a rap band.'

Julian's look darkened even more. This was the look he'd given me after I sent his Bruce Springsteen tour T-shirt to Oxfam. 'Can I talk to you behind our menu please? . . . *What are you doing?*'

'They're New Yorkers,' I bluffed, 'they hate sycophants.'

'Really?' he sounded dubious.

'Would I lie to you?' I lied.

Zachary re-emerged from behind his own massive bill of fare. 'Just bring me a burger with fries, man, and make it cry,' he announced to the startled waiter.

Chez Nico is the kind of poncey Park Lane eatery where you have to offer up your first-born child in order to get a reservation.

'Make it cry, Sir?'

'Onions and chilli,' Zachary deciphered.

The waiter curled a patronizing lip. 'Wouldn't Sir like to consult the menu again?'

'Naw. A menu's just a bit of paper that lists what the restaurant's just run out of, right? A burger's fine. Hold the ketchup.'

'I'm afraid we don't stretch to "burgers", Sir.' Condescension was positively dripping off this guy; there were little pools of it gathering around his hand-made Italian shoes.

'Okay then . . .' Zachary eyed the menu suspiciously, alighting with relief on something he recognized amongst the italicized verbiage. 'Steak. Yeah,' he indicated his choice with one hand, while squeezing my knee beneath the table with the other.

My response to his touch was reminiscent of Humphrey Bogart's reaction to the leeches he encountered on *The African Queen*. I dug my nails into his palm. With staggering impertinence, he then wrapped his wounded hand around my wrist. Like a handcuff.

'And what are you hungry for?' Zachary Burne asked me, in a parched voice.

I darted a nervous look at Julian. Preoccupied with placing his order, he hadn't noticed. I watched him turn to address Rotterman. But the entrepreneur was busy dismembering rolls with his stalactite teeth. Julian swivelled instead towards Zachary. 'So,' he small-talked. 'What were you saying about English women?'

'They jest want yer for yer body, man. That's what I'm sayin'.'

'But a shit-hot place to launch a career.' Rotty scatter-gunned breadcrumbs over the tablecloth as he spoke. 'Back home the authorities doan bother prosecutin' nobody for obscenity no more. Not even in the Bible Belt. Jesus Willy Christ, I've got big plans for this kid. Just like Hendrix! He was first appreciated in the Old Blighty!'

'The cultural bulimia of mainstream America must be quite a hindrance to a creative artist...' Julian paused to sip diagnostically at his wine, describing it as 'capricious in its affability'. Zachary turned his intense, dark gaze on to my Significant Other. With a disconcerting pang, I suddenly saw Julian through Zachary's eyes – middle class and middle-minded, predictable, pretentious, pinstriped. 'Not that we don't like Americans...' He added, darting a censorious look at me.

'The reason you English don't like us Yanks is 'cause

117

we know how to enjoy ourselves.' Zachary now centred me in his unblinking gaze. 'You Brits have no idea how badly yer live. I betcha in yer Constitution it promises "the pursuit of misery".'

'Yes,' laughed Julian. 'It's enshrined. "The Right to Life, Liberty and the Pursuit of Jellied Eels." But the pursuit of happiness can be used as a justification for the most appallingly selfish behaviour. For example – sexual incontinence.' I started to wince inwardly. 'One in three British couples has an adulterous partner, you know.' I gulped at my wine. 'A symptom of the *fin-de-siècle* angst of . . .'

'Darling, tell me, do you intend concluding that sentence any time in my life span, do you think? . . . Julian drowns in his own brainwaves, I'm afraid.'

'My fuckin' wife pursues happiness, Jeezus. She's near-on bankrupted me pursuin' happiness. Stoopid bitch,' added Eddy Rotterman superfluously. 'The only goddamn difference between my wife and my job, is that after five years, my job still sucks.'

Eddy Rotterman, it turned out, had begun his career in car rental before moving into entrepreneurial activities, representing – amongst a star-studded clientele – a Mexican transvestite who could fellate himself and a Peruvian dwarf who could haul a cart full of sumo wrestlers across the stage using only his teeth. Naturally, the world of rock and roll had beckoned. Having built up fledgling bands with names like 'The Butthole Sniffers', he now had

Zachary Phoenix Burne on his books complete with banned album, ensuring megabucks worth of publicity.

'So far the Stud here's only got a cult following . . .' Rotterman slapped Zachary on the back. 'Hell, the kid's so fresh he's still flappin'!' Zachary responded with an air of muted James Dean rebellion.

'Cult? You make it sound as though he sacrifices virgins, for God's sake,' I scoffed, dismissively. My wrist still burnt where he'd touched me.

'Mainly chicks,' Rotty jabbered. 'Women hear his music through their cunts, ya know?'

He was obviously the intellectual type. I risked eye contact with Julian, who reciprocated with a raised and querulous brow.

'But being banned! Those Scotland Yard fuckheads can blow me. I figger the publicity from this court case is gunna make him. Yer know Spike Lee? Well, I've already got him to cast Zachary in his next film. They're rewritin' the script, right now, to make his part larger.'

I myself could think of parts of him which it would be a pleasure to make larger. For God's sake, I told myself. Get a grip. I was merely lost in a fog of pheromones. I tried to think of unsexy things – corn pads, Anusol, Cliff Richard . . . But it was useless. Zachary Phoenix Burne was so sexy, he could open a deposit account at a sperm bank.

'Unfortunately, Mr Rotterman, the average judge

thinks "avant-garde" is a French football team.' Zachary stared at Julian, profoundly unimpressed at his little joke. 'Personally, I try to keep up with modern music . . .'

Modern music? The antiquated phrase belied the sentiment. I glared at Julian in disbelief, but not before I saw a wry smile play on Zachary's lips. This was too embarrassing.

'Julian . . . you hum along to supermarket muzak!'

'Well . . . it's not a crime, darling.'

'It is if the song is "Ob-la-de, Ob-la-dah".'

Thankfully the meal arrived. Zachary prodded a fork into his steak with repulsed disdain. 'I said rare man, not "grazin". The meat on this plate is tryin' to canter off to a rodeo.'

'But that's what you ordered, Sir.'

'I ordered steak.'

'Steak tartare,' explained Julian, 'is raw.'

'Jesus Christ.' Zachary recoiled in revulsion, pushed away his plate and lit up another roll your own.

'More wine?' Julian asked. 'Any favourites?'

'Wine's like women. The older the better, man.' With imperturbable poise, Zachary looked directly at me.

'Yes,' I rejoindered, gaping at him. 'Wine that's too young *lacks subtlety*.'

'So, Zachary?' Julian cross-examined, 'Are you implying a romantic attachment to an older woman?'

'Been playin' pocket pool over this babe I met just once. Redhead.' He surveyed me with those glinting eyes again. I studied my napkin with forensic absorption. 'Smart. Older. Pain in the ass.'

'*Older?*' I prickled. 'How much older? You make her sound as though she's on life-support.'

'Experienced. Tough. Takes no prisoners,' Zachary drawled. 'An', the best thing, she couldn't give a stuff about what I do. But like all nineties babes, she's lost the art of love.'

'Perhaps,' I countered, 'it's just that she expects so little from a rap star. Rap stars have Velcro dicks, do they not? Stick to any woman that passes. Rap stars, I'm told, change lovers more often than underwear.'

'Rappers get bad press,' Zachary asserted, strong-chinned and mutinous.

'Bad press? Naw. Don't shit me. No such thing . . .' said Rotterman, the Hype Meister. 'Now, Counsellor, how shall we handle those goddamn sonsofbitches?'

Julian and Rotterman bent their heads together to discuss the finer points of Scotland Yard versus Rottweiler Records, leaving me no conversational option other than Zachary. He was close enough for me to smell his skin. Not even the cigarette smoke could mask his particular aroma – cardamom and cinnamon and something else unsettling.

'And what would a rap star have to do to, like, prove himself to you?' He crossed one ankle over the opposite knee. His silver fly buttons meandered over his crotch. Lucky old fly buttons.

'If I *were* interested in one, improbable as it is, but

hypothetically speaking, I'd set him tasks to prove himself. You know, Herculean quests.'

'Like what?'

'I don't know ... Something unobtainable ... like Thomas Pynchon's signature ...'

'Who?'

'A writer. God, I forgot. A rock star's reading material is limited to his bank balance. Pynchon is a famous literary recluse.'

'What else?' A thin stream of smoke slipped from his luxuriant lips. Lips that could melt a woman at three hundred paces.

'I don't know. Home delivering twenty of her favourite Häagen-Dazs ice-cream flavours wouldn't go astray ... Renting a billboard and begging her to be your Love Goddess ... A gift-wrapped sea horse. A purple rose. Stuff like that.'

Rotty, having gorged his own meal, shoved an over-loaded forkful of Zachary's rejected steak tartare between his calamity of teeth and chomped with abandon, even though fleshy debris was spilling out in every direction and the rest of us were gagging into our napkins. 'Yer can never be too rich or too fat,' he chortled, spraying us with more half-masticated morsels.

'Well,' Julian turned to us desperately. 'What are you two talking about?'

'Love.' Zachary replied. He stole a gooseberry from my plate and slipped it into his mouth. I imagined that if he kissed me the taste would be moist and tart on his lips.

'I can't envisage having sex with someone you don't love,' volunteered Julian. 'Sex always begins in the head with me . . .'

Yes, I thought to myself, and ends there too, lately. Unlike the Man Who Took Women's Breath Away, whose hand had just stolen up beneath my leather skirt.

'People don't want invitations to orgies any more,' Julian added. 'People want invitations to dinner parties. Sex is so, well, *early eighties*.'

'Uh huh,' I mumbled. Well, it's hard to concentrate when your thigh is being caressed in long, silken sweeps by soft, warm fingers. I was rattled to realize that Rotterman was speaking to me. 'Pardon?'

'Get hubby here to set a court date soon. Jesus Willy Christ, I gotta holiday booked.'

'Where?' I asked in a jittery voice. 'Broadmoor Psychiatric Centre for the Criminally Insane?'

Julian drilled me with a stare.

Zachary, however, threw back his head and laughed. 'I prefer moister climates . . .' he deadpanned, sliding his finger under my pants' elastic.

I tried to picture him as old and decayed; losing hair on top and sprouting it from nose and ears. It was the only way I could summon the strength to push his hand away. I pinched him hard enough to make him cry out.

'Is everything all right?' Julian asked, alarmed.

'Cramp', said Zachary. 'Totally unexpected, man.'

'We're going to go away too, after this case.' Julian put his hand over mine. 'Somewhere romantic. Then you may finally marry me, Beck.'

I gulped at my wine again.

'No shit, you guys ain't married?' drawled Zachary, mock casual.

'Unfortunately, Rebecca is maritally impaired.'

'Oh, I thought you was married . . .' Zachary flashed a radiantly white smile. 'In-er-estin'.' He ever so slowly licked his wandering fingers. 'Great meal, by the way.'

I blotched fiercely. Blushing was not in my repertoire. My last blush was a pre-trainer bra. This was disturbing.

As Julian consulted the waiter about desserts, Zachary ostentatiously dipped an index finger into his glass, then slyly trailed a droplet on to my lap. 'I think yer should come back to my crib and get out of those wet things,' he whispered softly.

'I'd like to see you naked too – preferably with a tag on your toe. Don't ever speak to me again,' I seethed, sotto voce, the colour in my cheeks fading from crimson to a less life-threatening pink. 'And if you say anything I'll deny it. I'll sue, in fact, for defamation of character. I don't live with a shit-hot lawyer for nothing, you know.'

Feigning an early-morning start, I pushed up from

the table and made for the revolving door. While Julian and Rotterman loitered to discuss the size of the financial penalty if the case were lost, Zachary followed me out on to the street. He jammed the revolving door and pinned me to the glass. His groin torpedoed up against me, his lips a tongue's length from my mouth.

'See you after the "divorce",' he said coolly, before, smiling like a Cheshire Cat, he was swallowed by the dark.

As Julian's Saab negotiated the contours of Park Lane, he slotted a tape of Zachary's band into the deck. A filling-loosening cacophony haemorrhaged out of the speakers.

'GOOD GOD! ANOTHER TALENTLESS TEEN-AGER ABOUT TO SEND THE NATION' – he punched at the volume button – 'into a frenzy of indifference.'

'Oh, Jules. You're just down on anything you're not up on.'

'I'm in touch! I have my finger on the pulse – I can tell the difference between Noel and Liam Gallagher.' He rounded Hyde Park Corner, peeling off towards the Palace. 'Music was so much bloody better when I was young. We had better lyrics, better clothes, better habits, better hairdos . . .'

'Gee. They'll be making costume dramas about you soon.'

From the Mall, he cut down to the Embankment.

Strings of fairy lights flickered on the inky waters of the Thames. The boats' square windows, lit from within, made them look like illuminated harmonicas.

'Steak tartare!' Julian hooted. 'Waiter, I'll have some Mad Cow Disease, medium rare.' He slapped the steering wheel with mirth. 'Sir! This spongiform encephalopathy isn't cooked properly . . . You can just tell by his accent that he has rear-vision mirror ornaments. Dice probably. He no doubt drives a car with a bumper sticker advertising his illegal sexual practices. God only knows what other crimes he's committed.'

The perfect crime, I though to myself. Seduction. 'You're right. He's obviously into "rap" because it goes with his "sheet".'

Julian laughed. 'Yes. Rap-sheet music. Very good. You should come on my client dinners more often. You played the situation well.'

My mouth dried. I avoided eye contact. I scrutinized the Thames embankment with first-time-tourist intensity. 'Julian, I really think you should give the case to someone else.'

'Why? At least Rotterman's a paying customer. I thought you'd be pleased! The firm certainly are.'

'But it's so beneath you, Jules.'

'They're only hot-jacuzzi-habitués. Nothing too sinister.'

'Rotterman's natural habitat's a post-office tower with a machine-gun in his hand. He's the sort of guy who does terrible things to small animals.' I shivered.

'The clients may be reprehensible, Becky, but the principle is important. Freedom of speech. That's worth fighting for.'

I bit my lip. There was so much I wasn't telling him. Some freedom of speech could be very, very expensive.

At the Temple, Julian pulled over. He often did this, detouring to his office last thing at night to check for fresh fugitives from injustice. I walked to the office by his side, our heels castanetting on the cobblestones; the antique oil lamps flickering, my hand cosily cocooned in his.

In his office, he unexpectedly turned and nuzzled my neck.

'I have something for you,' he said, handing over a piece of paper.

'What is it?'

'A written invitation.'

I skimmed the spidery Mont Blanc writing, laughed out loud and RSVPed with a kiss. 'Turn off the light.'

As we made love on his desk, a prism of recollections put Zachary's face before me in a thousand ways. Images of him jostled each other for the most prominent position in the eye of my subconscious. They thrust themselves forward; a carnal kaleidoscope. It gave the sex a heated, startling frisson.

Julian's office has three arched windows, wide

panels of leaded glass, that yielded a small amount of warm light from the Temple's gas lamps. We lay for a while afterwards, the glow bathing our bodies a fiery gold.

Julian switched the desk lamp on, leant on one elbow and examined my face. 'You're thinking of somebody else, aren't you?'

The dream dissolved and I splashed up to consciousness, gasping for air in uneven spurts. 'Don't be ridiculous!'

'You're going to leave me one day,' he said ruefully.

'I will if you keep saying that!' I tousled his hair. 'You'll turn it into a self-fulfilling prophecy.'

'Aren't you worried *I'll* leave *you*?' he asked.

I thumped him good naturedly. 'Who'd have you?'

He retaliated, tickling my tummy. 'A plethora of female inamoratas awaits me. Oh, it's such a bore being perfect. Makes me wish I hadn't given up S and M.'

'You? Into bondage!? Don't make me laugh. You're way too straight to try anything weird like that. Your condoms are practically pinstriped.'

'*Do* you think I'm too straight? Is that why you didn't marry me, Becky?'

As he hovered above me, I noticed he'd left on his socks and that his clothes, as ever, were neatly folded over the chair. 'No.'

'Do you want me to develop a few illegal sexual preferences of my own? . . . I could, you know.'

'I like you just the way you are,' I said. And told myself I meant it. Told myself that I didn't want him to use ping-pong tables for purposes other than that for which they were originally intended; to have a definition of sexual athleticism that did not mean always coming first.

'Having lived together so long, Beck, being "good in bed" means I don't snore, right?'

'Absolutely,' I kissed his eyelids, reassuringly. But then why weren't my reassurances reassuring me? If I'd known what my sex drive had in store, I'd have got some steel-belted assurances for greater traction, because, believe me, I was about to hit a very bumpy road.

10

Resting On Your Orals

I detoured on to that bumpy course about a week later when I got a note from Harrods. There was a package awaiting collection. I forgot about it for a day or two until I was on the way home from a meeting with a conceptual artist – she was a 'holistic healer' who, proving that there is no end to the inventiveness of weird women wearing natural fibres to make money in their spare time, planned an interactive exhibition in which women burnt their contraceptives and reverted to pessaries of honey, gum and crocodile dung, as favoured by the Egyptians. Couldn't wait to promote *that* one.

As I was already on the Piccadilly Line, I got off at Knightsbridge – London's retirement village for seriously rich Arabs – and entered the crenellated department store otherwise known as 'Harabs'.

Because the one great difference between kids'

parties and grown-ups' parties is that kids always seem to know exactly what each other wants (you never see a child feigning delight over a Tupperware beetroot strainer or a coffee-table book entitled *Sweden – the View From Norway*) I shouldn't have been surprised when I bumped smack bang into Anouska, returning all the presents she'd gone orgasmic over days earlier.

'I thought you were in a meeting?' I said. 'I rang this morning . . .'

'What? Oh no. I've just trained my Portuguese maid to tell callers that I'm in meetings while I'm out shopping. You know. So that I don't feel so useless.'

Anouska had recently contracted Affluenza, a feeling of inadequacy and worthlessness brought on by wealth.

'Hell. You can have my job. I'm dying to feel useless.' I inquisitively prodded the sack she was carting.

'Well,' she said defensively. 'What on earth did Kate think I was going to do with a melon baller and Mexican tortilla press? I hate cooking. And Darius hasn't even *found* the kitchen yet.'

'How *is* the Prince of Darkness?'

'He cut short the honeymoon to go on a holiday to find himself. All he found out was that I'm mad and everything's my fault. Oh dear, here I am talking and talking about me. What about you, doll? I want to hear all about everything, okay? . . . Only tell me in ten seconds.'

'I saw my One-Lick Stand. At dinner. With Julian.'

'You're kidding?'

'No. Turns out he's a rap star.' I shoved her off the escalator at the second floor as directed. 'Did Darius mention any rap stars to you?'

'Maybe he came with the band? What's the name of *his* band? Let me guess. 'The Rock Hard Gonads . . . No . . . The Throbbing Gonads? . . .' she teased, thrilled by her own crudity. I dragged her through haberdashery, homeware and bed linen to what turned out to be the pet shop. 'I've got it. Pulsate and the Urgent Thrusting Gonads . . .'

I handed over the note to the sales assistant. He returned moments later with a small plastic bag containing one perfectly formed sea horse. Oh my god. The Knightly Quest. I burst out laughing. My rap star was obviously not content to rest on his orals.

'Oh,' Anouska trilled. 'Isn't it beautiful! There's a note . . .' She slit open the envelope with a neon-orange nail. '"Proceed to VIP florists",' she read. 'Kings Road. A treasure hunt. Oh goody. Come on. I'll drive.'

Even though driving around London in the late nineties amounts to the shortest point between two diversions, Anouska likes nothing better than putting pedal to metal. As usual, she was driving as though she was in the Starship Enterprise, i.e., warp factor ten. Tearing down Sloane Street, hand welded to the horn, she went straight through the red light at the intersection with Pont.

I adopted the brace position and Hail Mary-ed out loud. 'You know, we have a funny little tradition here on planet Earth, Annie, where red means stop.' We screeched into Sloane Square, running off the road at least six Land Rovers full of Sloane Rangers dashing to make their appointments for raspberry-flavoured colonics.

At VIP florists there was a rose waiting for me. Painted purple. And a note to go to Selfridges food hall.

Skidding around Hyde Park Corner at breakneck velocity, Anouska clocked my ashen visage. 'It's alright, doll. I always race through roundabouts to get out of the way of all the really bad drivers.'

'Oh well, that's okay then.'

At Selfridges, there were nineteen tubs of Häagen-Dazs ice-cream with my name on them. 'I'm dying, doll,' thrilled Anouska. 'Who is this guy?' This time the accompanying note advised me to look in my third desk drawer at work.

We were on our way back to the ICA, with me screaming 'slow down' every two seconds and Penelope Pit Stop explaining that she wasn't speeding; she was just driving fast enough for the speed cameras not to be able to get a snap of her . . . when we finally got pulled over by a cop.

Anouska lowered the window of her Mercedes

sports car, eyelashes on overdrive. 'Yes, Officer?'

'You're driving at 80 miles per hour in a 30 miles per hour zone,' the cop informed her.

'Officer, I wasn't doing more than 75. I must have had a tail wind.'

'And you went through a red light while I was pursuing you. I'm going to have to book you.'

'But what about all the green ones I've stopped at over the years? Doesn't that balance out? . . . Do you like ice-cream, by the way?'

Unable to contain my curiosity, I left Anouska to her bribery and my ice-cream and leapt on to the tube – which was just as well because at Charing Cross, in the advertising space usually reserved for warnings against casual sex, was a poster of Zachary's face, grinning wickedly. And a slogan, that said, simply 'Be My Love Goddess'. A squadron of butterflies took flight in my stomach.

In the third drawer of my desk was an envelope. Flustered with anticipation, I ripped it open. Inside was Thomas Pynchon's signature. And a phone number.

All afternoon as I sorted out gum and dung pessaries, I told myself that I wasn't hot and bothered. No. 'Hot' was definitely not the word. It was more like the surface temperature of the sun.

Kate accosted me by the bar. 'You're still thinking about Him, aren't you?'

'No.'

'Liar.'

'Okay. I am. But Jesus Christ, haven't you ever entertained the idea of wild, inventive, dangerous sex?'

'Yes, of course.'

'No. I mean, *with a partner*.'

'Ha de ha. You're not seriously considering seeing this . . . this *boy* again, are you?'

'No. Our paths will never, ever cross. We lead completely different lives.'

'Do you mean it?'

'Of course I do. Put it this way – he calls his penis a "love lance".'

Kate laughed. 'Say no more.'

'I never, ever want to see him again, okay?'

Sure, I could walk past the door of opportunity without knocking. But nobody said anything about not taking a tiny, teeny peek through the crack . . .

11

Eating The Arm Candy

Knock! Knock! Who's there? Opportunity. The very next day, Tuesday, Julian announced that he was off to Prague for two weeks to do some laps in a legal think-tank.

But in fact, Zachary opened the door *before* opportunity knocked. Who should I glimpse across a Tesco's pagoda of mangoes on Wednesday but the Rap God himself. Thursday, by a surprising twist of fate, he materialized in the bra-fitting section of Marks & Spencers – the natural haunt of a man. Friday, apparently, he was due for his cervical smear test. I looked up from my copy of *Hello!* magazine to find him standing over me in the Women's Health Clinic, in his scuffed workmen's boots, rodeo belt buckle and sideburns sharp enough to shave even Kate's underarms. Zachary always gave the impression of having been born in whatever he'd chosen to wear on any given day.

'Can't you ever turn up somewhere looking just a little mediocre? Do you have to look sensational at all times? I mean, *must* you?'

'Yer never rung me up.' He sweetened his impertinence with a dimpled smile.

'That's because I don't want to see you,' I said, dwelling on the delicious contours of his behind.

He just smiled, a warm, rich smile that made everybody else's smile look faded.

In the same way that mums tidy the house for the cleaning lady, I fully intended going to the gym more often once I'd lost weight; but I thought a workout might burn off some of my lust. The YMCA in Central London is Work-Out Heaven. All the men are gay. Which means you never have to bikini wax and there's not a matching leotard-tight ensemble in sight . . . at least not on the girls. Entering the building from Great Russell Street and walking down the sloping gang plank is like boarding an underground ocean liner. The brightly lit auditorium yawns before you, abuzz with basketball and squash games. The tiled grotto of a pool lies, blue and inviting, behind a long glass wall in the cafeteria.

I pressed my nose up to the smoky window, searching the lanes for Kate's lime-green swimming cap . . . my heart skipping a beat at the sudden sight of

Zachary Phoenix Burne. I watched him decant himself into a black Speedo. Undressed, he looked like Michelangelo's David, without the pigeon poop. I thought of Julian's detestation for swimming. 'Any pastime that requires you not to breathe for much of it fails to pique my interest,' he always said. But Zachary arced through the water with supple elegance.

Avoiding the pool, I attended a circuit-training class instead. He conjured himself up, bench-pressing effortlessly, while I panted asthmatically at his side. Belly dancing, beginners Judo, Tighten That Butt! – no matter what class I attended, he enigmatically surfaced, an avalanche of sexuality at my elbow waiting to engulf me.

'Why is it that every time I come to the gym, you're here exercising?' I finally acknowledged him, my voice saturated in sarcasm. 'I mean, what are you? A *hamster*?'

Oh no. Here it came again. The Look. His black hair flopped over one eye, giving him a piratical air. Unlike the other men in the club, Zachary's 'street' look wasn't assimilated. There really was something dangerous, something wildly intriguing about him.

Usually the very idea of jogging makes me break out into a sweat, but with Zachary haunting the gym I reluctantly took to running in Hyde Park after work; staggering down past Kensington Palace, hyperventilating around the Round Pond, dragging my weary bones along Rotton Row to Speaker's Corner.

One evening I was collapsed on the grass by the Serpentine, praying for death, when the membrane of sky split open and rain pelted down. Cursing, I crawled into the wood and crouched under a leafy canopy. Zachary was not far behind. For once I was happy to see him.

'I hope you've got a car?'

'Naw.' He hunkered down beside me.

'How'd you get here then?'

'Hitch-hiked.'

'You *hitch-hiked*?'

'Yeah, well, it's just like walkin' only sittin' down, ya know.'

Smartass.

'Can't even afford the tube, after forkin' out for that goddam signature. Had to track that Pynchon dude down through the internet. Search public records – yer know, for drivin' licence and birth certificate. Jesus. Why can't yer read comic books like everyone else?'

I bummed a cigarette off him – that's the kind of health nut I am. 'So, how's the case going?' I small-talked.

'Some motherfuckers called the Broadcastin' Standards Commission say my words are too fuckin' crude to play on air . . .'

'Fuckin' cheek . . .' I heckled. 'So, tell me, are you one of those singers who the critics all go apeshit over, or are you any good? . . . I mean, what sort of music *do* you play?'

'There's only two kinds of music. Good an' bad. But if the rap don't cut it back home, I'm gonna move into retro rock with soul elements.'

'So what does your mum make of your filthy lyrics then?' I said, in an effort to get away from the rock'n'roll Esperanto.

'Mom's dead. When I was ten. OD.'

My interest in him rose meteorically. But I wasn't going to say I was sorry. 'Is that what gave you the determination to succeed?'

'Naw ... It just gave me an instant way in with women.' He grinned broadly. It was the sort of smile that made you wish you were wearing Polaroids. 'They feel sorry for me, know what I'm sayin'?'

I shook my head in disbelief. 'Hardship *can* be character building, sure,' I said, a tight-lipped frugality to my tone. 'But you really require a character to begin with.'

'My family taught me everythin' I know. My Granmama was the first person I saw thievin' – robbin' candy for me. My Old Man bolted. Brought up to fight and steal and survive by a family that's as far from two-point-four cosy Bill Cosby land as you can imagine.' He fires up a joint.

I glanced up at the grey cauliflower clouds. Suddenly, it was as though a hole had been punched in the sky. We were drenched in pale sunshine. Steamy heat rose from the soil around us, which gave off a pungent, visceral smell.

'And what about you?' He offered me the joint. Usually I don't smoke dope. It dulls my sarcasm. Besides, Julian didn't like it. I surprised myself by taking a toke and even more by answering.

'Hated my parents. Dropped out of school. Travelled. Around Asia, backpacking. Grew a new layer of skin. A taste of something else.'

'Yer dropped out? How come yer talk so uptown then? You're such a lady. I mean, I can't even imagine yer takin' a crap. I bet when yer do, they're just tiny, delicate little party frankfurters.'

The man was a poet. I laughed, despite myself. 'I finally went to art school, on a grant,' I explained. Though really it was Julian who'd 'refained' me.

'That's what I wanna do. Grow a new layer of skin. An' play Madison Square Garden, of course.'

The horizon was fevered. Crimson welts scarred the sky. Beyond the line of trees, Telecom Tower rose like a swizzle stick in an exotic cocktail.

'See, that's one of the reasons I like yer. 'Cause yer know all them big words, an' 'cause yer one of the sweetest women I've ever had the pleasure to suck.'

I held my breath. Just as well we weren't sitting indoors because I would have just set off the smoke alarm. This had to stop.

'Look, I'm flattered, Zachary. Really I am. But it would never work between us. We're too different. I mean, you're American. You have perfect teeth. I've got fillings. Look.' I opened my mouth and turned towards him. 'Five.'

'Yer look pretty damn good to me.'

'And that's another thing. Americans are so polite. Whereas I'm a loudmouthed old slapper.'

'A slapper?'

'You see? You don't even speak my language.'

'I wanna fuck you. Is that plain enough English?'

I stubbed out my cigarette. Holy Hell.

The evening air, mysterious and satiny, was threaded with possibilities. Our thighs pressed conspiratorially together.

'This is just impossible. I'm in love with Julian. I can't see you again.' I said, holding on to him as though we were both covered in superglue. I smudged my heated face into his hot neck with a sigh.

But even as I spoke sane and sensible words – You're pubescent; I'm pensionable. You've got groupies; I'm practically married – my hormones were betraying me. The fact that I was now wearing nothing but a pair of Adidas running shoes should have been a clue.

'You had sex with him, didn't you?' Kate interrogated when I went back to the office to shower and change. She always worked late.

'How do you know?'

'The fact that you have half of Hyde Park in your hair is a teeny-weeny give away, you big boofhead.'

'Isn't sex the best, most wonderful thing in the entire world?'

Kate glared at me over her spectacles. 'Have you tried skydiving?'

'Don't tell Anouska, okay? I don't want it getting around.'

'Okay.'

'She rooted him.' Kate announced when Anouska dropped by the office half an hour later to return the ice-cream the cop hadn't eaten.

'No. What was it like? Are you going to tell Julian?'

'No. Absolutely not. Look, I had to do it once, just to get him out of my system. Okay? And now I'm cured. I'm not ever going to see him again.'

'Good,' said Kate.

'Good,' said Anouska.

'Yes,' I reiterated.

'So,' said Kate, after a pause. 'When are you going to see him again?'

'Just as soon as we finish this conversation,' I replied.

That night we made love in one of those seedy No Tell Motels in King's Cross. 'Can I see you again?' he asked.

'No. Absolutely not.'

'Can I just make ya come then?'

'Oh. Okay.'

* * *

The next day, we clung to each other in the sauna at the YMCA as though drowning.

'Do you know how long purely physical attraction lasts?'

'Um . . . I dunno. Five to six hours?'

'We'd better get cracking then.'

And, dissolving in an exchange of salty, smouldering kisses, we jammed the door

Over the next week, we had sex in every conceivable place and position. Only lab rabbits had more sex than us. We had phone sex – but *in* the booth. We did it while listening to music – but in the back row of Wembley stadium. Believe me, I was an FBI agent's wet dream – I had fingerprints all over me.

Zachary's hands located places on my body I didn't know existed. Whole erogenous topographies, as yet unconquered. Through all our fevered grapplings in twisted sheets, storeroom cupboards and on car bonnets – I had a BMW car-hood emblem imprint on my back for days – we lost grip on the passage of time. Mornings, afternoons, midnights . . . all telescoped into one another. Our warm, tangled toes became the edge of the world.

When I did return, reluctantly, to normal life, I felt groggy and disorientated, like a scuba diver leaving the bed of a spectacular ocean. The world seemed grey and drained of sensation; the air clammy. I missed the pure oxygen of lust.

'So, Beck, will you have an affair with me?' Zachary asked superfluously on day seven.

I was in a steady relationship. My fiancé was urbane, intelligent, sensitive, compassionate. This punk was a rap star, the lowest of the low. His hair was snarled; his tatty T-shirts torn. He smelt of Johnny Walker and had never read Thomas Pynchon. I told him – *hell yes*.

12

How Many Rock Stars Does It Take To Screw In A Light Bulb? *One*: Rock Stars Will Screw Anything

'An affair?' Kate's face fell, as though I'd just told her I had terminal cancer. 'I thought you said that once you screwed him, he'd be out of your bloody system?'

'It's only a fling. I've got my return ticket, okay?' Who knows? Maybe after this burns itself out, I'll be able to finally settle down?'

The black refracted lines on the bottom of the blue pool shimmied as Kate plunged into the 'fast lane'. As most of Australia seems to be situated outdoors, Kate, a dedicated sportswoman, was always hijacking us off to the pool. In my opinion if God had meant us to swim he would have given us waterproof cigarettes.

'But he's so young,' she chastised, as her head broke

the surface. 'I mean, what are you going to do? Date him or adopt him?'

'An affair! My God, doll. How grown up!' Anouska said, cringing at the insalubrious surroundings. (It was her first time at the YMCA. Darius was proving such a drain on her finances that she'd had to give up her Chelsea Harbour Club membership. Kate had greeted this economy drive with scorn. 'Don't you have a spare palace to fall back on?') 'I mean, Adulteress! It sounds so deliciously decadent, doll!'

'She is *not* an adulteress,' Kate reprimanded, licking the eye sockets of her anti-fog goggles. 'To be an adulteress, you have to be an *actual* adult first.'

'In all my girlfriends, you're the first Scarlet Woman,' Anouska thrilled, peeling off to a bikini so flimsy that any contact with water would reduce it to a piece of dental floss. She produced her mobile phone (we called it her 'It Girl Earring') and set off on the telephonic trail of her absentee husband.

'Sex with a lead singer does not mean you're a scarlet woman. It means you have a personality disorder.' Kate kicked off from the wall, showering me in a jet of spray.

I pursued her in a leisurely old-ladies breaststroke, neck periscoping above the water so as not to get my hair wet. Clinging to the lane rope, I tapped Kate on the shoulder as she tumble-turned and torpedoed past me.

'Jesus, Kate. When was the last time you did

something just for fun? Just for the hell of it? When was the last time you twanged a guy's jockstrap, huh?'

'I am not a Jockstrap Twanger, thank you very much,' she said, treading water.

'You're pleasure-deprived, that's your trouble.'

'This may come as a surprise, you big galah, but the rest of the world couldn't give a rat's arse about your imprudent dating habits.' She sprinted overarm towards the shallow end, capsizing me in her wake. I clawed at the air, spluttering like a spa pool. I was ready to send up a distress flare, when she powered past me again and I grabbed hold for a tow to shore. Swimming really would be fine, if it weren't for the water. 'So,' she pried, against her finer feelings, 'the sex is really that hot, huh?'

'Hot? My IUD smelted.'

'Jesus.'

'We've been through the *Kama Sutra*. Twice. We've done the revolving table with the melon, the flambéed banana. The lot. *The man licks out my naval lint*. If there were such a thing as Frequent Leg-Over points, he'd be flying Concorde, first class, for the rest of his natural life.'

'No wonder you look so damn happy, doll,' Anouska said enviously, dangling her legs in the tepid, chlorinated stew.

'Girls, on a cloud rating of one to nine, we're talking ten.'

Kate slammed her palm against her forehead. 'Why

is it that whenever a woman starts having great sex, her IQ goes down?'

'Why don't you start having great sex and find out? Just get yourself a man and . . .'

'The reason I can't get a man, Rebecca, is because you've got them all. But he's a rock star. We're talking about people who insert wildlife into their rectums. Jesus Christ, Becky. I hope you're using condoms . . .'

'He's not like that . . .'

'Oh yeah. I bet you can buy bumper stickers that say "Honk If You've Had Zachary".'

I retreated into the amniotic waters, ballet-kicking my way at glacial speed. A lap or two later I was prodded from above by a pedicured toe. Anouska giving up the hunt for her husband detached herself from her 'It Girl Earring'.

'But, doll, don't you feel guilty? About being unfaithful?'

'Gee, I dunno. If you're penetrated while having an out-of-body experience, does that count as being unfaithful?'

'To *die* for. Can I have him when you're finished? . . . Watch out!' Anouska shrieked. 'You nearly got my bikini wet!'

'Oh, God forbid,' said Kate with mock mortification. 'A wet swimming costume!' She was breaststroking towards us, her hands coming together as if in prayer. 'And what about Julian?' She trod water, hands on

Speedo-ed hips. 'He must have noticed you acting weird . . .'

'He's a man. He probably just thinks the goldfish's dead or I've got my period or something.'

Anouska's hand froze, mid-hoik of a wayward breast. 'Your goldfish is dead?'

Kate and I eye-rolled each other. Sometimes Anouska's brain waves didn't quite break on the beach.

'Besides, he's so busy liberating uniped Inuits or whoever that I hardly ever see him. Unless you're fleeing some Junta or other he's just not interested in you.'

Kate shook her head. 'Sometimes I think you only have a larval sense of what is right and wrong, Rebecca.'

'Oh Kate, why should I worry when you worry so well for me?' I playfully jettisoned a plume of pool water in her face. 'You're my surrogate. Anyway there's no need to get your Tampax in a twist. It's nothing. It's just a primitive urge. Hobbesian. Look, he makes me laugh, that's all. He says that cheese is nothing more than "grown-up" milk. Isn't that cute? He asked me why British mail comes in First and Second, but not Business Class?' Kate gave me a dubious stare. 'He calls the Millennium a creepy crawly thing with too many legs.'

'Oh God. You're falling in love with him, Becky. You are.' Kate surged towards me, eyes at water level, like a crocodile.

'That's not true. If you knew how I abuse him. Ignore him. How rude I've been . . .'

'But that's a bloody aphrodisiac for men. Since *you* don't love *him*, the Himbo invariably imagines *he's* in love with *you*! Soon he'll be swallowing you whole!'

'Yeah, well. I like that in a man.' Irritated, I pushed up on the side of the pool and made the toe-cringing cross over tinea-infested tiles to our towels which were nestled on the bench beneath a six-foot replica of a hammerhead shark, which seemed, in the half light, to be grinning lasciviously.

Kate began towelling herself dry with great ferocity, loofah-ing off layers of skin with each rub. 'But why, Becky?'

'I dunno. Excitement. Danger. It makes me feel sexy. Wanted. It makes me feel young. The question is not why am *I* having an affair, but why aren't *more* women having them? I can control my feelings for him, okay?'

'With what? . . . Medication?'

'It's no big deal. Nobody will get hurt.'

'No? What if Julian finds out?'

'Julian will never, ever know. Generally speaking, there are four words you don't want to hear whilst having oral sex. They are "Hi, darling. I'm home".'

'Yes. All it takes is a little planning,' encouraged Anouska, living vicariously. 'A little discretion . . .'

'How the hell do you know?' demanded Kate as we descended the mouldy spiral staircase.

'I . . . well . . . I think Darius is an infidel.'

151

'A what?'

'You know. Committing infidelity.' Cue eye-rolling from Kate and me. 'It's all a matter of not changing your behaviour in any way. That's what leads to suspicion . . .'

'Exactly. This will be a liaison planned with military precision. I mean, God, I don't want to lose Jules. Who would? If I did anything to jeopardize my relationship with Julian I'd need to have my head examined.'

But if I'd known then what I know now, I would have had only one thing to say. '*Paging Doctor Freud to reception . . .*'

13

How To Have An Affair.
A Beginner's Guide

'Listen,' I panted to the guy in the off-licence as I rummaged frantically through the champagne bottles in the fridge, 'just say a woman is going home to her partner, five hours late with no alibi, which vintage would reduce the chance of him breaking up with her?'

'Krug,' he said impassively. ' '86.'

Having An Affair – A Beginner's Guide

1) Beware the itemized telephone bill.
2) Don't suddenly abandon knickers with questionable elastic for more stimulating smalls.
3) Don't hide your spermicide in your toothpaste tube. You're sure to forget and end up with fluoride in your fallopian tubes, not to mention tooth decay.

4) Take up an evening exercise class, something energetic which definitely involves showering.

5) Choose a hobby with no obvious end product. A year of African craft with no woven baskets at the end of it could be a bit of a give-away.

6) Best not leave your lovers semen-stained black-leather-studded cock-pouch (two sizes bigger than your partner's) in your swimming bag . . . because yes, the dog is sure to sniff it out and bound into the lounge with it clenched between his teeth.

7) If this does happen, pretend you are a cross-dresser.

8) 'Slut', 'whore', 'trollop', 'tramp' – remember that these are words used to describe a woman who has the sexual appetites of a man.

9) When feeling cheap and nasty, remind yourself that without infidelity, literature and opera would be up shit creek. There would have been no siege of Troy for Homer to chronicle in the *Iliad*. No Anna Karenina. No Emma Bovary. And what the hell would Chaucer and Shakespeare have written about? Imagine if Cressida had stayed with Troilus? If Tristan had never played tonsil hockey with Isolde? What would Wagner have done then, hmmm?

10) Don't appear happier than usual. Nothing gives away an affair faster than frequent smiling for no ostensible reason.

11) Don't indulge in late-night whispered conversations on the phone. Can be just a bit embarrassing when you get caught saying 'I need your hot rod, you wild, satanic Sex Viking, you,' when you'd said you were just off to phone your dad.

12) Cover your tracks with Sherlock Holmes thoroughness. Nothing worse than driving along with your Significant Other and suddenly noticing your lover's upside-down footprints on the car window.

13) Be careful not to call out the wrong name when making love. Recurrent coital amnesia has blown the whistle on many an illicit love affair.

14) Plan your liaisons with military precision and don't change your behaviour in any way as this will lead to suspicion.

   And, most important of all,

15) Don't be five hours late coming home with no alibi.

'Where in God's name have you been, Becky? I've been frantic with worry.'

'Who the hell are *you* all of a sudden?' I laughed, stalling for time. 'The Director of Private Prosecutions?'

I moved down the hall, trying to dodge the prison search lights of Julian's eyes. But the heat of his scrutiny was making me sweat.

Which brings me to point number 16) Always lie.

An average person tells a lie every eight minutes. Do my hair plugs look real? Answer – *Yes*. Have I put on weight? Answer – *No*. 'Good Morning' is, in England, a lie for most mornings of the year. As is 'I hate to bother you but . . .' Blaming traffic when you're late; faking cystitis when you'd rather watch ER than have sex; pretending it was a mistake when billed for watching porn channels in your hotel room – society would be unliveable if people started telling the truth. Marriages would crumble. Friendships dissolve. As CVs are complete works of fiction, nobody would ever get a job. Not me, anyway. No. Honesty is way, way too subversive.

The only downside to lying is getting found out. Which brings me to –

Lying – A Beginner's Guide

1) Don't look down at your hand.
2) Don't cover your mouth with your hands.
3) Don't lick your lips a lot.
4) Don't breath erratically.
5) Don't nose rub, ear tug or fidget with clothing.
6) Don't forget what lies you've actually told.

'Oh, I had to chaperone an artist through a press interview over dinner.' I kept my eyes fixed on his.

'Didn't you promise always to tell me when you were going to be late?' His suit was as crumpled as his face and there was a whisky fog in the air.

'Did I?' I started to lick my lips and quickly bit my tongue.

'Yes, just last week, when you were late.'

'Sorry.' I forced my breath to stay even. 'I don't remember.'

'Well, why don't you look in that mental sieve where you keep all our conversations?' My nose got itchy; my ears cried out to be tugged, my clothes ached to be readjusted. 'And anyway, I rang the office. They said you left before lunch.'

'Oh yes. Well, I had a meeting with the Arts Council . . .'

'What? For eight hours?'

'. . . Then I had a swim.'

'You're always swimming, lately. You must have swum the equivalent of the Atlantic ten times in the last month. In case you hadn't noticed, mankind evolved *out* of the water. So why are you so desperate to get back *in*?'

Another trick up the adulterer's sleeve, well, trouser leg, is not to alleviate your guilt by being overly nice to the man you're cheating on or he'll really get suspicious. What you have to do is be really, really awful; awful enough to make him think that *he's* the one who's done something wrong.

'So what are you implying? That there's someone

else? God. I go to the effort of bringing home champagne to celebrate our life together and you just attack me.' What a fake. God, I was faker than a holiday rep for Club Ibiza. 'Of course there's no one else or I'd be off with him *right now*!'

Julian trailed me into the kitchen, his face pale as paper, his thin, dry fingers running anxiously through his hair. 'Becky, I'm only trying to talk to you. Lack of communication is the reason most relationships fail, don't you know that?'

'We talk all the time.'

'Rebecca, my small intestine communicates with me more than you do . . . It's just that, lately, well, you've changed.'

'Well of course I have. Any woman who's wrestled with a do-it-yourself bikini-wax-kit will never be quite the woman she once was.' I made myself busy, retrieving champagne glasses from the top cupboard.

'You are seeing someone else, aren't you?' he asked thickly.

I'm not a very nice person, I know. I ran out on my own wedding. My favourite pastime is to go up to supermodels and tell them they look so much better since they've put on weight. And worse than that, I was lying my lips off to the only man in the world who really loved me. Next thing I knew I'd be trying to sell people used cars. Regardless of gut-churning self-loathing, I resolutely set my lips and lied. 'No.'

'Then why have you taken to making love with your

eyes closed? . . . When you *do* deign to make love to me that is. During the past month I've tried to make love to you forty-two times. I've succeeded twice. Excuses have ranged from: "it's too hot" (5); facial mudpack (8); "You only ever touch me when you want sex" (12) . . .'

'Jesus, Julian. You're making me sound like an honorary Mouseketeer. Maybe if you tried a little fore-play first . . .' I counter-attacked.

'What are you saying?' One of the things I like most about lawyers is the big shock absorber they have strapped to their brains. Put it this way, if a lawyer's ego was hit by lightning, the lightning would be hospitalized. But I'd really hurt his feelings this time. 'That I reach my peak with a little too much alacrity?'

'Well, yes. You're usually showered and shaved and dictating three legal opinions while I'm still taking off my bra.'

'It's not that I come too quickly, Rebecca,' he said curtly. 'It's that *you* come too slowly.'

'Excuse me?'

'You do. I have to tickle *this*. And stroke *that*. And nibble the left and lick the right and lunge and plunge and whisper sweet everythings . . . and still nothing. All the pressure on men to make it last . . . It's time to put pressure on you women to crescendo sooner.'

'So what are *you* saying? That I'm a lousy lay? . . . But how can you tell *in ten seconds*?'

'Oh thank you for sharing that with me, Rebecca.'

'Well, you're the one who was worried about us not communicating enough.'

'Yes, but now I think we're communicating too much. Wouldn't it be an idea if we stopped talking about orgasms and actually started having some?'

I popped the champagne cork in reply, smiling suggestively. The other way to cover up the fact that you're having an affair is actually have sex with your partner now and then.

'Really?' he queried timorously. 'Right. Wait there.'

'Why?'

'Well, I took to heart what you said about getting too middle-aged and predictable . . .' his voice trailed off into the bedroom.

A few moments later, he re-entered the kitchen.

I think it's fair to say that Julian wasn't in his element in leopard-print lederhosen. He looked neither erotic or commanding. Just faintly ridiculous.

'Don't laugh,' I silently instructed my mouth. I mentally rearranged the bedroom furniture, planned a menu for a dinner party and composed a way of asking for thrush cream without humiliating myself at the pharmacy.

'There's more.' Fortified with Krug, he produced from behind his back a glow-in-the-dark condom in the shape of a Stealth Bomber called 'The Penetrator'. Great. Now I could read during the dull bits.

I employed the old 'thinking of unsexy things' technique. Episiotomies, callipers, Newt Gingrich naked.

'Well, what would you like to do? Whipped cream? Cling film? . . . Bondage?'

'Julian! The only thing I want tied are my tubes.'

He pressed on, ignoring me. 'We could do it right here on the floor.'

My body was starting to vibrate with pent-up laughter. I slurped at my champagne to disguise my erupting smile. But before I could swallow, a great guffaw escaped from my throat, jettisoning Krug all down his furry front.

Julian's face collapsed like a soufflé. Oh good one, Beck. Well done. I was a truly terrible person. I deserved to go to a wife-swapping party and end up with O. J. Simpson. But try as I might, I couldn't stop laughing.

Julian cocooned himself in his silk gown. 'We seem to be having a misunderstanding about what constitutes a laughing matter,' he said in an injured voice.

'Oh darling, I'm sorry.' I forced myself to stop sputtering. 'Come here . . . You don't need to perform any tricks. I love you just the way you are.'

'You . . . you do still love me then?'

'Of course I love you. There's nothing you wouldn't do for me,' I joshed, twanging a lederhosen brace. 'But sweetie, the only thing which should get laid on our floor are those imported terracotta tiles we've been talking about. Let's just finish this champagne, clean our teeth, put on our pyjamas and go to bed like a normal couple.

'Nothing like striking while the iron is lukewarm,' he quibbled, but joined me cosily on the couch.

'You were right about those rock people,' he volunteered a glass or two later. 'I should never have taken the case . . . They're philistines. Especially the juvenile delinquent . . .'

I smarted. 'He's not that young.' Adding quickly. 'Is he?'

'Young? I'm amazed his voice has broken.'

'The case is heard tomorrow, isn't it?' I enquired, casually. 'I thought I might come down to court.'

Julian did a double take. 'You? In court? You never come near the court.'

'Forget lederhosen, my love. Seeing you strut your legal stuff – that's the biggest turn on of all.' Oh, that was subtle. I possessed the subtlety of a cable game-show hostess. God, who was I turning into? *Richard Nixon?* I bemoaned, as I realized I'd stayed completely composed while lying my bloody head off. I was a bad, evil woman. I was a paragon of vice. I was Caligula's sister. I was the love child of Myra Hindley and Vlad the Impaler. I took back everything I said about fibs and rules of affairs and all the rest of it. I was a lowlife. I was lower than Pamela Anderson's bikini line. I mean, God counts adultery as one of the worst ten things in the world. It had a hell-fire quotient, for Christ's sake. Guilt – Life's back-seat driver – nagged me remorselessly.

Soaping my face in the bathroom, I couldn't look at

myself in the mirror. I kept the light off, just in case I inadvertently caught my own eye. Which is why I didn't notice that the toothpaste I was squeezing on to my brush did not come out in the usual iridescent peppermint curlicues. As I put the brush in my mouth and choked, Julian entered and flicked on the light. He raised a quizzical brow. Not wanting to arouse his suspicions, I was forced to keep cleaning my teeth in spermicide. It wasn't until we were having sex that I realized, through my champagne induced torpor, that I'd also inserted my cap in the darkness, which meant that my fallopians were probably fluorided.

As we made love, all I could hear was the sound of my teeth decaying.

I was a worm. I belonged in a bait bag. But, like a worm, I was hooked.

14

Courtus Interruptus

'Don't you think this is just a teeny-weeny bit completely bloody insane?' Kate queried, as we hurried through Covent Garden to the Bow Street Magistrate's Court.

'Not at all.' I ground the butt of the cigarette I still told myself I didn't smoke beneath my heel. 'Zack has promised not to tell anyone. He's the soul of discretion . . .'

'*Becky!*' Zack screamed, discreetly. We wheeled around to gawp at the vehicle from which my lover was emerging as it was still cruising up to the curb. It was the standard rock impresario penis replacement – sixteen feet of fogged glass. The limo's number plate read, appropriately, 'EGO'. Zack hit the pavement at a trot, sprinted towards us, circled me in his Herculean arms and twirled me ozone-ward. Before I could reprimand him, he kissed me. When I say 'kiss', I mean he dragged me into his mouth, descaled my teeth, tickled my tonsils and became intimately acquainted with both sets of molars before detaching himself from me with the sound of a squid being prised off glass.

'Zachary!'

'It's the only goddamn way I know to get you to shut the hell up,' he grinned. The baggy black suit couldn't disguise his lean-hipped, hard-muscled body, nor the nipple ring bulging beneath his tight cotton T-shirt. I was just tweaking his buttock cheek – when my Significant Other appeared around the corner of Long Acre pursued by a posse of press.

I sprang back as though electrocuted. Julian's eyebrows leapt towards his hairline. A puff of steam emitted from his magisterial nostrils. And then he was lost from sight momentarily, as a leather-jacketed rock and roll behemoth levered himself from the interior of Zachary's now stationary limousine. The bodyguard looked like the sort of swarthy fanatic who sits outside the Israeli embassy with an Uzi machine-gun in his hip pocket and a vest made from explosive plastique. He galumphed to Zack's side, allowing Kate and me the dubious advantage of being able to examine him at close range.

Zack introduced him as Danny (the Dog Fondler) de Litto. The six-foot yeti with a face foaming with beard wore four-inch steel-reinforced combat boots. His hair was so oily that any flies coming in for a landing would just lose control and crash-land right into his ear lobes. He stood beside Zachary with his hands clasped in front of him in the obsequious pose of a maid-in-waiting.

'You know, it's not mandatory to flirt with my clients, Rebecca,' Julian said sternly, taking my elbow.

'I didn't flirt.'

'Flirt? You turned into a Plantation Belle before my very eyes . . .'

'Sweet thang! Ain't that imagination runnin' away with ya'll. Jumpin' to conclusions is jest way to aerobic for *you*, honey-child,' I said with heightened breeziness, wondering if he could hear my heart executing its frenzied drum solo.

Julian admonished Zachary, who was straining to hear our conversation above the bleatings of journalists, with a suspicious glare. 'You look a little jumpy. Are you nervous?' he interrogated coldly.

'Does the Pope jerk-off?' Zachary's comment was accompanied by a primordial grunt and chest-puffed out swagger, neither of which exactly helped to suggest a Mensa qualification. Kate darted a disapproving look in my direction. I started to squirm.

As Julian, reassured, strode through the court doors, Zack and his bodyguard in tow, Kate shook her head in disbelief. I felt myself blushing. Toyboys really should be quarantined for six months until properly house-trained. This was proving excruciatingly embarrassing.

'Hey,' I said defensively, 'he's from out of town, okay?'

'Where? The Fifth Dimension? How can you even compare him to Julian?'

'Before you start, the Great Civil-Rights Lawyer appeared last night in leopardskin lederhosen,' I confided, defensively.

'Leopardskin lederhosen? Julian?' Kate snorted. 'You're kidding me, right?'

'No. With zips and studs and stuff. He's trying to be more of a groover . . .'

In the time-honoured tradition of best girlfriends, I was just about to tell Kate more things not to tell anyone, when we were distracted by the screeching arrival of a *super*-stretch limo. Until now, I'd always thought the word 'stretch' could only be twinned with the word 'marks'. This ridiculous vehicle was as long as the portals of the Royal Opera House opposite. The number plate read 'MEGABUX'. It was what Zach called Rotty's 'pick-em-up-truck'. Kate drew in her breath at the sight of the big Necklace Ape lumbering across the pavement towards us. Despite the suit and tie, Eddy Rotterman still looked like the off-spring of Quasimodo and a giant slug. Even the gargoyles on the surrounding rooftops seemed to shudder, involuntarily.

Seeing me, the yellow lozenges of his eyes lit up. 'Good to see yer, sweet cheeks,' he said with vote-winning sincerity. The man was so avuncular all of a sudden, I started looking around for long-lost cousins.

'So,' Rotterman said, heaving to a halt, a savage smile puckering his pocked face. 'Whyja think white chicks go out with black men? . . . To get their purses back maybe?' He winked implicitly. 'Or do you figure it might have more to do with the old beef bayonet?'

Kate suddenly remembered something pressing she had to do back at the office – like change some vase water – and departed forthwith. I too, headed with alacrity up the stone steps.

'I've got a good idea,' I said to him over my shoulder. 'Why don't you go test the resistance of that limo wheel with your body?'

I passed my bag into the black maw of the rapid-scan X-ray machine at the door and walked briskly under the metal detector. I made for the court at a trot but the lobby was crowded and Rotterman seized my wrist by the stairs. 'So, tell me? *Is* he the Pussy Master?' I felt my stomach sicken. When I didn't answer, he pressed on. 'The problem is, baby, an' I ain't jerkin' yer chain . . .' Rotty's eyes glistened wetly with secrets. My secrets. 'Yer know what they say, once you've had black, yer can neva go back.'

My nausea intensified. Zack had repaid my trust by giving his slimey agent a blow by blow-job account. Typical man – no sooner done than said. It was my fault for thinking that the guy had a brain. A rock star's brain is just that thing he thinks he thinks with.

'Let me get this straight. You're saying I slept with

your meal-ticket?' I dredged up as much indignation as my terror would allow.

'Oh, ya read my mind. Yer such a clever chick.'

I looked at him with contempt. 'Ah, actually that doesn't follow.'

I stomped ahead, hoping to lose him amongst the policemen, prostitutes and dangerous drivers who thronged the corridor nervously rehearsing the perjury they were about to proffer in the witness box. I scurried through the door to the public gallery of Court One. To my intense irritation, Rotterman intimidated the man sitting next to me into moving, then squeezed into the vacated leather chair.

'We have a sayin' in the music biz,' he whispered, clammily. 'Get yer end in, get yer friend in,' he hinted, his lips growing glutinous. 'A team cream, we call it. Or killin' two birds with one bone.'

His sidewalk brawler's laugh was cut short by the usher's cowering proclamation: 'All rise.'

Three lay magistrates tottered into court as if fresh from their third heart bypasses. There was a ritual exchange of courtesies with the lawyers, before Julian's opponent, a Marcia Clarke lookalike with the whiplash vowels of a young Margaret Thatcher, began hectoring the geriatrics on the bench as if they were wayward schoolchildren.

'This is a most disgusting case, in which it will be your duty to order the destruction, under Section Three of the Obscene Publications Act, of 25,000 compact discs seized by the police. The title of the album is, if you will excuse me, *Fuck the Cops.*'

She expelled the words with tingling pleasure – the high point of her career, the day she said 'Fuck' to a captive audience. For the next hour she spoke as rapidly as a sewing machine, threading words together, stitching Zachary up.

The beaks seemed ever so slightly to resent being told what to do.

When Julian rose to deliver the case for releasing the CDs to their owners – Rottweiler Records – he rocked on his feet, moving gently up and down in a graceful mesmerizing way. His hands were open, palms up, then, when making a particular point, palms inwards, fingers steepled. I hadn't seen him in court for so long I'd forgotten about these sure-footed intellectual arabesques. For two hours or more, he secreted verbal pearls around grains of fact. He spoke of Zachary as the authentic voice for the generation of disillusioned black teenagers looking for guidance in the face of the imminent urban apocalypse of the American ghettos.

He flattered the magistrates' intelligence. 'You,' he addressed them, 'are no doubt part of the generation that discovered in their youth the attraction of forbidden fruit. James Joyce, Henry Miller, D. H. Lawrence. Surely you've bequeathed to your children an equivalent curiosity?'

He conjured experts – a young, black, female BBC disc jockey to explain the harmless pleasures of rap concerts. Then, not to deprive the music of social significance, he called an earnest music critic from the *Guardian* who described rap as Street Journalism.

Julian brandished half a dozen adult magazines he'd purchased from the top shelf of the local newsagent. 'Magazines like these are freely available right here next to the Court. This pornography is designed to arouse lust. Zachary Burne's CD arouses fear, concern and distaste, certainly. But it does not arouse lust. It is often bitterly sarcastic and rude and will strike our ears as crude. So yes, the music may damage your ears, but not your mind. I'd like to put a stop to this music too, not by censorship, but by a social-welfare programme that gives the poor and oppressed a stake in our society.'

His master stroke, he admitted later, was to persuade the magistrates that the law of evidence did not permit them to read the transcript of the lyrics compiled with such care by the Obscenity Squad; instead they had to listen to the 'best evidence' – the music. The prosecution then made the mistake of playing the CD on a cheap portable player that had its modulation inexpertly turned to 'bass'. We all sat solemnly for fifty minutes while strange Afro-American gobbledegook was emitted from the witness box. There seemed to be only one audible lyric along the lines of 'Life Sucks, I Wanna Die', which, when repeated the customary three thousand times to a lolloping beast of a beat, was a sentiment soon shared by the entire courtroom. It was not so much music as a grunge noise edifice, filtered through a drain.

'Like the adolescent pimple, the unruly pop song is best left alone – though the temptation to pick it, causing it to fester and spread, may be overwhelming. But this noise is not "obscene" in law because it cannot conceivably deprave and corrupt.' Julian coaxed the Justices that they had no alternative but to acquit.

We hadn't even made it to the canteen for the obligatory cup of stewed tea when the three lay magistrates returned to reject Scotland Yard's invitation to destroy Zack's CD, adding their own coded version of 'Fuck the Cops' by awarding £2,000 in legal costs against them.

Outside the court, I tried to order Zack to call his Rottweiler to heel, but he and Julian had disappeared into the waiting arms of the paparazzi. I was madly May Day-ing with hand gestures when, with the speed of a ten-ton lorry, the bodyguard scooped me up and bundled me into the back seat of Rotty's pick-em-up truck. As he lumbered back to Zachary's side, the limo screeched away with both back doors flapping in a mockery of Prince Charles's ears.

'What the hell . . .'

'Victory lunch. The Ivy. Jest sent a message to the others to join us. Hungry?' I looked at Rotterman on the seat beside me. His mossy-looking tongue lolled lasciviously out of the left corner of his mouth. He was coiled, cobra-like, ready to strike. 'I ain't had no pussy for near on two months.'

'What?' I wedged myself up against the opposite door. 'Couldn't you afford it?' Steering the Olympic swimming pool of a car around the corners of Covent Garden was proving aerodynamically impossible. Every swerve sent me hurtling closer to him.

'Yer not gettin' any of this, are ya?' he grunted. 'I'm lookin' for a burrow for my purple-headed womb-ferret.' He lurched towards me and I was engulfed in a fug of bourboned breath.

'The thing is, Mr Rotterman, seeing you naked would almost certainly turn me into a lesbian.'

Rotterman's lips contracted like an irritated anus. Then light dawned in his eyes. 'Oh, don' tell me. Yer got the curse?'

'Yeah. *You.*' And a certain indiscreet Toyboy. How could Zachary have been so bloody stupid? He'd promised not to soil my reputation. Soil? Jesus. You could start plans for commercial agriculture in my reputation. You could feed the goddamn Third World. 'Don't you think I might be tempted to tell Zack about this? . . . And don't you think he may be tempted to use your testicles as maracas?'

'Naw. 'Cause then I'd be tempted to tell Julian that Zack's been shaftin' yer with his love-slug. His cranny-hunter, his donkey-kong . . . So, babe, whattaya say?' he demanded, a smirk in his hooded, jaundiced eyes. 'Yer place or mine?'

* * *

Dining with your lover and your betrothed is not a good idea. It's about as good an idea as, say, playing leapfrog with a rhinoceros. When Julian arrived twenty agonizing minutes later, a quick quizzical glance in my direction indicated he'd detected my discomfiture ... Perhaps the ten-inch sweat moustache I'd sprouted had given it away. I was in too deep. Deeper than the *Titanic*. How did men carry this affair thing off? *Cosmopolitan* reckoned that seventy-five per cent of men have affairs. So what did *they* know that *I* didn't? I'd just have to think like a bloke. Lie. Laugh. Not panic.

'Let's go,' I gasped, panic-stricken, the minute Julian sat down.

'What?' he joshed, buoyed up by victory. 'Haven't I sung for my supper?'

As he and Rotterman consulted the wine list, Zachary attempted to talk to me. I ignored him. There were just no words to describe my feelings about the guy without recourse to slang terms for faeces. *How could I ever have had sex with a man who had so little respect for my fiancé?*

When the waiter appeared with Julian's first course, Rotterman applauded the choice. 'Always a good sign in a man, ain't it?' he winked for my benefit.

'Ah, yes. The aphrodisiac powers of the oysters,' Julian laughed.

'Naw. Means he likes goin' down on his chick.'

Julian choked. I patted his back and passed him some water.

Rotterman ostentatiously pronged an oyster on a fork tine and inserted it lewdly between his lips.

'You know the oyster only dies when it's halfway down your throat,' I said coldly to my tormentor.

As I rhythmically soothed Julian's back with my hands, Zack's eyes burned; his breath slowed. Scowling darkly, he summoned the waiter and immediately changed his main-course order to a bed of rock oysters. A double bed.

Oh this was good. This was as good as it gets. No wonder Anna Karenina topped herself on the railway tracks of St Petersburg. Emma Bovary suicided as well. Tess of the D'Urbervilles got herself hung also, come to think of it. What a bunch of role models. I mopped at my Hercule Poirot of sweat moustaches. You could get this one waxed. What a day. It was like having root-canal work – only not as relaxing.

'The case went well,' I blurted, 'didn't it?'

'Justice ain't no more than a verdict delivered in *your* favour,' Zack sulked moodily.

'Where'ja dig up those "experts". Whiniest little fucks I ever saw,' Rotty scoffed, ungratefully.

'Yeah. An' what was all that "crude and rude", squeezed zit shit?' Zack demanded, chastising Julian with his butter knife.

I bridled. 'The reason you won today was more to

do with Julian's advocacy skills than your innocence, Mr Burne.'

'Yeah?' Zack brooded, pouting. 'Seems to me lawyers jest make a livin' outta lying.'

Suddenly I saw my lover through Julian's eyes – a jumped-up punk with a two-grunt vocabulary. A central-casting loser. Like a piece of coral removed from the tantalizing sea, he had lost all of his exotic allure and wondrous colour. Despite his cast-iron biceps, bedroom eyes and exquisite profile that went all the way down, suddenly Zachary Phoenix Burne possessed all the charm of a job at Kentucky Fried Chicken.

In the middle of my bleak ruminations, Rotty, still hell-bent on proving that Jurassic Park is no mere celluloid fantasy, leant towards me. 'FCK – the only thing missing is you,' he whispered, hoarsely.

I checked to make sure that Zack and Julian were still discussing the case. 'Um ... which part of the word "No" don't you understand?' I hissed.

'The part that says if yer don't let me stab yer whiskers, I may need to squeal to yer Learned Friend.'

The Ivy is the watering hole of London's artistic élite. The deals, the meals, the chattering, the flattering ... it's an excellent restaurant in which to exceed the feed limit, because you can lose weight whilst doing so. The search for celebrities requires a lot of energetic head swivelling. Peering around the Power Tables in the oak-panelled dining room this late Tuesday lunchtime, the famous patrons (so called because they are patronizing to anybody who *isn't* famous) seemed overwhelmingly underawed by our presence. Until, that is, I upended Julian's oysters into Rotterman's lap; toppling him backwards off his chair. In slow motion he cascaded on to the next table, sending their gourmet food into orbit, finally coming to land, spreadeagled as a bloated starfish, on the floor at the feet of Joan Collins. Suddenly it was Swivel City. Patrons would be in neck braces with whiplash for weeks.

Julian then did the most wonderful thing that anyone has ever done for me. He rose quietly to his feet and steered me by the elbow towards the door, only pausing to say matter-of-factly to the maître d' – 'Just put him on the bill.'

'Paul Revere has a lot to answer for,' Julian said calmly, once I was outside and moving, dazed and discombobulated, up the street. 'If Paul Revere had known one Edward Rotterman, he wouldn't have warned his ancestors of anything, I'm telling you.'

I took hold of him and kissed him full on his luscious lips.

'Let's get married.'

'What?'

'Let's get married.'

'When?'

'Now. All the paperwork's done. Let's just do it. For better or worse . . .'

'How much worse?' a pleasantly stunned Julian asked. 'I mean, are you going to start flossing your teeth in bed?'

The Registry Office in Rosebery Avenue gave my kind of service. Everyone who's no one was there – just two witnesses roped in off the street. No relatives. No garters. No flower girls. And the gay marriage celebrant said 'but no tongues' when he advised Julian that he could 'now kiss the bride'.

And while my darling did just that, long and lingeringly, I added a silent vow to the service – a vow more important than loving and honouring and till death us do parting . . . *And for God's sake, lead us not into toyboy temptation.*

15

The Mourning After The Knot Before

In the midst of life ... we are in marriage. It took a while for me to register that I actually was a Mrs. It took the entire honeymoon in fact. Well, it wasn't a honeymoon exactly. We called it our honeymoon, but really it was just the annual summer holiday with Vivian and Simon in a Tuscan villa.

What poor old Tuscany has done to deserve this summer influx of BBC producers, knighted playwrights and gin-and-tonic swilling advertising executives, remains a mystery. The pool at our villa looked like *Baywatch* gone wrong. It was the Brit version, complete with weedy white legs, wobbly thighs, lumpy bits and beer bellies – all boiled red in the sun, like the exotic salamis I'd seen hanging in Siena's markets.

Besides playing 'Spot the Italian' and screaming in agony from regularly scalping ourselves on the low beams, my main pastime was trying not to think about Zack.

I tried not to think of him when taking a daily constitutional to the local castle and back. 'So life affirming, Italy, don't you think?' Vivian pontificated, as we staggered along the dusty road, the olive trees flinching in the July heat.

'Yes,' I lied. To me, the Italian countryside reeks of death. At night all you can hear are the blood-curdling sound of things being killed. Wild pigs killing owls; owls killing rabbits; the housekeeper killing mice . . . In the morning we were always finding bones, picked clean. The whole area resounded to the sound of our next meal being butchered.

I tried not to think of him when we played anagram games after supper. 'Clitoris is almost an anagram of solicitor,' I exclaimed triumphantly, as we sipped our vintage San Gimignano.

'You've got clitoris on the brain,' Simon complained.

'Oh, so *that's* where it is!' Julian joked.

I tried not to think of him as I lay in bed waiting for Julian to stop working. (He had some hangings to delay in Belize, a country where justice comes with strings attached.)

'I have a really interesting question to put to you,' I said groggily when he rolled into bed around three. 'Is There Sex After Marriage? . . . I know Tuscany's having a drought. Are you complying with another kind of hosepipe ban?'

I tried not to think of him when a few minutes later Julian yawned halfway through my striptease. 'You yawned!'

'I did not!'

'You did. Your mouth just went like this . . .' I imitated a doughnut.

'I'm sorry, Becky, but I'm exhausted.' He began some perfunctory foreplay.

'Jesus, Julian. I'm so sick of you working. Put it off. At least until after the honeymoon.'

'Put it off?! The only thing about to be suspended indefinitely are those poor men. By the neck. I've finished the first written submission. That's why they need me. I get there faster than anyone else . . .'

'This is true of many things you do, Julian,' I said a few disappointed moments later – but he was already asleep.

I tried not to think of him as I opened the international edition of the *Guardian*, delivered a day late to the local trattoria. Until, that is, Zack's face peered back up at me from page three. The caption declared him a 'generic rock god in the making', all 'cascading hair and thrusting crotch'. The article went on to describe his lyrics as 'Shakespeare on Acid'.

The abiding irony of all censorship is that any attempt to ban artistic expression produces publicity which only serves to promote mind-bogglingly massive sales. Reports of the court case had given Zack's record the boost it needed to go into orbit. From then on I couldn't escape him. Publications as diverse as *The Face* and the *Daily Telegraph* were falling over each other to declare Zachary as a 'voodoo high priest', the 'new Lenny Kravitz', whose lyrics 'captured the nihilistic sentimentality of the Post-Diana, Pre-Millennium mood.'

There was no escaping him on satellite television either. There he was, giving the microphone the time of its life.

But fans weren't just mad for his music and macho posturing. The perfection of his buttocks was commanding, oh, 10,000 words a week. His posterior had a career of its own. It had its own publicist for Christ's sake. *Rolling Stone* listed him as one of the hundred most sexy men on the planet. Amidst the pretentious answers from other shortlisted bachelors, Zack elliptically listed his hobbies as 'not shaving'.

I still had a leather jacket of Zack's that I'd worn on the plane to Italy. I found myself touching it, reverently slipping my hand inside its cool interior, adoring the frisson it gave my palm, as though Zack himself were about to lift my hair and shiver-kiss my neck. I started to get an ache inside.

When Julian managed to tear himself away from his submissions and commissions and approached me amorously, I now found myself pushing him off with promises of 'Later'.

'Today later, or *some time in the new millennium later*?' he finally asked after the third brush-off. God, my worst fears were confirmed – I'd turned into a Fellatio Refusnik. And so I kept having sex with Julian, but my heart wasn't in it. It was as though a party was being thrown on my body to which I hadn't been invited.

Over the rest of that long, cool summer I realized, quite slowly, slow as rising damp, that I'd made a mistake. It was the same rising damp which had rotted the foundations of my parents' marriage. I could almost smell it.

Matrimony, I thought, needed a little something to break the monogamy.

16

To Love, Honour And Betray

I know I'd prayed in my marriage vows not to be led into temptation. But let's face it, I could find the way blindfolded.

'Don't you think discretion is the better part of middle age?' Kate said when I showed her the three tickets I'd just received in the mail to see Zack's new retro rock band playing at Wembley.

'I'm just curious. I mean, what harm can it do?' It was a rationalization nimble enough to qualify for the parallel bars finals. 'Go on, come with me.'

'I'd rather remove my own IUD with garden shears.'

'Where's your sense of adventure? He's a star now, you know.'

'A star, you big dag, is a gaseous state appearing as an apparently fixed luminous point.'

Exactly, I sighed to myself. A heavenly body.

'Just make sure you wear protective clothing. And if you pick up anything contagious, don't come back to the bloody office.' She was still mad at me for getting married behind her back.

'Please come, Kate. We'll stay downwind,' I promised.

'Oh, all right. But only because your hormones are in a bad neighbourhood, Rebecca, and it's best not to let you venture in there alone.'

'Oh, my *God*,' she said, eyeballing me as I tumbled into the back seat of Anouska's car two days later.

'What? Not subtle enough?'

'Subtle!' Kate looked me up and down – pausing with particular disdain at my thigh-high leather boots. 'In *that* outfit, you might as well be wearing a fluorescent T-shirt with "Root me now, you Cum-Coaxing-Fuck Pig!" written on it.'

'Two men. You're so lucky, doll!' Anouska took a swig of vodka. Since marrying Darius she'd come to see alcohol as a major food group.

'I do *not* have two men. I'm married. There's a dead-bolt on my knickers. If I ever get serious about a *rock star*, I want you to take me into a dark room and slap me repeatedly until I come to my senses. Okay?'

'Speaking of husbands, Anouska, have you actually seen yours since the wedding?' asked Kate. 'You know you're getting a little old to have an imaginary friend.'

Anouska floored the accelerator.

Once safely past the scalpers and inside the vast

auditorium, we were embalmed by the crowd.

'Do the words "cat" and "swing a" mean anything to you?' Kate asked as we fought our way to our freebie seats. The crowd had already begun the stubborn, staccato cry of 'Zack! Zack! Zack!'

The bass guitar started up like a Boeing 747 – with the audience as its flight path. There was the pheromonal rush of the lead electric guitars, then the nerve-jarring electronic squeal of the synthesizer. In time with the percussive undercurrent, the whole audience executed the kind of jubilant jump normally associated with winning the Lottery.

A guitar solo slithered across the stage. A cartwheel of light spurted from the wings ... and then there he was, undulating into the spotlight. With a great roar the crowd convulsed towards him. I felt a delightful throb of expectation not far from my naval.

'Oh my God, doll,' gasped Anouska. 'Could his pants be any tighter?'

Zack gave a petulant yowl – he wasn't just performing; that was a testosterone tornado out there. His body was pure energy; solidified light. I tried not to drool like Pavlov's dog. His voice was strong, raw. He'd mixed musical genres like pizza toppings ... soul, rap, rock. But the lyrics were consistent – assassinating all in their wake.

He prowled closer to the crowd. In the muffled blue light, the writhing audience looked like an octopoid creature. The sensation of peering into a rock pool was heightened by the sea anemone of swaying arms. Fans reached for him, then, as soon as Zack touched their fingers, retracted, enraptured.

I jumped as we came under scrutiny from the random gaze of the spotlight. Beneath its Cyclops surveillance I realized, with a sudden chill to the spine, that we were the oldest people in the audience.

Towards the end of the hypnotic set, he spoke for the first and only time in the microphone, besides the obligatory 'Hello, London!' and 'It's great to be here.'

'Becky, this song is for you, babe.'

My heart lurched. It trampolined, somersaulted and pogoed about in my chest.

Despite the syntactically bewildering title, 'Love You Much' was a slow song about love, or 'Lerve', rather, and how opposites attract. Not exactly Sondheim (looking good in latex seemed of more importance than an understanding of iambic pentameter), but there was an aching, inarticulate eloquence – a melancholy hunger to his words that burnt. I felt the familiar stirring of steamy anticipation. All around me, people were lip synching to the lyrics. Lyrics about me. Was this every girl's dream or what? I thought marriage had inoculated me against Zach's charms, but everything about him was thrillingly irresistible. A male Lorelei, he lured me on to his rocks.

In a collective whoosh, the audience were up on their feet, dancing on their chairs for the final song. It wasn't so much an auditorium as a *shrine*. Zack and his band were only the support act, but just being in Wembley bathed them in a deified light. There was an epileptic lighting effect – and then he'd gone. Evaporated. No encore.

The lights came up abruptly. The doors opened, disgorging the rock congregation into the bars.

'Jesus, doll,' Anouska gushed, as we filed down the stairs. 'Where'd you find *him*? A male-order catalogue?'

'You seem a tad underwhelmed, Kate . . .'

'What do you want me to do? Discharge small firearms into the air?'

'I loved the song about you, doll,' Anouska thrilled. 'It really lodges in your head . . .'

'Yeah,' said Kate, 'like a migraine.'

'I think the band is way ahead of its time . . .' Anouska enthused.

'Or maybe just late,' amended Kate, sulkily.

A bouncer with a black pompadour inspected our 'Access All Areas' passes before escorting us backstage through a tangle of cables and wires, thick and treacherous as eels. It was so crowded in the band's dressing room that the only way to survive was by holding our cocktail glasses ten feet above our heads . . . when I say cocktail, what I really mean is toxic defoliant. One sip and our tonsils were ricocheting around our upper brain lobes. The air was charged with emulation; as pungent as Rotty's aftershave, which assailed me shortly after our arrival.

'Jesus Willy Christ. What thuh fuck are you doin' here?'

'Nice to see you too.'

'Shaddup. I could've pressed GBH charges, yer know, yer loony bitch. Now stay away from my boy, yer little shit weasel.'

'I really don't think that's up to you,' I said, spying Zack. The sight of him took my breath away. He was ploughing through the leather jackets and lycra jumpsuits like Moses parting the waves.

'Remember me?'

We held each other as though it were freezing instead of ninety degrees in there.

'Tell me, is that a guitar you're carrying, or are you just pleased to see me?'

He laughed, a deep, wicked laugh with a promise of unmentionable sex acts in it. I broke free to introduce him to Kate and Anouska.

'So *you're* the one who defies description,' Anouska purred, flicking her hair. Anouska was a flick-teaser from way back. It Girls saw hair auto-manipulation as part of their sexual allure – not, like the rest of us, as dandruff-distribution.

Zack extended his hand to Anouska, who wrung it enthusiastically, and then to Kate who regarded it with the ocular zeal one would give a maggot in a jam jar. She shook Zack's fingers with limp reluctance and said sarcastically, 'I'm so nice to meet you.'

I elbowed her hard in the ribs. 'Don't worry about her,' I told Zack. 'She's *Australian*. Australia had a rough childhood, you know.'

But Zack just laughed and took my face in his hands. 'I've missed ya, Becky . . . I've missed sayin' yer name. I love the gentle sound of yer name. I love to put my tongue around it.'

Which reminded me of something *I'd* missed – that anaconda tongue of his.

'Your songs are amazing, doll.' Anouska was now follicular-flicking up to seven times per second.

'My songs are sex with you, Beck, set to music.'

I tell you what was amazing – the fact that he could say lines like that without making me want to throw up. No. It made me want to do other things all together . . .

'Why did you jest go an' dump me out like that?' Zack demanded, hurt.

'You told Rotterman!'

'Hell, you told *yer* friends, didn' cha?'

I looked at the fixed smiles of Kate and Anouska. Beaming like deranged orang-utans, they made for the bar.

'Becky, I need you. Yer different from all the other chicks I meet an' all . . .'

I glanced at the hordes of young women in awed orbit around the band. It looked like a training class for those innocuous, smiling female quiz-show sidekicks – 'Ladies and gentleman, a *car*.'

'No wonder. Most of *these* women look as though they just crawled out from under a rolling stone . . . probably Mick.'

'Yer make me think, yer know what I'm sayin'? And I've been thinkin' about this long and hard . . .' Oh God. Did he have to choose those exact words? 'An' I wantcha to move in with me.'

'What?' What was wrong with men all of a sudden? It must be the oestrogen in the drinking water or something. Overnight every man in the world wanted to commit all over the place.

'Yer make me happier than a dog with two dicks. I love yer, goddamn it.'

'You're a musician. Musicians don't love. Love is just a four letter word . . .'

He ran his thumb down my cheek. Two seconds and he had me humming like a stereo amplifier. I began to give myself over to the narcotic inertia of lust. But then my wedding ring nagged at me from my third finger and I pushed him away.

'I can't break up with Julian. Not now.'

'Why not? . . . Yer don't love him. End of story. If yer loved him, you'd have married him.'

'I did.'

'Do *what*? Sweet Jesus.' He reeled away from me. 'Well, yer *have* to leave him now. I ain't gonna be some married lady's boy toy.'

'I can't just *leave* him . . .' I gulped for air.

'Are yer happy to be where yer are when yer close

yer eyes at night an' when yer open 'em up in the mornin'?'

'Oh, let's start with the easy stuff.'

'Why are you Brits so goddamn strung out to bein' miserable? You're in Happiness Denial.' He turned me to face him. 'Be my destiny, Beck.'

'You know the judgement of a man willing to be seen in public wearing lamé loafers cannot really be trusted,' I said, mock-insouciantly, treading on his toes.

He stared at me intently as he rolled up his sleeve. There, in amongst a clump of barbed wire, a tattoo of my name coiled sinuously around his upper arm.

'I wanna be yer man. More than I wanna play Madison Square Garden, even.'

Oh God. So corny . . . So *horny*. What the hell was happening to me?

'Why are yer so scared to commit? . . . Most babes wanna be head over heels in love, yet you just want the heels over head bit.'

I took a step back which was when Rotterman propelled someone who *wasn't* frightened to commit, into my place.

The Suicide Blonde (she dyed by her own hand – actually, this girl's hair couldn't get back to its roots without a genealogist) was all of nineteen. Her sequinned boob tube and lycra hot pants (believe me, this was one girl who really *could* say 'read my lips') was a look that didn't quite come off . . . but definitely would later. Probably for the *whole band*. She gave Zack the kind of kiss you need a lifeguard for. I felt a stab of jealousy.

Celestia turned down the offer of Devils On Horseback, pronouncing herself a 'free-fall vegetarian'.

'And what pray tell is that?' I asked haughtily.

'She only eats vegetables an' fruit that have fallen to the earth,' Rotty said with counterfeit sincerity, 'an' not been cruelly plucked from branches. Ain't that right, sweet-cheeks?'

'And no meat of course,' she purred.

'Oh? So I suppose blow jobs are out of the question?' I said viciously.

Zack's fleshy lips tangoed across his face, settling into a wicked grin.

'Zachary had no complaints the other night,' Rotterman mentioned, as if in passing.

I reeled around to hiss at Zack – 'You've *slept* with her?'

'Well, you sleep with the *husband*, doan 'cha?'

'That's different. Why would you sleep with a . . . a . . . groupie?'

Zack shrugged. 'Because I can.'

And would again if I didn't move fast.

'Does "hubby" know you're here? snarled Rotterman poisonously.

'Zack, can we get out of here?'

'There's my dressin' room,' he pointed behind him. 'Come on in for coffee.'

Inside the poky little cupboard, he turned, leant down and kissed my inner thigh. Just once. It was then that the final G-string of restraint slipped nonchalantly to the floor.

The kettle didn't stand a chance.

17

The Fountain Of Age

'Something awful has happened,' I confessed as we piled into Anouska's car an hour or so later.

'You saw your bum from the back?' guessed Anouska, leaving the car park on two wheels and careering through an orange light (Amber is an 'It Girl Green'.)

'Well, not *awful* exactly. Amazing. Something amazing has happened.'

'You've had an Elvis Visitation?' asked Kate facetiously.

I flicked down the sun visor to gauge her reaction in the make-up mirror. I took a deep breath. 'Zachary has asked me to move in with him.'

Kate guffawed. 'Oh, lemme guess. Was this just right before he screwed you?'

'How did you know I . . .'

'And now you think you've been struck by love's arrow . . .'

'Javelin more like it,' Anouska snorted, hitting first the steering wheel with her palm and then, more alarmingly, the kerbstone with the car.

'Annie! For God's sake! . . . At first I kidded myself that it was just sex. Zack kept saying he loved me, but I never said it back. I thought if I didn't say it out loud, I'd be okay. But now I can't keep him out of my bed *or* my head. I . . . I think I do love him . . . Yes. That's what's awful.'

Kate guffawed again. 'That's what I like about you, you big dag. Your undies are always thinking.'

'I mean it, Kate.'

'I'm sorry, but people do not consummate "love" against a wall in a back alley of Wembley Stadium.'

'How do you *know*?' asked Anouska anxiously, glancing over at me. 'That you're in love, I mean?'

'Will you keep your goddamn eyes on the . . .' We caromed off the bumper of a parked car. 'I don't know. Love is like an orgasm,' I said. 'Hard to describe, but you know it when you feel it.'

'You're "in lust", Becky, that's all.' Kate flicked my head. 'You *always* fall in lust. The euphoria span usually lasts what? One to two months tops . . . Or until you meet his younger brother.'

'I'm thinking of leaving Julian.'

Anouska veered off the road altogether, collecting a post box en route.

Kate thumped her hand on Anouska's headrest. 'Pull over, you big dickhead. Pronto. Okay,' she said, once the car had screeched to a halt on a double-yellow line, 'it's official. Your brain has been surgically replaced by your G spot.'

'I know it's insane, but we just seem somehow . . . I dunno. Fated.'

'Oh yes. It's fate that forced you to fuck behind your husband's back. Then hey presto. Two houses you can't sell, two vacuum cleaners that don't work and his drummer moulting all over your mother at the wedding reception.'

'I think it's kind of romantic . . .' Anouska sniffled.

'Romance is a foolish bloody longing for life without mortgages and dentists. Romance is love without real life attached. What women need is equality, not romance.'

I ran a tongue over the lovebites on my lower lip. 'Kate, I want him so bad I can feel it.'

'. . . and lust is a low-down rotten trick played on us by Mother Nature to assure the continuation of the bloody species. It's hormonal hives. Curable only by a good dose of common bloody sense. Now go and get us some coffee,' she ordered Anouska. '. . . And one penis-on-rye, for the cradle-snatcher, here.' She hooked a thumb in my direction.

'It's not just sex,' I told Kate. 'He makes me feel, I dunno, brand new.'

'What the hell are you? An electrical appliance?'

'He makes me feel young, Kate.'

'Couldn't you just opt for a face cream? Or get breast implants? Or liposuction or something?'

'I am *not* having a mid-life crisis.'

'Bullshit. You want to trade in your old life for a new one, and *that's* a "midlife". If you were a man you'd be dying your chest hair or doing some red Ferrari thing. For God's sake, Becky, why don't you try acting like an adult? . . . Which ain't going to be easy in that bloody outfit.'

'He loves my laugh. He says it's like a smile that burst.'

'God, how nauseating. Can't you see that it's the secrecy and stuff which makes it exciting? What happens when that high voltage of sexual passion fizzes out? I mean, do you really want to share a toilet brush with this bloke? . . . Besides, how will you find the shoes to match your colostomy bag? I don't think Gucci do a range of colostomy bags, do they, Anouska?' she asked as two leaking Styrofoam cups of cappuccino passed through the window.

'It's a bit Freudian, doll,' Anouska commented, squeezing back behind the wheel.

'What?' I blew on my coffee.

'It's obvious. Didn't his mummy die when he was young?'

'Oh. Oh.' I put my hands up to cover my face as though reliving our recent car crash. 'I see. Of course, there has to be some distasteful psychological reason for a younger man to become involved with an older woman,' I snapped through foamy lips. 'Well, swap the genders for a second – thirty-two-year-old man runs off with twenty-two-year-old woman and the tolerance level instantly rises, am I right?'

'Running off?' Kate's coffee sprayed out of her mouth. 'You're seriously considering leaving Julian for this bit of . . . arm candy?'

'But *you're* the one who told me not to get married!'

'Yeah, yeah. But I definitely think marriage is more fun than divorce. You know what this is? It's a triumph of cunt over IQ. Julian is elegant, articulate, erudite . . . *Zachary*'s opening conversational gambit is to crush a bloody beer can on his forehead.'

'Oh that's rich. Spoken by an Aussie.'

'He is a Vulgarian, doll.'

'Big deal. Hell, I'd rather be with Falstaff than Hamlet. At least he knew how to have a good time. Julian can't have a good time unless it's scheduled in his diary.'

'Zack is beautiful, I admit,' conceded Kate. 'But you're much more likely to build a life with a man who wears chunky jumpers than one who leaps about on stage in a genital thong.'

'I think Julian *is* the right man for you, doll . . .'

'Yes, yes,' I snapped. 'We all know he's the right man. But have I had enough *wrong* ones? I want to have some regrets when I'm old, you know? I'm sick of Julian's PC World. I'm sick of unleaded, user-friendly, air-conditioned everythings . . .'

'Happiness is learning to be content with what you *don't* have,' Kate said sternly.

I clicked on my seat belt. 'If you feel that way, Kate, then I'm sorry for you, I really am.'

It was then she slapped me. Right across the face.

'Jesus. What the . . . ?'

'You told me that if you ever said you were getting serious about Zachary to take you into a dark room and slap you repeatedly until you come to your senses.' She slapped me again.

'Will you quit that?' Coffee sloshed on to the upholstery.

'Only if you promise to tell Julian. It's only fair to give him a fighting chance.'

'Okay. Okay. I will. I have to. Before Rotterman does. As soon as Julian can fit in a conversation between his cocktail party inspections of the Lord Chancellor's wallpaper in aid of the Educationally Non-gifted and Cross-Dressing Repeat Offenders gala balls . . .'

'You've got to make up your mind, doll . . . and fast.'

'I will.' Yeah. Easy-peasey . . . and why didn't I find a cure for Aids while I was at it?

For the next few days, my mind sort of sat on its hands. This was partly due to the fact that I was numb with shock at the situation I found myself in. Some women play hard to get. Well, I play hard to *want*.

Sure, I'd been pursued by desirable men before, but *this time I was actually awake*! Two blokes! It was a gift from the Self-Esteem Fairy . . . Obviously their Frosties had been laced with a strong hallucinogenic. Which meant I'd better act fast, before the effects wore off and I ended up losing them both.

Dog-paddling lengths of the Lido in Parliament Hill – Kate's favourite pool, despite the urine-count and concentration-camp architecture – I followed Anouska's pragmatic advice and drew up lists For and Against.

In the looks department, there was no competition. Sartorially they were both about to be arrested by the fashion police (Zack had a penchant for wearing baseball caps. Only spermicide tubes should wear caps. And Julian had his predilection for big, bulky jumpers. Peruvian jumpers that not even a Peruvian would wear). But the body beneath the clothes was a wholly different story. There was Zack's 'No Pain, No Gain' addiction to weight training and then there was Julian's exercise philosophy of 'No Pain, No Pain'. Sexually, you guessed it, there was no competition, either. While Jules had the motor skills of a rust-riddled Lada, Zack was the sort of man whose every sperm droplet you could enter individually in a rodeo.

But then there was the brain, I thought, as I dodged a floating Band-Aid. The trouble was, Zachary may have a strong libido, but could he spell it? He probably thought it meant the words in an opera. Except no, opera wasn't exactly in his vocabulary either. Except next to the word 'soap'. Julian, on the other hand, is a highbrow. Hell. He's the highest of broweries. The guy's a poetry-quoting brainiac. Been there, Donne that.

But still, Zack might have a vocabulary the equivalent of mental Novocaine, but believe me, he never put a tongue wrong in bed. The guy may not have any higher education but he had *heaps* of lower. Zack didn't want to save the globe, he just wanted to trot it. Julian's idea of living dangerously was to add a dash of whisky to his interminable honey and lemons – because he always has a cold, which he calls 'the flu' and which would no doubt develop into double pneumonia by morning. Yes! I thought, flailing around a child astride an inflatable dinosaur in the shallow end, that's what I wanted! A man who spends money recklessly and not on long-term pension plans.

Although, I ruminated, thinking of my childhood in that poky council flat, there was something to be said for financial security. I mean, Zack might be starting to do well now, but rock stars went through money like women. He'd clear the debts he'd no doubt accumulated, then blow the rest on champagne, guitars, crap oil paintings by art-school chums, indulge in some ridiculous obsessions – Thunderbirds memorabilia or first-edition Monopoly games – then give the rest away, first to drug dealers and then to rehabilitation charities and end up on the dole. I panicked inwardly.

At least Julian does my car tax.

Julian it was then, I informed the wild ducks bobbing, a little bamboozled, around the deep end.

But Christ. You can't live with a man because he renews your tax disc! Okay, he may check my oil filter, but we would never ever do it standing up backwards in doorways because we couldn't wait to get home.

All right, all right – I risked death by drifting too near the kamikaze diving board overloaded with Kentish Town yobs – what it all came down to was, which man would be least annoying to live with? As every woman knows, the minimum acceptable Hideous Habit Ratio between cohabiters is invariably about 100 to 1 in the man's favour. Julian's Hideous Habits I knew well. His anal retentiveness, for one. *The man hugs his shoe-trees.* I've forgotten what he looks like without a thermometer wedged between his teeth. 'I'm 104!' Julian, you're sitting on top of the Aga.'

But wait, I thought, braving the cold communal showers, at least he actually *did* the cooking. And a fair contribution to housework was not something to be swept under the carpet. Zack's domesticity? Well, the man couldn't turn down a bed.

Anybody's.

That was another drawback to living with a rock star. Julian may make Woody Allen look un-neurotic, but at least he wouldn't join the mile-high club with a total stranger. Even if Zack wasn't cheating on me, he'd be locking himself into the toilet with his mates for a competition of Death by Fart Inhalation. From what I'd glimpsed of Zack's friends, their idea of a good time is Indoor Football With a Gerbil.

The guy probably only has one clean pair of Y-fronts for those boringly formal occasions that actually require underwear – you know, like rectum surgery. So, on the one hand I had Julian who showered three times a day, and on the other Zack who told me he wouldn't shower in case it washed the smell of my cunt out of his hair.

Then there was Julian's tender side – and I don't mean the legal kind. He loved me, I knew that. Zack was a rock star. And they only loved their guitars, in sickness and in health, till death do they part. Didn't they? But he'd made up a song about little old me. And it was playing on the radio, making my heart expand like an accordion every time I heard it. And it wasn't just the tune I couldn't get out of my head. There was something he'd said about the English being addicted to misery; how if England had a constitution, 'the pursuit of *misery*' would be enshrined. Obviously he'd noticed the joyous vivacity of the tube commuter, the exuberant colour and exhibitionism displayed in the wearing of Barbour and tweed, the eager acceptance of newcomers and overwhelming hospitality towards strangers.

As I dressed in a cement cubicle littered with sweet wrappers and used condoms, I thought of my homeland: a nation of Eeyores; going for gold in the

Masochism Olympics. I mean, ours is the only country in the world which had a revolution, then *asked the Monarchy back*.

Unlike my fellow Brits, I'd always craved adventure. The vibrancy of the unknown beckoned. But would I have the guts to follow? One minute I saw Zachary Phoenix Burne as the water taxi out of my own Dead Sea and I would trample women and children to get aboard. A split second later, this decision was brusquely shouldered aside by a craving for Jules. He was, after all, a beaten path in my brain.

As I pushed through the turnstile at the end of the long corridor of changing rooms, out into the late-Saturday summer sunshine, I could see Kate and Anouska sprawled over the car bonnet waiting for me; waiting for my answer.

And what *was* my answer? Could I really exfoliate my old layer of emotional skin and find a new one? My mind said no, but my body said yes. What can I tell you? My clitoris and I were separating on the grounds of irreconcilable differences.

'Well, what the hell are you going to do?' Kate interrogated the moment I slid my bare thighs on to the hot car upholstery in the back seat.

'About what?'

Kate eye-rolled. 'About global warming, obviously, you big boofhead.'

'Come on, doll,' Anouska fired up the ignition. 'I'm not a mind-reader.'

'If you *were*, you'd only have to charge *half price*,' said Kate, belting up in the back.

'Either way, doll, you've got to tell him before Zack's agent does,' said Anouska, squealing out on to the main road.

'I know. I know. Besides, I'm not going to sneak around and lie about it any more. I'm not. I can't. I'm starting to hate myself.' Yes, it was time to go home and expose my Achilles' heel to my husband . . . then walk all over him with it.

But how to go about it? I'd never had a 'Things To Do Today' list which read: 1) Buy tampons. 2) Book eyebrow shaping. 3) *Leave husband*.

I mean, what do you say? Maybe I could borrow from the Male 'I'm Dumping You' Hall of Fame? The 'I need some space', 'I still love you – as a *friend*', 'I lied because I didn't want to hurt your feelings', 'I'm just not good enough for you', 'It's not you. It's *me*', 'But you never *asked* me if I was gay?' school.

I yearned for Zack. And cringed about hurting Julian. Yearn, cringe. Yearn, cringe. This was my seizured rumba all the way to Belsize Park. For a non-smoker, I also seemed to be trying to wrest the world nicotine-ingestion record from the beagle community.

At the sound of Anouska's car ricocheting off other vehicles as she dog-legged down the road, Julian bounded out of our house and opened the door, beaming. 'Hi. What took you so long? . . . Kate, Anouska, do come in for a drink.'

My two best friends swapped alarmed glances then widened their eyes at me in the rear-vision mirror.

'Julian,' I said urgently. 'We have to talk.'

'Sure . . . but let's have a drink first.' He opened the front car door and eased Anouska out on to the pavement. 'I insist. It's such a lovely evening. Kate, do come in.'

It'd been so long since he'd had a civil word to say to her that she followed automatically.

'Julian . . .' I slammed the passenger seat forward, hurled myself out of the sports car and scrambled up the front steps, my heart puncturing my ribcage with each fraught beat, practising the 'I need more space' spiel – space, friends, feelings, not good enough, it's not *you*, gay etc. – in my head . . . and scuttled after him down the hall. 'Julian . . .' It was time to empty out all my guilty little pockets. But could I really speak the unspeakable? 'Julian, there's something I need to tell you . . .'

The living-room door swung open to reveal every single one of our friends and family. They were beaming idiotically in my direction, wine glasses in hand. 'SURPRISE!' they gushed, in merry unison.

My face froze. Julian wrapped an arm around me. 'We never celebrated our wedding.' He kissed me. 'And, well, I just wanted you to know how much I love you.'

18

We Interrupt This Marriage To Bring You A News Bulletin

Surprise parties give you the kind of surprise that makes you drop dead of a heart attack.

'What were you going to say, darling?' Julian touched my face tenderly.

'Um . . . I was thinking that it was time we renewed our marriage vows!' I lied, lighting up ten cigarettes simultaneously.

'Friends . . . family . . .' *Oh Good God. He was going to make a speech. This was awful. This was like going to a school reunion when you're the only one still unemployed.* 'For those of you who didn't already know, I'd just like to announce that Becky here is madly in love with a married man . . . Her husband.' He kissed me. There was a gasp from those who didn't know we'd knotted our nuptials. 'I know this is not exactly the way we'd always planned to get married, but the truth is, Becky is a saint to marry me in any way at all.' *Oh this was unbearable. I hadn't felt more humiliated since that dog humped my leg at the reception to celebrate Julian's election as Deputy Vice President of the Law Society.* 'I work long hours, often for no money. I'm terribly neglectful.' *This was worse than that time a woman winked at me while I was naked in the YMCA showers.* 'And tonight, on our two month wedding anniversary, well, I just wanted to make it up to you, my darling.' He toasted me. 'The wittiest, prettiest woman in England.' *Oh, this was worse than buying Super Kotex and having the price checked at the supermarket till over the loudspeaker.* 'I love Rebecca Steele more than life itself.' *Female eyeballs moistened en masse. Oh great. Why not just go over and cut his balls off with a pair of nail scissors?* 'Remember, I'm a professional,' Julian said, to undercut the sentimentality. 'Do not try this pretentiousness at home!'

He kissed my hair. Gathered around us were solicitors and clerks from his law firm; my colleagues from the ICA, a sprinkling of London's Balsamic Vinegar Brigade, including the woman writer who was busy exhausting the literary possibilities of the labia; both sets of mutually loathing parents; Simon and Vivian and their gifted, unisex-clad children. They all applauded, then turned their collective, interrogative gaze upon moi. I realized with rampant horror that I was expected to say something. I also realized that I had goggle indentations around my eyes. Surprise parties really are the worst invention since the Femidom. All the guests have hours to preen and cream and Listerine while you get caught at the pool not having shaved your pits. My nails cut sickles of fear in each palm.

'I didn't *marry* Julian. He just came with the house.'

There was a surprised beat, then a gradual relaxation into laughter. Anouska shoved a glass of champagne into my trembling hand and Julian ruffled my shrubbery of red hair affectionately.

'If you had any idea about this,' I hissed to Kate and Annie through a lacquered smile of simulated gratitude, 'I'll kill you.' But they looked as shell-shocked as I did. Obviously Julian knew that 'Besties' tell each other everything.

I intuited that my mother was on the guest list by the Chihuahua that had just zoomed straight up my trouser leg. It was the first time I'd seen my parents since the wedding debacle. Mum was wearing a black-bordered T-shirt emblazoned with the death mask of Frank Sinatra. Her massive bosom distorted his face, drunkenly.

'Placements, sugared almonds. Ya could've 'ad the lot. 'Cept yer bottled out. I wanted it more than I want yer farver to quit playin' lawn bowls.' She jabbed an elbow into my father's scrawny ribs. Still lingering in that twilight stage between living and dying – 'Died of boredom' they'll write on his death certificate – 'he twitched'. I know Julian works hard an' that, but he's a good provider . . . Nothin' wrong with bein' effluent.'

Julian winked at me as he smothered a laugh.

Julian's mother – a petit-point-footstool, dried-flowers-in-the-grate, stripped-pine-mug-tree kind of Wimbledon woman – kissed me coldly somewhere near my ear. 'Hello, Rebecca,' she said, in that voice that implied that the greetee has just been diagnosed a cholera carrier. Horrified by the gene pool, the gene *paddling* pool, into which her eldest son had waded, my mother-in-law's lips protruded into a pout of indignation, then sank, the folds at the corners of her mouth filling with disapproval and cake crumbs.

'Stuck-up cow,' my mother said loudly, her vinyl high-heels squeaking with sale-price defiance as she bee-lined for the taut-bunned waiter behind the bar.

Smiling jovially, Julian was moving around the room, rubbing his hands together and briskly repeating the mantra 'Isn't this *fun*?' I followed, grinning and nodding, my face glaciered into a Doris Day rapture of marital euphoria. It was like playing charades when sober.

I retreated as soon as I could to the garden to find a quiet place to throw up. This was awful. This was excrutiating. If we'd been on an aeroplane, it was a 'Please Return To Your Seats, Extinguish Your Cigarettes And Put On Your Life Jackets' kind of moment.

A hand tendrilled out of the dark, twined around my waist and dragged me into the garden shed. Well, it used to be a shed, but Julian had DIYed it into a little clematis-clad folly with mosaics and mock-Roman pillars. A hot, wet mouth was on mine.

'What the hell . . . Oh God,' I said, trying to kick-start my heart into beating again. 'Julian's here. In fact, everyone's here . . .'

'I know. He invited me. To DJ. Thought yer might be havin' second thoughts, an' well, I came by to persuade yer that yer first thoughts were better.'

Despite my feeble protestations, Zack proceeded to do just that with hands and tongue and cinnamon breath, spinning us into a cocoon of heat and skin and lust.

Which is exactly how Julian found us ten minutes later.

Getting back to those etiquette points; exactly what *is* the correct behaviour when your husband catches you with your teeth in the fly of another man? Spontaneous Combustion was the only appropriate reaction I could come up with at short notice.

Julian stood there, a chocolate fudge cake in his arms, sparklers fizzing around a marzipan bride and groom as his face caved in. He gasped, pain flooding in like the sea gushing into a scuttled boat. It was pointless lying. An erection cannot be hurriedly disguised in a snakeskin jockstrap. I looked up into my husband's eyes with a mix of dread and relief.

'I suppose when you file for divorce, this will be the first incident you'll mention to the judge,' I ventured.

Julian composed himself faster than an Andrew Lloyd Webber musical. 'Oh. I didn't realize the invitation dress code read "Trousers Optional".'

'Jules . . . I . . .'

'I believe, Rebecca, we've reached a turning point in our marriage.'

'Julian, I'm . . . I'm leaving you.'

'Oh . . . So does that mean the wedding waltz is off? . . . Happy Anniversary,' he said, and hurled the chocolate fudge cake into my face.

Part Two
The Affair

19

Breaking Up Is Hard To Do – But Dividing The Book Collection? Unbearable

Until my husband caught me in the arms of my lover at our wedding party, my only experience of hell had been the time I bumped into my prospective father-in-law at a nudist beach.

Julian's reaction to my infidelity had been understandably Vesuvial. First the cake in the face, then, failing in his attempt to remove Zachary's brain by pulling it through his nostrils, he flounced out of the party – leaving me with a house full of spellbound guests. I took the only course open to a woman in such a position and hid in the bathroom where immediate members of my family were less likely to mug me.

After I'd kissed the porcelain for a few hours and Kate and Anouska had smuggled Zachary over the garden wall, marshalled the guests out the door and cleaned up the worst of the debris (including my howling mother) I set about moving out – lock, stock and CD-ROM.

It was three a.m. when I heard Julian's key in the lock. My intestines macraméd instantly. I stood stock still in the middle of the living room to face him for the traditional fusillade of crockery and recriminations. He appeared, half moons of grief beneath both eyes.

'Funny,' he said, tossing his car keys in the vague vicinity of the couch, 'but I don't remember our marriage vows saying, "Till Death Us Do Part . . . *Or Till Someone Younger Comes Along*".'

'Julian, I'm so sorry.'

'Actually I knew you were going to leave me.' He crouched down to peer tipsily into the cardboard box I'd been packing.

'How?'

'All the "Her" towels were missing from the linen press.'

'That's not true. I hadn't planned it to happen this . . .'

'True? True? I'm sorry, but I think that word should be excised from your puny vocabulary.'

The knot in my stomach was working its way up into my throat. I swallowed back tears. 'It's my fault, Jules. Not yours. Please don't take it personally.'

'Don't take it personally! How can I *not* take it personally? You're my *wife*, for Christ's sake!' Julian kicked over the cardboard box scattering my essential running-away items – the portable Dorothy Parker, the non-stick wok, the Patsy Kline albums. 'So,' he said, his voice dripping in sarcasm, 'do you think this is what they mean by the "Honeymoon Period being over"? . . . But Jesus, Becky.' He bent double as if from a flying tackle. 'A black man! Did he have to be black?'

'Oh,' I commented, quietly squirrelling my possessions, 'spoken by the great Civil Rights Lawyer.'

'Believe me, Zachary Burne is the only person I've ever met who's made me rethink my views on Capital Punishment.' He rummaged disdainfully through my effects with the toe of his shoe. 'He should rename that awful album of his "Desperately Seeking Brain Cells".'

My contrition started to sour. 'Excuse me, but you recently spent several hours in court convincing three justices that . . .'

'Speaking of which, when *did* the idea of infidelity first thrust itself between your legs? Before or after I saved your lover from deportation?'

'. . . that Zack is a serious artist . . .'

'Artist! Huh! An advanced tadpole could do what he does. If you'd left me for a nuclear physicist, okay.' He plucked the Beatles' 'White' album from a pile of old records and CDs I was sorting and clutched it to his chest. 'But God, the humiliation of being left for a monosyllabic singer . . . The Titanic vulgarity of it is . . .'

'Zack is not monosyllabic.' I wrested the record from him. 'He just has occasional flashes of silence, that's all . . . Unlike *someone I know*.'

'The man needs Berlitz lessons – in *English*.' He

yanked back on the double album which swung open like a book. 'He couldn't double an entendre if he tried. He gropes towards a *single* entendre.'

Julian grappled more fiercely, tug-of-warring until the double album tore down the middle; the records frisbeeing stereophonically wall-wards.

We faced each other despondently, each clutching one limp collectible cardboard sleeve. 'So, that went well, Jules. Shall we divide the stereo next?'

'First you broke my heart and your marriage vows and *now* my favourite album . . .'

'*Your* favourite . . .?'

'And I won't be able to afford another because no doubt you will need help with the child support.' Julian drained the dregs of four abandoned champagne glasses.

'Zack's not *that* young . . .'

'Young? Huh! You'll have to carry him on your shoulders around EuroDisney.' He criss-crossed the room, siphoning every glass in sight. 'You'll have to get stationery with wise-cracks printed round the borders and start putting a circle above your 'i's and buying multi-coloured drinks.' He was rooting out crockery and cooking utensils from my paltry possessions and piling them up in his arms.

'Age doesn't matter. Not unless you're a building or a grapevine or something. I mean, *you* make *God* look young. And yet do I ever mention it? You can't even name the Top Ten.'

'Um . . . the Spice Girls . . . ?'

'That's last year's Top *One*.'

'At least I can remember all the names of the Beatles' wives. But don't worry. Just because you're running around with a man old enough to be your son doesn't mean our friends are sniggering behind your back . . . They're *guffawing*. Out loud. To your face. I mean, where's your self respect . . . ?'

'I don't know.' I undermined him with frosty efficiency. '*You're* the one who puts everything away.'

Now *I* began drinking dregs. 'My God. You're making me feel as though I'm about to start hobbling around in a walker with drool on my chin.'

'You'll be fine,' he retaliated bitterly. 'Just make sure he doesn't catch his fly zipper in a stretch mark.'

The living-room door swung petulantly behind him.

'Stretch marks!' I barged after him into the kitchen. 'I do not have stretch marks! Where?' I tugged down my jeans and scrutinized my thighs. 'I dare you to find one stretch mark on my body! . . . Hey I bought that . . .' I snatched the wok from his arms. 'Just because he's a decade younger, doesn't mean Zack and I don't have a lot in common, you know . . .'

Julian surveyed me, thoughtfully. 'You're both protein-based life forms, yes that's true,' he said, before wrestling the wok from my grasp. 'This is mine, thank you very much. Mail-ordered from Perugia.'

'Like me, he likes to share his feelings,' I persevered. 'The only thing *he'll* share with you, you'll need penicillin for. How can you swap our marriage for that kind of tawdry, passionless carnality?'

'I wear flannelette pyjamas to bed. What does that tell you about our marriage?'

'Um . . . that we need to turn up the heating? . . . So, it *is* just sex,' he gloated triumphantly. 'I kind of guessed you hadn't outgrown me mentally.'

'What's that supposed to mean?' I bristled.

'Before you met me, the only thing you'd read from beginning to end were your vibrator instructions, apparently.'

'That's hitting below the belt . . . Though you need an anatomical orienteering course these days to remember where *that* is.'

'And *you* need a shrink. The only balanced thing about you is your cheque book, thanks to me. I plan all your holidays.' He ripped the calendar off the wall and threw it at me. 'I pay your bills.' He rifled through a kitchen drawer and pelted me in envelopes with cellophane windows. 'I file all your appliance warranties . . .'

'Then let me put this in language you'll understand. The warranty on our sex life has expired. Last time I tried to seduce you in the shower, you stopped to de-mildew the tiles. Every time I want to have sex, you're off in some supermarket somewhere, fingering kiwis. Ouch!' I banged my head on the Italian kitchenware Julian delighted in hanging upside down, for some bizarre reason, from a fully retractable stainless-steel ceiling rack. 'You take the Christmas tree down on

Boxing Day so the carpet won't get dirty. You get mortally offended if I use the wrong towel. Or leave it on the bed . . .'

'Wet towels on the bed create an ecosystem that supports the growth of entire populations of microscopic spore.'

'*You sorted my tights by denier number.* You have a cardiac arrest if a shirt gets hung on a wire hanger. You once yelled at me for draining the asparagus too roughly. Honestly,' I swigged at somebody's wine then slammed the glass down on to the oak table. 'If you didn't fuck women you'd be gay, do you know that?'

'Could you puh-lease put a coaster under that?' He swooped on the offending wine glass.

'You see?' I groaned, fighting my way through the jungle of dried organic herbs suspended from his faux seventeenth-century beams. 'You're spontaneity-impaired. I want a man who doesn't worry whether or not his decay-preventative dentifrice oral hygiene programme is effective enough . . .'

'Oh, right, you want a rock star with *pool algae* on his teeth,' he said, squeegeeing up stains and food crumbs left over from the party. 'You might as well go and roll yourself naked over the floor of a public toilet and tongue kiss the lavatory seat. I just hope you contract a disease that requires a completely humiliating treatment.'

'The only sick person around here is *you*. Terminal

workaholism. We never go anywhere,' I ranted. 'We never see anyone. Unless it's related to Bisexual Dwarves with Learning Difficulties seeking refugee status. This is not so much the end of a marriage as *Case Closed*.'

'I'm dedicated to my work. Oh! Let me do the honourable thing and Suicide now. Well, we know one thing for sure. *You'll* never be spoiled by success.'

He stomped out of the kitchen. I galloped after him, spinning him around. 'What's that supposed to mean?'

'You're thirty-two years old and still don't know what you're going to do when you grow up. If it weren't for Kate's kindness you'd have no career to speak of. All that creativity and cleverness squandered. Why? Because you're so spectacularly lazy. If you had your way, fingernails would come already painted, martinis pre-stirred . . .' He entwined the iron in its own cord. 'You approach ironing with the firm belief that the rumpled look must soon make a comeback. Which is why you won't be needing this . . .' He shoved the iron back into the cupboard in the hall. 'You're impatient . . .'

'I'm not impatient!' I trailed after him. 'I just wait in a hurry.'

Julian sprang up the stairs, with me on his heels, strode into our bedroom and began shedding clothes. He shucked off his shoes. 'You're dishonest, dysfunctional . . .'

'Well if I'm dysfunctional, who dysfuncted me? You,

that's who. I mean, I've been with you nearly all my adult life . . .'

'Oh yes, it must be my fault,' he said flippantly. 'It must be the surplus of culture I've forced you to endure . . . the chamber music, the opera, the literature, the poetry . . .'

'But can't you see?' I gestured despondently towards the shoe-trees, which, even mid-anguish, he didn't forget to insert in his footwear. 'All the poetry has gone out of our relationship. It's now like prose. Bad prose. Or worse – Jeffrey Archer.'

'No,' Julian sighed. 'Our marriage is like a romance novel . . . where the hero dies in the first chapter . . .'

I looked down at my hands. 'I . . . I didn't mean to fall in love with him. It just happened.'

'But I *was* your hero once, wasn't I?' he said in a wistful voice, sinking on to the end of the brass bed in his underwear.

'Oh yes. And you still are . . .' I drooped down beside him. 'We're fighting over a non-stick wok. It's unfathomable, isn't it? Look, Jules. It's just a trial separation, that's all. Until I sort myself out.'

'No, Rebecca. We can get past this. Let's analyse your feelings.'

'No! Let's analyse why you want to analyse everything! I'm sick of love from the eyebrows up. Animal magnetism, that's what I want.'

'I can be animal. I can! I can change!'

'Oh where have I heard that before? It'll just

disappear into the Bermuda Triangle of promises along with "I'll join a gym", "I won't work so hard", "I won't correct your grammar in public . . ." Please, Jules. I need some time.'

'You'd really trade in warmth, friendship, intimacy for a . . .'

'Intimacy? The most intimate moment we've had all year was when I had to check you for an anal fissure.'

'I was in pain.'

'Hey, so was *I*.'

We both laughed, an exhausted, convulsive explosion of tension.

'Can't you see? We know everything about each other.' His voice was plaintive with defeat. 'Please don't go, Beck.' He grabbed my hand. It suddenly felt inappropriate and awkward to be in a bedroom with my husband.

My taxi was muttering outside. I picked up my suitcase and moved towards the stairs.

'Rebecca, why do you have this illogical desire to be the butt of people's jokes?'

I scooped up the wok and my half of the 'White' album.

'Answer carefully. I'm a lawyer, remember. I only need another two signatures to put you away.'

'Oh yes. I *must* be mad if I want to leave *you*,' I said sarcastically.

'You're the only woman in the world who's looking for love without commitment, do you know that?'

'I'll . . . I'll call you.'

His face slammed shut. 'Make sure it's long distance.'

The door echoed his sentiments with a bang.

Zack was waiting on the threshold of his Brixton flat, the door wide open. Once inside, I collapsed on to the couch, lethargy clinging to me like satin in summer. The wind shuddered against the window pane.

'I can't believe what I've just done.' I began to weep at my own audacity. 'I know nothing about you. Except you're way too young. And a rock star. I know nothing about rock and roll. I was never part of a garage band . . . We never even had a garage. The only "acid" I know about is in my stomach from the stress of leaving my husband for a rock'n'roller. Maybe I'm having an early menopause? And *you're* my hot flush? Maybe you're just like plastic surgery, only not as painful . . . ?'

Zachary cradled me, his touch sending splinters of desire down through my whole body. He swept me up in his arms and carried me, like the cover of some gaudy romance novel, into the bedroom.

Later, when Zack went to mix me his favourite drink – an ambrosial concoction involving amaretto, sweet vermouth and gin – I rolled over on to his side of the bed, all warm from his body. I felt his contours in the way the mattress moulded under me.

It felt right. It felt good . . . It felt like bungee jumping without a rope.

20

The Trophy Bonk

When leaving a marriage, many problems arise. The most serious of these, apart from who gets custody of the cat, is Friend Division. Which is why, a week later, when Zack and I woke in the late afternoon, legs entwined in velvet torpor, I kissed his sleepy, creamy eyelids and informed him that we were getting dressed for a dinner party at Vivian and Simon's place.

'A dinner party?' He opened one steely eye. 'Ain't that where people yer hate come round, drink up all yer beer, toke all yer dope, up chuck on yer sofa, stay till, like, dawn ... then bitch about yer at the next dinner party yer not at?'

'Well, yes. But it's a tradition. You're my partner now, and you've got to fit in with my friends. I want them to understand what it is I see in you. It's time you lost your social virginity.'

So, I led Zachary down Ladbroke Grove – the Couple Who Do Everything More Successfully And Fabulously Than Every Other Couple in the Known Universe lived in the heart of the Home-Made Pasta Belt in Notting Hill Gate.

'They'll adore you,' I reassured him with a kiss.

Simon, wearing an embroidered Ghanaian shirt, met us at the threshold of their Feng-Shui-ed, four-storey terrace. He ushered us into the stark, pared-down 'living space', decorated in mandatory cool grey and creams with polished blond floor-boards and a minimum of spare, modern furniture. Even the pot plants had that 'talked-to' look.

I noticed, to my amusement, that Simon had left copies of books by Ben Okri, Toni Morrison and Maya Angelou conspicuously on the coffee table and that African music was throbbing out of the speakers.

In the kitchen Kate, Anouska and Vivian were muttering over the bouillabaisse like the witches in Macbeth. When Zack entered, the conversation stopped abruptly. At her first sighting of Zachary, Vivian's eyes whirled like plates on a magician's stick. She was wearing a vivid turban with matching beads and big dangly earrings, upstaged by some sort of batik Kaftan in boisterous primary colours.

'So pleased you could join us in our humble home,' Vivian said, with the diction and demeanour of a progressive nursery-school teacher. 'I *love* black people. I love *Africa*. I feel so rooted to

Africa. That wonderful warmth and enthusiasm!'

Zack surveyed her with the enthusiasm one gives an approaching traffic warden.

'One of your *brothers* works in our law firm, you know,' Vivian prattled.

'Ah . . . I'm an only child . . .'

'I'll introduce you. He's from Nigeria,' she clarified.

Zack shrugged his massive shoulders. There was a cumbersome silence.

'I love that film starring Denzel Washington,' Anouska giddily volunteered.

Once we were seated according to placement (honestly, Vivian would have a placement at a picnic) I realized that everyone was wearing some hint of African Urban Chic. Fierce loyalty to Julian was wrestling with an overzealous desire to prove how relaxed they were around black people, which meant that within minutes all the guests were boasting about what wonderful affirmative action policies they'd personally implemented in their workplaces, some-how managing to touch on an unbridled admiration for Tiger Woods's golfing technique or Linford Christie's track speed en conversational route.

'I hate sports,' Zack replied. He caught my eye across the black-eyed beans – yes, even the food was ethnic – and I suddenly knew, with a sickening turn of the stomach, that this dinner party was going to become like one of those meetings between Hutus and Tutsis, with the UN vainly trying to turn the conversation to the weather.

'I believe we met briefly. At my wedding,' trilled Darius who'd deigned to join us for the first time since his marriage.

Zack shrugged. 'All you white guys look alike to me.'

'What about that old weather . . .' I hazarded. 'So cold for September . . .'

Couples consulted each other with their eyes, then, deciding Zack was joking, laughed immoderately.

'Black is such a reductive term,' Simon pontificated, passing me what looked like pâté, but in this household could easily have been Vivian's placenta. 'Any label, any category that reduces people to one thing, what they look like – Jew, black, woman, gay – is so patronizing.'

'Yeah? I lerve bein' niggah black . . .' The guests leant towards Zachary in a condescending choreography of sympathy. '. . . Great for gettin' laid. Guilt trips white chicks *so* fast.'

Eyebrows were semaphoring all around the table. We're talking Oscar-Winning Eyebrow Performances. I quailed inwardly. My partner's tongue was now practically protruding through his cheek.

'S'pecially if yer pretend to be from the Third World.'

A frisson of shock rippled through the room. Surely he meant to say 'developing countries'?

Vivian realigned her cutlery on the Designers Guild tablecloth. Silence collected between the dinner guests like drifts of snow. I couldn't believe Vivian had bothered with the wretched placement. Nobody was going to stay long enough for Zack to learn their names.

When Zack used the fish knife to butter his roll and flossed his teeth with a matchstick, you could sense the contempt being kept in check. But when he poured the Armagnac he chose to drink with his main meal into a parfait glass and played table quoits with the onion rings, restrained disapproval bulged like an abscess in the room. I tried to escape, I truly did. But every time I made a move, out would come another course. This was turning into the longest dinner party in the history of the world. It was the Hundred Years War of dinner parties.

'We can't stay too long, I'm afraid. Zack thinks that a dinner party is a perfectly good way of wrecking a perfectly good evening.' My words were strung together on a taut wire of nervous gaiety.

'Naw, I don't. I see dinner parties as, like foreplay . . .' he said, hell-bent on mischief. 'Somewhere's I can be thinkin' about those crotchless panties that I gave yer earlier.'

It was Eyebrow Oscars again. Personally I felt a loo trip coming on to search for some serious substances to abuse. But when I got back, with only half an expired cold capsule in my system, things had got worse. Zack was toying with my friends, the way a cat toys with a mouse.

232

'Drug dealers ain't so bad. Ain't it a relief for your parents to know that the guys hangin' around the school gates ain't all child molesters?'

I guzzled my wine in one gulp.

'. . . Hey. *Animals* wear fur an' nobody complains. As for testin'? All that shampoo keeps their fur real shiny, yer know . . .'

At that point I commandeered the whole bottle, crawled inside and just tried to remember what my name was. When I reemerged it was to hear Vivian exclaim to her designer lettuce with great indignation, 'Oh no, Zachary. You must never strike a child in anger.'

'Yeah?' Zack asked. 'Well, *when* then?'

Needless to say, a gap in the conversation opened up. During dessert, I exhausted myself acting as a conversation gap filler. Just when I thought we could exit without insulting anyone more than we had already, Vivian announced that Zack just had to lead us in a little dancing.

'I've got rap, funk, jazz. I've got Ladysmith Black Mambazo!' Determined to show just how hip and cool a hostess she really was, Vivian hijacked Zachary into the living room. As they ground pelvises, Simon looked on, his repugnance masked by a thin blade of a smile – a smile that sliced the air as Zack danced more erotically and Vivian swooned more besottedly with every funky jungle beat.

Later, over the hiss of the espresso machine, Vivian

cornered me in the kitchen. Her mouth was swollen with the need to talk, to probe, to know all. 'I didn't understand you leaving Julian, but I do now. When you've got a trophy bonk, who cares about the brain? No wonder he charmed the pants off you . . .'

'The elastic wasn't too strong to begin with, though, was it?' Simon said, appearing behind us, armed to the teeth with cold, glinting words. 'Have you read my publication on the importance of intellectual bonding,' he turned to Zack, who'd just sauntered into the kitchen in the search for ice, 'over purely ephemeral physical attraction?'

'I'm sorry, man,' Zack replied, raiding the freezer. 'But, like the Voyager Spacecraft – that's way the fuck over my head.'

Simon rankled. 'We don't use that uncouth word in this house.'

'Fuck? You're right, man. Fuck is such a cunt of a word.' As Zack rubbed an ice cube across the base of his throat, a look reminiscent of a dieter faced with a plate of chocolate éclairs flashed across Vivian's flushed countenance.

'Well, Rebecca,' Simon said curtly. 'It's been a real experience meeting the man for whom you dumped my best friend. And when you take your leave, we'll be more than grateful.'

Zachary turned to me. 'Would it be a real breach of that precious dinner-party tradition of yours if I kneed the host in the nuts?'

I placed myself bodily between them.

'You do teach harmony and reconciliation, remember, Simon . . .'

'I do *not* refer to myself as a teacher, thank you very much. I am a learning coordinator. An educational enhancer.'

'Yeah?' said Zack. 'Well, I refer to yer as a grade-A mother-fuckin' dipshit.'

The odour of violence was dissipated by the sound of a Janet Jackson hit single being warbled through the letter box in male falsetto. As Vivian dragged Zack off for more dancing, Simon flung open the front door to reveal Julian crouching on the threshold. The fact that he was wearing boxer shorts, a dinner jacket and a pair of antlers on his head was probably *not* a good sign.

'Where the hell is that melanin-over-endowed, intellectually challenged, phallocentric, bastard of African-American extraction you left me for?' he demanded. 'It's time I showed him a thing or two . . .' He swerved into the hall.

His breath, up close, was strong enough to melt your nostril lining. 'Jules,' I placed a restraining hand on his arm, 'you're drunk.'

'Drunk? I'm not as think as you drunk I am . . .' He shook me off and lurched in the direction of the music. 'Madonna, U2, The Bearded Clams . . . you see? I know the Top Forty off by heart. I forsook Classic FM for Capital Radio, all the way over here . . . Greater love hath no man, believe me.'

'You *drove*?'

'Good God yes. I have to keep my car with me at all times. I'm frightened it'll leave me for a younger owner.'

'You could have got yourself killed!'

'Oh well. Save me suiciding. Single men are twice as likely to commit suicide, you know,' he hiccoughed.

'Jules . . .' I tried to hold him back, but he veered into the living room, barging through Darius, Anouska, Vivian and Kate who were all dancing self-consciously to some bongo beat, climbed on to the coffee table and started doing the lambada.

Sober, Julian is a terrible dancer. But drunk he resembled Isadora Duncan with stomach cramps. Zack watched, bemused, from the sidelines, while Julian incorporated vigorous knee and elbow jerks with a lot of Bacchanalian flinging to the floor.

'You see? I'm not always excessively biased in favour of rational and tasteful behaviour,' he cried out, snogging every inanimate object in sight. 'I'm not an anathema to everything you find proposable to after all, eh Beck?'

Watching Julian pinballing about the room, I was well aware that I was the one who'd jilted his game. It was then I knew that Catholics and Jews do not have a patent on guilt.

Julian wheeled drunkenly to the left, colliding smack bang into the muscular arms of Zachary. Julian looked up woozily.

'Oh . . . it's the Thinking Woman's Crumpet. Nice to see you. Though I nearly didn't recognize you without my wife attached to your genitalia.'

The dancers stood, motionless. Zack took a step back.

'How many wives can you blokes actually have? It's odd, but we more civilized types believe that matrimony is a library where the members are obliged to return one spouse,' he swayed, 'before taking another.'

'Yeah?' said Zack, the steam of anger rising off him. 'Maybe I can learn from that . . . I'm nearly over the cannibalism too, yer know.'

'Zack,' I steered him towards the door. 'You know, us being here is making it really, really hard for them to talk about us behind our backs . . .'

'Name me one of the Beatles' wives,' Julian prodded him in the chest. 'Go on. Just one . . .'

We had to get out of there. 'Come on,' I plucked at Zachary's sleeve.

Julian let out a bestial cry. 'Rebecca, I forbid you to go.' I turned and looked into his aching eyes. 'Okay . . . I beg,' he amended, a funereal droop to his shoulders. 'I don't wanna walk down life's lonely highway, holding hands with myself.'

Jeepers, he *had* been listening to the Top Forty. 'Oh, Jules . . .' It was me who'd done this to him. I was the Princess of Darkness. Not even Johnny Cochrane could defend me on this one. 'Don't let Julian drive home,' I ordered Kate as I heaved open the front door.

Julian, tortured by loss and misery, seized my arm. 'Isn't this what you wanted?' He was gesticulating wildly, as though presenting News For The Deaf. 'A man who can show his feelings?' Sentiments sloshed over his face.

Yes, I thought woefully. But this was an arterial wound to the emotions. 'Jules, get some sleep.'

'Typical,' pontificated Simon. 'Women like you spend years telling men to undo our buttoned-up macho silence, advocating the catharsis and closeness to be had when sharing deepest, darkest fears . . . then you leave us for a man who's perfecting the art of being a vegetable.' He pointed at Zack.

'You people shit me, j'know that?' Zack slewed around to face the gawking throng. 'Yer fuckin' noses are so fuckin' high in the air you'd think you was sniffin' God's socks.'

'*Were* sniffing,' Simon corrected automatically.

A bone-brattling punch sent Simon hurtling backwards into a hall wall smothered in framed photographs of the famous couples whose marriages he claimed to have saved. They toppled en masse on to the trendily bare floorboards, shattering on impact.

'There was no need to do that,' I screamed at Zack. Julian staggered to where Simon lay, curled up like a broiled prawn, porcupined in glass shards amongst a Cubist assortment of facial fragments of Britain's Fashionista. As Julian drunkenly administered the kiss of life, Vivian, howling, hit Zack over the head with a

Conran vase. In the ensuing chaos – believe me, even the talked-to plants were trying to strangle each other – the Infant Prodigies rushed down the stairs and bit Kate on the leg.

'Oh grow up,' Kate snapped illogically, slapping their bums. This prompted a decibel-melting duet of wails, soon tried by Vivian, then counterpointed with Simon's threats of lawsuits and a solo falsetto from Darius – 'You're behaving like Savages!' – a howler that would require a Witness Protection Scheme to have saved him from Zachary's flying fists.

'This has gone far enough!' Kate exploded at me. 'For once I agree with Simon. How could you leave Julian for this bit of fluff? Everything about him is odious. What he says. How he says it . . .'

'Where he lives,' Anouska shuddered. 'Nipping out for a carton of milk in Brixton is an act of heroism!'

'I couldn't care where he lives as long as it's with me.' And I meant it. 'You're just jealous, Kate, because since "Married with Children" dumped you, your diaphragm's been growing lichen!'

So much for Zack losing his social virginity, I thought as we escaped in the minicab. This had been more of a gangbang at Caligula's orgy.

I vowed there and then to never, ever mind when Zack used a preposition to end a sentence with . . .

But little did I know the amount of crap up with which I would have to put . . .

21

How Gauche It With You?

It would be fair to say that at first glance, South London lacks charm. At second and third glance as well, actually. The streets sprawl about like an old drunk. The exhausted tenements whose rickety verandas bloom with grey washing exhale a stale, insipid odour. Pedestrians tread carefully through the rubbish, like novice rollerbladers. The local charity shop has bars on its windows. This is Hell's kitchenette.

Until Kate's outburst, a miasma of lust had blinded me to my surroundings. But on the way home that night, I suddenly saw it all through my friend's eyes.

Zachary lived in Brixton, which is twinned with Eritrea. The minicab shuddered to a halt in front of a hairdressing salon whose sign read 'Bobbitts – For The Best Cut In Town'. As Zack and I crossed the potholed street, I was aware of eyes, hostile predatory eyes, following me. It felt like insects running up and down bare legs.

'Now that you're starting to make it big, Zack, perhaps you could consider a move?'

'Move? I like it round here. It's kinda funky, yer know what I'm sayin'?' He led me up the doddery staircase above the salon. 'Real arty.'

'Um . . . Zack, men with underpants on their heads yodelling "Kill All Bitches" are probably not buskers, you know.'

'Besides, I'm broke. I blew all my dead presidents on my goddamn Herculean quests.'

Zack's flat, which I had previously seen as a love nest, was also losing its allure. For the first time I noticed how the walls were varicose-veined with damp. Mould bulged beneath the flaky skin of wallpaper. The edges of the mangy, fungal carpet were curling inwards like sandwich crusts. I also became aware of the thrum of hungry, multiplying bacteria; bacteria so big you could net them individually and shoot them with a tranquillizer gun.

Cobwebs billowed from the ceiling, illuminated by bare light bulbs. The plumbing had developed a smoker's cough and the loo was blocked up. Actually the entire bathroom should have been cordoned off with 'Crime Scene' Police tape.

Not wanting to look middle class, I said nothing. But by the end of September I was desperately missing

Julian's house with the John Lewis shag pile, crisp sheets and central heating warm enough to ripen a guava plantation.

Yes, love kept you warm . . . but so did a goosedown duvet, I thought, as I was skewered by invisible daggers of draughts.

The food situation was just as grim. At Zack's, we didn't so much eat as *forage*.

'Um . . . peanut butter spooned directly from the jar is not a meal, in the true sense of the word,' I told him the next night – then shut up abruptly in case he took the hint and actually cooked. Cooking here could kill. The stove was so greasy it looked like another Exxon disaster. *E-coli* the size of semi-trailers were idling in every corner of this lamentable kitchen. Besides, I was in love, wasn't I? And when you're in love, you're not supposed to notice these things. Right?

I tried to ignore it, truly I did. I was in Domestication Denial. But on my third week as a rock chick, I could stand it no longer. We were necking in the bedroom when I abruptly came up for air.

'Don't you think it's starting to get a little Quentin Crisp around here? It would help, you know, if you stopped putting wet towels on the bed. They create an ecosystem that supports the growth of entire populations of microscopic spores.' *Where'd I heard that before?* 'I don't know how to tell you this, Zack, but closing the lid of the toilet does not equate with cleaning the bathroom, either.'

'So? *You* clean it then. Women are better at house-work. Kitchen surfaces are just at the right height for yer to clean,' he smirked.

I shoved a pair of discarded boxer shorts into his hands. 'And while you're washing your clothes, why not throw yourself in with them?' I crossed into the kitchen. 'There's enough dirt under your nails to support organic farming on a commercial scale.'

'I'll feel demeaned, man.' Following, he pressed up against me. 'My masculinity will suffer an' I'll need Viagra to get it up again . . .'

I pushed him away. 'You won't *need* to if you don't clean the fridge now and then.' I promptly threw out anything that moved before I prodded it. Zack's refrigerator was a penitentiary for food sentenced to life imprisonment. I found yoghurt whose expiry date read 'When Dinosaurs Roamed The Earth' I found chutney bottled during the reign of Elizabeth I. 'Honestly, not even the homeless would live in this flat. They'd walk in and just bend double with derision.'

'Is that all, babe?' he said, mildly irritated. 'Or is there some other little thing?'

'Well, now you mention it. Do you *have* to hold your knife like a fencing foil? And chewing with your mouth wide open. That's got to go. As does calling me "babe". As does belching . . .'

'Hey, where I come from that's a goddamn after-dinner speech.'

'. . . And then there's the clothes. How can I put this? There's a refugee in Bosnia who needs those clothes. No, come to think of it, refugees would send them back.'

'I s'pose you want me to start wearin' Haute-Couture threads. Haute Couture is just a big fat nothin' with its nose in the air.'

'I just want you to stop wearing black. Why do musicians always dress as though somebody just died?'

'This is all to do with that dinner party the other week, ain't it? Yer tryin' to turn me into one of them limp-dick limo-liberals lippin' on about edible fungi and how much Islam has to offer the West, 'ain't yer?'

'It's just that there are certain rules of behaviour . . .'

'What?' he said flippantly, moving his languidly athletic body close to mine. 'Like not going down on a woman on a first date?'

I held him at arm's length. 'Manners maketh record deals you know, Zack?'

Peeved, he slewed open the door of the fridge I'd just cleared out and cracked open a beer. That was all that was left, besides three rolls of film and a half-empty bottle of bison grass vodka. 'Bullshit, man. Good manners are what you Brits use instead of brains.' He picked up a pen and paper and started scribbling.

'What are you doing?'

'Writin' a letter to my agent . . . Would yer mind

tellin' me how to spell conde-fucking-scending?'

I knew it was asking a lot. In the rock and roll world, the only social gaffe is to think that there are any social gaffes. Training your pet dog not to sniff the labias of the back-up singers is about as well mannered as most musicians get. At first, Zachary refused to allow me to Pygmalion him. But then, Julian started ringing in the middle of the night to swear undying love. He sent flowers daily. I woke one morning to the exquisite caress of a string quartet playing beneath our bedroom window. Two movements into a Schubert variation, Zachary finally agreed to be tutored.

Lesson one, he had to stop beating up on the English language. 'You could be had up for assault . . . GBH, of the mother tongue.'

'Okay. Okay. Stop dissin' . . . Naggin,' he translated, '-ing' he reluctantly kowtowed.

But for a guy with no education he was still out-smarting me. When I gave him a *Roget's Thesaurus* he only wanted to know one thing. Why there was only one word for thesaurus.

I turned his mono eyebrows into two separate ones. I sent him off for a facial with lime-scented towels.

'That's not hair,' I said, ordering Vidal Sassoon to run a mower through it. 'That's a lawn. That hair could have garden gnomes in it.'

After convincing him that his clothes should never be louder than his music, I coaxed his Atlantean physique into a sharp, tailored suit. He even agreed to an opera excursion. 'Opera's cool. It's the only place in the world where the fat chick gets laid.'

Okay, so I had a way to go. But hell, it was definitely a beginning.

It also had to be the beginning of the end of Julian's presidency of the Wife From Hell fan club. The poor angel was going for a medal in the Men's Long-Distance Cross Bearing. My guilt gland throbbed at the thought of what I'd done to him. I was a monster. Any minute now I'd be sprouting bolts from each side of my neck.

Vivian had let slip that Julian had a Privy Council case pleading for the lives of dissidents on death row in Anguilla. I accosted him there, outside the main gates of Downing Street.

'You have to stop the flowers and the phone calls, Jules. A separation usually actually means Being Separate.'

'Separate? What am I? An egg white?' he looked pallid, stooped, worn.

'I'm not worth it. I'm trash, no kidding. Soon I'll be moving into a trailer park and wearing white stilettos with no stockings.'

'I must see you. Come out with me. Tonight.'

'Oh, Jules, you never wanted to take me out when we lived together. Except to benefits for torture victims. I never knew whether to talk to them during the pre-dinner cocktails and get indigestion ... or over the port and get insomnia. Besides, I'm going to an awards ceremony with Zack tonight.'

'What? His high-school graduation?'

'The British Music Awards, if you must know.'

'The British Music Awards? Oh yes,' Julian mocked. 'They're just like the Oscars, aren't they ... only without the *subtlety, flair and sophistication.*'

Julian's bewigged colleague prissily reminded him that if it wasn't too inconvenient, would he mind stepping inside to help save a few lives?

Watching Julian trudge down the cobbled cul-de-sac towards the Privy Council, I felt wracked with contrition. I truly did. Then I thought of arriving at the Docklands Studios on my rock star's arm – was this every girl's wet dream since puberty, or what? Was I going to indulge in a night of glamour and hedonism? Or should I show a bit of character? 'Call out to him! Beg for forgiveness,' I lectured myself sternly. My brain was threatening to secede from my body. It was time I listened to my conscience!

But then I thought – hey. You really shouldn't take advice from strangers – and went to get a leg wax.

22

Welcome to Tonsil-Town!

A music awards ceremony is the place a girl goes when she has nothing to wear. Literally. I had never, ever seen so much naked flesh.

I was sizzling with excitement. All those teenage years singing into a hairbrush in front of the bathroom mirror. All those posters of unobtainable Rock Gods on the bedroom wall. The first love of my life had been David Bowie. When he didn't reciprocate, probably something to do with the fact that he was a multimillionaire megastar and I was an acned trainer-bra-ee, I thought I'd never get over it. And in a way I hadn't. Which was why I was here, welded to the arm of the most gorgeous man on Earth. Although the word 'gorgeous' withered next to Zachary Phoenix Burne. Knowing that I was doing what squillions of women could only dream of doing whilst half-naked in their hot-tubs, and clocking the envious female stares in the street outside, put a certain spring into my step. Wasn't this why I'd abandoned the fusty, rusty rituals of marriage? To sample this elixir of lust?

Not everyone was as thrilled about my arrival as I was. Eddy Rotterman, for one, looked like a man who'd realized too late that wearing nylon undies while sporting testicle rings will give you a violent electric shock when you least expect it.

'What thuh fuck . . . ?!' he greeted us eloquently.

As we moved down the red carpet along with the flotsam and jet set, with paparazzi running backwards in front of us like eighteenth-century French courtiers, I felt Rotty's breath on the back of my neck.

'Thought I told you to stay away,' he harangued. 'Yer little shit weazil.'

I half turned, a smile acid-etched on to my face. 'You know they found a cure for baldness? . . . Hair.'

Everyone was kissing everyone else. At a do like this, when in doubt, just keep on kissing. French kiss twice, thrice. Basically you just keep on kissing until your lips go numb. This was not Tinsel but Tonsil-Town.

A complete stranger, wearing a mock-croc mini and silver reflector stilettos, engaged me in a lip lock. As I prised myself free, I saw Rotterman's face gored red with anger. 'And forget blackmail,' I hissed. 'I've left Julian.'

'Yer an old mutt. J'know that?'

'Yeah? Well if I'm a dog, then *you're* a post,' I replied, outwardly calm, while inwardly panicking. Old dog? Moi? What about *him*? Think pot, think kettle, think black. Rotterman's buttocks, in tan suede flares, resembled a two-car garage. The man could be arrested for persistent chest-hair exposure. Chest hair *with* gold chain. Zachary's manager was single-handedly keeping the gold jewellery market buoyant.

But his words curdled my confidence. I looked at the women around me. They were blonde, blue-eyed, beautiful – proof that Barbie and Ken dolls do have sex.

Feeling self-conscious in an outfit that suddenly seemed implausible for a woman out of puberty – thigh-high boots and leather hot pants (I'd mistakenly presumed that my pre-Julian wardrobe was so out-dated it'd be fashionable again) – I clung to Zachary with life-raft tenacity as we thronged into the auditorium.

The awards ceremony was like upmarket karaoke, except that the musicians' lips were out of synch with their brains. Despite this, every single laborious mime-to-playback was described in the mirthless humour of the host as a 'phenomenon' – which kind of belied the adjective. The Phenomenon next to me spoke to the Phenomenon on my right, 'Zack, man. He's a Phenomenon,' he said, phenomenally.

An hour or so later I found myself curiously dis-enchanted with public displays of rhythm. Maybe if I just concentrated on Zachary's shapely lips and ignored the thumping music, I could avoid narcosis?

'And *coming up . . .*' the autocue-ist was oozing charisma on to television screens, live across the country. 'Zachary Burne is *in the house*! So, don't touch that nob!' he gushingly *double-entendre'd*.

'Now I've repositioned him in the white rock market, yer bad for his image,' Rotterman sneered when Zack had kissed me and made his way back-stage. 'I have ways of keepin' yer away, yer know,' he said darkly, arching a brow towards Zack's body-guard. I quailed as Danny (the Dog Fondler) de Litto flexed his rent-a-muscles. This was the sort of guy who mouthwashed in battery acid and gargled with lighter fuel, a man who'd been rejected by the SAS for being too aggressive.

After a live performance by a band called 'Neuronal Meltdown' at a volume capable of atomizing igneous rock – the only award *this* band was likely to win was in the 'Crappy, Inaudible Lyrics in Pseudo Bondage Wear' category – Zack slunk on stage in a pair of cling-film satin trousers hugging what the British tabloid press universally claimed to be the most prodigious organ outside Westminster Abbey. As he sang, live, the song he'd dedicated to me, my fantasy fulfilment was dampened by two things. First, the nit-infested pony tail of the man next to me that kept flicking into my beer as he head-banged in time to Zack's beat. Flick. Flick. It was frothing it up like a cappuccino. And secondly, the Agent from Hell, who lectured me for the entire duration of the performance about the brilliant future Zack now had behind him, thanks to me.

'He ain't nothin' without a celebrity girlfriend, see? Some leggy supermodel. A celebrity chick is as much of an accessory as a Prada bag. Somethin' yer change each season. Then when they break up, they each get fifty per cent of the publicity. Geddit? Rock stars don't marry for life, only until they get a new record label. Don'cha want him to be bigger 'n' better 'n all the rest? To make it in America?' His jabbering suddenly stopped. 'Holy Mamma! Now *that's* fuckable.' Celestia, the free-fall vegetarian, meandered past our table. 'Now, *she's* in the give-her-one category . . . what a bod.'

'That's not a body,' I sulked. 'It's a biro.' Apart from her breasts, that is. Celestia's mammary glands were encased in bra cups big enough to house Pavarotti and his twin brother.

The awards being given out in the background (Most Creative Nipple Realignment on a Back-Up Singer; Best Penis Bulge in Tight Pants Amounting to Nothing More than Sheer Technology) were so bum-numbingly interminable that I missed the moment when Zack's career took a precipitate leap from controversial debutante to Best Newcomer. It was only the fact that he was Pompeii-ed in a lava flood of fans, that I knew at all.

'Oh, darling . . . Sweetie . . . You are soooo *fabu*lous,'

came the glissando of sycophantic reassurances as he left the stage. Lips sucked at his face from the left. Lips sucked at his face from the right. It must have been like falling into a vat of leeches. Moving back towards our table he left trails of saliva; whole rivulets.

The evening wrapped up for the televisual audience. Zack, swept me up on his way to the *VIP* VIP party where the winners were being corralled.

'Gosh,' I teased him, looking at my watch. 'Are you sure we're going to be late enough. I mean it is only *midnight*.' Unlike everyone else in the room I had to work in the morning. The autumn budget meeting. Missing it would mean the sack. Though tempted to go out in a final blaze of incompetence, I couldn't let Kate down.

As Zack opened his lovely mouth to retort, he was whisked from my presence by a ferocious PA into a convoy of fake fur, cigar smoke, vinyl pants and peroxided hair for an urgent press call. As she was bundling off into the exclusive zone, he managed to shove his two allotted *VIP* VIP tickets into Rotterman's grubby, outstretched hand.

Once Zack was safely out of earshot, Rotterman vipered in my direction. 'So are yer gonna make nice and fuck off back to hubby?'

I picked up some china from the table. 'How would you like a second plate in your head?' I said, *nicely*.

But if I wasn't going to give up Zack voluntarily, Rotty had a secret weapon. She came in a size 8 with a flawlessly waxed bikini line, unchipped nail varnish, a pliant smile and 'beg for it, baby' breasts. As we approached the bouncer-flanked, velvet-roped barrier to the inner sanctum, his eyes glittered maliciously. When the bouncer, frills foaming down the front of his shirt, asked for the *VIP* VIP passes, Rotty shoved me aside and tugged Celestia from the giant cobweb of the crowd, and over the privileged threshold.

'Hey. That ticket was meant for me!'

'Forget it, babe!' Her voice was a car-alarm whine and she talked in exclamation marks!

'You know, Celestia, Rotterman is only nice to women if he has a weird sexual request to make later. If it's really weird, he'll offer coke and a recording contract.'

'Bye-bye . . .' Rotterman mouthed, waving limply.

And so I stood there in exile with the other nonetities as the Illiterati – the micro-celebs and coke-hooverers, all with an excess of ill-conceived hairstyles – sauntered by me. A rock star in an 'Urban Decay, Stop Poverty' T-shirt was loudly boasting about how he books a seat for his guitar on Concorde. Pseudo Hard Men from Manchester bragged about drug busts and Borstal stretches; when driving an uninsured car would be their only brush with the law. Looking like extras who'd escaped from a Stephen King novel, they stared dismissively as they stepped right over me.

This was toe-plaitingly embarrassing. 'Okay,' I whispered, 'what will it take to get in?'

The bouncer waggled his preposterous Groucho Marx eyebrows. 'Hey – anyone game enough to wear that outfit deserves to get in.'

The cobweb vibrated with taunting laughter. Other performers, among whom Elton John shall remain nameless, were also busily committing fashion *faux pas*, but *they* didn't have bouncers pointing it out to them in BOOMING BASS BARITONES.

Once inside, I seemed to be a castaway in a sea of Celestia-clones; attention-craving, cheekbone-owning, talented model types with visible hip bones who were also athletic. I tried to console myself with the thought that JFK and John Lennon had wanted to be the centre of attention, too.

'Exactly how long have you had that outfit?' the real Celestia asked – she dropped the vocal exclamation marks, I noticed, when there were no men around. 'I mean, what exactly is it saying?'

I eyed Celestia's outfit. She was wearing what looked like a red lurex condom. 'I don't know. But *yours* seems to be saying "I'm going straight from here to an orgy and there's no time to stop off at my brothel on the way".'

'At least it's in fashion,' she bitched, in her Essex twang.

'Yes, but fashionable clothes do date one so quickly,' I retorted.

'As do *some dates*,' she touchéd.

Celestia sashayed on to the dance floor, immediately

grabbing the limelight with some high-risk bottom manoeuvres. A tension headache began to throb in my mid-temple, in time to the music. The other guests seemed to be having a group hallucination that the music was good. I started a frantic search through the jouncing bodies for Zack. I glimpsed him finally, at the far end of the dance floor. He was moving so quickly the silver heels of his boots were only a metallic flash, the flick of a fish's tail in the sun. When he saw me, cringing on the sidelines, he boogied over.

'Dance with me, Beck.'

'That's not dancing. That's a contact sport.'

'Come on, girl.'

'There's no winners out there, only survivors. Besides, I only know two types of dances. One of them is the go-go and the other isn't.' *Where had I heard that before?*

'I'll dance with you!' It was Celestia. I glanced at her red lurex condom. It was the kind of dress designed to 'accidentally' expose your breasts while jiving.

Immediately I led Zack in between the heaving flesh and began a few preliminary gyrations. I tried to copy Zack's movements. One, two, swivel, shake . . . One, two, swivel . . . It was like chess with sweat; I could actually hear my feet thinking. On either side of me women danced as though they had Tina Turner trapped in their knickers. Celestia was effortlessly executing some sort of synchronized quadruple reverse pike with a lot of sticky-out-pelvis-manoeuvres thrown in. It was like finding yourself standing naked next to Kate Moss in a communal changing room – and you're both trying on the same dress. Just as Zack was distracted by the sight of Celestia's breasts accidentally popping out, she also accidentally impaled my arch on the steel of her stiletto, tripping me up and sending me sprawling.

As my nose grazed the parquet, I catalogued my woes. I had 'clubber's nipple' – the dancer's equivalent to jogger's nipple, caused by constant friction against the mesh panelling of my top. I had PVC bottom – from crotch-hugging hot pants with no knickers in that tropical clime. I had curvature of the spine from wearing orthopaedic nightmare, sky-rise footwear and now an instep as crushed as my ego.

'It's been nice, Zack,' I whimpered, staggering to standing. 'But I really have to go and have a nervous breakdown now.' I limped towards the exit.

He caught me up. 'Wassup?'

I rubbed my wounded foot. 'That woman! I can't believe you slept with her. Her main lamentation in life is that she has only ten toenails to varnish.'

Zack cackled. 'Love the way you sisters stick together.'

A PR lit up with hostess wattage. 'Thank you for coming,' she purred as we moved out into the street.

'She certainly *should* thank us for coming.'

'You Brits don't need etiquette books on how to behave well,' Zachary chided. 'You need etiquette books on how to behave *badly*. Stay. Come on.'

Outside, black cabs swarmed the street like an outbreak of beetles. I flagged one down. 'I've got to work tomorrow. I mean what are you people? . . . Vampires?'
Where'd I heard that before?

'J'mind if I hang?'

'Of course not.' I hoped my smile was on straight. Watching Zack dwindling in the rear-vision mirror I reflected on the fun, relaxing night I'd envisaged . . . Watching Zack relax was exhausting. The whole night had been about as relaxing as amateur ovarian cyst removal. But it was positively painless compared to what happened next . . .

23

Liberated, Hip, Post-Feminist . . . ?
Or Amoral Slut? Defend Your Answer

Until I fell in love with Zachary Burne, I thought 'paparazzi' was some fancy pizza topping. The irony of being famous is that celebrities spend half their careers fighting to get their faces *in* the paper, then the second half fighting to keep them *out*.

'I know the camera never lies,' I told myself on the tube on the way to work next morning, 'but couldn't it be a little bit *discreet* now and then?'

Two of the tabloids were carrying the same picture of my face contorted in pain at the precise moment Celestia had shish-kebabed my foot. She, however, had been captured at her most radiantly beautiful with her arm snugly around the waist of my boyfriend.

Worse than the picture was the prose. The *Express* described Celestia as Zachary's girlfriend and me as Celestia's *mother*.

If I ever saw Celestia again, believe me, air heads would roll.

Despite the overcast autumnal weather, I slipped on my dark shades. Invasion of privacy was a side of life with Zachary which I hadn't counted on. Put it this way, I was now too frightened to have a cervical smear test in case they published the slides.

I slunk into my third-floor office two hours late, shed my glasses and poured stale coffee from the pot.

'Well,' said Kate, 'it could be worse. You could be Fergie.' She glared at her watch. I'd missed the budget meeting. Since falling for Zack I'd been spectacularly lax about work attendance. Having worn out the bad cold/waited in for plumbers/dental appointment run-of-the-mill excuses, my alibis had become weirder and wilder. I'd been kidnapped by extraterrestrials. I'd been held at knife point by Mafia hitmen in a Bizarre Mistaken-Identity Accident. But I couldn't fly by the seat of my hot pants today, as I was pictured wearing them in the papers.

'Um . . . remember how I couldn't come into work yesterday because I went into an unexpected coma and was in Intensive Care being read the Last Rites? Well, last night I made the most amazing recovery just in time to attend the British Music Awards.'

'Gee, just think,' said Kate sardonically. 'Somewhere right now *your next lover* is being potty-trained.'

'Look, I know you and Zack got off to a bad start, but I'm working on him. I'm helping to kindle his appreciation for the finer things in life . . . '

'Like what? Doing his homework? Just stop acting like a brain-dead dag and ditch him. Otherwise you may have to find a more suitable career, say, *Life-Saver at a sewage plant.*'

All morning I lectured myself that the age difference shouldn't get to me – while secretly poring over magazines for beauty tips, haemorrhoid cream to tighten eye bags; a flesh-eating virus for immediate weight loss.

During my lunch break, I was just squeezing the life out of a tea bag with a fork on the side of a mug when I heard Zack's voice in the hall.

'She's not in,' Kate declared. 'Would you like to leave your fingerprints?'

With the restraint of an Exocet missile, I was around the partition and into his arms. Kate groaned in disgust as we kissed. 'New lovers really should have a minimum isolation period of say, six months so as not to nauseate everyone they meet.'

Coming up for air, Zack handed me another newspaper plastered with photographs of us embracing. I scanned the article. The gossip columnist maliciously described me as a 'cradle snatcher' and Zack as a 'grave robber'. 'Wife stealer' and 'Home wrecker' Zack had circled in red ink. Although personally I was more exercised by 'mutton dressed as lamb'.

'Yer know what this means, don'cha? . . . It means yer gotta get a divorce.'

'A *what*?'

'I ain't . . . I'm *not*,' he corrected himself, 'going to sleep in some other dude's crib, okay. Yer gotta put a stop to it.'

'What? Straight away? Do you have to be so exigent?'

'Do you have to be so married?'

'Ahhmmm.' Kate cleared her throat, ostentatiously. 'Rebecca, can I talk to you for a moment. *Exigently!*'

With great reluctance I trailed her downstairs to Reception – to see Julian standing by the ticket office, a bouquet of roses in his arms.

'I just came to say goodbye. Despite all you've done to me, I do still love you.'

'Goodbye?'

He looked at me with bruised, sorrowful eyes. 'I have bowel cancer.'

My heart lurched. 'You have what?'

'Well it *could* be cancer . . . or maybe another anal fissure.'

'Your ability to cheat death is awesome,' I said flippantly. 'You just have haemorrhoids, Julian, because you won't exercise.'

'Could I have a glass of water?' he asked weakly. I fetched him one from the bar. 'To take my pills,' he volunteered feebly. When I didn't ask what for, he added, 'It's probably nothing, but on my chest X-ray I seem to be missing a bit of lung.' When I folded my arms but made no comment, he proffered more information. 'The doctor has made me an urgent appointment with a specialist, so, you know . . .' He put a finger to his temples as if to blow his brains out.

'Oh, so they've finally found a cure for hypochondria,' I said coolly. 'Death.'

Julian changed psychological gear immediately. 'You don't look too well yourself, actually. Your complexion is showing a vampirical aversion to daylight. Are you eating correctly? Are you getting your greens?'

'Julian, you are not respecting my boundaries!'

'Boundaries? What are you all of a sudden? A *ranch*? Come back to me, Becky!'

'Remember the "for better of worse" part of our marriage vows? Well, it was never for better. It was always for worse.'

'If you don't stop this ludicrous genuflection to youth, I'll tell the entire world that you pluck that hair on your chin.'

'You wouldn't dare!'

'Try me.'

I steered him towards the exit. 'This is exactly why I left you. You're more controlling than a pair of Elizabeth Taylor's pantyhose.' I attempted to edge him out into the street. 'I know I've hurt and betrayed you. Hell, I could win a Monica-Lewinsky-Behave-Alike Contest. And I'm desperately sorry, but we agreed that I could have some space . . .'

'Space?' Julian wheeled. 'Oh, well, may I suggest

that you look between the ears of your toyboy.'

The look of aggrieved vexation that came over my husband's face told me that my lover had appeared behind me. I turned to find Zachary absorbing the scenario, hands on his sturdy hips.

'Did you know she plucks a hair from her chin every second day? She also lies about her age. Did you know *that*? How old did she tell you she is? Twenty-five? Twenty-six? Well she's nearly thirty-three. The woman needs sheltered housing.'

'Julian.'

'Her hair is turning from grey to red.'

'I do *not* dye my hair . . . much.'

'You can't trust a woman who lies about her age. If she cheated on me, what makes you think she won't cheat on you? Have you thought about that, huh?'

'Can it, libel-breath.'

'Oh amazing!' shouted Julian. 'A rock star with the power of speech. That's the only reason she's picking this fight with me you know.' Coils of anger loosened from his tongue. '. . . Just so that she can get to use words of more than one syllable – like promiscuous, ephemeral . . .'

Zack took a deep breath, controlling himself. He spread his hands wide in appeasement. 'Becky has something she wants to tell you. I know it's hard, man, but . . .'

'*Please* don't attempt to venture into psychology. It'll be a nerve-racking experience for both of us,' Julian retorted bitterly. 'The point is, if you don't stop committing marital vandalism and give me back my wife, then I'll have to insist on a bit of practical negative reinforcement.'

Zack looked at me perplexed. 'Say what?'

'A traditional English term for beating the shit out of you,' he said uncharacteristically.

This sent Zack into an explosion of derisive laughter. Julian took a shaky step closer to him, prompting Danny (the Dog Fondler) de Litto to heave into sight from behind the bookshop.

'And what pray tell are you?' Kate demanded of him. 'Some kind of bouncer?'

'Naw. I'm a gi-normous cupcake. What thuh fuck do yer think I am?'

'I just hope you've planned on your next album being posthumous,' Julian said, his face working with emotion. 'Because of course you'll be dead by then.'

'It's just . . .' Kate, undaunted, prodded Danny de Litto, who was now in a predatory crouch position, ready to pounce. 'We usually check our machine-guns at the door. It's just a quaint little British custom.'

Drawing on my fine command of diplomacy, I did nothing.

The two men drew closer to each other. I placed my hands over my eyes. As I waited for the crunch of bone on bone, I was staggered to hear instead my mother's brittle voice breaking the silence. I peeked between my fingers to see her sashaying into the foyer brandishing today's tabloids.

'Re*bec*ca,' she demanded, as the entire gathering quaked before her brutal cockney consonants. 'Were you present when these photographs were taken?'

Kate suppressed a giggle. My father was cocker-spanieling close to heel. He was wearing a T-shirt as faded as he was, the message indecipherable; although 'I'm With This Idiot' would have summed things up.

Mum, in a dress that was strapless and a bra which wasn't, flung the papers down on to the floor at Julian's feet. Julian let out a desolate whimper as he saw the headlines.

'Becky.' I did a double take. My father, usually operating on auxiliary plankton power, had actually spoken, unprompted. 'If you buy a car, he'll treble your insurance, you know.'

'It's all *'er* fault,' my mother rounded on Kate. 'Youse feminists. Wouldn't be 'appy till you ruined 'er marriage. Until she was emaciated.'

Even Danny the Dog Fondler snickered at that one.

'E*man*cipated, I think you mean, Mum.'

Perching on the ticket desk, my mother fired off a barrage of disapproval about Zack. Despite this verbal volley, I noticed that she surreptitiously flashed him her camiknickers as she crossed her legs.

Oh, God. Here we go again. That was it. I'd had enough. Thinking with my feet, I made for the door at a trot. Julian grabbed my arm in a quivering, feverish grip. I turned. The muscles of his face were numb with despair; his eyes ringed by the strain of estrangement.

'You're really not coming back?'

I'd always thought that life was a bitch, but it struck me suddenly that maybe I was. Zachary's eyebrows urged me to go on, the set of his jaw indicating that he wouldn't tolerate any procrastination.

'I . . . I . . .' I guzzled air. I'd presumed separation from Julian was merely a symptom of my PMT (Pre-Monogamy Tension); symptoms for which Zack would be the cure. Then what the hell was I doing? Of course I shouldn't split finally and for ever from my dear, sweet husband. I loved him. But rationality had gone cold turkey on me. I needed to attend a small, anonymous meeting. 'Hi, my name is Rebecca. And I'm a Zack-aholic.' Which way to the Linda-Trip-Double-Crossing-Two-Faced-Bitch Seminar? My God. If I wanted to self-destruct, why didn't I just become a crack addict or a car salesman or something?

Zack gave a determined nod.

'I want a divorce.' I said shakily, then left my husband standing there, like a man waiting for a train.

24

Better Latent Than Never

'Divorced?' squealed Anouska. 'It sounds so glamorous, doesn't it? So Somerset Maugham. It's rattan pine chairs on colonial verandas, Gauloises, vodka neat and slowly whirring fans . . .'

'You can't get divorced,' exclaimed Kate, craning her head between the two front car seats. 'You're not out of love with Julian, are you?'

I paused. 'No. But I'm also *in* love with someone else.'

Anouska dented a bollard in a heart-stopping, paint-scraping manoeuvre which Houdinied her into a disabled parking space in the car park beneath the YMCA.

'If only men came with hallmarks, so you'd know his real value,' Kate lamented, un-impaling herself from the gearstick.

'*What?*' I swivelled around to face her over the back

seat. 'Could it be! A malfunction in the Kate McCready All-Men-Are-Bastards Prototype Factory! You're the one who told me not to marry him!'

'But if I'd known you were going to turn around and pick an unripe lemon from the tree of life . . .'

'Zack is not a lemon. He's conjugating verbs now, you know.'

Anouska locked the car and we trudged across the concrete tarmac to the rickety lift.

'Oh, ye Gods! A Verb-Conjugator! Wow! . . . Rebecca, the guy's an embarrassment socially. If Zachary were a dog, he'd need a lead. If he were a drink, he'd need a coaster. If he were a . . .'

The lift doors yawned open.

'I do still love Julian. But the trouble is, he's too nice.'

'Yes. I hate that in a man,' said Kate sarcastically. 'Get out now while you still have some self-respect.'

'I want you to go and talk to Jules about giving me an early divorce,' I interrupted, punching the ground-level button.

'Just make sure you get a lawyer, doll. Britain's husband-friendly in divorce settlements,' Anouska moaned as we shuddered surfaceward. 'You want to make sure everything gets shared equally . . .'

'Yeah,' Kate scoffed. 'Between your lawyers. Lawyers just charge a humungous amount to tell you what you already know, except they tell it to you in Latin. Divorcus Alimony Maximus.'

'It won't come to that. Besides, there's nothing to share . . . We threw it all at each other weeks ago.'

The Ladies' changing rooms were shrouded in a fog of talcum powder, fem-fresh spray and hair volumizer. We jammed our plastic membership cards into the locker slots and started to disrobe.

'But why divorce?' Kate sat on the wooden bench that ran the length of the locker aisle to peel off her jeans. 'Oh my God!' She lifted her head so quickly she took a chunk out of her skull on the sharp edge of a locker door. 'You're not going to marry Zack, are you? I wouldn't put it past you. In your book being single is just the shortest space between two marriages.'

'Well, *you're* never even going to get close to matrimony wearing *those*.' I flicked the elastic of her M&S bloomers. 'Nothing could get inside them. Those knickers could deflect machine-gun fire.'

'Bugger me! You are going to marry him, aren't you? You collect unsuitable men the way, I dunno, fly-paper collects blowies!' She gave a retaliatory flick to the lace on my G-string. 'Tell me, do these come in thermal? Winter's coming, you know. How can you *wear* them? I mean, they're not *undies*. They're a *curette*!'

'Elasticated waistbands are completely incompatible with foreplay,' I counter-attacked.

Kate stepped out of the offending bloomers and shoved them into her duffel bag. 'Petting, I'll have you know, is only for animals.'

'And if the knickers don't stop him, battling his way

through the pubic undergrowth will. That bikini line could be gainfully trained up the side of a house! I mean when are you going to start waxing, Kate?'

'She's right, doll,' Anouska decried. 'That's not pubic hair. That's a hearth rug.'

'Just tell me you're not going to get hitched to the mongrel?'

'I may have to marry him if we go to the States. For a Green Card.'

'Ah-huh,' Kate sing-songed. 'And so that *he* can come back and stay in England without being an illegal immigrant.' She gave me a knowing look before crunching into a Kit Kat. 'Now it's becoming clear. A fish out of water is an easy catch, you know, Rebecca.'

'. . . Not to mention those love handles, Kate' – I slapped her rump – '. . . It's pointless exercising if you then go and mainline chocolate. Though I suppose eating *is* the safest sex in the world.'

'They are *not* love handles. These' – she placed her hands matter-of-factly on her hips – 'are protein storage . . . Marry Zack? Christ. Although hey! Why am I getting my tits in a twist over this? It'll never happen. He'll fail the written exam for the marriage certificate. I mean, he hasn't even reached the age of consent.'

'Protein storage my ass. There probably was a thin person inside you trying to get out, Kate, but you ate her. Zack is not a kid!'

'Really? I bet he wears pyjamas with *feet*.' Kate

hoiked up the stretchy trainer pants bucketing her ponderous buttocks. 'And anyway, I'm not fat. It's just period bloating.'

'*Four weeks a month?*'

'It's water retention.'

'If *that's* water retention, then the Pacific ocean must have run dry last time you went for a dip, doll.' Anouska, busy threading her spindly legs into a Gucci leotard with matching lycra tights, did not see the thunderous look that crept over Kate's countenance. 'I mean Rebecca's right. You must start looking after yourself. You don't even moisturize. Your skin is so scaly, doll, my crocodile handbag gets a hard-on just looking at you,' she said, daringly.

'Yeah? Well I bet it's the only bloody male excitation in your household, you great galah.'

Anouska stopped laughing. 'What's that supposed to mean?'

'Well, I wasn't going to say anything, but now you've bloody well asked for it.'

Kate yanked Anouska out through the changing-room door and pressed her pert nose up to the window of the Free Weights room.

'What?' demanded Anouska, irritatedly.

Kate pointed at the thigh-extension machine. Sprawled before the mirror, legs splayed, was the Prince of Darkness himself.

'Darius? What's *he* doing here. He never fraternizes with the Great Unwashed.'

272

'Keep watching, dag-features.'

'This is silly. I'm going in to say hello . . .'

'Anouska, how can I phrase this? . . . It's a bloody Ken and Ken kind of situation, savvy?'

'What?'

'Well, let me try and put this in an English kind of way,' Kate elaborated. 'Your husband is a middle order batsperson *for the other side . . .*'

'Oh my God,' I shrieked. 'Are you serious? How do you know?' Our breath fogged the glass.

'I still have no idea what you're talking about,' Anouska whined.

'What Kate is trying to say is that she thinks Darius might have effete of clay . . .' Anouska's face was still resembling a piece of blank paper.

'He's sailing up the windward passage,' thundered Kate impatiently.

'The man leaves no buttock unturned . . .' I added.

'He drinks at the Hot Cock Tavern . . . The Bun Boy Bar.' Kate exploded with frustration. 'He lunches at the Rim Café, goddamn it!'

The colour drained out of Anouska's face as a tanned personal trainer hooked his finger in the front of her husband's shorts and tugged him close. Darius clenched his trainer's buns and darted his tongue into the Adonis's ear.

'My husband picks up men at the YMCA?' she gasped.

'Unfair, isn't it,' said Kate. 'The only thing I've ever picked up here is tinea.'

Anouska collapsed back on me. 'But he's straight.'

'Your husband makes Liberace look heterosexual,' Kate said, exasperated. 'I've been watching him for days.'

'I had no idea . . .' Anouska stammered.

I placed an arm tenderly about her thin shoulders. 'Didn't wearing the bridesmaid's dress to the wedding rehearsal kind of give you a clue?'

'I just thought it was some kind of public-school thing,' she snivelled. 'He said they were always dressing up as women at school.' She dabbed at her eyes with her sweat towel.

'Has sex been a bit of a game of Orifice Roulette?' I prompted.

'I just thought his aim was off,' Anouska whimpered.

I rolled my eyes. That's definitely the trouble with upper-class Englishmen – they just can't drive past a perversion without pulling over.

'What are you going to do now?' I asked Anouska soothingly. 'You know, besides putting in a call to Jeffrey Dahmer?'

'Come to think of it, *Priscilla Queen of the Desert*, *The Way We Were* and *Maurice* are his three favourite films. Do you think it's grounds for divorce?' Anouska queried, pitifully.

'What? Liking *The Way We Were*? I think it's grounds for manslaughter,' I told her.

'But my "thank-you" letters for the wedding presents are still warm!' she sobbed. 'Besides, the social embarrassment of it! Maybe we can go on as if nothing's happened?'

'Anouska, your husband is coming out,' Kate remonstrated.

'Well, I'll just push him back in again!'

'Anouska, Kate's right. Can you imagine what it'll be like having sex with someone when you know that you're both fantasizing about the same person?'

'Tom Cruise,' she clarified, absent-mindedly.

'Just divorce him. Rebecca sure as hell makes it sound easy enough.'

'I can't. He'll take me for every penny I've got.'

'He'll screw you for palimony, no doubt about it. Money can't buy love, but it can definitely rent it by the hour,' I said, inclining my head in Darius's direction. The trainer was kneeling between Anouska's husband's legs. On the pretext of checking the strain on abdominal muscles during sit-ups, he pressed his hand lower and lower on Darius's dank belly, surreptitiously tweaking his penis at every opportunity.

Anouska burst through the door. Kate and I followed at a sprint, but couldn't catch up with her. It was the first time I'd ever actually seen her take any exercise. By the time we got to the Nautilus machines, a shame-faced Darius was stammering out the usual excuses. 1) I was thinking of a girl – of *you*, I mean – the whole time! 2) You're not gay if you don't kiss. 3) It's just there are so few women in the Y. 4) I was just curious. 5) Every man has at least one gay encounter: Voltaire, Tolstoy, Winston Churchill, Tiny Tim … 6) I'm calling my lawyer.

That made two of us. I only knew one thing for sure. Marriage was definitely the chief cause of divorce.

25

Warning. The Following Sexual Positions Are Not For Amateurs. Do Not Try This In Your Own Home

The good thing about rock and roll, is that having the charisma of a crash dummy and being the offspring of two siblings, only enhances your chances of being a thunderous success.

This is what I thought as I was formally introduced to Zachary's band for the first time. Besides Zack, there was lead guitarist Ace (the mandatory Vaguely Sinister One); bass guitarist Mr Dee (the compulsory Deep and Earnest One) and Skunk the drummer (the obligatory Prankster). Between them they were wearing enough mousse to sprout antlers. As I entered Rotty's office, they blinked and recoiled from the light like nocturnal worms dug up with a garden trowel. This wasn't a band. This was an eight-legged intestinal parasite. This was Journey To The Centre Of The Earth.

'Have you seen Zachary?'

Their befogged synapses tried to communicate with each other, bogging down in a linguistic quagmire of grunts and 'yeah man's' and 'got any blow?'s. Only Rock and Roll English spoken here.

Having given up on trying to bring Zachary's flat up to sanitary standards, I'd talked him into a move. When he'd missed our rendezvous at an estate agent's office in St John's Wood, I'd tracked him here. Rotterman single-handedly ruled over his musical fiefdom from an office in Soho that could only be reached by picking your way up a tottery staircase over needles and crisp packets and towards a door with 'ROTTWEILER RECORDS' written on it in wonky purple felt tip. When I knocked, my knuckles came away sticky with paint. Oh, this was definitely Big Time.

'Um . . . Have you seen him or not?' I painstakingly enunciated.

The band's springy black cowlicks boinged about as their brains broiled . . . Five minutes later, after a great deal of wiry-armed semaphore and 'fugedabowdit's I was still none the wiser.

I was about to start checking under the floorboards when Rotterman crashed through the door with a demonic swagger. Registering my presence, he pulled up short. An excess of unconvincing toupee sat askew on his cranium. Bald, Rotterman was homely. But now, he was uglier than a caravan park.

I laughed out loud. 'What the hell have you got on your head? It looks like a bit of road kill scraped off the pavement and then glued on!'

Rotterman's slobbering mouth eroded a cigar as he spoke. 'Zack's busy ... like *for the rest of his life*, yer know? *This*,' he informed the band, hooking a gnarled thumb in my direction, 'is Zack's screw. I'm sure yer noticed her in the budget for quite some time now.'

'I am *not* an unremunerative outlay of capital, thank you very much. I'm an independent career woman,' I said huffily.

Suffice to say that Rotterman and I were still finding each other spectacularly unendearing.

Rotterman threw a thick leg over the arm of his beige easy chair. 'Do the words "Yoko Ono" mean anything to you?' he drawled.

'Do the words "agent rip off?" mean anything to you?' I sat on the vinyl lounger puckered with plastic blisters opposite his desk.

'Shaddup. I'm peddlin' a whole Lenny Kravitz lifestyle here and an old douchebag ain't it. Yer saw the tabloids.'

'The tabloids, yes. But the eye of the real press is not that short-sighted.'

'Yer can blow me, okay? I've been told by the record company at the most senior goddamn levels that Zack needs Image. For starters, we gotta take all the seventh chords and all the minor chords outta his songs. Get in ghost writers for the lyrics. Then I can go the cross-promotional Pepsi and Nike mega-endorsement route. Maybe even change his nose. Do his lips. Lighten his skin a little.' I looked at him aghast. Honestly, it was all I could do to keep from spewing on his shoes. 'Hell. The Bee Gees underwent castration as a career move.' He re-fired his cigar.

'Dumb him down and you'll be cutting off his dick, too, metaphorically speaking. Gives a whole new meaning to severance pay,' I shot back. 'Speaking of pay, why is it that Zack's records are selling but he's still on subsistence wages? A complimentary prawn sandwich seems scant compensation for the merciless grind you subject him to. If you're so obsessed with Image then you can pay for the Big Fuck Off Rock-Star Residence I intend moving us into.'

Rotterman snapped his fingers and it suddenly got very Jurassic Park in there. Danny (the Dog Fondler) de Litto blundered to his side. His body looked even more pumped up than last time I'd seen it. It was Invasion of the Michelin Man.

'The bottom of the Thames is a notoriously cold kinda place, yer know,' Rotterman remarked, digging last night's meal out from between his yellow fangs. No kidding. Zachary's agent has all the charm of a Mafia hitman – possibly because he *is* one.

'Keep your polyester pants on. Why don't we let Zack decide for himself?'

I barged my way into an inner lair, calling out Zack's name. I located him seated at a desk staring at a legal contract of some kind. Two men in Armani suits with strenuously flamboyant ties were hovering: Suit No. One, clutching a pen like a hypodermic needle, jabbed it in Zack's direction.

'Oh, your record contract.' I picked it up between my fingertips as though it were radioactive. 'So *that's* what an oily rag smells like. I wouldn't sign that until you get a lawyer to read it from covert to covert.'

'Yeah,' panted Rotterman, behind me. 'Not if yer don't wanna sell, like, a gazillion records.' He snatched it back and slapped it on to the table. 'Sign the sonofabitch.'

Zack looked from me to Rotterman, uncertainty flickering in his eyes.

'She's Delilah to your Samson, ja'know that? You're losing yer edge, yer animal magnetism . . .'

'But not the fleas it attracts,' I interjected, glowering at Rotterman.

'Well?' Suit No. Two demanded impatiently.

'I dunno, Beck. Rotty's my main man . . . He has heaps of contacts an' that . . .'

'Yes. I'm sure – like Satan's unlisted phone number.'

'Sign, for Chrissakes,' Rotterman hissed. 'No sonofabitch artist has ever found difficulty in selling fewer albums, yer know.'

'Sign and you'll have an ulcer from saying Yes Sir, No Sir, Lick your bum, Sir,' I warned Zack.

'Shaddup! . . .' He shoved Zack back into his chair. 'Sign!'

'They want a ghost writer . . . so you can write without moving your lips. If you really do love me, Zack, you won't do it.'

Rotterman ground his prognathous jaw. 'How could you screw such a dog?'

'Hey,' I shrugged. 'I'm handy for sniffing luggage at airports . . . and . . .'

My retort was cut short as Zachary cut a swashbuckling swathe towards his wilting agent. Looming over Rotterman, his powerful torso seemed to occupy half the room. Up to this point, Rotterman had been acting so tough. Now, suddenly, it was trousers-down-and-face-the-carpet. He grovelled. He simpered. He blubberingly begged Zachary for forgiveness. Like all cruel men, Rotterman was the type to cry buckets at funerals and 'This is Your Life' reunions. No doubt he also adored animals.

'We're goin' house huntin',' Zachary announced, turning his back on the sabre-toothed tapeworm and leading me to the door.

Round one – to me, I thought, and followed, relieved.

The rest of the day we spent poking through other people's homes in St John's Wood. We learnt a lot of things. That 'cosy' means small. That 'deliciously cool in summer' means dark and arctic. 'That 'retains excitingly authentic features' decodes as an unrenovated cesspit. We also learnt that you could talk the estate agents into waiting in their cars and letting you view the house alone, ostensibly to get 'a feel for it'. Or, more to the point, for each other.

On the kitchen table of a semi-detached in Circus Road, Zack dusted me with icing sugar then wrote love obscenities on my naked body with an ice cube. 'We'll have to put up a blue plaque to say that we slept here,' I panted, as he propped up a mirror so I could watch him making love to me.

By the end of the afternoon, we would have to put up a lot of blue plaques.

Finally, within spitting distance of Abbey Road recording studios, serious house lust set in.

'Four bathrooms! We're going to have to get incontinent to enjoy them all. I'll be the cleanest person you know,' I told Zack.

'Yeah, with the dirtiest mind.'

'Do you think our relationship is just sex?' I asked as he sat me naked and blindfolded on a chair, massaged peaches into my thighs and ate fruit salad off my flesh.

I even declined the joint Zack produced post-coitally, fearful that drugs would make me forget how happy I was.

'Come. On the tour?' Zack pleaded, as we taxied it back to Rotterman's office to secure the deposit. (The estate agents wanted an advance that made Bill Clinton look celibate.)

'Zachary, the only way I'd spend more of my leisure time with Rotterman would be if we were both kidnapped by Osama Bin Laden terrorists. Besides, I can't just drop everything for a man.' Nothing, I thought, would induce me to go.

'Isn't it exciting!' Celestia exclaimed in her thin bat squeak as we entered the office unannounced to find her signing a contract to provide what Rotterman referred to as 'backstage ambience'. 'Our star signs are terrifically compatible. Great for when we're on the road.'

'On the road?' I tried to keep the jealousy out of my voice.

'Look, Zack,' Celestia poked out her pink tongue to reveal a round metallic stud. 'I got this for you.'

'Um, a tongue stud weeping pus does not enhance fellatio, you know,' I said redundantly, as every male in the office drooled in Celestia's direction. 'If you wanted to make a hole in your head, wouldn't it have been easier for all concerned if you'd used an AK47?'

'It's so hard being beautiful,' Celestia confided to the band. 'Other women just want to kill you.'

'Maybe that can be arranged while we're on tour,' I said cheerfully.

Rotterman's grin soured with contempt. 'We're? . . . Well 'aint you the "independent career girl",' he taunted, flipping me the finger.

'That's great, babe.' Zack kissed me. 'Ain't ya excited?'

'Excited?' I replied half-heartedly, as I imagined the

scene when I told Kate. 'Oh yeah, I think I have a goose bump.'

Round two, I thought despondently, to the Scum-Master General.

Kate was predictably scathing. 'Make sure you get Zack a booster-seat for the tour bus. I imagine you'll be on a bus, 'cause he can't fly, of course. Well, not without Hostess Accompaniment.'

But as I packed for the tour later that night, excitement did bubble up. 'On the road' – it sounded so thrillingly Jack Kerouac. Wasn't this every female's fantasy? Turning the hotel swimming pool into a giant punch bowl, then diving in? Fully clothed. From the first-floor balcony. Tequila-fuelled fandangos at dawn whilst rhyming couplets which would be worked into lyrics later? Waking up at midday and complaining that we have to get up so early? How wild and rebellious ... God, I hoped the rooms would have blow-dryers. Of course they would. Those penthouse toilets seat six!

Julian was on the phone before I'd finished packing. 'Touring? With a remedial rock band? That'll be about as interesting as Bulgarian daytime television.'

'Have you spoken to Kate?' I enquired tentatively. 'Is that why you're ringing?'

'I'm ringing because I've been doing a bit of checking up on my former client, Mr Rotterman and his spectacularly untalented protégé. Lover boy's mentor has very close connections to the New York drug barons. There's even some suggestion that he's under investigation in the States for racketeering. Why do you think Rotterman brought the band to Britain? This is serious stuff, Rebecca. One of his former associates is wanted for murder in the first degree.'

'Oh, Jules . . .'

'Becky, the man's business address is a *wharf*. And do you know, it was Rotterman himself who lodged the obscenity complaint with Scotland Yard. For the publicity, of course.'

'Then why don't you tell the authorities?'

'Because it would be a breach of lawyer-client confidentiality. The one professional obligation I dare not break, even after the client's death, which will, I hope, be soon.'

'Hello? Earth to Julian. This is *me* you're talking to. I know you're making this up.'

'For your own good, promise me you'll keep away from him. Swear you will, Becky . . . Unlike a wedding vow *this must actually count*.'

'How's the cancer?' I asked harshly.

'Fine.' His voice went cold. 'Find out the hard way then.' He hung up.

I shrugged off his caution. Hell. I had a one-way ticket to Hedonism Valhalla. And I was going to take it. Besides, finding out the hard way was what I did best. In my book, you never know what you're incapable of until you try.

26

The Dark Side Of The Tune

The reason rock and roll bands tour is because no one knows what a non-entity they are back home, and no one back home knows what a non-entity they are on tour.

Despite Zachary's Best-Newcomer award, the tour Rotterman had booked for him consisted of hotels with beds rejected by the Salvation Army as being too uncomfortable, gigs in clubs that were nothing more than urinals with feedback and guest appearances on cable chat shows in between ads for halitosis cures and hair transplants.

For all of November we criss-crossed the British Isles via a double helix of roundabouts. After spending what seemed like an entire week on one seven-lane sub-orbital ring road, everyone on the bus was starting to resemble a passenger on the *Raft of the Medusa*.

Sprouting a haemorrhoid the size of Helmut Kohl, I was missing Julian's fan-warmed Saab more than I liked to admit. But whenever I got off the bloody tour bus, I was very quickly desperate to get back *on* again. In Manchester the decrepit hotel we were staying in made sleeping under the Cornish pasty van at rock festivals feel like the ritz. Although 'sleep' is too optimistic a word. It was impossible to get any rest. Mainly because some insect was always blinking it's 9,000,624,439,002 eyes at me in the dark.

The thrilling highlight of each day was if no one flushed the toilet while I was in the shower. What with three-course meals of vending-machine food and watching television repeats of badminton matches between Romanians and North Koreans I'd never heard of, the time just raced by as though it were only *a year or two*.

But no matter how great my detestation, I couldn't leave. Having been hired on the spurious pretext of media liaison, the delectable Celestia was proving to be more adept at private than public relations. With this groupie on board the bus, it was a case of Meals on Wheels.

When Zack opted to return to me at nights, Celestia decided to bring the party to him. After a dreary gig in Bristol she bounded into our hotel room, beaming like an over-refreshed game-show hostess, an entourage of hangers-on and the hangers on's hangers-on at her heels.

288

'Um, occupancy of this hotel room by more than 200 people is not only dangerous but probably unlawful,' I said to no one in particular as Celestia, wearing a dress that revealed parts of her only an obstetrician should see, started dancing.

Rotterman rolled his eyes. The more I nagged and ragged, the more Rotty spoon-fed Zack's ego. He'd been chopping up little nourishing press morsels and presenting them decoratively on a plate. He'd been taste-testing every interview. He'd cuddled and mollycoddled. And Zachary was starting to get an appetite for the attention.

'I told yer that a girlfriend on tour is bad luck, Zack,' he exulted. 'I mean, how can yer trust anythin' that bleeds for five days and doesn't like, *die* . . . ?'

Retreating to the dreary lobby, I checked my watch. Even though it wasn't yet six a.m., I rang Anouska.

'Really?' she yawned down the line. 'You haven't been to bed yet? You must be having the most glamorous time, doll!'

'What? Oh yes. I've made three triple scores in Scrabble and won Park Lane from myself eighty-six times.'

'The hotels must be to diiiie for, though, aren't they?'

'Well I'm standing by the foyer windows, drinking in a splendid view of the toxic waste dump site as we speak.'

'You're just playing it down to make me feel better. On tour! God. It must be *sooooo* exciting.'

289

'If you call "exciting" the band's foreskin rings setting off the metal detectors at a local television station in front of a Girl Guide Troupe, then yes. But why do you need cheering up?' I fed more coins into the slot. 'Has Darius admitted he's gay yet?'

'His new best friend is a male flight attendant. He's doing everything but flower arranging.'

'Divorce him then.'

'Can't, doll. He wants palimony. Both of us made a mistake, but only one of us is going to pay for it. I hate to admit it, but you and Kate were so right about him.'

'Speaking of Kate, could you go into the ICA occasionally and mess up my office for me? You know, put coffee cups on my desk, turn off my light at six p.m., make it look as though I'm turning up occasionally? I did say I'd only be gone for a couple of weeks . . .'

My money cut out. 'Annie?' I'd been about to tell her how much I missed her. I listened to the dismal dial tone. Through the double-glazed hotel windows the December sky was breaking into a weak, wan light. I watched the wind-whipped pedestrians struggling up the pavement to the station, men in pin-striped suits. Just like Julian's. My lover was leaving me for far too many hours on my own, hours in which I could dwell on my husband. I was tempting to get some more change and ring Jules, just to make sure it really was nothing more serious than an anal fissure. I wanted to let him know I was worrying about him, without rekindling his expectations. But how? I decided to send him some bran muffins. As a get-well present. It was impossible to read romance into bran muffins.

Numb with fatigue, I trudged back to my room. I was so tired I'd have to hire someone to have orgasms for me. Opening the door, I snapped off the music and peeled Celestia out of my bed.

'I don't know how to tell you this, Celestia, but oral sex is not a spectator sport. Any groupies still here in two minutes will be towed away at the owner's expense,' I commanded, forcing open the bathroom door. Skunk was slouched on the floor. Rotty was sprawled across the closed lid of the loo, a McDonald's carton spread open on his knees. It was packed with packets of white powder. 'Now that's what I call a "happy meal".'

'It's to cure a goddamn affliction of mine, wise ass,' Rotterman snarled.

'What? – Reality?'

'Nasal diabetes,' he said smugly, before gesturing at Skunk. 'We both got it bad, ain't we, buddy?'

Before Rotterman kicked the door shut in my face, I caught sight of the teenager drummer's arm which was tourniqueted tightly, a needle puncturing his patchy, purply skin.

'I want all you people – whoever you are – out of my room,' I shouted. 'Right now.'

'Don't you just love a woman who speaks her

mind . . .' Celestia said sarcastically to the snickering band.

'That's because I've got one,' I snapped, glaring at her as she rustled venomously away.

Zack appeared with fresh supplies of cigarettes just as the last human dregs leaked out into the hallway. 'Tell me, with your goddamn diplomacy skills, have you ever, like, considered a career in hostage negotiation?'

'I can't stand it any more, Zack. Look at me! A diet of stale kebabs and hotel-fridge peanuts and my skin is taking on the pallor of a long-term prisoner. I haven't seen daylight for weeks. I'm about to start hanging upside down to go to sleep.'

Zack laughed. 'Come on. It ain't *all* bad on the road. At least we've learnt some stuff. You know, like, that cat food is the basis of all English roadside curries,' he grinned. 'Let's go get breakfast.'

He led me over the road to a dockside greasy café whose taupe walls were tragically plastered with yellowing photos of exotic places. As we waited for meatballs they must have been flying in from Naples, I tried to manufacture a smile that aborted, halfway through, into a long-suffering sigh.

'So what's eating you, 'zackly?'

I gestured around me. 'This never-ending barf buffet for one thing. Backstage I have seen things done to other things on crackers that will haunt me in my nightmares. Crummy hotel rooms with nylon sheets – my pubes have been standing on end for weeks. The fart-fog surrounding the tour bus. We're talking gale-force farts. Especially Rotterman. Not to mention the *band* . . .'

Zack's yellow-flecked eyes, the eyes of a stray cat, fixed me defiantly. 'They're okay.'

'*Okay?* Their main entertainment is trying to pee in a pot plant through a key hole.'

'You know, if you hate it so much, go back to London then,' he said coolly.

'Yeah, *right*.' I sipped at a glass of apple juice that was warm enough to shave your legs in.

'Just because you're on tour with a woman who, whenever she walks into a room all the men get erections for the next three months, shouldn't give me any reason to doubt your fidelity, I know, but if it's all the same to you, I think I'll stay.'

Zachary leant back in his chair and gave his famous slow, honeyed smirk. 'What? You think I'd cheat on you?' he said in a smoky voice. The grey water beneath the dock made a carnal, sucking sound.

'Zachary, my darling, you have a penis that is always ready to party.'

'I don't want *her*. Why would I want her when I have you?' The naughty-boy mischief in his eyes teamed up with that crooked grin and ruffled hair – he was edible, at least more edible than the two plates of congealed spaghetti and meatballs which were plonked down before us. We stared at them dubiously.

'Um, how would Madam like her dog balls?' asked

Zack, pronging a specimen and devouring it whole.

'You do want her. Every time you see each other, you launch into a vigorous exchange of saliva.'

'That don't mean nuthin'. . . . Anything,' he corrected. 'It's in our recordin' contracts that we have to keep kissin' each other. Kiss*ing*. And flirting. I'm nothing but a clit-tease,' he laughed.

I cringed. 'Another reason I can't leave you. You'll slip straight back into all your old linguistic crudities.'

'Hey, leave my crude, indigenous ghetto speech patterns to me, okay?' he said, a smile not quite masking the slight irritation in his eyes.

'Besides, who's going to do your thinking for you if I go?'

Zack bristled. 'You're my lover, not my owner, yer know what I mean? In my opinion . . .'

'I hate the way you say "you know what I mean", all the time . . . And if I want your opinion I'll give it to you, *you know what I mean?*' I prodded at a cold meatball with a plastic fork.

'I'm getting sick of this crap,' Zachary snapped. 'Getting' sick of these honky threads too.' He tugged his Calvin Klein sweatshirt over his head. 'I'm gonna have to wear a T-shirt that says "Dressed by Girlfriend". Though technically you ain't my girlfriend, but *the wife of some other dude.*'

'*Ex*-girlfriend,' I said, averting my eyes. Like looking at an eclipse, gazing at the warm, sleek skin of his torso was way too dangerous.

It was our first fight. So much for Hedonism Valhalla. Walking back to the hotel, I realized that the only way to survive a rock tour is to dread one second at a time.

Fortuitously, that very morning Celestia's tongue stud got infected. She was in great pain and could put nothing in her mouth other than warm, salty water for the next four weeks, making it safe for me to abandon the tour.

Even though some synchronized swimming in a pool of each others' sweat had reconciled us, on the train back to London I found myself having to subdue a sense of rising panic. I clung to the reassurance that I still loved *Zack*; I just didn't love his lifestyle. Which was fine because as soon as he hit the Big Time I would never, ever have to see a complimentary miniature Cadbury's chocolate on my pillow again as long as I lived.

But the rail tracks were fringed with rust-coloured pine needles. Opening the rain-splashed windows, the pungent effluvium of fallen leaves caused a fog of melancholy to steal in over me. I looked at the clouds churned by the bitter wind into a dull grey cream. As the train slammed into a tunnel, I realized with a jolt on what thin ice I was skating. And what dark waters lurked beneath. I heard the surface crack, but it was too late to go back. I skidded on.

27

Till Divorce Us Do Part

The ice began to shatter sooner than I'd thought possible.

'Where to first, doll?' Anouska was driving me away from Waterloo Station through the Christmas rush hour in a not altogether successful combination of first gear and reverse.

'A doctor.'

'Good God. Are you ill?'

'Yes. I have a terminal attack of everything a doctor will find plausible enough to write me a note saying I had to be off work for the last six weeks.' My credibility with Kate was stretched to Twanging point.

I'd only been at my desk for five minutes when she tacked across Reception, as though into a gale. 'Where the hell have you been? . . . I only gave you two weeks' leave.'

'Would you believe menstrual problems?' It had proven an above-average excuse with other bosses.

'You don't have PMT. You're just a rotten cow. Period.' She flicked at the paperclip chain I'd begun on my desk. 'Well, that's the most productive twenty seconds you've had since you met Zachary Burne. I'm telling you, Beck, I can't lie for you any more. One more day off work and the Board is going to give you the sack.'

'The Board? Didn't you cover for me?'

'Yes. But you don't have enough toes, teeth, intestines or eyes for all the chiropody, periodontistry, endocrinology and ophthalmology you're supposed to have had lately. You'd have to have vertebrae stretching from here to Paris for the amount of osteopathic hours you've had out of this bloody office.'

'You can't sack me! I was just about to ask for a ten-year advance on my salary.'

'Don't give me that starving artist in the garret routine.'

'I'm not ... I couldn't afford one. Not until the divorce anyway. So, how did Julian take it? That I want a divorce?'

She drummed her fingers on my battered, antique desktop. 'Oh, as calmly and rationally as could be expected ... Last time I saw him he was running his car back and forth over your wedding dress.'

'What did he say?'

Kate sighed. 'He said that he felt a visceral revulsion

to the idea of you naked and ecstatic in the arms of a lower life form. He said that marriage brought into play the basest impulses . . .'

'So . . . that's a yes?'

'. . . as well as the highest aspirations.'

'So what's that?' I looked up at her. 'A no?'

The roll Kate gave to her eyes was magnified by her specs. 'Maybe you can get the marriage annulled on the grounds that the immaturity of the female petitioner made you incapable of giving informed consent?'

'With friends like you, who needs mothers? . . . What else did he say?'

Kate sat on the edge of my desk, slewed a foot sideways, heel hooked over the rung of my chair. 'That you have to be married for a year before you can get a divorce. So you can't give up your day job just yet. But believe me, anything you want from your old house you should take now. Blokes get really ugly during a divorce.'

Anouska appeared in my office doorway, signing into her mobile phone. She acknowledged us with a jaded flutter of a manicured hand.

'How can you think so little of Julian?' I reprimanded. 'He'd never do anything unscrupulous.'

'Sure, he's at stage one now. The hurt, "I-Want-You-Back-I'm-Dog-Meat" stage. But soon he'll reach the "You Bitch" stage. Followed by the "*Every* Woman Is A Bitch" stage. Followed by "Even Though All Women

Are Bitches, I'm Going Out to get Laid" stage. And then, finally, stage five, when you'll get a wedding invitation. I mean, how will you feel when Julian finds someone else?'

'He's a workaholic who dresses in lederhosen. Who'd have him?' I joshed.

'He may advertise,' Kate devils-advocated. ' "For Sale: One Husband. Has Had Only One Careful Lady Owner".'

'At least I now know what keeps couples together,' sighed Anouska, detaching herself from her 'It-Girl Earring'. 'The cost of divorce. I've just been speaking to my lawyer. Darius is determined to take my purse to the dry-cleaners. He's insisting I pay for him and Norbett, the South African towel attendant, to go on a holiday to recover from my shattering request for a divorce. Can you believe that . . . that . . . *bum-bandit*?' She exclaimed, blushing at her own linguistic audacity.

What I couldn't believe was the miserable prediction Kate had made about Julian. 'What makes you such an expert on men?' I asked her, heatedly. 'I mean, hello.'

'For the last time, Becky. I didn't give up on sex; sex gave up on me. Okay? So, are you happy now?' she said despondently. 'So shut up about it. All right?'

There was a bleak silence while this sorry revelation was fully absorbed.

Kate stomped towards the door. 'Jesus Christ. I wish I could divorce my bloody friends.'

But Kate was wrong about Julian. I knew it better than I knew anything. He was Mr Ethical. He was unswervingly honest and honourable. He was a Human Rights Lawyer, for God's sake. He would never run me through with the sword of justice.

'He's changed the locks! I don't believe it!'

We were standing outside the house I'd shared with Julian. It was midnight on New Year's Eve. Earlier in the evening I'd made a New Year's Resolution not to make any New Year's Resolutions. But now, with Anouska standing next to me and humiliation imminent, resolutions were tumbling through my head – to go to fewer parties, to aid World Peace . . . *for my key to turn in this goddamned lock*.

We'd spent the earlier part of the night at Darius's New Year's Eve Party, which had become way too *La Cage aux Folles* for Annie's liking. Zack was playing in Aberdeen, and so – emboldened by alcohol – I'd decided to pick up some of my old possessions. Anouska had offered to drive me to Belsize Park.

'You're too drive to drunk.'

'Of course I can drive. Hell, I'm in no condition to walk, now am I?'

'If only Kate were here so *she* could drive,' I lamented as we collapsed into the car. Kate refused to attend a New Year's Eve party so close to the

Millenium. She said she saw little to celebrate in a century that had given us the Holocaust, Hiroshima and the H-bomb.

'Stop taking those bends so fast, doll,' Anouska shrieked, as we nearly demolished Marble Arch, 'I'm spilling my drink.'

'Annie, um, *you're* driving.'

The unexpected pang of nostalgia I'd felt as we juddered to a halt outside my old ivy-throttled house had quickly turned to dismay when I realized Julian had locked me out.

I leant on the bell. I banged on the door. I peered through the living-room window. The Christmas tree, or 'horticultural festive element', as Julian called it, was still standing and a confusion of pink and silver paper chains dangled from the chandelier like the toils of a gigantic spider on acid. Christmas decorations? *A week after Christmas?* What *was* this?

I buzzed again. No answer. I checked my watch. Five to twelve. Julian never went to bed this early. He had at least ten Belizean tribesmen to save from extinction before dawn. My finger had a buzzer indentation by the time I finally roused him. He didn't open the door, but spoke to me through the letter box.

'Your possessions are boxed up down the side of the house, Rebecca. And your Christmas present is behind the rhododendron.'

'Can I come in . . .'

'No.'

'Is that your New Year's Resolution?' I said, with false gaiety. 'To be a bastard? ... Come on, Jules. I'm freezing my tits off out here. And I'm absolutely starving.'

'Sorry. The only thing I'm serving is a divorce petition.'

'*What?*' I crouched down to peer through the slit at a silken pyjamed knee.

'If you're determined to make such a big fool of yourself, Rebecca, why should I stand in your way? I'm willing to divorce you. On the grounds of unreasonable behaviour.'

Unreasonable? Had he actually *seen* Zachary? It would have been unreasonable *not* to have an affair with such a man.

'And for mental cruelty. In the shape of bran muffins.'

I guess the 'not-reading-romance-into-this' present had really worked then. Heavy skeins of fog hung in the damp air. The steps were draughty. In the sickly light from the street lamp Anouska and I looked grimy and grey-hued. 'Great,' I said neutrally. 'Fine.'

'Fine.'

I'd imagined this moment a hundred times – I'd feel sad and remorseful for, oh, about 2.6 seconds before it all fell away, like snow off a roof. But instead, the moment was tinctured by thoughts of the warm symbiosis we'd enjoyed. I started calculating how many hectares of honey on toast I'd buttered for him;

how many socks I'd paired for him, how many vests I'd turned right-side out for him, how many ear hairs I'd trimmed for him. I even calculated the mountains of his dead skin cells I'd vacuumed over the years.

Nostalgia is that weird emotion which makes things seem a million times more wonderful now than they did when they were actually taking place. What makes 'the good old days' is a really really bad memory. This is what I told myself as I slipped off my sapphire ring and wedding band and passed them through the letter box.

'Goodnight then,' I said, adding ludicrously, 'Happy New Year.'

'Happy New Year,' he replied formally.

Silk pyjamas, the whole house lankly strung with tinsel and streamers in January ... 'You don't think he's seeing someone else, do you?' I asked Anouska, stopping dead in my tracks as we lugged my worldly possessions into her car.

'An eligible heterosexual man in London? I would have thought he'd have been stripped down and sold for parts by now, doll.'

Dropping a box, I seized hold of her arm. 'Do you like Zack?'

'Yes, he's lovely.'

'Tell me the truth. Am I making a complete ass of myself? Am I too old for him?'

'No.' Her thin stream of breath dissolved in the air.

'Please, Annie. What I value most about our friendship is your straight talking.'

'Okay, he's too young. You're making a fool of yourself.'

'So you think I'm too old, huh! Have *you* looked in the mirror lately, *wrinkle-breath*?'

I flounced off to search behind the rhododendron. Wrapped in black paper were the mouldy bran muffins and our wedding photo, shredded. I think it was safe to conclude that Julian had reached stage two.

28

Survival Of The Hippest

When contemplating living with your Stud-Puppy,
five issues invariably arise – gynaecological thigh
abductors, the Haircut From Outer Space, goats' milk,
a shaved pudenda and dimmer switches.

Let's take them individually.

Months of all-night partying, irregular meals and
too much alcohol, and not only will your liver be flying a white flag of surrender, but you'll look as though
you've been held captive at gunpoint by a group of
deranged jungle revolutionaries. The only way to get
rid of that look is to use every second you've got to
beautify yourself.

When dating a younger man, the brain is obliged to
cut a new deal with the body. And a hard bargain it is.
Most of January, February and March, I spent in
London ostensibly doing up Zack's new house in St

John's Wood, but in reality renovating my own ageing façade.

'Sorry, sorry, sorry,' I wheezed, staggering into the office three hours late. 'Would you believe, Kate, that I was abducted by aliens to their Mother Ship for bizarre scientific purposes?' Actually this wasn't far from the truth as I was spending all my time in beauty parlours being tweezed in placed I'd never even noticed before. Any time left over I spent contorting myself masochistically at the gym.

'Not the gym again,' wailed Anouska as I dragged her off the tube at Tottenham Court Road. 'Why?'

'Because I want to be young and firm.'

'What are you, doll? A tomato?'

A faster technique for looking young, of course, is to be seen out with much uglier women. 'Kate, please come to Zachary's gigs with me . . .'

'Absolutely not.'

'If you won't come I'll have to resort to plastic surgery,' I moaned, sweating my way through my sixth set of abdominal crunches.

'Yeah? What about the nasty side effects? Plastic surgery can lead to women developing thick Californian accents. Anyway, you big dag. There's nothing wrong with your face. It's a nice, lived-in face . . .'

'Yeah, lived in by an old bag lady. Look at me!' I peered at my reflection in the chrome frame of the nautilus machine. 'I've seen better heads on a pimple.'

To lift my spirits even further, the horrifically gynaecological thigh abductor, on which I had to do sixty repetitions daily, was situated directly opposite the bench press. Every time I opened my legs it was to see a drooling insurance salesman staring directly at my vulva.

I now had more money invested in Estée Lauder products than in my pension plan. I seemed to have a special Swiss beauty treatment for each individual pore. I was buying only makeup with 'concealer' in the blurb. Pretty soon I'd be so concealed I'd be bloody invisible.

Which would not be a bad thing considering the Haircut From Outer Space. The disaster occurred when, in an effort to look younger, I abandoned my usual hairdresser for one of the trendiest, most expensive hair boutiques in London.

'What look would'ja like, sweet'eart?' the stylist lazily enquired.

I looked at his stringy, purple, raggedly razored crop. 'Um . . . show me something you really loathe,' I suggested.

The Haircut From Outer Space that followed meant that I then had to spend yet more money I didn't have on 'talking point' hats, wigs and hair extensions.

Maybe I could distract from my hair by shifting the focus on to something I was wearing? Say a belly-button stud?

'Abso-bloody-lutely not,' ordered Kate. 'A woman does not need any holes in her other than those which are strictly speaking necessary.'

'What about a new dress?' Anouska pointed out a diaphanous shift in a Soho shop window. 'That would look great on you, doll.'

'Yeah. As long as I keep my weight down to *one stone*.'

Which segues me neatly on to point number three.

It's impossible not to feel fat in the company of groupies half your age. A couple of minutes with these anorexic girls and you'll want to rent space on the side of your arse to advertise major consumer goods.

Consequently, for three months I drank nothing but goats' milk. No kidding. By the end of March I couldn't pass a piece of furniture without scaling it.

'What kind of bloody Feminist are you?' Kate scolded me. 'You're obsessed with thinness.'

'I'm not.'

'You won't even cook with thick-bottomed saucepans!'

No matter how many pounds I lost, it was never enough. Maybe bulimia was the way to go? This is one of the few diets that actually *does* work. Bulimia would give me a figure to die for – *literally*.

Which brings me to the next point. Malnourishment and a nocturnal social life produces a state of chronic fatigue.

'Ironic, isn't it?' I yawned, when Kate prodded me

awake at work one day. '*You* have no life. And I have too much . . . I'm so exhausted, I sleep when I'm awake so I won't be so exhausted when I get back into bed.'

As if it weren't arduous enough ricocheting back and forth from London to rendezvous with Zack on the road, I had to be a Love Goddess when I reached him. My sex drive had worn out its gearbox. Perhaps it was the constant migraines from inflating my plastic sexual pleasure enhancers? Perhaps it was the persistent pneumonia from dressing provocatively (as a lead singer's girlfriend, you're constantly having to slip into something less comfortable). Perhaps it was the third-degree carpet burns on bits of my anatomy that I couldn't explain away as a housework-related incident? Or the rope burns that came under the category of The Most Humiliating Chafe Mark in The History of The Universe? Fishnet friction can inflict a nasty wound on your groin area, you know. And believe me, a shaved pudenda may sound erotic, but when it's growing back it looks like a shag pile that has been terrorized.

I found myself getting desperate desires to do it in the missionary position. Preferably inside. Frostbite of the breasts, leeches on the labia, neck cramp from trying to keep one eye peeled for wandering psychopaths does not get a girl as aroused as her partner might think.

Nor does making love in daylight. If the Nobel Prize was awarded by a woman, it would go to the inventor of the dimmer switch. This is the greatest sex aid known to women-kind. Well, to women over a certain age, say *sixteen*.

'This is getting ridiculous,' Kate said as I pored over photos of supermodels to compare their primary and secondary sex organs with my own. We were sprawled around Anouska's living room prodding half-heartedly at a lukewarm takeaway.

'You don't know what the competition's like.' I curled up into a little ball on the couch. 'When Zack and I go out, women 4,000 years younger than me shove their phone numbers into his trouser pockets. Even when he introduces me as his girlfriend, their eyes don't flicker. "Well, let's meet up when she's not around," they say, "Well let's just go outside then, right now." Everywhere I go, I see older men with younger women. Nobody cares. It's okay for *them* . . . But the glares I get strolling down the street with Zachary on my arm! The whisperings in restaurants! The pressure on me to be equally as glamorous. I mustn't get fat. Mustn't slob around in old clothes. Mustn't forget to trim my split ends or push back my cuticles or . . .'

'Get a grip, doll,' counselled Anouska, between mouthfuls of chicken tikka. 'There are lots of older women who are still attractive. There's Goldie Hawn and that woman who was in the *First Wives Club*, what's her name? Oh, hold on. That *was* Goldie Hawn . . . and then there was, um . . .'

'Goldie Hawn,' I moaned bleakly, nibbling guiltily on naan bread. 'I've started doing sums in my head. When *I* was having my first sexual encounter, *he* was teething. When *he's* ready for kids, will *I* still have a workable womb? . . . I mean, what if Julian's right?' I started chewing holes in the upholstery. 'What if I am too old for all this? . . . I'll be senile, cavorting naked with my toyboy . . . but not able to remember *why* . . . Is it love? Or am I just flattered that somebody wants me . . . And terrified that nobody else will? You don't think Julian's having an affair, do you?' I asked Kate suddenly.

'What? So soon?' She didn't take her eyes off *News at Ten*. 'Not even amoebic disorders move that fast.' She sniffed suspiciously at an onion bhaji.

'Are you sure?'

'Yes, I'm sure. I can read that man like a book. Julian couldn't pick up anyone. Not without crib notes. Do you think we could have a conversation about something else once in a while?' There was a sharp, querulous edge to her voice. 'There is a big, wide world out there, you know.' Zapping off the television with the remote, she got up to go home. She'd been walking out on me a lot lately. I jumped as the door slammed. I felt as crushed as the poppadom in my hands.

'But, Annie, I definitely can't rage and relate for seven nights running and live to tell the tale. I mean, look at me. I'm a basket case. I also have grave misgivings about the joys of rap dancing. I like to drink coke, not do it. I no longer consider hitch-hiking a means of transport. Making love in the back of a car has lost its appeal. I don't want to use aphrodisiacal oils every night, either. They stain the sheets. And sometimes, just sometimes, I'd rather sleep. I'm convinced astrology and numerology are bullshit. That *must* make me old, goddamn it! At Zachary's concerts I even find it reassuring to see cops around!' Where had I heard *that* before?

Anouska promised me that I wasn't prehistoric, but a few days later when I forgot to attend the premiere of a live art event at the ICA (although, to me, sitting naked in a bowl of your own body fluids is not an expression of artistic integrity, it's a cry for help, goddamn it) I was convinced that I was hovering between menopause and senility.

'God. I'm losing my memory,' I grovelled, rushing in with Anouska as the last guests left. 'I've got all the first signs of . . . of . . . what's the name of that disease again?'

'Alzheimer's,' said Kate, coldly. She was often cold lately.

'See? . . . I couldn't even remember that? Apparently, after thirty, you lose up to 100,000 brain cells a day.'

'Riveting,' Kate drawled half-heartedly, mop in hand.

'It's all right for you,' I darted about the gallery, trying to help clean up but just getting underfoot. '*You've* graduated from university. You've got plenty to spare. *I* dropped out. I need all the brain cells I can get.'

'Why? The biggest bloody decision *you* ever have to make is whether to do it standing up or backwards.'

'Well, why the hell not? Another year and nobody will want my body. Not even medical science. My confidence is so low, Kate. I'll only be seen after dark. I won't even stand beside someone with a bright personality.'

'Which is why you're spending so much time with Anouska,' Kate said bluntly.

Anouska drunkenly swapped her mobile phone from one ear to the other and announced funereally, 'I'm getting a list from the Foreign Office of dangerous holiday places, where Darius and Norbett can die a hideous death and end up in an unmarked pauper's grave. In Bogota one person gets murdered every hour!'

'Why not just let him commit suicide by inhaling next to Zack's drummer after a gig?' I joked, trying to win back Kate's affections.

'How would you know, doll? It's not as though you've been to any gigs lately.'

Zachary agreed. 'You still doin' up that dive?' he grumbled on the phone from Edinburgh later that night.

'Yes. I'm afraid Michelangelo and Co. haven't finished painting the walls, yet.'

'Who?'

'Michelangelo and . . . I mean, they're taking so long

they may as well be painting the Sistine Chapel . . .' It was a crack Julian would have enjoyed. 'Oh, forget it.'

I'd expected to miss my old life – the house, the herb garden – but I hadn't expected to miss Julian quite so much. Little things. The verbal shorthand, the 'in' jokes, the pet names. An icy premonition shuddered through my body.

'Do yer reckon they might finish, like, this side of Armageddon . . . ?' Zack's voice crackled down the line. 'Ain't . . . *haven't* seen you for that long I'm about to put your picture on a goddamn milk carton.'

I laughed. What was I doing? I had a funny, sexy, famous Love God panting for me and I was whingeing and whining around the place feeling sorry for myself. It was birthday blues, that was all. There was one thing for sure, nothing ages you so much as a birthday. I was about to celebrate the third anniversary of my thirtieth.

Hanging up, I determined Zack and I would not lose our footing on Cloud Ten. Hell, we'd have to look *down* to see Cloud Ten. With renewed verve, I vowed to prove them all wrong. I glanced down at the flesh rising over my lacy stocking tops like cheese soufflés. Okay, I may have to spend all my waking hours reversing out of rooms so that he couldn't see the backs of my thighs and compare them to the last supermodel he'd dated, but Christ, it was worth it. I'd run away from my marriage to live on the edge, not at the gym. I was going to be an adventuress, with a daring capacity for lavish gratification. I would be a slave to my passion. I would be coquettish, charming, extravagant. I would be a vamp and a tramp. Nothing, but nothing, would stand between me and my pleasure. I'd left Julian to be a Steaming Jezebel and I was going to steam, goddamn it.

29

I'm Not Pleased To See You –
It's A Gun In My Pocket

Despite the fact that it was my birthday, the only party on offer was a coming-out party for a ghost.

When Zack's drummer, Skunk, was found dead in the toilet of his Dublin hotel room, I didn't immediately suspect Rotterman. Not even when Zack told me that Skunk had been insured by Rottweiler Records for £500,000 and that a replacement drummer had been hired before his death. But at the Brompton Cemetery, a long overdue alarm bell went off in my self-centred cranium.

As the paparazzi swarmed like ferrets in a septic tank to get the best positions graveside, Rotterman couldn't disguise his thrill. 'What a publicity stunt!'

'Rotterman, a boy's dead!' I reminded him in disgust. 'I doubt it was a career move.'

'Yeah, but think of the record sales!' Rotterman was

always encouraging Zack to get caught in an act of auto-eroticism or survive an assassination attempt from some right-wing extremist. As far as he was concerned, it was a rock star's duty to expire weirdly. He skulked off behind a headstone to huddle in menacing collusion with 'an associate' who'd jetted in that morning from New York. Catching a glimpse of a handgun in the waist band of the associate's trousers, all the idle threats Zack's agent had made to me over the months suddenly became more ominous and Julian's warning less fanciful.

Funerals of rock stars attract celebrities like flies to a dropped chop. As the coffin was lowered into the earth, paunchy, grey-templed record executives in lemon cashmere and aftershave strong enough to, well, wake the dead, cut record deals. High-heeled 'mourners', bitching about who got to go to the wake – 'I knew him better than *she* did' – made dates with the surviving band members.

After the funeral the simulated grief continued at our house off Abbey Road. Record bigwigs (compensating for physical inadequacies by wearing bulging money belts at groin level – the male version of the Wonderbra), and bohemian band members, sporting the 'I'm too Creative to Shave' look (yet, curiously, their stubble stayed at exactly the same length all year round) swapped Skunk anecdotes as tasteless as the finger food – it was death by vol-au-vent.

When I located Zachary in the newly renovated kitchen, the two Armani suits were waving another contract under his nose.

'Zachary!' I exclaimed, in a voice to rattle china. 'Don't sign that! Not unless you want to find yourself having to flee to some remote Argentinian fishing village at short notice!'

Zachary frogmarched me into a secluded part of the garden. 'Quit motherin' me, would ja,' he ordered, his diction deteriorating.

'I am not mothering you although, now you mention it – you're grounded for three weeks,' I said, feebly.

He smiled tightly. 'You know I'm splittin' for Budapest in an hour.' He tugged me down on to the lawn 'An' you should be comin' with me.'

'Um . . . I don't think so. Knowing Rotterman he'll have you booked on to the sort of airline where the cargo door has a habit of opening at unexpected times, ensuring that the passengers land slightly ahead of their aircraft.'

'Yeah? The only time in yer life that yer don't wanna be informed that a man's *goin' down*.' Although his hand was under my bra, I detected a note of weariness in the innuendo. 'Yer should come, Beck . . . I mean, we're like growin' apart in little ways, girl.'

'I know. You sleep when I'm awake. You're awake when I'm asleep. Your brothel bill . . .' He laughed, but half-heartedly, and stopped caressing my breasts. 'We don't talk any more, either,' I added, stroking his face. For once, body language would not be eloquent enough.

'You're right. I don't talk to you enough . . . See you later, babe. Gotta go pack.'

'Oh. Typical. You can't even talk about not talking enough.'

'Then come on with me! Yer s'posed to be my woman.'

'If I'm that important to you, then stay. I mean it, Zack. I don't think you should go. Listen to me. You know the company collects on the insurance money. When we were in Bristol I saw Rotterman giving heroin to Skunk.'

I waited for his nuclear reaction. But Zack merely lit a roll your own and dragged on it indolently.

'What's wrong with you? I'm more upset about Rotty giving that poor kid drugs and then him *overdosing shortly afterwards* than *you* are – and *I* didn't even know him.'

'I'm upset, okay.' His eyes flashed angrily. 'I just don't choose to show it.'

'I'll never understand men. You won't ring your mothers, you don't cry at *Sleepless in Seattle*, you can't say "I love you" to the woman who bears your children, you can't cry at a friend's funeral and yet you weep blood when the Rolling Stones revival tour is rained off.'

'Look, in the music business it ain't whether yer a

motherfucker. It's whether yer less of a motherfucker than some other motherfucker. The man's gonna get me heavy coin to pose for a Calvin Klein ad.'

'God! Do you really want to become a Spice Boy? You really want your success to be gauged by the number of puppy-fat midriffs you autograph? I don't want to live out our life in the tabloids – "the Zack and Becky Show! Join them on their Journey To The Centre Of Pop".' Zack smiled. 'Don't smile! I can't bear you smiling at home. Your smile is now owned by all those other people. It's copyrighted, for Christ's sake.'

'Aw, man. Quit bein' so damn English. Nuthin' fails like success, right? Rotty's got the Garden booked. Can you imagine what that means to me? I'm an artist, an' artists are driven.'

'Yes. In an air-conditioned limo. Julian says Rotterman lodged the obscenity complaint with Scotland Yard.'

'Julian? When were yer talkin' to him? An' what the fuck would he know?' He parted my thighs brutally.

'Zack, if you have any feelings for me at all, you'll leave Rotterman.'

'You forget. I'm a guy. I ain't got none!' he said sarcastically.

'Some day you'll go far, Zack . . . and I hope you stay there,' I said, and regretted it instantly.

'Yeah, well, see you around.' He left me lying there, skirt rucked up around my waist.

Inside the house, laughter and music percolated,

mocking my misery and Skunk's death. I rallied my flagging spirits. All Zack needed was more proof.

Across the living room, I saw Rotterman beckon Celestia. She fluttered towards him obediently. They indulged in a little whispered conversation before Celestia padded off to the upstairs bathroom. When I burst in after her she gazed at me with glazed eyes. There was an automatic air of dull perkiness about her. I looked at her beneath the harsh fluorescents; skinny child-legs encased in fishnet tights; red-veined, kohl-rimmed eyes; dirty hair hanging like limp linguine. Detecting a faint reek of vomit, I pushed past her and peered into the sink to see a little bit of regurgitated lettuce and carrot. God, I winced. If you were going to be bulimic, you'd think you'd eat a chocolate pudding first. To be throwing up even this meagre amount seemed pitiful beyond words.

'Why do you do this to yourself?' I said quietly. 'You must get help.'

She looked at me blankly. It was silly asking her to get in touch with her inner child. She'd no doubt thrown her up already.

I would just have to confront Rotterman. He was nowhere in the throng. I checked each room before finally peering into the murky, submarine light of the garage.

Flicking on the faint overhead bulb, I discovered the hunched malevolent shape of the newly arrived 'associate' counting money into piles of fifty-pound notes on the bonnet of Zachary's new sports car.

'J'mind?' Rotty spat. 'We're havin' a meetin' here.'

'Really? What's the agenda? The advantages of moving to Italy where crime really pays; the hours are good and all the judges are dead . . . ?'

'Actually, it's good that yer here.' Balancing a plate of hors d'oeuvres, Rotterman reclined across the bonnet like a bloated lizard. 'There's somethin' I wanted to tell yer.'

'Let me guess. Your mother drank during pregnancy?' I stared into a volcanic pore as he shoved his face into mine.

'I should just kill you for that.'

'If I had a corpse for every time you've said that . . .' Despite my bravado it *was* getting a little Quentin Tarantino around here. 'Now get out of my house,' I bluffed. I opened the garage door. Light flooded in. Rotterman's sleek limousine was slowly sharking up and down the street. 'There's a limo leaving in two minutes,' I said. 'Be under it . . . Otherwise, I bet Zachary would be interested in this little "meeting" of yours.'

'Ha!' Rotterman gloated. 'Now that Zack's finally signed his freakin' contact ya can't touch me, ya little shit weasel. I own him!'

'He signed?' My mouth dropped open.

'Jest now, on the way to the airport.' The carnivorous agent bit smugly into a priapic sausage.

'He wouldn't do that, not without consulting me.'

Rotterman flaunted a pile of paper in my face. 'Read 'em and weep.'

Round three to Attila the Agent.

Zack had put me in a hairy situation. Hell. This situation needed depilation. And when it came to depilation, there was only one person to turn to . . .

30

I Waxed My Bikini Line For *This*?

I am as fond of beauty spas as I am of being flayed alive with barbed wire. But Anouska was going to Champneys for a few days to recover from the news of Darius's near-death experience ('I'm so sorry.' 'Me too,' she'd sobbed. 'He *lived*. How could anyone survive Srebrenica?') and the loyal, long-suffering Kate had given me a few days off to mourn for the drummer. I didn't tell her I'd booked in for a boob and lube job.

Champneys is a luxurious health farm full to bursting with elephantine Saudi princesses bobbing about in the indoor pool, detoxing soap stars and a depressingly large number of newly divorced matrons getting in shape before heading back out into the Marriage Market.

After the customary bale of hay for lunch, we were

pounced upon by broad-shouldered, Amazonian therapists, brandishing colonic irrigation nozzles. Opting for something less Gothic, I was counselled to apply aluminium oxide to my neck through a disposable syringe and advised to have an urgent consultation on cosmetic enhancement. ('What? Like leg lengthening? My main problem is that I'm 5' 3".') I was also instructed to inject purified botulism to inhibit muscle movement and so stop me from frowning. 'I'm frowning because I can't believe what a moron you'd have to be to do that.'

An hour later a micro-current facial toning machine had me down to about one double chin. Add a marine algae skin peel and my face would soon be too small for my hair. I was saved further shrinkage by the apparition of a seaweed-wrapped Anouska, with one half-tweezed eyebrow, bursting into my therapy room.

I levered myself up on to one elbow. 'What's the matter?'

'I was just having my eyebrows arched . . .'

'Why bother, Annie? You're posh. They arched at birth.'

'. . . when Julian walked by.'

I sat bolt upright. '*Julian?*' Here? He hates exercise. Nearly as much as he hates wealthy, pampered people.'

'And he's not alone. He's booked into a double room. With *his wife*.'

I lurched off the treatment table, grabbed a robe and

staggered after her, somewhat burdened by the discovery that two tubs of avocado face-rehydration mud weigh more than I do.

When I barged into room 32 on the east wing, the first words out of my mouth were 'What the *hell* do you think you're doing?' Although seeing my best friend's legs wrapped around my husband's ears like the ends of a stethoscope should have given me a vague indication.

Kate and Julian un-suctioned their faces from each other's groins and catapulted off the bed.

'What the fuck are you doing?' I screamed at Julian. 'You loathe Kate.'

'Um ... would you believe, airing our differences ...?' He shrugged on a fluffy white gown.

The shock was physical as well as mental. I felt the pain of it jackknife through my body.

Kate's eyes scurried like mice back and forth across the carpet. She groped for her spectacles.

'Do you want to have your last words now, or save it for your epitaph?' I lunged at her, but Julian restrained me.

'If she disappears without trace, people will notice,' he said calmly. 'Particularly me.'

'Well then you'd better get her into some kind of MI5 Relocation Programme for Adulterous Best Friends, and soon. *How could you?*' I roared at her. There are some things a Feminist should never do. And not sleeping with your best friend's husband is about 100 of them. Besides which, you hate each other. You always have!'

'Platonic friendship,' said Julian, struggling to keep hold of me as I squirmed furiously. 'It's the gun you didn't realize was loaded.'

'Anyway, it's *your* fault,' Kate whimpered, shrouding herself in a blanket. '*You're* the one who made me go and see Julian on your behalf. And, well, then I got to know him better and . . .' she faltered.

'You told me you could "read him like a book". But I didn't expect you to thumb the goddamn pages! And what the hell's that on your tits?'

'What?' She glanced down. 'Oh. Nipple rouge,' she said too shell-shocked to sham.

'Nipple rouge!' I reeled back in astonishment. 'You didn't even wear a *bra* until last week.' I followed the seam of her stocking to its erotic conclusion in a pair of shimmeringly shiny patent-leather 'follow-me-home-and-fuck-me's'. 'I thought you said high heels dehumanized women?' Breaking free of Julian's grasp, I rummaged through the tangled sheets looking for other signs of Kate's hypocrisy.

She scurried up the bed away from me. 'It can be a sign of female empowerment too,' she tentatively rallied.

Finding the His and Her leopardskin lederhosen beneath the pillows, I uttered the kind of long, loud groan which in these surroundings would have been instantly mistaken for a post-enema high. Passing therapists would have been giving each other smug congratulatory beams. 'Lederhosen! I told you about the lederhosen! You . . . My God. You've just pretended to be my friend in order to glean that sort of inside information so you could steal my husband. No. No. This is *not* in the Best-Friend Charter.' I lunged at her again. 'This is a breach of the "Besties" Code. This is Best-Friend Divorce!!'

'Ah . . . The D word,' Julian twisted one arm up behind my back and spun me around to face him. 'You may have forgotten, but we are about to divorce. At *your* instigation.' The robe I'd flung on in the therapy room gaped open. Julian glanced at my naked form without a flicker of interest. I'm not kidding. The guy mentally *dressed* me. 'Kate and I are not doing anything wrong. Nothing at all. That's *your* department. Now kindly get out of our room or I'll call security and have you removed.'

'Removed? What am I? A melanoma?' I lashed out at Kate again. 'I'm still his wife, goddamn it.' Kate howled as my foot made contact with her shin; her *shaved* shin. 'You've shaved your legs?! I don't bloody believe it!'

'Get out.' There was a steeliness in Julian's blue eyes that I'd never seen outside the courtroom. 'Or I'll have you arrested for unlawful wounding and affray.' He placed a protective arm around Kate who'd un-characteristically retreated.

'I'm sorry I didn't tell you, Becky, but I knew you'd

go ballistic. The thing is, Jules was so vulnerable, thanks to the way you'd treated him, and ... well, things just escalated. We didn't mean to fall in . . .' she pulled up short.

'A clot of dread rose in my throat. 'Love? You and Julian? Oh excuse me while I wipe these tears of laughter out of my eyes.'

'It's true,' said Julian calmly. 'Kate is everything you're not. She's reliable, unselfish, honest . . .'

'Honest! Huh! I thought you were being kind, giving me all that time off, but you just wanted to get me out of the way! Exactly when did this, this . . .' I didn't know what to call it. 'How long?' I demanded.

'New Year's Eve, actually,' Julian said in measured, even tones.

'*New Year's Eve?*' Take knife. Plunge into heart. Twist. The streamers, the silk pyjamas, Kate's party refusal. A frightened, disbelieving laugh heaved out of my chest. Oh, this was a Kodak moment if ever there was one.

'Look on the positive side,' Kate said appeasingly. 'Finally it's *me* doing something irresponsible and completely bloody insane.'

I caught sight of my reflection in the hotel mirror. I'd forgotten about the algae mask. My face was bright Martian green, my skull encased in a Mrs Norman Bates hairnet. Globs of avocado neck wrap were sliding dismally down on to my chest. 'But ... but I thought you loved *me*?'

'It'll be hell surviving without you, Rebecca.' Julian jostled me towards the door. 'But let me give it a go.'

'Becky . . .' Kate scrambled for her vest. 'We can get past this, mate, we can. *You're* the one who told me to get a man . . .'

'Sure, I wanted you to get laid. *But not by my own husband!*'

'I'm not yours. You sent me back, remember? Let's spend some time together really soon . . .' Julian continued mercilessly. 'Have a nice century.' And with that he shoved me unceremoniously out the door, slamming it in my face.

'Let me go order you a colonic irrigation, Kate, *with cement*,' I screeched, pounding my fists on the door.

At the approach of two evangelistic therapists with that 'aggressive behaviour indicates you need a good purging' look in their eyes, I followed Anouska, who'd been hovering helplessly in the doorway to pilot me into the dining room. 'Look on the bright side,' she said. 'Brilliant Karma points.'

In a daze I sat down amongst the honed and toned healthy people. Their high-tech, all-in-one tracksuits and complicated air-cushioned training shoes with self-cleaning tread patterns gave them the look of Captain Kirk's crew. My algae-green face pack made me the alien on Planet Betrayal. With Kate the Klingon on my starboard bow.

This was *definitely* the downside of love affairs. I'd been so busy being duplicitous that I'd failed to notice my husband cheating on me! I failed to notice my best friend cheating on me too. Kate's treachery, utterly at odds with my deepest expectations, was cataclysmic. Girlfriends are supposed to get you through the tough times, not contribute to them. God. My best friend had run away with my husband – and I missed her awfully already.

Anouska, in an effort to distract me, rabbited on about how, from now on, she was only booking Darius on dodgy airlines – anything Colombian to Honduras and absolutely *any*where mountains ring the runway – 'Terminals must be so-called for a reason, right, doll?' I nibbled on a salad valued at a tenner per leaf and absorbed the full impact of what I'd lost. It hit me like a body blow. Kate and Julian! Oh, lust had found a new sewerage outlet. I'd sent her to provide comfort and she'd promptly melted him in the warmth of her sympathy. It was like buying someone a lottery ticket as a present, only for it to win.

With a sickening jolt, I realized that I wanted my husband back. I didn't know what had got into me! Yes, I did. Ten throbbing inches. But I was now living with the fixtures of an outgrown fantasy. My heart contracted. *I still loved Julian*. I'd made the terrible mistake of looking at our marriage through the fog of habit – only to find myself now missing his hypochondria, his opera addiction, his relatives, the way he sucked on the end of his pen, the way he never ate his crusts. I even missed his vocabulary, for Christ's sake.

But it was useless. Romantically, I'd vanished from his emotional radar.

But red-eyed remorse was not enough to get him back. I would have to try much harder than that.

Calling for double cream for my coffee and slathering butter on to a bread roll with a sacrilegious fervour that caused audible gasps of dismay from the dieting diners, I vowed to win him back, fair and square . . . even if I had to cheat to do so.

Part Three
The Divorce

31

An Impediment Of Reach

Life is full of frustrating and infuriating things. Treading in a puddle in the aeroplane toilet in absorbent airline socks and realizing that it's *not your own*; bumping into a bloke you've got the hots for in the waiting room of the Pox Doctor's Clinic ... But finding the man you love in the arms and legs of your best friend had to top the Devastation-ometer.

I was tortured by images of them making love, searing images of legs and lips entwined. Shadowing him seemed the only way I could cauterize such festering emotions. And so, with Zack away on his European tour, I dedicated myself to stalking.

Huddling into Zack's black leather jacket in the shadows beneath Julian's office, or opposite his favourite restaurants, or outside the gates of Pentonville Prison while he visited clients, I tried to ignore Care-In-the-Community types talking to their fish and chips, whilst reassuring myself that I had not turned into a bunny boiler.

'Got any bunnies, doll?' Anouska asked pointedly as I directed her to drive, headlamps off, down Julian's street, so I could train binoculars on my old bedroom window. 'This is OTT, doll ... And I want you to appreciate that this comment is from a woman who sent her husband for a holiday to Kosovo.'

'This is *not* over the top,' I seethed, hauling on a balaclava. 'Just curious ... Creeping into the garden and pressing a glass up against their window, now *that's* going to be OTT.'

With my ear pressed to the cold base of a glass tumbler, I could hear them laughing but their words were lost in the television hiss. Detecting movement through the wooden slats of the bedroom blind, I shinnied up the tree in the front garden in time to see the Venetian blind suddenly coagulate.

For the first few weeks, I soothed myself that Kate would soon become dismayed with Julian's workaholic tendencies. But then, *he stopped working*. I watched in horrified amazement as he set about cramming a decade's worth of social occasions into one season. Labour Party galas, a Salman Rushdie book launch, fund-raisers for One World Action, opening nights at ENO, Glyndebourne excursions, an informal dinner at Chequers; same outings, same seats at Wimbledon, same friends. All through June and July I observed Kate stepping into my old life as if it were a pair of warm slippers I'd lovingly worn in for her. I fantasized about revenge.

First I spread a rumour around our Feminist-inclined work-place that Kate was having liposuction and nipple enlargement surgery. Next I put Nair hair-removal cream on the panty liners in her desk drawer. Okay, it was a tacky, petty, little revenge. But hey, it's a tacky, petty, little world.

When Julian refused to answer any of my calls, I realized that I needed to pull out all the wooing stops. I started off with Killer Bouquets.

'What kind of flowers do you suggest for the husband you dumped and now want back again?'

In response to my floral tributes, I wasn't so much as inundated with a single postcard. This only served to make him more desirable and to make me more determined. I *bombarded* him with bouquets. I opened an account with the florist. She took to sighing when I rang and saying, 'Okay. How sorry are you *this* time?'

When he had a newsworthy case, I pretended to be a journalist so that I could 'interview' him.

When Julian took on a client who was clairvoyant, I bribed her to mention my name.

I tried to apply mental calamine to my burning jealousy by soothing myself with the notion that Julian and Kate would soon become disenchanted with each other's sartorial solecisms . . . But more and more often

I found myself trailing them to Harvey Nichols, Versace, Armani. It was as if they'd both been put on probation by the fashion police. Those Peruvian jumpers that not even Peruvians would wear were a thing of the past. Kate, who'd always been lamb dressed as mutton, was suddenly mutton dressed as fox.

It was six weeks before I saw the whole transformation. Kate, who hadn't had a holiday since the Bronze Age, suddenly took off, leaving me as Acting Head of Everything. When she finally reappeared in the office, I didn't recognize her. Her svelte bottom wiggled when she walked. Her cleavage peeka-booed above a push-up bra. Even the glittering lenses of her famous bug spectacles were gone, replaced by eye-colour-enhancing contact lenses, you know, to make her look less intelligent. To complete the dumbing-down exercise she was reading – and even laughing at – *Bridget Jones's Diary*.

I gasped like a deflating Lilo. 'Oh you are so transparent, Kate.'

'No. Just thin,' she rejoindered.

'I thought you said that your weight was a terrorist act against fascist stereotyping?' I exploded.

Before she could retort, Julian appeared behind her. My heart catapulted into my throat. He'd grown his hair out into Byronic, collar-length curls which made him look ten years younger. Until now, all Julian had required of his skin was that it grew hair and, when shaved, stopped bleeding before he got to the office. But his face now sported a moisturized, sunbed glow. Also missing were the traditional pleat-fronted pin-stripes and Jermyn Street double-cuff shirts. My jaw dropped as I took in the details of his Gucci leather suit, black Armani T-shirt and Patrick Cox shoes which looked as though they'd been made from the hides of hand-reared steers and stitched by brain surgeons.

When he saw me his smile congealed on his lips. The wads of his jaw muscle thickened. 'Hello.' His mellifluous voice took on the impersonal tone of a speak-your-weight bathroom scale.

'Hi!' I squealed. I was twitching with espresso, having been up all night stalking. As Kate and Julian had become healthier and happier, my late-night vigils and full working days had left me looking more and more haggard. How quickly I had gone from dumper to dumpette. Rejection was hanging off me like the stink of a dead animal.

'It's good to see you,' Julian said with the blandness of a popular, easily spreadable luncheon substance.

Kate kissed him territorially. They kissed the whole bloody time they were at the ICA.

'You know, new lovers really should have a minimum isolation period of say, six months so as not to nauseate absolutely everyone they meet,' I said snidely. *Where'd I heard that before?*

When Kate went into the toilets, I followed her,

kicking the door closed behind me with my battered regulation stalker's Doc Martens. 'In the parlance of trained marriage-guidance counsellors – 'You *slut*! You *whore*! You double-crossing *Jezebel*!!'

' "Whore" . . . that's the definition of a woman who gets the bloke *you* want, right?' Kate tried to push past me, but I wedged myself into the door frame to block her way.

'I thought you said romance was a trick mother nature plays on us? A lie?' Ignoring me, Kate turned to the mirror to re-scrunch her newly streaked, styled and root-lifted locks. 'I thought a woman needs a man like a cow needs an abattoir?'

'But Julian is not just *any man*.'

'No. He's my man.'

'Becky, make like a turtle and pull your head in.' She squared her fuck-off shoulder pads. 'Julian doesn't want to see you ever again – not without an electrified fence and a German police dog present. He doesn't love you any more.'

The two worst things that can ever be said to a woman are 1) 'Yoo-hoo – hey, listen to that echo!' in the middle of oral sex. And 2) I don't love you any more.

I sank into a crumpled position on the cold, white tiles. Was she lying? She had to be lying. But what could I do? I kept telling Julian that he loved me, but he wouldn't believe me! Having tried all the usual getting-the-love-of-your-life-back techniques – begging, grovelling, blackmail threats, lying down on the road in front of his car – I'd just have to resort to more drastic measures. I started by stepping up my surveillance. I hired a van, and staked out Julian's house morning, noon and night. I never left my post, not even when I had chair-lock and could only walk like a crab – knees bent, hands frozen at dashboard level.

When I could no longer afford the van, I got an accomplice. Anouska, an insomniac due to Darius's snoring ('sleeping out loud', she called it) fitted the bill nicely. She swung her Mercedes into a disabled-parking spot in Connaught Road and cut the engine.

'Annie, you can't park here!'

She levelled me with a dubious stare. 'Call me old-fashioned, but we're *stalking*. We're breaking about 400 rules *for which we could be put in prison* and you're worried about a parking ticket?'

'Oh my God,' I shrieked, focusing the binoculars. 'He's given her a whole shelf in the bathroom!'

'A whole shelf? Jesus, doll, that *is* serious.' Anouska commandeered the field glasses.

'Bloody hell. I think she's moving in.' I unclicked my seatbelt. 'I'm going to go in for a closer look.'

'Oh no, you're not. This past-husband regression's gone far enough, Becky.' Anouska pressed down on the automatic door locks. 'You have got to get on with your life.'

I rested my head wearily on the dashboard. I'd tried, truly I had. But I was like a big piece of blotting paper, craving moisture. Without him, the world seemed to have taken on the exhausted sepia of an old photograph.

Things to do today. 1) Stop thinking of Julian. 2) Buy Julian an expensive present. 3) Break into house to see if best friend is moving in with husband.

'I can't, Annie. I've tried.'

'There is a good side to this, you know, doll.'

'There is?'

'If they do move in together it'll mean a considerable saving on Chrissy cards.'

With Anouska in recalcitrant tow, I scurried across to the dank alleyway that runs beside my old house. For the next hour we haunted those windswept shadows, warding off horny dogs and carnivorous bugs.

'I'm cold,' Anouska whinged.

'Sshhh.'

'Let's go.'

'No.'

'Becky, there's a dog romancing my leg!' she said delicately.

I gazed at the signature of the city against the horizon, written in landmarks of skyscrapers and monuments – places I'd been to, with him – and gnawed the inside of my cheek so as not to cry.

When Julian and Kate finally left – strolling arm in arm, I noted painfully – and the summer light had dwindled sufficiently, I prised open the laundry window which had the dud lock.

'Becky! When you said "closer look", I didn't realize you meant breaking in!!' Anouska gasped. 'I am *so* out of here! . . . You should know better, doll.'

I was half squeezed through the window when I heard my accomplice floor the accelerator and skid, burning rubber, down the street. Scrambling for purchase, I grazed my shin and, cussing loudly, pondered the one true lesson I had learnt of late – that no woman is ever old enough to know better.

32

Remembrance Of Flings Past

Home is definitely where the heartache is. The house smelt of freshly ground coffee and leather-bound books. It was an olfactory ambush which brought on a haemorrhage of nostalgia.

After poking through kitchen utensils (the espresso machine and pasta maker were *definitely* hers) and bedroom cupboards (she'd colonized one whole drawer for underwear – not a good sign), I made the mistake of burying my face in Julian's dressing gown. The aroma of him sparked a throb of loss and longing. In my mind's eye I could see him coiled in sleep, sheets twisted and kicked aside, his hair pressed by the pillow into a crazy coiffure: a coronet fit for a king. And there, next to him, the empty pillow where my head should be; now bearing the indentation of my best friend's cranium.

I was so lost in regrets that I didn't hear their key in the lock. When the creak of the stairs jerked me from my sentimental reverie, I punched out the light and, dextrous as Kate's cat (whose bowl had taken up smelly residency on the window sill) shot beneath the brass bed.

When the light flickered on, my whole body jumped, causing me to snag my hair on the bed-springs. For a few moments there was a disquieting silence. I felt sure I'd been rumbled. My pulse was beating loud enough to be coming over a PA system. Lying there in the dust balls and rank Kleenex, trying not to sneeze, my eyes lit upon items given up as missing in action – one satin slipper, *Kobbe's Opera Guide*, a copy of *Thinner Thighs in Thirty Days*.

I strained to decipher the audial hieroglyphics beyond the valance ... And then the noises began to take nauseating shape.

Is there anything worse than listening to other people having sex? To the wet gasping sounds of harpooned whales surfacing simultaneously? Especially when each bounce of the bed is pulling your hair out by the roots. When I realized what was happening above, I made that involuntary 'Ugh' noise, the sort of air exhalation you make when you witness a car accident.

The harpooned whale noises beached themselves disconcertingly.

'Did you hear something?' Kate's Aussie drawl drifted down to me.

Blood tattooed a terrified rhythm in my temples.

'No,' mumbled Julian, a mumble that quickly turned into a long, low, luxurious moan.

The thought of Kate as an erotic enchantress filled me with equal amounts of wonder and despair. How could Julian be in a state of sexual thrall to *her*? What was left of my mind boggled. I put my fingers in my ears but the sounds they made during orgasm reached ten on the Richter scale. At first I was appalled. *God! Did they have to have sex so loudly?* Then distressed. *God! Was he that loud with me?*

As if listening to the act hadn't been humiliating enough, I now had to endure the encore.

'Sweet lips.'

Sweet lips. God, I think I'm going to throw up.

'That was great,' Julian purred.

'You mean *you* were.'

Yep. Throwing up time.

'Really? Becky thought I was too passive in bed. "It's lonely on the top", she always said.'

Verballed! And by my own husband! I bit my hand so I wouldn't call out.

'Yeah. She's hard to please all right. She was always whingeing. About you, about the wedding, about marriage, about not wanting children . . .'

. . . About what a bitch my best friend turned out to be!

'I feel so comfortable with you, Kate. I was thinking,

346

we should go on holiday together. Somewhere romantic. The Seychelles, Mauritius, Virgin Gorda . . .'

The Seychelles, Mauritius, Virgin Gorda . . . ?! What? No Death Row? No famines? No tsetse flies?

'I've worked so hard all my life, Kate, and for what? I've paid my dues. I want to enjoy myself. I've carried the weight of the world on my shoulders and now, well, it's time to get a porter.'

A porter? Oh, where'd I heard that before?

'And when we get back, well, I was thinking. Why don't you move in?'

Move in? I knew it. Oh God, Oh God. They were going to move in together. My ribcage contracted around my lungs.

'Move in together? . . . Cripes. I hadn't even thought about it.'

Yeah, right. Which is why you've accidentally left your espresso machine in the kitchen. Why your underpants are breeding in the drawer. Why your cat's bowl is in my bloody bedroom. Why you're pretending to be a nice person.

'Maybe even get married . . . Married men are mentally healthier and have less heart disease than single men. I'm at that stage in life where I need to be married.'

Married? I nearly bit through my wedding finger.

'I mean, neither of us is getting any younger,' Julian added. 'I definitely want children. If I wait much longer we'll be in nappies together!'

Children?! . . . That made two fingers for urgent digital replacement surgery.

'Maybe yours could be the next ovary off the rank, Katie-pie?'

'Well, to tell the truth, Julie-poolie, I have, of late, been hearing the old fallopian tubes calling . . .'

Katie-pie? Julie-poolie? This time I 'ughed' loudly enough to attract Kate's cat. It slunk beneath the bed and appraised me with a superior eye. I dislike the company of cats. And not just because of my allergy. I felt the tingle of dread in my nose. The need to sneeze animated the hairs on the back of my neck. My eyes watered in an effort to control it. I sniffed. I snuffled. I prayed. With cool malevolence the cat sashayed forward and flicked its tail in my face.

When I recovered from my nasal detonation, it was to see two heads, inverted, peering at my contorted form cloistered beneath their bed. It was now Kate's turn to make the car-accident noise. Julian, white with anger, hauled me out by one denimed leg, leaving half my scalp behind.

'Jesus Christ, Rebecca! What the *hell* are you trying to do? You could have given me a heart attack!'

'Me too,' chorused Kate, saronging herself in a sheet.

'Oh God. Maybe you two *are* meant to be together. Two hypochondriacs. The two of you should get married and just move into a hospital.' I sneezed and coughed with abandon, as I brushed dust balls off my clothes and out of what was left of my hair.

'What in God's name do you think you're doing?'

Julian yanked me on to my feet. I stared at his naked body in awe. One of the things I hate about men is that depression makes them eat less. He's lost at least two stone since I'd last seen him in the flesh. And I liked what I saw.

'Look, I had to break in. Kate, well, she's turning you against me!' I frantically groped for an excuse. 'You've just heard the sort of things she says about me behind my back. I need to be in front of her at all times.'

Julian pressed the palm of his hand against my forehead. 'This is psychotic. You need help. Why are you hounding me like this?'

'Well, the thing is . . .' I took a deep breath. 'I want you back, Julian.'

'But you were tired of me! That's what you said. "I'm tired of you".'

'Yeah, well, now I'm rested.'

Kate, rummaging for knickers in her underwear drawer, screeched indignantly. 'Shit a brick! You've been going through my things, haven't you?'

'I rifled the odd drawer, yes, but I didn't read that diary entry on butt-fucking, so there's no need to feel awkward.'

'That's it. I'm calling the police,' Julian threatened. 'I'll get a restraining order!'

But I'd had enough. Though up against the wall, literally, the window was open. I Geronimo-ed out of it. Scrabbling at branches and clutching at drainpipes I realized that love, if done right, can definitely kill you. I managed the descent with only serious-to-middling injuries, watched, with veiled amusement, by Kate's wretched feline, poised agilely on the sill. Exit, pursued by a cat.

33

Nocturnal Omission

Pop lyricists have been curiously silent on the joys of being the girlfriend of a famous rock star. Staggering home to find Zack's house being ransacked room by room by an infestation of police explained why really.

A Detective met me at the door. 'Are you Miss Steele?'

'Yes.'

'Is this yours?' he boomed, holding up my handbag. The man was irrepressibly loud. His voice was loud, his tie was loud – even his silences.

I nodded.

'Then I'm arresting you on suspicion of possession of a classified drug.'

'What? Period painkillers? That's the hardest drug *I* do.'

'You have the right to remain silent. You do not have

to say anything, but anything you do say may be taken . . .'

'Hello? I don't even drink coffee after seven p.m.'

'. . . down. It may harm your defence if you fail to mention when questioned . . .'

My first fevered thought was that the drugs were Zachary's. My second thought was to wonder exactly how tall Zack was *so I could order his body bag*. How could he have done this to me?

'. . . anything you later rely on in your defence. Please accompany me to the station.' The boa-constrictor grip on my arm kind of decided me. Besides, I was innocent. What did I have to worry about?

A terrifying interview with an officious custody sergeant at Marylebone Police Station, one strip-search, sixteen Styrofoam cups of cold coffee, three panicked calls to Zack in Amsterdam, a six-hour stay in a cell with the ambience of a gas chamber and a charge of possessing fifteen grammes of cocaine and I was not as enchanted by the British legal system as I'd previously imagined.

'For the millionth time, I don't do drugs,' I insisted in the interview room. Although, after *this* experience, I was certainly going to need some.

The Detective smirked and folded his hirsute arms across his polyester-shirted chest. 'Why don't you plead innocent, lassie, and give us all a good laugh?' He flicked on the tape-recorder for the inquisition.

'How did you know drugs were even *in* my bag?' I agitated. By now my blood pressure was reaching thermo-nuclear levels.

'Tip-off. From a concerned citizen,' the detective thundered in his ten-pack-a-day voice.

'Oh my God.' My stomach soured. 'Am I going to go to *prison*?'

By some staggering oversight on behalf of legal aid, I'd actually been assigned a sober duty solicitor. She explained that, as it was a first-time offence, and as the amount of cocaine was only on the cusp of intent to supply, I might just get off with a fine. The only real punishment would be that imposed by the American Government. 'Visas aren't granted to anyone who's been arrested, charged or convicted on a drugs charge,' she clarified.

My twitchy apprehension suddenly crystallized into clear, cold understanding. 'Let me guess, Detective. The "concerned citizen" . . . ? Was it a man with an American accent?' I don't know why I was surprised. It was your standard Dastardly Villain behaviour. Honestly, Zack's agent was like some creature from a horror flick who just won't die.

I was in the process of being granted police bail when Zack barged into the station, straight from Heathrow. I hadn't seen him for two months. He threw his arms around me protectively and pressed his mouth to mine, his skin warm as sun-kissed aubergine.

'Now do you believe me ... about Rotterman?' I asked, as the custody sergeant, informed me that I'd be advised of a court date, and handed back my possessions.

'That scumbag dropped the dime on you all right.'

'He did it so I can't go with you to America ... and for the publicity, no doubt. If only you hadn't signed that bloody recording contract!'

Zack signed resignedly. 'Do you know a good lawyer?' he asked facetiously.

The news that Zachary Phoenix Burne's girlfriend had been arrested on a drugs charge had made the evening papers, which meant that groupies now knew our address. We arrived home to the incessant cater-wauling of 'Zack! Zack! Zack!'

By this stage of my life not only did I know all of the deadly sins but I could personally demonstrate at least six of them. A police record for narcotics abuse would make it seven. But the icing on the angst pie was yet to come. We made it through the blizzard of paparazzi bulbs and up the front steps. Once inside, I had my heart set on some analgesic sex. After two months, cravings for my particular hard drug were insatiable. But when I started tearing at Zack's clothes with my teeth, he tenderly pushed me aside.

'Later. I need your advice first, Beck. On the album sleeve notes. I have to get them in tomorrow.' He began to read to me from his torturously scripted prose.

'Zack, it's only a CD blurb. It's not the Rosetta Stone.'

'I'm taking my career seriously now. You was ... *were*, right. From now on I'm gonna ... *going to* be a Serious Artist.' I found myself jeering inwardly at Zack's absurdities. What once entranced me, I now felt a great desire to mock. 'I've lined up an Amnesty gig and a Landmine benefit,' he boasted.

I buried my face in the kilim cushions. Oh great. Another selfless career-junkie. Another lover determined that on our evenings out together, I'd be the only one present with a full set of limbs.

I listened to Zack ring around to all the band members to rubbish Rotterman. When, with Born-Again certainty, he corrected the guitarist, 'It ain't "in-erestin'"', it's interesting,' I knew just how Doctor Frankenstein must have felt.

To make matters worse, he then offered me a glass of Puligny-Montrachet '88, proudly describing it as being 'capricious in its affability'. I watched in amazement as he blotted his lips with his napkin in the recommended fashion and placed his knife and fork in the internationally approved twenty past four. He then set about cleaning up, complete with a lecture on dishcloth hygiene. 'Will you stop fluffing pillows?' I begged him. But it wasn't until he took the batteries out of our vibrator to put in the television remote to watch *Newsnight* that I knew with grim certainty that I really had created a monster. What I'd created, in fact, with the white designer shirt cuffs, reuniting split infinitives and pretending not to like ethnic jokes, was another Julian. The old version. Great. Now I had Julian taking life too frivolously and Zack taking life too seriously. It made me miss his more monosyllabic days. I mean, here I was panting for some hot jungle sex while he preferred to ponder why the word 'mono-syllabic' has five syllables. Hell. The guy was conjugating *nouns*, for Christ's sake.

'Do we have to talk all the time?' I finally snapped. 'Couldn't we just have sex? . . . I mean, "words" are just those things we use to kill time until we fuck, remember?' It was something he'd once said to me.

But when we did finally make love that night, the images crowding my mind were of Julian. It was going to be difficult, I mused, for a guy with an LL B, a Ph.D. and a D.Phil. to get used to being wanted for his body and not his brain . . .

The light snapped on. 'You're thinking of somebody else, aren't you?' Zachary accused me.

Zachary's allegation and the lamp's interrogative spotlight wrenched me out of Julian-land. 'I'm not,' I dissembled. 'Don't be silly.' With the light banishing all furtive fantasies, I had sex as though under anaesthetic.

'Oh God, what have I done?' I silently addressed the ceiling. 'And how on earth will I undo it?'

It was time to draw the line . . . Pretty hard though when you've already stepped over them all.

34

Cross My Legs And Hope To Die

A 'hostage' is the term for a woman who invites guests into her own house. Is there anything worse than spending a night making strangers feel at home – which is precisely where you wish they bloody well were?

Despite this, Anouska was throwing a summer party. 'I've given up on dangerous destinations, by the way. I'm now concentrating on dangerous sports,' she'd thrilled down the phone when she rang to invite me. 'I've got Darius shooting rapids, wrestling piranhas and generally heading for an early death.' A 'sudden debt pay-off', she called it.

After lunch, I'd returned to my desk to find a scribbled telephone message from Anouska. 'PS. Party's fancy dress. Theme – Kitschy-Kitschy-Koo.' . . . Which is why, a few days later, I was sitting in the back of a minicab dressed as a garden gnome, a string of sausages on a pole draped over one shoulder.

Now the one thing that's worse than actually attending a fancy-dress party, is realizing that you're the only person who's fancily dressed. As the front door opened, I shuddered to a halt, my eyes desperately scanning the famous, glamorous throng. But no. All the other women were in little black cocktail dresses.

Anouska sprinted across the living room to my side. 'It's a *look*, doll, it's a *choice*.'

'But I got a message! From you! Saying it was fancy dress!'

'Revenge, dag-features,' purred Kate, materializing eerily at my side, 'for the panty liners.'

'Yeah, well, I hope you're wearing your bullet-proof bra, Kate, 'cause this is war!'

Anouska gestured toward the tanned and taut entourage of men hovering around her husband. 'If I had a sex change so I could go out with all those delicious men over there, would that make me gay?' she asked plaintively.

But Kate and I still had our invisible antlers locked. '*You're* the one who told me to get laid,' my ex-best friend rebuked. 'You did everything but coat me in vasso and heli-drop me, starkers, into a maximum security-prison for men! You told me to change. And I have. And what's more –' she flicked her hair coquettishly '– a whole new world is opening up to me.'

'Yeah ... Like Sharon Stone's legs.' I snagged my finger through her fishnet stockings. 'You know who you're turning into? The very sort of woman you've always loathed.'

But my train of spite was derailed by the appearance of Julian, bursting in from the garden through the French windows in a flurry of other guests caught in a sudden summer downpour. His hair, slicked wet from the rain, was brushed back, giving him the appearance of a Mafioso. This new, devilish air was enhanced by a fringe of five-day growth accessorising his top lip. He looked, I thought sadly, like a perfect stranger.

'You've got Julian growing a moustache?' Anouska commented redundantly.

'Why?' I said curtly to Kate. '*Now nobody will be able to tell you apart.*'

'Why don't you two just duel with pistols at dawn and get it over with?' suggested Anouska, so irritated that she rushed off to greet old, old friends – whom she'd never met before.

The party, much like the marriage, seemed to be operating in parallel universes. The couple's friends regarded each other with counterfeit enthusiasm. While Anouska's monied chums compared the springiness of their sprung ballrooms, Darius's friends were discussing nipple-chafing and penis-piercing.

Cast off into sartorial Siberia, I spent a fascinating evening watching a bowl of guacamole go black. I examined the art on the wall with a slight tilt to my head and an absorbed facial expression. Pretty soon my nerves were in a blender and switched on to Fine Chop. I crouched out of view behind the couch and tried not to cry.

'Dah-ling.' Darius stopped dead in his tracks at the sight of me and my wilted sausage string. 'Why don't you pop upstairs and put on something of Anouska's?'

'Um . . . As you've never seen her naked, you probably haven't noticed but your wife is actually a size "anorexic".'

Darius chortled. 'This is killing you, isn't it?' he chortled.

'Not quickly enough.'

'Borrow something of mine. I do have the odd frock, dah-ling. Well, what can I do?' he replied to my raised brow. 'I was born with the sort of legs that simply *demand* mesh stockings and high heels. Help yourself.'

'Thank you.' Inching my way towards the staircase, I made a mental note to tell Anouska not to kill him off. Darius really was much nicer gay than straight. I nearly made it to the first step, except for a Rolexed wrist tentacling out of the throng and suctioning on to my upper arm.

Nobody knows who invented marriage counsellors, but the Devil is the chief suspect. Simon, leading the 'I'm So Sorry I'm Not A Woman Brigade', was always on the look out for an oppressed female to whom he could offer his solidarity.

'I heard about the break and enter.' Simon tightened

his grip on my arm until I yelped in pain. 'You need physical pain to cauterize the emotional pain. It's symbolic. Remember the Sioux Indians? Hanging upside down with bear claws through their chests in order to make a request to the Gods?' He squeezed again. Tears were springing to my eyes. 'Now you can make a request to be free of emotional pain.'

'The only request I'd like to make is that you stop self-medicating.' I stomped on his toe, forcing him to pogo backwards.

By a curious combination of snow-ploughing and side-stepping, I ascended the stairs in my long pointy slippers. Once changed, I could slip past Julian into the night, with a shred of self-respect . . .

If ever I am a contestant on *Mastermind*, social humiliation will be my specialist subject. This was my only thought when I bumped smack bang into my Significant Ex, on the first-floor landing.

When Julian saw me, his scowl was on autopilot. The caviar spilt off the cracker in his hand and on to the white rug, a little congo line of black dots in search of a stave. We instantaneously launched into one of those sub-titled conversations between exes.

'Hi,' I said, 'How's my waffle-iron?' Which meant – *Oh God, I miss you.*

'Fine. How's my non-stick wok?' Which meant – *Please get the fuck out of my life.* He glanced at my costume and said 'That's a bold choice.' Which meant

– What the hell are you wearing? And How Could I Ever, Ever, Ever Have Married You?

'I'm sorry. About the other night,' I said, which meant – *Oh, oh, I love you, I love you, I love you. Please, please, please, take me back.*

'Look. I'm sure in time we can still be friends, okay?' Which meant – Y*ou are nothing but an inverted image on my retina, detected by light-sensitive cells. Consequently you exist only as a series of impulses and you will cease to exist when I close my eyes.*

He made to move past me. It was a now or never kind of a moment. And I now-ed. 'Julian.' In a clumsy attempt to clutch-start a reconciliation, I wrapped my fingers around the small, exquisite patch of exposed skin beneath the cuff of his shirt. 'Can't you ever forgive me?'

'Forgive? Well actually I wasn't planning to *speak* to you for, oh, *the rest of my life.*'

Remembering that I was probably not at my most alluring, I wrenched off the false beard. 'As they say in the marriage guidance business – you now have the whip hand, Julian.' Despite his air of weary nonchalance, one of his caramel-coloured eyebrows crept up his broad forehead. 'I was weak. I thought it was love. But it was only lust, after all. I'll never make the same mistake again. Promise . . . Cross my legs and hope to die.'

Julian gave a tetchy sigh. 'Rebecca, infidelity is not exactly where it's at, troth-wise, you know.'

I felt a hot pang of desire. My Prince Charming had got his swashbuckler back. 'You're so attractive when you're angry, Jules.'

'Well I must be *irresistible* now. Infidelity hurts deeply, Rebecca. Forever. And in ways that can't be rationalized away. You weren't just my "wife". You were my best friend. How do you think that made me feel?'

'I know I behaved abominably. But so do lots of other people,' I pleaded. 'Cheating on your spouse . . . it's so common, it's *un*original sin. I mean, you said that marriage brings into play the lowest impulses . . . But you also said it brings into play the highest aspirations. Like forgiveness . . .'

'But I don't like you any more.'

'That doesn't preclude loving me.'

'I did love you once,' he admitted, in a tone of jaded chagrin.

'Only once?' I smiled sheepishly.

'. . . But not now. Besides, I'm kind of in the middle of someone.' He prised my fingers from his arm and manoeuvred me out of his way. I held on to his belt with both hands and, in my felt boots, slalomed after him along the polished wooden floors.

'Okay, you don't love me. But who exactly is it you're not loving?' I stem-christied, forcing him to stop and face me. 'Certainly not the woman in front of you because you don't know this person.'

'Oh, *please*. Let me guess. You're a Born-Again

Human Being? . . . You're a Born-Again Human Being trapped in a gnome's body.' He looked me up and down reprovingly. 'I imagine those clothes have some kind of pharmaceutical explanation?'

'Kate told me it was fancy dress. I'm so embarrassed . . .'

'Really?' he scoffed. 'I thought you'd be numbed to shame by now.'

'Oh, Jules. I've changed. I have. I've grown up. I've got a Ph.D. in guilt. When it comes to remorse, we're talking encyclopaedic knowledge.'

'Abridged.'

'Well, we'll cross that abridgement when we come to it.'

When he smiled at me again, it was like opening up the windows of a locked-up house; light rushed into dark corners and the smell of rich earth filled my senses. At the sound of Kate's voice ascending I nudged him into the spare bedroom decorated in textbook Ye Olde English. The quilted, canopied four-poster was bathed in light from a pale, lopsided moon. The July air was warm as bathwater.

I closed the door behind me and darted a soft-focus glance in his direction. 'The truth is, I'm madly in love with a married man.'

'Really?'

'Yes. My husband.' I trembled in anticipation of his touch like some wan heroine from a Mills & Boon novel – except that I was emitting lust rays visible to the naked eye.

'That's downright kinky . . . and a shame,' he replied in a silky voice. 'Because I'm completely over you. I haven't given you a moment's thought for, oh, minutes at a time.'

His hand on my waist was warm and familiar. We melted into a romantic embrace worthy of the frilly décor.

'I have to tell you that my intentions are strictly dishonourable.' I ran my hands down the bony Braille of his spine and squeezed his buttocks. Gone were the customary buns-of-custard, replaced with mouth-wateringly taut musculature. 'I want to perform serious and wilful misconduct on your corpus delicti . . . An indictable offence, no? May I kiss you?'

'Objection.' He pulled me towards him. The best thing about body language is that it doesn't need any subtitles. Even for exes.

'Overruled,' I said, as we dissolved into a swirl of limbs and wet kisses; coiled and knitted together by longing. I think it's fairly safe to say that it was the first time Julian had ever made love with a garden gnome.

And so it was that I began an affair with my husband.

35

The Three Of Us Make
A Really Good Pair

From the moment I started cheating on my lover with
my husband, events in my life took on the speed and
danger and out-of-control quality that required runway foam.

All the clandestine thrill and general gusset-
marinating I'd once enjoyed with Zack, I now shared
with Julian. My once strait-laced spouse became a
heat-seeking moisture missile. He was no mouth and
all trousers.

When Zack accused me again of seeing someone, I
lied: po-faced, no fidgeting. 'Who the hell is it?' he
demanded. I must have hesitated a fraction too long,
or maybe he picked up on my nervousness – Nervous?
Hell. I was smoking *during* sex – because he added,
'Hey it isn't like I'm asking you the identity of
Watergate's Deep Throat.'

Gratifying Zack sexually (in between discussing the linguistic dangers of a dangling participle) was the only way to alleviate his doubts. Which is why I was soon twirling from partner to partner in a sexual cotillion which was burning holes in my soles and other parts of my anatomy.

Anouska, tweezing my eyebrows one night, casually informed me that Kate was eaten up with suspicion that Julian was having an affair.

'*What?*' I squeezed open one eye and looked up at her from my prone position upon a pillow in her lap.

'We were discussing Darius – he's just laughing in the face of death, doll. It's terrifying. He survived catapulting, hang-gliding and micro-lighting. Cave-diving, that's next. You're wedged in a damp, dark crevice . . .'

'Sounds like something he might enjoy,' I knocked the tweezers impatiently to one side. 'Could we cut to the chase here?'

'All right . . . All right . . . Anyway, then she told me she was convinced Julian had a woman on the side and did I have any clues.'

I made a split-second decision that telling Anouska would be bad. It would be like swimming after you've eaten. Under no circumstances would I breathe a word.

'It's me,' I dived right in. 'He's having an affair with me.'

'*You?* You mean . . . a *ménage à trois*. Why?'

I shrugged. 'Well, it gives me a chance to practise my French accent.' Anouska made a moue of disgust. 'It's great,' I elaborated glibly, slightly peeved by her disapproval. 'I now have two men around to fix fuses and change car tyres.'

'Yes, doll, and there's now twice as many men to be amused by your big bum.' Her upside-down face was a mask of censoriousness – it was as though I'd told her I was eating seal-pup sandwiches.

'Relax. We're not actually having sex all at the same time.'

'Well, why not? You'd save on sheets,' she snapped uncharacteristically.

'Why is the spectre of women having their cake and eating it so unbearable for those who aren't?' I said bitchily. 'And what do you mean by "big bum", exactly?'

She flopped my head out of her lap as though it were a rancid cabbage. 'It's just not very nice, Becky.'

'Oh, and where had being nice got women, huh?' I propped myself up on one elbow on Anouska's four-poster. 'Still no equal pay. Still doing all the housework . . . You should stop being so nice all the time, Annie. Being nice all the time is best left to moonies, monarchs or heirs-a-bloody-pparent.'

'Nice?' she squealed before flouncing towards the door. 'I'm currently deliberating whether to send my husband white-river rafting – which offers maximum cranial damage, or shark-diving – that's the art of keeping one inch of rubber between you and 670 ravaging incisors. Yes. You don't get much nicer than that, doll,' she said bitterly.

'And I do not have a big bum!' I called out after her.

Julian didn't think our arrangement was all that 'nice' either.

'I'm glad in a way that Kate got back in touch with her sexuality,' I purred post-coitally one afternoon, smugness fuelling my magnanimity. We'd tumbled into an orange-chenille-bedspreaded Bloomsbury Hotel within staggering distance of a luncheon restaurant named, appropriately, A Wok on the Wildside.

Julian bristled slightly. 'She's actually a very warm woman.'

'Warm?' I rolled on to my belly to watch him more carefully. 'In bed, you mean?'

'No . . . Well, yes, that too, I suppose.'

I tried to keep my voice casual. 'Really? What was she like? . . . In bed?'

'What?' Julian fumbled with a mini-bar vacuum-packed tin of cashews. 'Oh. Average. You know.'

'Average . . . Oh. Well, what am *I* like in bed?'

'You're good. You know you are. Ouch!' He dropped the tin. Nuts scatter-gunned across the acrylic carpet. He sucked the fingertip he'd caught on the serrated lip. 'Look, can we please not have this conversation?'

I plumped up a punctured pillow. 'So, *she's* average and *I'm* good . . . But isn't good just average?'

'Do you think we could just have sex without Kate coming between us? . . . I mean, you brought her up in the first place . . .'

'You mean *you* did. Silently. She's always on your mind.' Julian didn't deny it. He looked away. 'Stop saying nothing in such an awful tone.'

'She's on my mind because I've never cheated on anybody before. Yet here I am, having an affair with my wife. I'm finding it hard to be a Scarlet Man.'

'Affairs aren't that hard. In fact they're quite easy . . .' I said without thinking.

Julian shot me a witheringly injured look. 'I know the downside of what it's like to be cheated on, Rebecca. I had plenty of time to get used to it and it's hideous. It's time for Zachary Burne's education to embrace the concept of oxymorons.'

'Such as?'

'Oh . . . "womankind" springs to mind.'

. . . And 'liberal sensibilities', I thought to myself, as Julian pored over his current case. He was prosecuting (I noticed in amazement) some unfortunate minicab driver who accidentally slapped his passenger across the face when attempting to get hold of her handbag to assist her in paying the fare.

'The police are our friends now, are they?' I asked sarcastically, leaning over his shoulder. 'Next you'll be putting men on death row, rather than getting them off it.'

'Actually, our firm's been approached by the Government of Trinidad to uphold the sentences on some of their more unpleasant murderers,' he replied absent-mindedly. 'We are considering it. Lots of money, of course.'

My stomach knotted. What had happened to my psychological Superman who fought for Truth, Justice and the Legal way? Kryptonited, that's what. By Yours Truly. And I didn't feel good about it. I mean, what was Clark Kent without the bionic underpants? Who was Bruce Wayne without the Caped Crusader? I'm afraid my legal eagle had turned Vulture like all the rest.

In fact, our clandestine days were over faster than either of us had planned when Kate extracted a confession – a voluntary admission obtained with a stun gun – from Julian. This meant an immediate career change for moi.

'You are like, *so* fired,' she spat when I arrived in the office one morning in August. In contrast to her bombast and bravado, I noted a forlorn dab of lipstick on her eye tooth.

'Kate, we need to talk about this . . .'

'I'd love to discuss this with you, I really would, but I don't have anything to throw up into right now.'

'Well just remember,' I warned, clearing out my

desk. 'that I'm now a DE – Disgruntled Employee. Meaning that I'm soon to gun down several of my co-workers, starting with a certain loud-mouthed Aussie I know.'

'Go plait your shit,' she dismissed me eloquently.

'Feel like having a powerless lunch?' I suggested when Anouska opened her door an hour later.

'You're not working, doll? Anouska enquired, wrapping her kimono around her.

'Um . . . no. I'm um . . . downsizing.'

'Ah, so Kate finally found out about your adultery with your husband and sacked you?' she decoded.

'I don't look on it as "sacked". I look on it more as being self-employed. You should see me suck up to myself.' I made a stab at joviality. 'Not a pretty sight.'

Nor was confessing to Zachary. It would be the most nerve-racking event of my life, well, which didn't involve gynaecologists. I was going to tell him, truly I was, but when I got back to his house that night, Zachary scooped me up in his arms and carried me into the bedroom, as though he'd just popped in from the Ottoman Empire.

'Come with me to France, Becky, for the Amnesty gig,' he said between caresses.

'No. I'm not glamorous enough. The French don't let you in if you're ugly. Honestly. They run you over in their Citroëns.'

'But you're beautiful, Beck.' He took my face in his hands and kissed my mouth, thawing my resolution with the tip of his tongue. The heat of his touch flowed over me, soaking into my skin like melted butter. Morals just couldn't keep in that climate. He gave me an indolent smile. The air was charged with his aroma. His jeans fitted like a suntan. The trouble was Zack's chocolate-milk skin. It was so moreish. And I was far from lactose-intolerant. My mouth watered insubordinately.

The truth is, I'm lousy at making decisions. When shopping, I always come home with the same pair of shoes in black *and* red. When dining out, I pick at the other person's meal. I channel surf. I hedge bets. I like opera *and* rap music. Yet now I had to decide which man was going to be my 'A' and which my 'B' side.

But why should I *have* to choose? An 'A' side is not complete without a 'B' side. Right? When looked at that way . . . Okay, you had to squint quite hard, but why couldn't I have both? Hell, men did. All the bloody time. Prostitutes for pleasure, concubines for service, wives for breeding – that's the magical sexual sleight of hand men have performed for centuries. Why should I have to look a gift horse in any of its apertures? Why couldn't love have a multiple-choice answer? I told myself that I wasn't self-centred – I just had a larger capacity for pleasure. What harm could it do, I thought, as Zachary covered my body in kisses? How could I leave him? It would be a rat deserting a floating ship. If it was lust I was addicted to, at least it wasn't as bad as heroin or cake. Right?

With his tongue in my navel it took me, oh, about 3.6 seconds to convince myself that the edifice of my crumbling life needed to be held up by the twin beams of Julian *and* Zack. And was that such a bad thing? To choose to be Courtney Love over Celine Dion? Why couldn't women be selfish for a while? Hell, it was our turn. Why couldn't we take lovers? And award ourselves huge salaries for doodling on a blotter? The secret was to just never, ever, ever let them know about each other.

But while it's true that the stoning of adulteresses is generally frowned upon in the West, a 'wanton' woman is still universally condemned. Unless, that is, she's seen to suffer.

And suffer I most surely would.

If Life were a slice of toast, mine was about to hit the linoleum, butter-side down.

In this world there are 1,100 ejaculations every second, with nearly one million conceptions every day – half of them unplanned.

When I realized that I was just one measly bit of maths in this staggering evolutionary equation, my problem should have paled. But it just loomed larger. So much for equality. What was the point of thinking like a man when my body was still thinking like a woman?

'Jesus, doll,' Anouska exclaimed, as I collapsed into the worn chair next to her after being told the result of my test. We were in a doctor's shabby, beige-carpeted waiting room in Belsize Road, amid the gridlock of buggies and electronic wheelchairs and a United Nations of patients all jostling and jockeying for the next appointment. 'Were you using contraceptives?'

'Yes,' I replied snarkily. 'On all conceivable occasions.' I bent my mouth towards her ear, whispering – 'It's just that one of these men should have a bumper sticker on his penis saying "Caution: Baby on Board".'

'Excuse me . . . But *you don't know whose it is?!*'

Anouska's fog-horned announcement succeeded where modern medicine had failed. Tubercular coughing gave way to a prurient silence, as patients swivelled in my cringing direction.

'Not without DNA.'

'Well, you must tell them, doll.'

'Of course I will. After all, I knocked them up. I'd better do the right thing by them.' I escaped down the ramp into the treacly August heat, dazed by more than just the sunshine. 'Besides, one of them's going to have to pay for the termination. I'm currently suffering from an ingrown income.'

'Termination? Becky, you can't. The miracle of life is stirring inside you.'

'Hey, Kate is wearing high heels and mascara. I've already witnessed my miracle for the year.'

As it was, Anouska had a little retroactive birth control of her own to attend to. In her continued attempts at widowhood, she had drag-racing, paragliding, bicycle-abseiling and sky-surfing excursions to organize.

To aid my sexual kleptomania, both the men in my life were under the impression that I was staying with Anouska. I'd told them that she was taking life too easily – i.e. Darius's – and needed to be watched. But approaching her car, which was sporting the customary literature affixed to the windscreen by a traffic warden, I decided I'd had enough terror for one day. I opted, instead, to walk to Zack's house.

My shoes rang out on the concrete, scabbed with cracks and crevices. Designer jeeps crammed with horn-happy mothers late for pre-school runs, snaked down Abbey Road. My legs leaden, I plodded towards the famous Beatles recording studio, the zebra crossing outside it cluttered with Japanese tourists posing for polaroids. I thought at first I would not tell either man. But since I was developing penchants for pickle sandwiches, pedicures and holidays in the Hebrides (well, they're the pregnancy cravings *I* got) – it would not take long for the penny to drop. But how to break the news?

Maybe next time I was vomiting and either man asked if there was anything he could do . . . I could simply reply 'Um . . . how about carry our child to full term?'

Subtle, yet dramatic. And more direct than a sudden declaration that I'd be declining all bungee-jumping invitations for the next nine months.

A summer storm was boiling on the horizon. Breaking into a shambling trot, I reheared the dialogue in my head ... It would be just like the baby in my belly; so easy to conceive, but so hard to deliver.

36

Ping! There Go Those Elastic Morals Again!

Although employing all the traditional anti-baby, pro-abortion techniques – like sharing with the father-to-be (or in this case, fathers-to-be) my newly discovered Islamic fundamentalist religious convictions – *the ones I wanted to share with my children*, both Zachary and Julian were euphoric at my embryonic news.

'Isn't there anything I can do?' asked Zack, holding my hair back as I stared down the throat of the toilet for the tenth time that morning.

'Um . . . How about carry our child to full term?'

'We're having a baby?' Zack whooped like a Californian aerobics instructor.

'Don't get excited. I don't think I'll be keeping it.'

''Course we will, babe,' he teased. He mussed my hair, before enquiring what I'd like for breakfast.

'What do you feel like?' he insisted after carrying me back to bed.

'I don't know.'

'Just listen to your uterus,' Zack said. 'It'll tell you what it needs.'

I screwed up my eyes. 'I'm listening.'

'Well,' he said, after a pause, 'what's it saying?'

'Leonardo DiCaprio.'

He laughed, tickling my rib cage.

Julian responded by conforming to the well-established upper-class ritual of putting the embryo down for Eton.

For the next two weeks, I listed my worries and fears to both men. Firstly I did not want my body to be stolen by aliens and replaced with the body of Marlon Brando. Just trying to sit down on public transport would require torches and flares, as if landing a jet. I did not want to have to wear a 'sheep dog' – you know – the sort of bra that rounds 'em up and herds 'em in. I wouldn't even be able to dull the humiliation with alcohol. Mind you, once the baby realized who her mother was, the poor kid would *need* a drink.

And then there was the birth. I told them both that I didn't even want to do anything which felt *good* for thirty-three hours!

I told them both that I didn't feel at one with the universe; I felt at one with the toilet bowl. I told them both that an abortion, statistically, carried less risk to the woman than going through pregnancy and birth. I told them that I didn't feel guilty about wanting to have an abortion. I told them to stop making me feel guilty about not feeling guilty. I informed them that there was nothing earth-movingly romantic about the conception. I explained that the sperm probably hit the egg while I was killing cockroaches behind the cooker.

The one thing I didn't tell them was that I had no bloody idea whatsoever which of them was the Dad.

With time running out I spent day after nauseating day procrastinating about procreating. I tried role-playing.

I tried playing the role of a demented parent – untangling the same mobile for thirteen years and arranging to have my salary paid directly to Osh Kosh. I tried playing the role of a demented non-parent: a vegetable in a nursing home with nobody to slip me morphine surreptitiously.

I tried playing the role of a decisive person.

But in the end nature decided for me. When the bleeding started, I rang the doctor. 'Spotting,' he called it euphemistically. 'Are you cramping?'

'No.'

But as the day wore on I felt bloated, enervated, peculiar. After the stabbing cramps took hold came the nag of backache. By midnight I was bleeding heavily and curled into a foetal ball around a hot-water bottle in Anouska's spare bed.

At dawn Anouska drove me to the hospital, a sooty Victorian building in central London, for an ultrasound. The white-coated gynaecologist arrived about three centuries later.

The springs of the examination table seemed to mourn as they took my weight. The room smelt of corroding rubber, decades of damp fears and stale farts, with a noxious overlay of Domestos.

As the doctor dolloped a globule of cold jelly on to my abdomen I gazed at his third coat button as though it were the eighth wonder of the world. While he ran the scanner over my belly, my mind was as blank as the screen. There was a whooshy echo – but no tattoo of tiny heartbeats. I turned my head. In the bleary black and white of a scratchy pre-war newsreel, tenuous images began to emerge. I peered in on the water-bottle world where my baby should have bobbed, buoyant with life. I searched the little black sack for a grainy profile. Empty. I heard the doctor's voice from a long way off telling me, kindly, that one in eight pregnancies ended in miscarriage. It was probably a genetic fault. 'It (he called the baby 'It') would have perished a few weeks ago, he said, but it took the body a while to understand. 'Your hormone levels drop slowly. Why not wait a month, then try again?'

'Try again?'

On the way home I opened the car window and

breathed deeply. The air was sharp as lemon juice. For most women this would be the time to draw on inner reserves of strength and integrity and re-examine life's priorities . . . but what, I wondered, should *I* do?

'Well, doll, I think the warranty on your double life has well and truly expired,' Anouska volunteered.

'Great. Tell me something I *don't* know.'

'Um . . . I'm going to murder my husband? If I shoot him I get life, but if I run him over with my car I'll be out in six months. Especially if I'm ovulating at the time,' Anouska added, veering erratically towards a group of pedestrians on the cement apron who scattered, diving into ditches and local hospital emergency rooms.

'Hey, don't worry. You'll be acquitted on the grounds of insanity. The proof being that you married Darius in the first place.'

And let's face it, grounds for insanity were something I knew a lot about. Still holding the World Indoor Record for Self-Delusion, I started to tell myself how good it would be to have my body back. Not to feel ill; not to feel caged. 'Let's go out on the town,' I suggested spontaneously. 'I've only got this cleavage for another few hours. *This*,' I pointed out my bust line to a startled motorist at the traffic lights on Marylebone Road, 'is *not* a Wonderbra.'

But first I had to tell Julian and Zack that I'd lost the baby. I winced at the thought. God, I was gutless. That's what I *should* have asked for at the hospital – a spine donor. And maybe scruples transplant. It's just that I needed more time. My body would withdraw slowly from the hormonal high. I, however, would go cold turkey from the drip-feed of attention I'd been taking intravenously. But not, I baulked, if I didn't tell them straight away ... It was a wayward, irresponsible thought. But why not delay, for just a few days, until I got used to the idea myself? It was, after all, only a small fib. And, I duped myself, fibbing is only like a parking infringement on the moral rap sheet. Isn't it? Providing ultimate proof that the flow of oxygen had been cut off from my brain, I made Anouska promise not to tell Julian or Zack about the miscarriage. At least, not just yet. Okay so it wasn't exactly rising to the occasion. Show me an occasion and I won't rise to it. As the Devil will no doubt discover when he surveys my CV, I could hold workshops on non-occasion-rising. But Anouska was unquestioning.

'Listen, doll. I learnt a long time ago not to repeat anything you ever tell me. And I never will. Not till hell freezes over.'

'Thanks.'

If I'd had a psychological barometer I'd have been better prepared for what was in store.

Put it this way. 'Weather Warning. Hell Frozen.'

37

Laugh? I Almost Died

The tampon has done more than any other invention to liberate women. The most obvious thing about it is that it isn't. It's complete freedom – with only one string attached. But it wasn't until Anouska thumped on Zachary's front door at dawn a week later, that I realized just how versatile the tampon truly is.

I looked at her blearily whilst wondering what triviality could be upsetting her now. A scratch on her nail varnish perhaps? 'What?' I yawned, shrugging Zack's leather jacket over my knickers. 'Is the bat signal up?'

Her answer came in spasms between shuddering intakes of breath. 'Remember how I told you that unless I go off to sleep before Darius, he starts snoring? Keeping me wider and wider awake? Until I am forced to kick and punch and scream that I am going to kill him? . . . Well, *I killed him.*'

'*What?*' I yanked her in over the threshold.

'Well, he was snoring and I couldn't sleep and . . . Anyway, I put two tampons up his nose. You know. To make him breath through his mouth? But when I woke an hour ago, he . . . he . . . well he wasn't breathing at all!'

'Are you sure?'

She unscrewed the cap from the Jack Daniel's bottle she was clutching and swigged down a hefty draught. 'I didn't mean to kill him. Actually, doll, we've been getting on much better lately. I'm a regular fag-hag. But the thing is, I've talked so much about murdering him that no one will believe it was an accident!'

I gawped at her. 'Where is he?'

'I just left him in the bed.'

'We'd better get an ambulance around there.' I dialled 999 with shaking fingers. The Boston Strangler. The Yorkshire Ripper. The Chelsea Tamponist? 'Toxic Snot Syndrome' . . . It somehow didn't have the same menacing ring. After giving the paramedics a minimal amount of the more believable details, I scraped Anouska up off the floor. 'Don't worry, Vivian will be able to get the sentence commuted to a couple of sessions with a Harley Street quack and a Jerry Springer appearance.' I thrust my legs into a pair of jeans and steered her towards the door. 'We'll collect Vivian at Ladbroke Grove – it's virtually on the way to Chelsea – then go on to meet the ambulance.'

'No!' Anouska's heels left skid marks on the hall floor. 'Not my perfect sister. With the perfect marriage!' She chugg-a-lugged more whisky.

'Flattered as I am that you've chosen my company over, say, a *psychiatrist* – we really need the big guns now.' There were times, I reassured her, when there was nothing like having a lawyer in the family.

. . . What a shame this was not one of those times.

The domestic chaos we encountered at Ladbroke Grove was like World War Two, without the fun. The usually pristine house looked as though a herd of incontinent wildebeest had stampeded through it. Furniture was upended, children were squealing, phones were ripped from walls as Vivian, spinning Simon around on the stripped-pine floor, stomped on his abdomen.

In the corner of a couch, the sound of creaking leather trousers alerted me to the presence of Celestia, the free-fall vegetarian.

'What the . . . ?'

'Apparently,' a dishevelled Vivian elaborated shrilly, 'she came here for bulimia counselling during which Simon told her that he'd discovered a new multi-orgasmic erogenous zone between the G spot and the cervix.'

'The AFE,' Celestia clarified. 'The Anterior Fornix Erotic zone.'

'And naturally she wanted to find out if he was right. Unfortunately for her, my legal conference in Manchester unexpectedly finished in time for me to catch the last train – and she was in my bed when I arrived home.'

Simon, who seemed to be wearing the kind of outfit more at home on an Abba comeback tour, then made the mistake of suggesting his wife calm down and get back in touch with her 'inner earth mother'. But Vivian's inner earth mother had forged a volatile bond with her inner Hellcat, and the two of them seemed determined to 'out' Simon as a hypocritical bastard.

'Sweetie-pie, pumpkin, little lamb chop. Please. Not in front of the children . . .'

'The children?! What do *you* care about the children?' Vivian pursued him around the room, jabbing his chest with her wedding finger. 'You can't keep your hands off the help. The nannies and au pairs demand combat pay.'

'Well,' he scuttled backwards, 'if you hadn't let yourself go, I wouldn't need to spice up my sex life!'

'Let myself go? Where do you think I got these hips? From bearing your genetic line. That's where!'

'My genetic line did not tell you to eat three Ben 'n' Jerry cartons of ice-cream in one sitting, three times a day.'

'I was pregnant! I had cravings!'

'Cravings to eat between meals *after* they were born?'

'If you'd ever given me a satisfying orgasm in all the years we've been married, I wouldn't have *had* to eat.'

'*What?* But what about all that moaning . . . ?'

'Those were moans of pain; the emotional pain of having married a big, fat phoney like you!'

In the stunned silence that followed, the only sound I could hear was what I thought was hail; indoor hail. My eyes darted about the room to alight finally on the fridge door. Painted lentils dropped forlornly on to the floor from the latest finger-painted mosaic stuck to it by a magnetic pineapple.

As Anouska and I bundled Vivian out of the house and into the car, a bleary-eyed Celestia piped up dimly. 'So, um . . . does this mean you and your wife *don't* share a transcendental fidelity of the spirit which liberates you from monogamy?' She really was pitiful – a moth drawn to a fraudulent flame.

In all the mayhem, I hadn't quite realized how drunk Anouska was until she jumped a red light in the Mall and almost collected an early-morning jogger. Anouska's only reaction was a demand to breath test the pedestrian. 'She ran into my car!' she protested.

'We're going miles out of our way. We'll never beat the ambulance at this rate. Pull over,' I ordered. I yanked at the wheel of the rear-demisted, power-steered juggernaut. Anouska yanked back, sending us veering out into the rush-hour traffic.

The roundabout outside Buckingham Palace is a place where the motoring customs of a dozen

Mediterranean and Arabic and Caribbean nations fuse into a cacophonous whirlpool of screeching brakes, blaring horns and dodgem-car bumper-ramming. But as far as I know, nobody had ever seen anything like Anouska's two-wheeled, airborne collision with the giant, inverted shower fitting known as the Victoria Monument. As the windscreen shattered and coruscations of spray jetted into my face and water gushed into the car's crushed interior, it wasn't my life that flashed before my eyes. It was Mary-Jo Kopechne's.

38

Not The Full Matinee Jacket

There's a lot of things which frighten the tits off a girl.
The Taliban invading London, trying on swimming
costumes, wasps (not the ones with wings, but the
snooty Mayfair Ladies Who Lunch) ... But nothing,
absolutely not one thing could be as terrifying as the
vision that hit me when I levered open my eyes five
hours later in ward twelve of London's University
College Hospital. I saw both my lovers, as I still
described them, in a momentary proprietorial
delusion, one on each side of the bed. They were
glowering at me, then at each other. I slammed my
eyelids closed again and feigned catatonia. Did they
know about each other? I panicked. I squeezed open
one eye and peeked at them both. All was revealed in
their eyebrows, and from the air in the room, quivering with a heat haze of tension and anger.

'Well,' said Julian in a brittle voice. 'Don't you have anything to say?'

My throat was scratchy, my mouth sour, my tongue swollen and dry. I noticed a plaster cast on my wrist.

'Um . . . Toto. I think we're no longer in Kansas?' I hazarded.

'Would you mind enlightening me, if it's not too inconvenient, as to which of us is the father of our child?'

I felt the heat of shame flush across my neck and chest and seep upwards into my complexion. The fluorescent-lit hospital room was like a tourist brochure for Albania. I tried to lean forward but found myself imprisoned behind a metallic tray, one arm tethered to an IV drip. 'I've died, haven't I? . . . And this is Limbo.'

'You know what, Ms High and Mighty Moral Superiority?' Zack seethed. 'You're getting less and less reason to look down on me, you know that?'

The door creaked enquiringly and Kate's hesitant head peeped around it. She and Julian held eyes briefly before darting downwards simultaneously to scrutinize their respective footwear. 'Is everybody all right? Simon rang me . . .'

'Ms . . .' A clipboard-clutching nurse wielding a thermometer, bounced into the room before anyone could answer. '. . . Steele. Feeling any pain?'

What I felt was that I was going to implode, like one of those deep-sea divers with the bends.

'Just a few formalities . . . Marital status?'

I looked at her blankly. Zachary's dark eyes were jumping around the room. Fumes of rage seemed to be smoking forth from his skull.

'Are you married?'

'Well. Yes. No. Kind of. Though, I have a feeling that it's about to be annulled. I don't suppose you want my parents, do you, Julian? In the divorce?' Jesus Christ. What was wrong with me? Could I not stop making cracks? Even *now*?

'Occupation?' I looked at the Nurse as though she were speaking some intergalactic-pidgin. 'What do you do for a living?' she spelt out. I glanced self-consciously at Kate to find all traces of friendship extinct in her face. She regarded me with dignified disdain. The nurse looked impatiently to Julian. 'So what did your wife do before you annulled her?' she asked freshly.

'A lot of things I didn't know about,' Julian replied tartly, before steeling himself. 'Look. The most important thing is the baby. Is the baby all right. Can you tell us that?'

'Baby?' Kate said in a strained, long-haul air-hostess accent. Her eyes vainly sought an explanation from Anouska, who was slumped in an armchair under the window; her only apparent injury a lethal hangover.

'Listen, Rebecca,' Julian sighed with wistful resignation. 'Despite your appalling behaviour, your deceitful, duplicitous dealings and the flagrant flouting of road-safety rules by not wearing a seatbelt, I am willing to stand by you and the baby.' He made an attempt at a smile. 'After all, my mother is crocheting herself into a coma as we speak.'

'I gnawed the inside of my cheek. A thumping headache was zigzagging through my temples; each breath, a rasping ache. Zack was about to make a declaration of similar purport, when a doctor hurtled through the door and launched into his rote exhortation.

'This patient has sustained a chest injury,' he lectured the nurse in an accent thick with kilts and sporrans. 'That, combined with abdominal pain and her swinging pyrexia,' (he indicated the Pyrenean mountain range stencilled on to my temperature chart), 'could indicate a sub-phrenic abscess.' He peered at me over his bifocals. I'm going to inject a radio labelled isotope which . . .'

The minute he said the word 'inject' both men wheeled around to snap at him in unison. 'She's pregnant!'

'Actually, I'd like to be discharged.' My armpits were sweating buckets. I had a body odour which could stop armoured tanks in their tracks. 'Like, right now.'

Light struggled through the grimy windows, highlighting the many handprints on the smeary glass, making it look as if thousands had clawed to get out of here. I knew just how they felt.

The doctor gave us all the bifocal treatment, as if we were minor bacteria beneath a microscope.

'I have examined Ms Steele thoroughly and she is not pregnant.'

If Life imitates art, mine had just become a Hieronymus Bosch exhibition.

Julian's tenderish expression decomposed into a look of detestation. 'Are you sure, Doctor?'

'Quite sure.'

'I was going to tell you. I was.' I tried to take refuge in Julian's eyes. He turned away. 'Really. I lost it, a week ago . . .'

That was when Hieronymus Bosch came to life in the form of Darius and a squad of policemen.

Anouska's husband, looking like an expensive and very peeved pet, led them into the room and pointed at his wife, who started twitching like a frog in a science experiment.

'She's the one, Officers. You should charge her with attempted murder.'

The eyes of the other patients ping-ponged around the ward. Even Doctor Dour stopped peering over the tops of his glasses.

'I was only trying to stop you snoring. Julian . . . help me,' she implored, oscillating her hand through her hair as though auditioning for a shampoo advertisement.

My Knight in Shining Armani moved swiftly to her side. 'Of course I will, Anouska. Just as soon as we get out of here.'

The thin mattress was like a soggy slice of white bread. I struggled into a sitting position. Wincing with pain, I hurled myself at Julian, toppling both the tray and the IV. I clung to him like a punch-drunk boxer in the final seconds of an exhausting round. 'Don't leave me!'

I caught sight of myself in the mirror. I had the fixed facial expression and Einstein hair of someone who has just put a knife in a toaster.

'She's all yours,' said Julian to Zachary, coldly extricating himself from my embrace. 'But be warned. This woman is like radiation. It may take you twenty years to get over her, and you'll *still* be paying the price for that exposure.'

'Would it change anything if I told you that when I slept with Zack I was thinking of you?'

Zack's eyes narrowed to two hard slits of fury. He stabbed his arms into the sleeves of his leather jacket. 'What a goddamn love story this turned out to be. It's a "Girl Eats Boy" kinda scenario, right?'

'Zack, I'm sorry,' I beseeched in a tourniqueted voice. 'I didn't mean . . .'

Julian was at the door, his arm around the sobbing Anouska. 'I'll leave you to do some soul-searching,' he said witheringly. 'Of course it does help to have a soul to search.' The door slammed shut like a trap.

'Zack, let me explain . . .'

Zack flipped a fifty-pence piece on to the bed. 'Call somebody who gives a fuck.'

Once the Police had taken everyone else off for questioning, I was left weary and waterlogged in the storm's debris. Lifting my head up from the bed I saw only Kate, sprawled high and dry in the armchair by the window.

'Need anything?' she asked with poised lucidity.

'Yeah. Menopause.'

She swung her denimed legs to the floor. 'You were *pregnant*?'

'I . . . I didn't want it.'

Kate shook her head in disbelief. 'And here am I, so desperate to be a mother that I weep if they serve me up baby corn in a restaurant . . .'

'Um . . . wake up and smell the pooey nappies, Kate. You hate children. Remember? You're a . . . what's the word for kid-haters? A childophobe. A kinder-thrope.'

'I was once, I know. But, like all women, I did vaguely plan a sprog sometime in the future. And then it hit me. There isn't much "sometime" left. I used to think it was selfish to have a baby. But you know what? All the reasons I *didn't* want to have a baby were *selfish* – my health, my career, my reputation, my future. Me, me, me . . . Am I happy? Am I fulfilled? The best thing about kids is that you're too busy to keep asking yourself those bloody questions.' She calmed her T-shirt creases with open palms. 'You know your trouble, Rebecca?'

'No. But I feel sure you're going to tell me.'

'You are a woman who has everything ... You just don't know how to use it.'

'Yes, yes. I feel guilty, okay? I've cheated. I've lied. Hell. I'm probably responsible for the war in Bosnia. There. Happy now?'

But Kate, too, was making to leave.

'Come and see me soon!' I quipped. 'I'll be the one sitting in the corner, drooling and braiding my hair.'

'Don't be ridiculous,' she said, flinging the words over her shoulder. 'To have a nervous breakdown you actually have to have a central nervous system.'

The door springs hummed and twanged and fell silent.

39

I'm Not Waving

Laugh and the world laughs with you. Cry and your mascara runs. Lying in that hospital ward, inhaling air full of other people's, *sick* people's, recycled breath, I quickly came to the conclusion that Life was Mike Tyson – and I was a club bantam-weight.

I fiddled with the name tag on my wrist. In hospital they label you in case you forget who you are or (in my situation) no one claims you. On the baggage carousel of life, I was no Vuitton valise. I was the beaten-up rucksack that comes down the chute right at the end and circles, forlorn and uncollected. I stared at the phone by the bed but couldn't think of one single person to call. In the end I dialled the speaking clock. At least the time would talk to me every ten seconds.

Come evening I had a case of the blues. Two dozen cases. Vintage blues. I had been juggling faster and faster with more and more balls, and it was only now I realized it was inevitable that they would all come crashing down on my noggin. Why did sex have to complicate everything? If only we could be asexual, I thought, as a nurse changed my bandages, rolling me this way and that like a piece of dough. Dandelions, elm trees and tiny single-cell algae simply divide themselves. The greenfly has *really* got it sussed. It only has sex once every six generations. And we're supposed to be the highest on the evolutionary scale? *I don't think so.* Why can't we simply form a bud or split our bodies in half or lay some bloody eggs? Then I wouldn't be in this God-awful frigging mess.

Across the hall in another ward, the violet flicker of televisions ghosted eerily on to the walls. Below the grimy windows, London scrolled out as far as the eye could see, cramped, crotchety little streets, beneath an irritable sky. The woman in the bed next to me unloaded a throat load of streptococci into the spittoon by my head. At least, I pondered, it couldn't get worse than this.

That was when my mother walked in. She was wearing an animal-print miniskirt of uncertain zoo-logical provenance and a T-shirt at least five sizes too small, featuring the gold-embossed face of Julio Inglesias picked out in sequins. She beamed insincere concern in my direction. It had been nearly a year since I'd seen her.

'You've done something to your hair.'

'No, I haven't.'

'Well, you *should*.'

My mother always had the knack of making me feel like the Elephant Man. *I am a human being*, I reminded myself. I glanced for moral support towards my father, his Brylcreemed hair parted at the customary two o'clock, but he was staring into the nebulous mid-distance, taking a rain check on life as usual.

'Nice furniture,' my mother said, shimmying into the armchair beneath the window, allowing maximum exposure of her lace scanties to the entire ward. 'Stimulated leather.'

'*Sim*ulated,' I corrected her half-heartedly.

'Anouska rang and tol' me 'bout the sprog.' I looked at her warily. Surely, she wasn't going to be sympathetic? For the first time in her life? 'An', frankly, I'm that relieved. I refuse to become a gran'muvver, ya 'ear me?' she lectured in her skidding, slovenly vowels. 'We've come 'ere, ya dad an' me, to tell ya somfink.'

Please, please let it be that I'm adopted, I thought desperately.

'Let's face it, ya not the muvvering type, Rebecca. I fink it'd be wise to get the doc to cut them bits outta ya, while ya in 'ere.'

I honestly thought I had astonishment fatigue, but this floored me. Although I shouldn't have. This was how she had always treated people; as dispensable and disposable. A lot like me, I thought with a sickening shudder. A half-hour later, she broke off from talking with the nurses about her complex gynaecological problems to say goodbye.

'Anythin' you'd like me to bring ya?'

'A life?' I suggested sadly.

As soon as they departed, I retreated to the communal bathroom, ran a bath and, broken wrist extended, sank into the grimy tub. My lips skimmed the surface of the scummy water, sending tiny waves out towards my toes, capsizing the soap. I let the babble from the outside ward wash through the flimsy walls and right over me; the forced jollity of exhausted medics, the happy squawk of Hindu and Bengali, the jabber of visiting children. 'Ladies and jelly-men,' said a boy's voice. 'My bottom's burping,' said a little girl. The little boy was explaining that he had a headache in his foot and didn't think Father Christmas believed in him. The little girl queried, in a lisping falsetto, whether the dead squirrel they'd seen on the road was going to heaven, or hell? Hell, her brother felt sure and 'of course the devil has a wife!' he added emphatically. 'Everyone has one of those!'

I found myself ambushed by an unexpected longing for domestic conviviality.

The hospital ward was an eighty-degree womb, connected to the heating system by an umbilical cord of pipes. As they shuddered and juddered, pulsing water around the building, it made me think of what the doctor had described as the 'uterine material' that had been pulsing within me. I'd wanted to pretend that it was just a missed period, just a tiny bunch of cells, just a blue line on a bit of blotting paper. But listening to the childish banter I began to realize that it hadn't just been a hiccup in my quest for personal fulfilment. I couldn't help thinking that the thin, blue line announcing the baby's presence was one that I should not have crossed. The knowledge that Anouska had been right punched me in the guts – there had been a little commonplace miracle stirring inside me. A miracle I'd wished away. How callously I'd marked the gift 'return to sender'.

Waves of remorse began to replace the waves of nausea I'd felt when pregnant. All the stupid jokes I'd made, about how the baby would be the only infant on the block wearing black baby clothes and so on, began to hammer on my mind's door. Logic battled emotion. Get real, I lectured myself. If women could 'wish' away their pregnancies, there would have been no backyard abortions. I told myself that losing the baby had been for the best. But the trouble was, I'd spent the last four weeks secretly adjusting. The hormones had kicked in. I'd become a furtive pram-peerer. I'd made whispered clandestine confessions to other mothers, who'd confided back about how fulfilled they felt.

So, what had gone wrong? Was it the sleeping pills I'd taken before I'd known? The aerobics and weight training I'd done afterwards? The cracks I'd made at the baby's expense – 'Sure I wouldn't mind children . . .' I'd said to anyone who asked, '*if someone would have them for me.*'

But it wasn't anything I'd done. It was something I *hadn't* done that was starting to worry me deeply. I hadn't told anyone that I wanted the baby. That I was already fantasizing about her little face. The tiny clenched fist. The mouth puckered at my breast. The hushed excitement of the ultrasound as the doctor tried to discover the sex. The euphoria, post-birth. The friendly invasion of friends and family. Dressing her up in kangaroo Babygros with a pouch and pointy ears – photos that would humiliate her on her twenty-first birthday. I'd started to think about the Mothers' Day cards glued in macaroni and string.

I'd pretended that losing the baby was on a par with – I dunno – having it rain before a pool party, nixing my bikini wax. Oh yes, I, Becky Steele, had been blessed at birth with a double genetic whammy. Not only was I as shallow and selfish as my ghastly mother, but I was as emotionally stunted as my poor father. I was a callow youth, at *thirty-three*. Living proof that you may only be young once . . . but you can be immature forever.

A throbbing inner emptiness began to eclipse the pain from my accident abrasions. Emotions began to tear at my throat. What had I done with my life? I could probably have damaged and disfigured myself more, but only if I'd used a chainsaw and a bath of acid. I'd always thought of myself as tough, caustic, durable, full of common sense. But that was before I'd lost everything. Not lost, but thrown away. Common sense? Well, it's not so common. Self-disgust has a taste. Acrid and hot. A thick, black self-loathing gurgled up in the back of my throat.

I had to get out of my life! But in all the aching void of the world, where did I belong? I got an overwhelming urge to run – just as I had from the wedding, from Julian, from a career, from motherhood – from me. Because that was the truth of it. Like my mother, I was completely wrapped up in myself . . . And it was such a teeny, weeny package.

Though the bathwater was getting cold and my fingers were papery, I was immobilized by contrition. Embracing remorse like a long-lost lover, I was thick-throated with sobs. But there was no catharsis, no release, no relief in it. Just gut-wrenching despair and self-hatred. I'd been annoyed with myself before, ticking off, chastising. But had never felt the poisonous, toxic fumes of ignominy.

When my crying finally modulated into low-level keening, I lay in the drained bathtub, a body washed to shore. I was the hypochondriac now, with a terminal disease called Life. It was time to join Social Lepers Anonymous.

I soaked a facecloth in cold water and pressed it into stinging eye sockets before leaving the bathroom and limping across the ward. The last rays of the sun lit my red hair, igniting me into a bonfire. The hair colour was mine, but the pyre was made up of my friends, my family, my future.

And so the monstrous night crowded in around me.

Numb, I lay down on the most inhospitable bed in the world – the one I'd made myself.

40

For Sale. One Husband. Has Had Only One Careful Lady Owner

At this stage of my life I think it's fair to say that opportunity had stopped knocking. I had no place to live except at my parent's flat; my lover was consoling himself with groupies; I'd lost the baby I'd learnt too late to cherish; Anouska had been so devastated by events that she'd disappeared to have a lobotomy or join the Scientologists – her maid had forgotten which; I had been framed for possession of class-A drugs; and my best friend had run away with my husband. As we'd now been separated for the requisite year, a divorce petition alleging adultery plopped on to my parents' doormat bearing Julian's robust signature in brown ink – the colour, I noted desolately, of dried blood. A dismal little postscript requested speedy execution as he was planning to remarry as soon as possible.

A Decree Nisi takes six weeks ... but the heartache goes on forever. The day I was half of one of thirty couples pronounced divorced at Somerset House in the Strand, I took to sitting around in my parents' Islington flat in my wedding dress answering only to the name of Miss Havisham. I sent out un-wedding invitations. I baked un-wedding cake and sawed the plastic bride and groom decoration in half. I played Patsy Kline until my ear lobes fell off.

I tried to convince myself that mistakes are part of the dues I'd paid for an interesting life. I tried to convince myself that being single would be an adventure. It struck me that I'd never been without a man in my entire adult life. Living alone would mean never having to dash home from work to thaw the dinner in two minutes flat. It meant never being caught defrosting bread with the blow-dryer, a packet of icy lasagne wedged between my legs. It meant never having to listen to reminiscences about how some ex-defacto painstakingly mixed individual tabbouleh salads for his three pet guinea pigs. No snoring, no boring, no irritated wails of 'What are you? Premenstrual?' Living alone meant peace and quiet ... But, quiet enough for what? ... To hear myself crying, that's what. Believe me, I needed wader boots.

Who was I trying to kid? The realization that I'd turned into my mother meant I was now carrying around so much emotional baggage I needed a skycap porter. I'd become the sort of person I would normally flee at parties. Sentiment would seize me un-expectedly; while ploughing my trolley through the hordes of conceited, happy couples in supermarkets; whilst eating mixed nuts and glancing down to see a cashew coiled in foetal position in my palm . . .

The weather matched my mood. All through October and November the sky was a grey catheter bag, leaking sour, sooty rain over London. It had been raining so hard and for so long that animals were start-ing to pair off and bleat for Noah.

It was at the YMCA on one of these dreary days when I looked up through the steam of the communal showers to see Kate's freckled face studying me from behind her red-framed spectacles.

'Oh!' I felt winded. Water beat down my back for a full minute before I remembered some greeting was required. 'Hi.'

'G'day . . . Um . . . am I interrupting . . . ?'

'No, no. I'm just absent-mindedly pummelling my cellulite blobs.'

Kate removed her glasses, slung her towel over a hook and stepped on to the green plastic matting. 'So . . . how are you?'

I shrugged a soapy shoulder. 'Not good. I've been renting *Bridges of Madison County* and weeping all the way through it.'

'Oh, you *are* ill.'

'Basically, I've tried to commit suicide so many times I've nearly killed myself.'

'Just as well you've been working out so much.' Kate turned on the tap opposite me and stood under the corroded nozzle. 'At least now you can commit suicide naked.'

The plastic bottle farted as she squeezed herbal shampoo into her hand. I watched as she lathered her hair into a stiff meringue before I blurted – 'What you said in the hospital . . .? Well, it was all true. The trouble is, all my life I've been so flip; a walking chat show, paying the host *and* the guests.

Kate peered myopically through the steam. 'Would you quit putting yourself down, you big dag? You're going to wreck the fun for the rest of us.'

'You have every right to hate me,' I replied, despondently. 'I took advantage of you at work. I lied. I put Nair hair-removal cream on your panty liners, for God's sake! Running two lovers at once . . . Jesus! I was acting just like a man. Not a nice man, either. A Neanderthal. I . . .'

Kate put her hand up like a cop stopping traffic. 'You think you own the copyright on self-loathing? I was wearing false eyelashes. In *public*, for Christ's sake . . .'

'You did . . . change a little, yes,' I said tactfully.

'but now I've changed back . . . To tell you the truth,' she admitted, lifting an arm to reveal a reassuringly hirsute pit, 'I was finding all that bloody optimism a bit tiring. Cheerful people underestimate the complexity of problems. Einstein said that he was in a

409

really sad mood the day he came up with the theory of relativity, did you know that?'

'It's good to have you back, Kate.' Though naked and slippery with soap, we tentatively hugged.

'Actually, it was always your life. I was only keeping it warm for you . . .'

'How is Julian?

We pulled apart from our reorientating hug-fest. 'I was about to ask *you*.'

'Me?' I exclaimed. 'I'm in a holding pattern, man-wise . . . But you two are back together, right?'

'Good God, no. I've sworn off men. I'm still looking for a man who can excite me as much as a crème brûlée.'

This information amazed. 'You're not marrying him then?'

'Me? I thought *you* were.'

'I haven't seen him since the hospital.'

'Neither have I.' We turned off our taps, the plumbing wheezing emphysemically, and looked at each other in a state of Advanced Disbelief. 'At least he's being scrupulously bloody impartial in his anomie,' she said, Julian-like.

I towelled dry, absorbing at the same time this perplexing news. 'Personally, I'm pleased,' I bluffed. 'I'm so relieved not to be in any kind of relationship that I could just wake up each morning and . . . *applaud*.'

'Me too,' Kate agreed glumly, climbing into her customary flame-retardant clothing. We regarded each other with the animation of a couple of taxidermied trout.

An hour in a pizza bar in Leicester Square where you can eat all you want for £2.85 and our love for humanity, not to mention each other, was somewhat restored. Whilst reassured that while it would be nice to find True Love, at least we would always have each other, there was a dirigible-sized question hanging over us both – if neither of *us* was marrying Julian, then who the hell was?

'Vivian,' Kate conjectured, three pizzas down. 'It has to be Vivian. I mean in the piety stakes the bloody woman is hovering somewhere between Florence Nightingale and Mother bloody Teresa.'

'It can't be Vivian!' I bellowed. 'The woman wears culottes!'

'Doesn't Julian always go on about her being so perfect? And isn't she vulnerable right now? And needy? And victimized by a bastard husband . . .?'

'Kate, the woman buys her sex aids from a surgical supply shop!'

'Think about it! They're both lawyers, they're both family orientated. Christ Almighty! She's probably expecting his child . . .'

'To do what?' I interrupted cynically.

'They're homebodies . . . They both love cooking. They're probably having a bit of light banter in the heavy-appliances section of John Lewis *as we speak*. You know how bloody desperate Julian is now for

Rings and Strings . . .' She waggled her wedding
finger in the air. 'We've got to find out.'

Kate, commando-like, listed the paraphernalia she
needed – a microphone powerful enough to hear the
mould spores multiplying in his salad crisper; a
camera strong enough to photograph the plaque on
his teeth. Meanwhile, I took the simpler option of ringing his office. His secretary told me that he was
meeting 'Ms de Kock' for a fitting in Tatters, the bridal-
wear section of Harrods, at one p.m. There was no
time to lose: Vivian had already reverted to her
maiden name. We hailed a taxi, and a few moments
after our arrival, amidst the cumulus formations of
fluffy white frocks, my life took the kind of dramatic
turn that causes whiplash.

'Becky! Kate! Oh, hiya, dolls,' Anouska squeaked,
three octaves above a coloratura. 'Listen, Beck, thanks
for helping me that night,' she stammered. 'I'll do the
same thing for you . . . if you ever stick tampons up
your husband's nostrils and he suffocates, that is . . .'

'Hi.' The hug I gave her was only half reciprocated.
'Your maid said you were out of town?' I probed.

'Oh well, I'm back . . .' Sitting down, she knotted
one waxed leg around the other, over and over and
over until they were plaited.

'I know. For your sister's wedding . . .'

'Oh.' She nervously picked mascara clumps off her
eyelashes. 'You know about the wedding?' Her eyes
roved anxiously towards the escalators. She was

wearing a nervous grin, the one reserved for announcements preceding the words 'It wasn't my fault.'

'Is that why you've been avoiding us?' I insisted. 'Because of Vivian and Julian?'

Before she could answer, the shop assistant pootled into the changing area, an acreage of creaking satin in her arms. She smiled the wide, convulsive smile – all mouth, no eyes – of a car salesman. 'Miss de Kock, or should that be Mrs Julian Blake-Bovington-Smythe? *Your wedding dress!*'

A catastrophe is a furnace in whose heat identities buckle into entirely new shapes. When I wheeled around to confront my friend, her face was so hard and her eyes so cold that she was a stranger to me.

'But ... she's ... You're ...' The room tilted. 'This woman's already married!' I informed the Convulsive Smile, once the crashing in my ears had subsided.

'Annulled.' Anouska unwound her spaghetti legs and snatched up the taffeta veil from the chair. It rustled like a snake in the grass. 'Darius is now happily playing house with Norbett the South African towel attendant.'

'Annulled?'

'A decree of nullity,' elaborated Kate, 'because of wilful refusal to consummate. Prima facie grounds for ...'

'I know what it means!' Pain I thought blunted, pierced my solar plexus. 'You're marrying Julian

413

... without even ringing me for a reference?'

'Listen, doll. *You're* the one who told me to stop being nice all the time.' She gave me a scalding look. '*You're* the one who said that being nice had got women absolutely nowhere. *You're* the one who said that being nice all the time is best left to Moonies or monarchs . . .'

'You're obviously running late for your Dysfunctional Friend Support Group, *doll*,' Kate said facetiously, towering over her.

'*You* can talk . . . I'm sick of you two telling me what to do all the time. Julian is perfect Husband Material. For all your book reading and big words, you were just too stupid to see it,' Anouska said, a treasonous curl to her painted lips.

I shook her by the shoulders. 'You are *not* Anouska de Kock. You're an evil pod person. The real Annie is Out There Somewhere, isn't she?'

She brushed me aside. 'Plus he's a brilliant lawyer. Julian got my marriage to Darius tippexed out of legal history. Meaning no palimony. And all those awful motoring convictions quashed. Besides, silly me! I've been barking up the wrong family trees! New Labour are going to abolish hereditary peers. But with all Julian's donations to the party . . .' she said with cold-blooded complacency, running a pink tongue over a picket fence of perfectly capped teeth, 'and work with torture victims, I'm sure he'll be rewarded . . . A life Baronetcy at the very least!'

I gave a bitter laugh – the sort of laugh Rhett Butler gave when he realized his beloved South had been barbecued and his wife was a bimbo. In the cold light of logic, it was obvious. As far as an 'It Girl' is concerned, marriage is like a horse; you have to get straight back on after a fall. She was also man-hungry. Believe me, Anouska made cannibals look vegetarian. The woman's love letters were addressed 'to whom it may concern'. Julian, the Hypochondria King, was desperate to marry and so lower his risk of heart disease. He would have been weak before her Hair-Flicking Offensive. The Mountie had got her man again.

I looked at her sadly, all the fight knocked out of me. 'It must be so tiring having to put make-up on two faces every day,' was all I managed.

'Oh, go throw yourself into a vat of Clarins de-aging cream, lizard-neck,' Anouska spat.

The one thing I'd learnt of late is that dealing with loss and heartache doesn't make you stronger. It only makes people think you are. As Anouska pivoted past me, shimmying into the inner sanctum of the luxurious fitting rooms, I barely recognized myself in the giant gilt-edged mirror. The face belonged to a prior incarnation – a life from which I was now removed by whole galaxies of grief. If they were making a TV programme about me, it wouldn't be *This Is Your Life* but *This* is Your *Life*?

Any more down and out and Zack would have to play a benefit concert for me, no kidding.

41

A Pina Colada, A Non-stick Wok and Thou

By December, my Life imitated Art in only one respect. I'd been framed.

The morning of my court case, the air was tart. As I dragged myself into the Bow Street Magistrate's Court, it was also heavy with the odour of a very large rodent. Dominating the windowless courtroom, Rotterman was fatter than ever. His immense accretion of flesh avalanched on to the bench next to me.

'Guess what?' Rotterman drawled excitedly.

'Um . . . You slept with someone you're not related to?'

'Yer goin' to jail!' Gone was the road-kill toupe. Rotterman now sported a hair transplant in its place. It looked as though pubic hair had been sutured to his skull. 'No one can save yer sorry ass. With a criminal record there ain't no chance of yer gettin' back with

Zack, once we're Stateside. I jest came by to gloat.'

This was no surprise. I knew exactly what page Rotterman was up to in the 'How To Be A Complete Bastard' manual. 'I know my rights! And legally, well, legally . . .' I floundered 'this sucks.'

What I also *knew*, was that I was in deep doo-doo. Circumstances had boxed me in like the sides of a coffin. Fear coated my tongue. If only I could once again enjoy the peace and tranquillity of a panic attack. Trying to block out the cumulative strength of anxiety, I kept my eyes focused on the spearmint-green linoleum beneath my feet. I wasn't feeling so cynical about lawyers now, believe me . . . except for my legal-aid appointed barrister, who seemed more concerned with the wax he'd just extracted from his ear than with my innocence.

Maybe the truth could save me, I thought hopefully . . . Yeah right. And O. J. Simpson doesn't own any Bruno Magli shoes.

Looking up to see Julian striding into court, my blood left skid marks in my veins. Zack's agent was as thrown by Julian's appearance as I was. Rotterman's Adam's apple positively leapt over his gold chain. 'How'd the divorce go?' he blustered. 'J'know why they call all hurricanes chick's names? . . . They're wet when they come and they take the house when they go!' His guffaw was as fake as his hideous hair.

As my brain tried to kick-start my heart again, Julian

executed a slow, top-to-toe body scan with his eyes, before laughing out loud. At first I thought it was my Lufthansa-stewardess look – scarf, pearl earrings and sensible wool suit in neutral tones – that had tickled him, until I remembered my hair. My hands flew to my head in embarrassment. Kate had predicted that the court might order a DNA hair-strand analysis to ascertain whether or not I was a drug taker. Trawling the internet, she'd discovered that dyeing my hair would destroy all evidence of the odd joint I'd smoked with Zachary. Needless to say, I'd been up all night at her place, bleaching. Not the type to overreact, I'd also shaved every hair off my entire body. Kate had to call in Dyno-rod that morning to de-pube her drains.

'So, where's your pimp?' was Julian's cold appraisal of my new look. I noticed, with relief, that he spoke through lips no longer shag-piled with moustache. 'Now if you'll excuse me, I have work to do,' he said with a grim smile, before marching over to a lawyer from the Crown Prosecution Service who was standing at the bar table with my barrister, several grey men in grey suits and the cop who'd arrested me. Julian conversed with them quietly and then pointed in my direction. The cop nodded and detached himself from the confab. My Hellfire Pageant continued as he advanced towards me. I tensed involuntarily for the handcuffs he was removing from his belt. Looming over me, he cleared his throat as his shadow fell to obliterate me once and for all.

'Mr Rotterman, I presume?' he enquired of the suppurating lump beside me. 'I have a warrant for your arrest for extradition to the United States for trial on charges of racketeering, blackmail and trafficking in narcotics across State lines.'

Notwithstanding his gaseous torrent of obscenities, Rotterman was dragged in handcuffs down to the Dickensian cells of Bow Street police station.

'How did you *do* that?' I asked Julian, once I'd recovered the Power of Speech.

'I rang the case officer at the CPS last week and told him everything I knew from my old client files about Rotterman and his gang and their problems in the States. They checked with the FBI and found out his real name. He's on the run and they want him extradited. We figured he might be malicious enough to turn up in Court this morning to gloat over your conviction. It turns out he was Scotland Yard's informant about the drugs, so he must have planted them on you.' His hand on the small of my back was steady. 'I also persuaded Danny (the Dog Fondler) de Litto to turn Queen's evidence. He's currently on a witness protection scheme and will only answer to the name of "Cheryl" . . .' He steered me, symbolically, towards the light at the end of the foyer and pushed open the heavy doors. 'The charge against you will be dropped, Beck.'

'But, Jules.' I was overwhelmed; disorientated. 'You shouldn't be here. I mean, this is your wedding day isn't it?'

He shrugged. 'There's no law against us being friendly.'

'Yes, I mean, what have we got to lose? We're already divorced . . .' We faced each other formally, like foreign dignitaries. 'I've . . . I've missed you,' I admitted. 'You were the best husband I ever had.'

'I still miss you, too, but my aim is improving,' he quipped. His tone was remote, but friendly, like a tour guide. 'So?' he teased. 'Were you going to state your age *before* you were sworn in on the bible?'

'Actually, I've discovered a way to grow older gracefully . . . plastic surgery.'

That inveigled a smile out of him. 'The way to stay young is to get older friends.'

'So *that's* why Anouska's marrying you. I mean, what is the priest going to say? ". . . I now pronounce you Father Figure and Wife"?' I bit my tongue. I'd promised myself I'd walk the tact tightrope for once; to rise to the wretched occasion.

'So you're against it?' Julian fastened his eyes on me. 'Give me a reason not to marry her,' he said in grave, low tones.

My perceptions had been so skewed for so long that I dismissed the note of ambiguity I thought I detected in his words. My lips were stiff with the effort not to cry out – *Because she doesn't really love you! . . . Because I really do!* Instead, I gave a restrained smile. 'Is Simon going to be your best man?' I said, polite to the point of insignificance.

He nodded. 'You know he's with Celestia now?'

'Yes. I seem to remember him promising to find her Anterior Fornix Erotic Zone.'

'Oh God. Not another erogenous spot. I'm still looking for the *last* one.'

'*You've found it*, I wanted to say, touching my head and heart, like some demented Barbara Cartland clone. But I resolutely set my lips and said nothing. Hadn't I sabotaged his life enough already? What on earth could Julian see in a frequenter of the moral low ground like me? An entry in 'Who's *Not* Who'? A bleached-craniumed, career-deficient (I was so broke I'd soon have to break into my facelift fund) disaster-magnet with the selfish ability always to land on somebody else's feet?

'Becky . . .' He turned to me, an unfathomable expression in his blue eyes. Unspoken feelings hovered in the air between us. But the warmth in Julian's face faded as his eyes focused on something behind me. His brows went up reflectively for a moment – then disappointment flowed down his face.

I swivelled to see Zachary executing his head-turning, high-bummed strut past the canary-yellow offices of the *Herald Tribune* towards us. In his torn T-shirt emblazoned with a cobra poised to strike, his Medusa hair and three days worth of stubble, he looked like a barbarian raider come to rape and pillage.

'Thanks, man,' Zachary extended his hand towards

Julian, who shook it automatically. 'I'm free!!' Zack jerked his fist back, hard. 'Yeeess! . . . The FBI interviewed me. They said I'm in the clear. Rotty's contracts ain't gonna be legally bindin' now, are they, not now the gangster's gonna be jailed, right, Counsellor?'

Julian nodded almost imperceptibly. His face had gone the colour of the fog.

'Rotty's dead as a dodo, man . . . The dodo. That was a real crap bird, weren't it?' he said, lighting up. 'No wonder the sucker's like, extinct . . .'

I grinned. Two grammatical errors, a mispronunciation and a totally politically incorrect sentiment. Thank God. Finally Zack too was back to normal.

'Anyways, Beck, at least I'm still gonna be doin' that gig at Madison Square Garden. I'm leavin' for home. Tonight. An' I ain't comin' back. Anyways, I was wonderin' . . .' He glanced at his gleaming sports car, cosied illegally up to the kerb. 'I know yer don't like bein' seen in a car shaped like a sex aid,' he zapped a smile in my direction, 'although it does kinda go with yer new hair, babe, but do yer wanna join me? Yer can have Rotty's seat beside me on Concorde.'

I spun urgently towards Julian . . . to find him gone – evaporated into the milky mist. I peered frantically up and down the street, but could see nothing. The whole of Covent Garden seemed to be lit by a forty-watt bulb.

'Oh, Zack.' I took a deep breath. The man was still so sexy I could only look at bits of him at a time. Neck.

Ankle. Calf. Buns. Is there anything more aesthetically pleasing than lip-smackingly sweet buns in a pair of tight 501s? 'You've got such verve, such élan, such panache . . . not to mention your irresistible libidinousness, but . . .'

Zackary regarded me with quizzical affection. 'When I get home and look all them words up, I'm gonna be pleased, right?'

'Yeah, you'll be pleased.' I kissed his cheek, demurely. He smelled of woodsmoke and caramel toffee. But my tourist visa on Planet Libido had expired.

He tossed his car keys high into the air, then caught them effortlessly with one hand. 'Well?'

'I wonder whether you have any songs about self-indulgent, thirty-three-year-old disillusioned females who left their husbands for a fantasy . . . and now want to go back?'

'So.' He centred me in his topaz gaze. 'Yer ain't got no more in yer heart for me?'

I tugged playfully on a dreadlock. 'Trust you to turn a perfectly good one-night stand into a year-long Meaningful Relationship . . .'

'It was meaningful, weren't it?'

'Yeah. It was . . . But I'll only cramp your style, Zack. Why don't you sing me something in the key of "I'm so sorry, it was wonderful, but it would never work out between us" . . . ?'

Zack hugged me to his hot body for one brief

second, sidled up to his car, inserted himself behind the wheel, gunned the motor and was gone. I watched his yolk-yellow headlamps wavering in the greasy light before it swallowed him up.

I slumped down on to the icy kerb beside a woman in a stained slip and greying bra, wrapped in a Salvation Army blanket, muttering to herself. Loneliness roared at me. I could feel myself draining away. I started to shake then, in shuddering, palsied spasms. The old woman offered me a swig from her bottle . . . But what was the point? It would only come straight out of my eyes.

When Kate barrelled into her Bloomsbury flat a few hours later, she found me crumpled on the living-room floor, providing a scratching post for her hateful cat. 'What happened?'

'Julian spilled the beans on Rotterman – to the CPS, the FBI, the CIA – they all came to take him away. My charges got dropped in the excitement.'

'He did that? Wow! Did you tell him you still love him?' she demanded.

'No.'

'Why the hell not?'

'Because he doesn't love me. Not after all I've done to him.'

'You big boofhead! Rotterman was his client, wasn't he? And Julian's a lawyer. The bloke's just broken his duty of confidentiality. He's a solicitor who's ratted on a client! He could be struck off for that, you know!'

'Struck off? . . .' I looked at her in the vivid light, aghast. A shock wave of nuclear-test intensity went through my body. 'But he loves his work!'

'Not as much as he loves you. Shit a brick, Becky, you two are meant for each other. Your problem's not irreconcilable differences . . . it's irreconcilable similarities. You both wake up in mid-sentence, for God's sake . . . Do you really want to become the pleasure-deprived Commitment Phobe I was for all those years? Sex *is* better than skydiving. But love is even more wonderful. You were right about something else too. Happiness is *not* learning to be content with what you don't have,' Kate said staunchly. She pointed dramatically to the door. 'If you pull your finger out, you can still make it to the church on time.'

My abstract feeling of despair solidified into a raw voltage of alarm. I sprinted down the stairs and dived headlong into the nearest cab.

Lately I'd been swallowing my pride so often I was getting a taste for it. Mmmm. More pride please. It took me a moment or two to digest it . . . but by the time the taxi was tearing through Camden, I'd admitted that my terror of being a bad wife and mother were ill-founded. Let's face it, there's no such thing as a functional family. The only rule for achieving a good marriage is never to claim that you have one. And to love realistically, with the inoculation of experience. Sure, it was okay to have a fantasy about

Tarzan swinging down on a vine and having his way with you ... as long as you were prepared for the armpit odour. As if I finally abandoned my role as Supreme Commander of Spaceship Stupid, I also realized that my terror of losing my identity in marriage was ludicrous. Of course you can have it all ... just not all at once.

With my usual knack for making enemies, I barged straight through the throng on the pavement outside the little church on the edge of Regent's Park; right past Darius and his fiancé Norbett, the South African towel attendant; straight past The Woman Who *Used* To Do Everything More Successfully and Fabulously Than Every Other Woman in the Known Universe but was now as Demented, Ineffectual, Underachieving and Real as the rest of us; past Celestia, the bulimic Free-Fall Vegetarian who was flirting with Anouska's father by telling him that she didn't mind him calling her 'honey' as long as he didn't eat it (worker bee exploitation).

I vaulted the fence into the pocket-handkerchief park, darted across the well-mown billiard baize and, dodging tombstones, skidded down the path pumiced by generations of parishioners. Inside the vestry, Simon was pinning the obligatory carnation to Julian's grey, swallow-tailed coat.

'What on earth ...' the Best Man began.

Before he could launch into another of his hypo-critical castigations, I kneed him in the groin. 'You need physical pain to cauterize the emotional pain. Remember the Sioux Indians? It's symbolic,' I explained, propelling him into the graveyard at a reluctant gallop. The oak door slapped shut and I turned the giant key clockwise in the lock.

Julian swept his buttery hair back from his broad forehead, revealing the first flecks of grey. 'Rebecca! . . . Whatever happened to the sanctity of divorce?'

I put my hand over his mouth. 'Don't speak to me until you're ready to listen . . . !' I said illogically. 'I came to tell you that I've realized that, well, *every* marriage is a mixed marriage. Two foreign cultures. In every couple, there's one who roots through the mixed nuts and steals all the cashews . . . One drives too fast and one drives too slow . . . One likes the window open . . . One likes it closed. You see!' I enthused evangelically. 'Every couple is incompatible!'

'Excuse me.' He prised my fingers from his lips. 'But it's only *you* who's incompatible, Rebecca.'

'Another good reason why we should have children,' I said, with a tentative smile. 'Kids keep their parents way too busy to fight with each other.'

'Children?' Julian reeled backwards. 'Why are you here exactly?' I stepped closer to him. He inched away. I approached. He inched. Soon we were gyring round each other, clouds of dust rising out of the oriental carpet.

'I'm here to tell you that wedding vows are misleading. It's not illness, infidelity or lack of money that breaks marriages up. It's cellulite, clipping toenails in bed, interrupting each other's anecdotes. Or worse! Correcting anecdotes. Vicars should forget about sickness and health, and say "in irritating, snorty laughing noises" and in "thickening thighs" I now pronounce you man and wife.'

A reluctant smirk tugged at Julian's lips. 'Yes. Till Gastroenteritis us do part.'

'And relative reunions.'

'Absolutely. Especially *your* relatives.'

'There should also be a Snoring Clause in all wedding contracts. And a Forgetting-Your-Birthday-Clause.'

'And an "I Will Not Discuss The Size Of My Husband's Genitals With My Girlfriends" clause . . .'

'We do not *just* discuss your anatomy . . . We also talk about your emotional shortcomings, balding angst, nocturnal intestinal activity, revolting personal hygiene habits, pet names you have for your penis, mother complexes, gym-shoe odour, loo-reading material and the taste of your ejaculatory fluid.'

'Oh, well, that's a comfort,' Julian said sarcastically, throwing his eyes up to the ceiling.

'But, Jules . . . I'm cured. My PMT – Pre-Monogamy Tension – well, it's gone. For ever.'

He stopped circling. 'It's too late, Becky. I mean, there's Annie to consider . . .'

'You don't love her! She's Rebound Woman, that's all! And Annie doesn't want *you*. You're the Duke of

Wrong. You have a real life, Julian. Something Anouska knows nothing about. Real life, to Annie, is just something to do between shopping hours. Her father's about to be indicted and Darius has spent all her money. Don't stand between Anouska and what she's always wanted – a man she can really bank on.'

'Oh this is typical!' Julian tugged violently at his buff-coloured waistcoat. 'Why did you have to wait until *now*? You really are the most selfish, arrogant, childish, megalomaniacal, irresponsible, irrational . . .'

'So you *do* still care!'

'Rebecca,' he sighed, exasperatedly. He placed his hands on my waist, ready to launch into a lecture. But the touch was urgent; sensual, not censorious.

I looked at where his long, pale fingers pressed into my body. 'In your learned opinion, would you agree that you are flirting?'

'I am not.' Julian jammed his hands back into his pocket. '*You* are.'

'You touched me, like this . . .' I mirrored his movement, sliding my hands along the warm raspberry lining of his jacket.

'I didn't do it like *that*. I did it like *this*.' He demonstrated, drawing me closer to him. 'And that's definitely not flirting. *This* would be flirting.' He brushed my neck with his lips. A pulse of sexual excitement surged through me.

'*That's* not flirting.' I pressed my mouth hard against his and tickled his tonsils with my tongue. 'Now *that's* what I call flirting,' I announced, as we surfaced, breathless, minutes later.

There was a yammering on the side door. 'Julian? Julian!' It was the unmistakably plump vowels of his mother; the sort of voice which made your scalp crawl. 'Rebecca Steele! I know you're in there. Leave this church immediately. Who do you think you are? . . . *Zsa Zsa Gabor*?'

Julian and I looked at each other. The absurdity of the remark startled a laugh out of both of us – unstoppered laughter, a vortex of guffaws which left us panting.

'Do you want to go get a coffee?' I asked him, once we'd curbed our convulsions. There were more people thumping and pounding on the vestry door now. It added a strange syncopated rhythm to the organ music pumping away in the church beyond. The bride was no doubt out there in her father's limousine, circling maniacally.

'*Coffee?*'

'Yes, it's made from beans, grown in Brazil . . . We need to go somewhere and talk,' I urged. 'No strings attached . . . except marriage and babies.'

He drummed his fingers on his silk top hat. 'My God, Rebecca! In the "Just Cause", "Does Anyone Know Any Reason These Two Should Not Marry" *everyone we know* will put their hands up!'

'But, the thing is, Jules, I love you. There's never been anyone else for me. It just took me a while to realize it.' I flung open the creaky window. Light poured in. I swung my legs over the sill. Below lay the canal, bordered by wintry flower beds. 'Just think of it Jules; love, marriage . . . a surrogate mother to carry our child . . .'

'I'm over you,' Julian protested, all the time inching closer to the window. 'I'm out of your jurisdiction . . .'

I stretched my hand towards him. 'I don't mind you saving the world. But promise me for our honeymoon that we'll go somewhere where there are no death rows, no dissidents . . . Just a place where I can be draped attractively around a pina colada.'

'I'm a lawyer!' Julian's beaded brow furrowed. 'I can't elope out of a window on my own wedding day! It's undignified.'

'Julian, if you don't jump out of this window, I'm leaving you.'

'Hey,' he rallied, 'it's my turn to leave *you* . . . Remember? . . . Pity you don't have any other friends I could leave you for!'

'And then, when we get back, well . . . it's time I cancelled that audition for catwalk model.'

Julian blinked in astonishment. 'You're going to get a real job?'

I nodded, 'Maybe even finish art school.'

'Rebecca Steele, I think you're finally Growing Up.'

I held my breath as he gave into the dizzying impulse and levered his legs over the window sill. 'And I think *you're* finally Growing Down.'

The chaos inside the church crescendoed.

We squinted out at the dazzling day. It seemed to have started without us. Despite it being a December afternoon, the sky was a deep, still blue – the storm completely past. I laced a finger through his button-hole.

'I don't deserve you, I know. But hell. I don't deserve cystitis either. And I've got that as well.' I kissed his lovely mouth. 'Jules, before we jump, there is one thing we must vow to each other. We must vow never again to put the other on a pedestal. Promise?'

'Absolutely.' He slipped his hand down the inside of my air-hostess blouse. '. . . It's so hard to make love on a pedestal.'

And then, to the strains of 'Why are we waiting?' – Oh God, it was that Humerous Organist again – we joined hands. And jumped.